One

Toward a Civilization of Light.

Mark Kimmel

Book III of the Paradigm Trilogy

One
Toward a Civilization of Light.

Mark Kimmel

Printed in the United States of America

www.cosmicparadigm.com

Kimmel, Mark
One / Mark Kimmel - 1st Edition
p.cm

ISBN NUMBER
0-9720151-8-3
978-0-9720151-8-9

1. Paranormal
2. Metaphysical
3. Human/extraterrestrial

I. Title

First Printing
September 2008

PARADIGM BOOKS
FORT COLLINS, COLORADO

For Amber,
for my wife, Heidi,
and for the countless beings who assist us all.

*Your sisters and brothers from other star civilizations await your call
to bring their light to your home.*

-- *Sarah Smith*

AUTHOR'S NOTE

The President of the United States, the Secret Service, the Federal Bureau of Investigation, Central Intelligence Agency, National Security Agency, Defense Intelligence Agency, Air Force, Army, Navy, Customs and Border protection Agency, various media organizations, and the Boulder County Sheriff's Department are, of course, real in this 3rd dimension. While based in this reality, the humans, organizations, and events in this book are fiction. The technology described either exists or is being developed. I have depicted non-human life forms as accurately as my present understanding permits. I have taken liberties in creating individuals, places, organizations, and procedures to facilitate the telling of this story.

PREFACE

One, Toward a Civilization of Light, the third book of the Paradigm Trilogy, is a story about the changes that will take place as Earth-humans transform themselves. This book weaves together a number of concepts and truths, all of which must be comprehended to truly appreciate the larger reality.

I have waited several years to write *One*, gathering material for it from many sources, most importantly, information from spirit guides and our brothers and sisters from other star systems. These intervening years were also filled with presentations and interviews about my earlier books, and conversations about their contact experiences with many people. Most importantly, I waited until certain information, not previously known to non-humans, was available for inclusion in this book.

The second book of the trilogy, *Decimal*, was published in mid-2004, the first, *Trillion*, in 2002. These earlier books represented my understanding of the larger reality as of that time. During the interposed years, my experience of the larger reality, and who we really are, has grown by leaps and bounds. There is little doubt that if I were to re-write those two earlier books using my new understanding, they would now read somewhat differently. Rather than do that, I have decided that it will be more fun and informative for readers of the earlier books to explore my expanded reality through Ryan Drake, Sarah Smith, and the other characters in *One*.

As I wrote the words of *One*, I was amazed how characters and circumstances in books from over five years ago dovetailed into what exactly was needed for this new manuscript.

Many readers of *Trillion* and *Decimal* believe the tales told in those books are mostly true. I still insist that these books are works of fiction, products of my imagination. Most readers found that the messages in those earlier books presented them with hope for the future. It is my desire that *One* continue in that vein. Enjoy it as a story as well as discovering the insights presented herein.

On a personal note, my job in this grand adventure of Earth's transition has been to anchor the energy of certain truths contained in *One* in this 3rd dimension, and to deliver a new paradigm for humanity during the interim time. I hope, by the time you finish reading *One*, that you will comprehend that to which I refer.

Mark Kimmel
September 2008

SYNOPSIS OF *Trillion* AND *Decimal*

In a remote corner of the Navajo Reservation in northwest Arizona, Ryan Drake, a successful businessman, becomes acquainted with Sarah Smith. He visits her home, an underground facility, Harmony Center. Soon after, he helps her escape from a raid by rogue government agents. As they are fleeing through the desert, he discovers that his beautiful companion is from another planet, Phantia.

When they finally evade their pursuers, he takes Sarah to his home near Boulder, Colorado. The group that controls the major media in the United States, and has been covering-up extraterrestrial contact for the past fifty years, kidnaps her.

After rescuing Sarah, they return to his home, only to find it has been rigged with explosives. Narrowly escaping, they are interrogated by government agents about three deaths that had occurred in connection with the raid on Harmony Center.

Meanwhile the shadow government continues to find ways to disable Sarah's mission. John deBeque, an important man in the media affiliates, defects to join the humans at Harmony. The shadow government has reverse-engineered ET craft, as part of a plan to challenge beings from other star systems who are working to help the people of Earth overcome their enslavement.

Sarah goes public in an attempt to wake up people, as well as shield herself in publicity. This only serves to increase the pressure on her safety while the media discredits her. Sarah and Ryan meet with the beings from other star systems and celestials on board a starship. Ethete, another beautiful Phantian, and Ajax, Sarah's brother, join her at Harmony Center.

Just when things had started out so well for newly elected President Carlton Boyle, he is feared dead, lost in the tsunami that has surged over the coast of Oregon. Unbeknown to the outside world, Sarah and Ryan had rescued the President.

Believing the President dead, Richard Tyler, Vice President, seizes the Presidency, becoming a virtual dictator. A few days later, President Boyle is discovered alive and returns to the White House.

ONE

"Now is not a good time." The President of the United States said in a brusque voice. "I'm too busy bringing this country back to life."

At the other end of the conversation, Sarah Smith said, "I understand, Mr. President."

Carlton Boyle said, "If it's all right with you, I'm going to put you on the speaker phone; Henry is here with me." Without waiting for her reply there was a click, and then the President continued, "Sarah this is Henry Bustamonte, my new Chief of Staff."

After brief acknowledgments, Sarah said, "Mr. President, my visit can be private if you wish."

"I just can't afford to get things off track right now. As you know, it remains the official position of this government that extraterrestrials do not exist."

Sarah said, "Mr. President, in time, the truth will become known."

"...President," Bustamonte broke in. "With an economy damaged by the tsunami, with that nuclear explosion out west, with terrorists attacking our supply of oil, and with getting this government back on track, you have a lot on your plate."

"Yes, Henry, it is a lot," the President conceded. "Sarah, what exactly do you want to discuss?"

She replied. "I wish to help you restructure your civilization."

"Restructure our civilization?" The President gasped. "I'm just trying to get this government back on track after Tyler wrecked it, and after the tsunami ruined the economy."

"Look around you, all institutions that serve the needs of the powerful and wealthy are disintegrating. Replace them..."

"Sarah," President Boyle interrupted, "hold on a minute."

Then there was only static on the line.

Published articles reported that Carlton Boyle was hustling to repair the damage done when Vice President Richard Tyler had seized control of the Presidency. Since several of his former cabinet members had followed along with Tyler, he had invited new people into his administration. Sarah had read that Henry Bustamonte was one of these.

Carlton Boyle had seen his re-insertion into the Office of the President as an opportunity to clean house. The media had quoted him as saying, "I am going to get things on the right track." The Right Track had since become the theme that Boyle's revitalized administration was cultivating.

During his brief reign as President, Richard Tyler had demonstrated how quickly the United States could become a dictatorship. Threats and imprisonments had effectively squashed dissent. His first day back, President Boyle had taken decisive actions to undo the damage, and plug the flaws that his former Vice President had used to consolidate power.

The satellite telephone felt clumsy and cold as Sarah held it to her head. She had removed her western hat to make room for its antenna. As she stood facing the desert sun this morning, a cool breeze whipped her long blonde hair. She switched the instrument to her other hand. Glancing at its display she noted the time: 7:14.

Standing next to what appeared to be a large Navajo hogan, she glanced up at the sheer rock face of Fortress Mesa. Despite its awesome face, the energy of the mesa was warm and inviting. Because she had experienced it, she knew that atop this formidable plateau there was a pristine wilderness. Plants and animals lived as they had for a thousand years.

Turning to her immediate surroundings, she drank in the blossoms of the cacti. Blooming earlier than usual this year, they covered the landscape with delicate flowers of white, yellow, and orange. She glanced at the sagebrush. Its normal bluish color had turned a dusty grey, a condition normally reserved for the hot summer months. She had been in this desert place a little over eighteen months now; it was so very different from the lush green of her home on Phantia.

Sarah felt herself adjusting, once again, to the density of her new home. The process of sliding in and out of Earth's reality had been ongoing since she had arrived here. Now, each time she became conscious of the process, she reminded herself that its slower density was merely slower energy.

A large array of photovoltaic solar cells, off to the south from where Sarah stood, powered Harmony Center's facility. The nearest electrical distribution lines were a mile away; connecting to them would have been expensive, but not out of the question. However, Dr. Victor Adamson, Harmony's architect, had chosen solar, both as a more reliable source and one that demonstrated his commitment to a lower impact on the planet. They had never burned wood as so many others on the reservation did. The only petroleum product they burned was for cooking. It was supplied from a propane tank buried to the left of the parking area.

Water came from two deep wells. Because most of Harmony Center was underground, only minimal heating and air-conditioning was required. Communications with the outside world were via a satellite dish, or the Navajos who staffed the facility. A variety of vegetables, and a few fruits, were grown under the nearby geodesic dome; Navajos supplied eggs and milk to them.

As Sarah looked across the valley to the west, she saw little traffic on the highway that ran along the floor of the valley. Farther west she noted the dark slope of Black Mesa and knew immediately that Peabody Coal was still mining on its top. The mesa transmitted a sad energy, sad at man's destruction of her once beautiful wilderness.

Sarah enjoyed the solitude of Harmony; she was glad their front gate discouraged reporters. Ryan Drake had installed it where their road branched off the dirt road that headed to Ben Tsotsie's archeological dig. From that road only the top of Harmony's large hogan could be seen. With no smoke coming from its chimney, it was difficult to determine if anyone was home.

She glanced up at the desert sky. Even in this desert climate, the sky seemed hazier than on Phantia, where the sky was a pristine azure blue. She saw X's being traced by high-flying jets. When she had spoken with those who monitored Earth, she had learned these trails were connected to the planet's increasingly caustic atmosphere. She applied special lotion to diminish the damage to her skin, and in turn to her internal organs, that was coming from the air of her new home planet.

"Are you there?" Boyle's words interrupted her thoughts.

"Yes."

"What do you mean restructure?" he asked.

She spoke with words from a lighter density, "To become citizens of the cosmos, your civilization must be restructured to become sustainable, to include all people, to operate from a new basis."

"What do you mean sustainable?" Bustamonte broke in, his voice gruff with anger.

"Wealth and power are concentrated in the hands of a few, at the expense of the many. Corporations plunder the lands of indigenous peoples. Religions convince people that they are helpless. Burning the planet's hydrocarbon reserves rather than developing new energy technologies is short sighted. All of these are not in the best interests of your children, your grandchildren. Shall I go on?"

"What would government look like under this?" Boyle asked.

"It will be restructured to be a government by consensus, a government that considers all people of the planet as equals, and a government that recognizes the connectedness of all."

"How can you believe that such a government could possibly work?" Bustamonte asked. "People depend on strong leaders to solve problems, to take care of them." His words sought to pull Sarah into a lower density argument.

"It is the way of enlightened planets," Sarah replied.

"Boy, we are a long, long ways from your utopian ideal," Boyle said. "The only way I know is to force things through negotiations and majority rule."

Bustamonte interjected, "How could we possibly defend ourselves?"

Staying with the lighter density Sarah replied, "The transformation from a fear-based civilization to one that is light-based is more fundamental than most people can imagine. For thousands of years, the people of this planet have based their civilizations on fear; it has become ingrained in their DNA. In the new civilization, each person will be operating from a place of freedom, each will care as much about others as themselves. Since all will be adequately provided for, there would be no enmity, no need for military defense."

"Pure fantasy," Bustamonte blustered.

"And this is how your friends want to see things develop?" Boyle asked.

"Your world is already moving in this direction; it is but a matter of time. With our advice plus your consent we wish to speed that process."

The President said, "Sarah, I'd like to be part of your vision, but I don't think I'm the...

The phone abruptly went to static.

Sarah knew that Carlton Boyle, President of the United States of America, remembered the pictioning she had given him as they waited in the cave in Oregon. Her pictioning had displayed, in lifelike clarity, the civilization of her home planet, a planet that enjoyed "utopia."

They had spoken by phone eighteen days ago, the day after Boyle had resumed his duties as President; she from a pay phone in Kayenta, he from the White House. That time he had been most cordial. He had renewed his promise to have her visit him in Washington, DC. "You can stay at the White House," he had said. "As soon as I take care of a few emergencies, we'll set a date."

Then he had requested a means of getting in touch with her and had suggested the satellite phone she now held. Three days later one of the Secret Service agents who had been assigned to her presented her with the instrument. "A direct line to the President," the agent had said as she handed the box to Sarah, and had given her the number to dial. The agent had also announced that she and the other female Secret Service agent would no longer be guarding her.

The following day, Sarah had dialed the number she had been given and was told that the President was extremely busy. She was invited to call back in a week. When she did that, she was told that he would talk with her today, March 9th, six days hence, at 9:00 AM, Eastern Time.

Now as she waited for the conversation to resume, Sarah closed her eyes and directed her etheric body to visit the Oval Office. Such out-of-body traveling, using one of her energy bodies, not her soul, was a skill that she, J'Li D'Rona, had learned on her home planet.

She positioned herself behind President Boyle as he sat at his desk, a desk without a single scrap of paper on it, but arrayed with mementos of earlier Presidents. The President's suit coat was of dark blue material; a rim of white shirt showed above it. Every strand of his neatly trimmed hair was in place; the frame of the glasses he wore protruded behind his left ear.

She had expected to see only Bustamonte with him; when she viewed a total of seven people, it startled her. They were engaged in a heated discussion. Four of the five other men were also dressed in coats and ties; one wore a military uniform. She guessed from the decorations that he was a high-ranking officer. The men appeared a little strange, but she dismissed it as her less than perfect visioning of the scene.

Sarah realized that she was no longer a confidant of the President. He had been sharing their conversation with this entire group.

The voice of a heavy-set man standing alongside the President's desk pegged him as Henry Bustamonte. His hand was poised over the phone. The Chief of Staff had dark wavy hair and prominent dark eyebrows. He wore a white shirt and red tie under a charcoal gray suit.

"She understands," someone said. Sarah could not determine who had spoken the words.

She saw a tall man of medium stature. Standing very erect, he pointed to the President and said, "We can't allow a damn alien visitor to 'advise' you. This is our planet. We'll run it however we damn well please." The man wore a dark blue suit. His sun-bleached hair was swept back from a face dominated by a prominent nose. His smooth deeply tanned skin spoke of physical fitness and a luxurious lifestyle.

"What happens if we don't cooperate, don't take her advice?" the man in the uniform asked. He stood behind one of the sofas in the Oval office. His mottled complexion indicated that he probably consumed too much alcohol. The buttons on his uniform strained to confine an ample stomach.

"She trusts you." Bustamonte directed his comment to Carlton Boyle. "Keep her talking. Pump her for all she knows. Meanwhile we'll keep the media focused on the terrorist threat."

"Government by consensus, bull, we eviscerated that notion a long time ago." With a wave of his hand, the dark blue suit motioned to the room in which they stood. "I don't know about the rest of you, but I'm ready to finish privatizing the rest of the planet."

A thin man stood and spoke. His voice was much louder than might be expected from one of his small stature. He wore a tweed sport coat and sported a Van Dyke. "Our decision to prevent her from coming to Washington was correct." Pointing to the President he said, "You must not meet with her; it would confirm things that she would then pass on."

"What does she look like?" The man in the dark suit asked.

"Quite attractive," Bustamonte replied. "I remember the picture of her with Carlton as they emerged from the cave, tall slim blonde, with big eyes."

"Oh yes, quite beautiful. Where is she from?"

"Some planet on other side of the galaxy. They imported her a couple of years ago."

"For a visitor, she sure wasn't very insightful when Ernest Steiger kidnapped her," the military man chuckled. "I say we get her here."

"She is now without fear," the thin man insisted. "Her energy is increasingly intense. She also has another visitor with her."

"She saved my life," Boyle said. "Aren't I supposed to recognize that?"

"I know what I recognize, she is one good looking broad," Bustamonte laughed. "I'd like to spend some quality time on top of her, pump her for information."

J'Li D'Rona winced at these last words. It was strange being an observer of this conversation; at the same time she was thankful that she was not physically present.

A large man, seated on one of the sofas held up his hand. Bustamonte stopped talking; the others silenced their remarks. The size of the man reminded her of Dr. Adamson the architect of Harmony Center, but in this man she did not sense the light that infused Victor Adamson.

His thinning gray hair and weathered face made him appear to be old by the standards of this planet, but she sensed an inner vitality, a powerful personality. His words came out with an accent that made them hard for her to understand. "We must stay the course; allow this country to continue to believe that it's a democracy. Tyler's reign created fear and confusion; we made good use of it, as well as the chaos from the tsunami. The explosion in Utah was a setback, but we have other plans.

"As for this city, salt water already seeps into underground levels. Our new headquarters on higher ground are ready; prepare yourselves to move there."

Sarah realized that this man was the leader of the group, not the President.

Straightening slightly, the seated man continued, "Gentlemen, nothing has changed. I don't care one wit how things look right now; we are still in charge, and I intend to keep it that way." He pointed a stubby finger at the President. "Just keep doing as instructed." Dismissively he added, "Soon we'll all be in Colorado."

She watched the President slump at these words. "Yes," he mumbled.

Sarah felt her stomach tighten. How had President Carlton Boyle come to this? When they were holding out against the tsunami, he had been so sure of himself, so alive.

She noted the man seated on the sofa opposite the heavy-set man. He had a strikingly handsome profile with dark hair, a dark blue suit. From her angle of observation, she could not see his shirt or tie. He moved his head to follow the words of the others, but did not speak.

The man in the military uniform said, "We must preserve our nuclear option."

"Consensus be damned," the blue suit injected. "We have always made good use of economic turmoil. I say bring it on."

The handsome profile seated on the sofa smiled and nodded once.

When the leader nodded to Bustamonte; he pushed the talk button on the phone.

In a split second J'Li D'Rona was back at the hogan, and the President was saying, "Sarah, give me a few days to get things sorted out."

"Mr. President, I believe you have forgotten who you really are."

"Sarah, I am the President of the United States of America."

"Very well, I will wait to hear from you. Good bye, Mr. President."

She pushed the disconnect button on her satellite phone. Shaking at what she had just experienced, she took a deep breath. Carlton Boyle seemed so different. And who were those men in his office?

TWO

Still shaken from the conversation, Sarah replaced her hat and walked slowly to the door of the hogan. Before opening it, she paused to center herself in a place of love. As she was doing so, she recalled how Ryan Drake and she had sheltered President Carlton Boyle from the tsunami.

The group of five, President Carlton Boyle, two secret Service agents, Glenn Koslowski, and Tony Santori, along with Ryan Drake and she had found the "cave" on the hill above the Boyle family's ranch house, not far inland from the coast of Oregon. They were barely inside when she had felt the ground shudder as the force of the tsunami swept over the land. In their black vault, there was little they could do but wait. When Glenn and Tony went to examine the entrance, they found three huge boulders wedged into it.

She remembered Ryan snuggling close to her on the soft dirt of the floor. They used their jackets as pillows. Despite the surrounding rock, the temperature in the cave was amazingly comfortable.

The next morning, sunlight shining through an opening at the top dimly illuminated the cave. She had estimated that the area in which they were trapped was an oval about sixty feet by thirty. The rounded top of the cave looked to be about thirty feet above its floor.

She had touched Ryan's cheek and communicated, *'I think we did well.'*

'Pretty close call if you ask me.' Ryan replied in the mind-to-mind communication she had taught him.

"Any idea how we get out of here?" Carlton Boyle asked.

"Mr. President, I'm sure they'll come looking," Tony said with an air of bravado.

Glenn checked his two-way communicator, but received only static in response to repeated attempts to call.

President Carlton Boyle sat on the dirt floor of the cave and buried his head. "What a disaster. And I'm not out there to help. That's what they elected me to do, help. And I'm trapped in this damn cave."

After a while, Sarah sat down next to Carlton Boyle and said, "Mr. President, may I tell you of my home?" For the next hour she talked about her home on Phantia, about the family she had left behind, about her friends, and about her teaching career.

Taking Carlton Boyle's hand in hers, she had asked, "May I show you a picture of my planet? Close your eyes. It will appear."

Thirty minutes later Carlton Boyle's eyes blinked wide open. "I had no idea." Amidst tears rolling down his cheeks, he said, "I had no idea how beautiful it could be. There is no violence, no pollution. It is so peaceful." His ramblings and questions flowed for an hour.

"So is the President okay?" Glenn asked. Tony and he sat nearby. Neither had been trained for these circumstances; neither had been trained to handle someone from another planet.

By the time the light faded from the hole in the ceiling, President Boyle had talked to Ryan Drake not only about the media affiliates, but also about the World League. Sarah had pictioned Phantia for both Glenn and Tony.

On their second day in the cave, she had mentioned the actions of Richard Tyler as he turned the Presidency into a dictatorship.

"How do you know?" Boyle had asked. Then he had caught himself, "Oh, I guess you just do."

Lost in the contradiction between this recollection and what she had just visioned in the Oval Office, Sarah pulled open the door of the large hogan. After President Boyle's rescue from the tsunami on the coast of Oregon, and the ensuing attempt on the President's life, Secret Service agents had been assigned to guard her. Now she wished they were still around, maybe one of them could help her understand what had gone on in the Oval Office. Better yet, maybe Glenn Koslowski or Tony Santori would help.

She walked a few steps across the tiled floor of the hogan then descended a long, green-carpeted stairway until she reached twenty feet below ground level. Pushing open one of the massive oak doors, she entered the great room of Harmony Center. The lighter density of the space enveloped her.

Ryan Drake sat alone in one corner of the great room. He was sipping hot chai, a combination of black tea and spices he had concocted, and reading pages he had printed from the internet. This was the second phase of his daily ritual. The first was meditating, a practice he had adopted, at Sarah's urging, while they were in the cave in Oregon. He had begun to use the meditation corner of Harmony's great room as soon as they returned.

With meditation, a new adventure had begun for Ryan. He had learned to center himself, to reduce anxiety, and, on occasion, spirit guides made their presence known giving him a series of very clear "messages." The messages came to him in the form of a concept or a vision. He crafted the messages into words as he jotted them in a notebook. With these experiences, Ryan Drake had begun working in the lighter densities.

Reluctant to disturb him, Sarah hung back. His salt and pepper hair, just touching the collar of a plaid long sleeved shirt, was combed, but he had not showered.

After a minute or two, she took the chair next to him and leaned over to kiss him lightly on the day-old stubble of his cheek. The unique smell of this human was always greatest first thing in the morning. On her home planet, men smelled the same all day long.

In moments like this, she wondered what it would take for Ryan to release the rest of his ingrained fears, fears that were the legacy of all natives of this planet. He had made strides over the past months, but there were still parts of him that clung to the old ways of seeing. What would it take for him to turn his back on the consensus reality that defined Earth, to embrace the lighter densities?

Sensing Sarah was there, Ryan stabbed at the sheets before him, "Can you believe this? The government is now admitting that its earlier estimates of casualties due to the tsunami were off by a huge factor. And I quote, 'Government officials admit that, in the panic surrounding the worst tsunami to ever hit the United States, and the subsequent electrical blackout of the entire West Coast, their estimates of casualties had been based on projections by people at the United States Geological Service's National Earthquake Center and at the National Atmospheric and Oceanic Administration, both located in Colorado, a thousand miles away from the nearest ocean.'"

As they waited in the cave, Sarah's off-planet allies had told her about the destruction being caused by the tsunami. When the newspapers had published their estimates of millions of casualties, she had told Ryan that they were way off, but until this moment he had clung to the earlier numbers, after all, he kept insisting, they had witnessed the tsunami's destruction first hand.

"They have reestablished communications with most of Oregon and Washington," Ryan said. "Portland was largely unscathed by the tidal wave, just damage around the port and loss of power. Astoria was wiped out, as were most of the towns on the coasts of Oregon and Washington. From what I can gather, Boyle's ranch was at the southern end of the tsunami's impact. The big thing is that the destruction was nothing like previously reported.

"And the reports about volcanoes erupting along the Cascades were similarly exaggerated by the U.S.G.S. Significant eruptions were seen at Mount Rainier where a new shoulder to the mountain was created, at Mount Adams, and in the Three Sisters Wilderness Area. There were minor eruptions elsewhere, but these caused few reported deaths. The main catastrophe was shutting down the electrical generating plant at Bonneville. Looks like it'll take another week or two to put it back on line. John deBeque told me that he figured some of the less-seasoned employees at the media affiliates had gotten hold of the initial reports out of Colorado and had inflated the casualties.

"And, look at all the other stuff coming out." With his hands, he made a motion like bubbles rising to the surface. "The U.S. economy is in the pits; just look at the numbers. The exchange rate for the dollar is thirty percent of what it was a year ago."

He pointed to another page. "It's right in front of everybody: Oil is running everything. Governments invading countries in a mad scramble to secure the last reserves." Since returning to Harmony, and finding quiet time, Ryan had begun to pay attention to the news that filled the lives of those who were not involved with off-planet beings and with saving the life of a President. It had not taken him long to find the truth behind the national media at alternative news sites.

John deBeque and he were busy creating a web site to publish information from Sarah and Ethete, another visitor from Phantia, on views of this planet from an off-planet perspective. Through one of his old contacts, John deBeque had recovered a copy of the video from Peter Jones' speech in Denver. The broadcasting of Sarah and Peter's admission that they were not of this world had been blocked. Although he was somewhat reluctant to do so, primarily because he had learned so much that was new, they were also going to post the video of the news conference that Ryan had staged a short time later.

Ryan had become concerned about his own financial health. On a chart labeled TTT INSTRUMENTS, the squiggly line was consistently downward. It was not that his life revolved around that particular stock, since he had taken mostly cash rather than shares of TTT when he sold Sanitas Technologies, but for him it was a bellwether, albeit at the moment a rather depressing one. He congratulated himself that his timing on the sale of Sanitas had been so superb.

He took a sip of chai and said. "And, despite a tsunami that did kill thousands of people, and pushed this country into a depression, nobody's doing anything to prepare for another one."

Then, as if just recognizing that Sarah had joined him, he casually asked, "So, how'd your conversation with the President go?"

She placed a hand on his arm. "Something is very wrong. President Boyle never asked how I was doing, or about you. My 'private' conversation with him was shared with six others."

"Six others?" Ryan turned to look into her large eyes.

"He kept putting the phone on mute, so I traveled to the Oval Office. There were six other people discussing what I had said to the President." A tear welled up at the corner of one large gray eye; her shoulders slumped.

"Sorry you lost your connection with him." Ryan reached his arm around her. "He seemed like a pretty decent guy -- when we had him alone. Who were the others?"

"I didn't recognize any of them. On the phone, Boyle introduced me to one, Henry Bustamonte, his new Chief of Staff. But it's more than that; I sense that President Boyle has undergone some sort of a change. He acts like he has totally forgotten what we discussed. The others treated him like he was working for them, not like the leader of this country. Let me piction it for you."

She reached for Ryan's hand and held it tightly. When Ryan closed his eyes, he was transported to the Oval Office as Sarah had viewed it earlier. After a few minutes, she released his hand; the pictioning stopped.

Ryan looked at her. She looked at him. They slumped together in an embrace.

After a full minute, Ryan whispered in her ear, "So what are we going to do now?"

"You continue with what you are working on, the web site, other projects, and I find out what our allies suggest."

"I feel this all raises another concern." Ryan straightened. Pointing to her satellite phone, he said, "I don't think those men who were with the President are going to be satisfied with letting him query you over the phone. And your old Secret Service guardians certainly know where to find you.

"We must not operate from fear." Sarah turned her large gray eyes to stare into his. "We both have fallen into that trap, and look where it has led. I appreciate your concern, but no more fear-based anything. No more. Okay? If we are pursuing the right course, no harm will come to us."

"You really believe that, don't you?" he asked.

"Yes. From now forward I will come from my center, come from a place of love."

"What happens if you're wrong?"

"Then I die." Sarah shrugged her shoulders. "I died to my old life as J'Li D'Rona of Phantia when I agreed to become Sarah Smith, a resident of Earth. I have lived many lives on many different planets. My soul goes on, cumulating my various experiences."

"And you think you can turn fear off just like that?" Ryan snapped his fingers.

"Yes. Death is not a big deal when you realize you've done it before. Fear is a choice; it can be replaced by the energy of love. At every instant we are creating our experiences, creating the world around us. Every thought we have, every judgment we make is having an effect on other people, on other things. I am going to create my experience without fear."

"I don't think that I'm ready to ignore all the bad guys," Ryan said. "What about Peter's death? And the guys who tried to kill me? And Aza, what about Aza? And the raid on this place? No, I'm pretty sure I'm not ready to roll over."

"This is coming from your imagination." She kissed him lightly on his lips.

"Hey, my imagination is pretty imaginative."

"Your imagination is carrying remnants of the dark energy; its tentacles are still active on this planet." Then Sarah smiled and said, "Ryan, when you were an entrepreneur, how much energy did you spend worrying about the competition?"

"Not very much."

"As an entrepreneur, how did you approach solving problems?"

He thought for a moment. "I just outlined the situation, and set off to deal with it. I had a few failures, but it worked most of the time. Hey, this is different -- we're playing with people's lives here."

"True, but the same principle holds," a newly invigorated J'Li D'Rona of Phantia said. She felt herself coming from that place of lighter density, what people on this planet called the fourth or fifth dimension. "You were successful because you sent out the energy of success. You ignored your fears. You acted as if it were true. I suspect there were times it seemed almost magical, right?"

"Yeah, okay. I still say this is different."

"And I say it's the same. We must change the energy we radiate -- before we attract a whole new set of problems. And we must not let what I saw this morning influence what is good and right about this planet.

"We are going to model for others, showing them how to secure control of an enlightened destiny by radiating the energy of truth and love. As people wake up to who they really are, and begin to add their collective energies, the transformation of this planet will accelerate. Your energy, your thoughts, and your intentions are just as important as mine."

"And you think we have a chance to wake up this whole planet?" Ryan asked? "That if we get enough light energy everything is going to flip to a better place? As I see it, we are a long ways off."

"It will be a gradual process for Earth-humans as more and more of them see that living from the light is best, as they move away from fear. Earth is already on her way to transitioning into a higher dimension," Sarah said. "She would like to take as many of her people with her as possible. This is the reason I volunteered to come here -- to help with this transition. Other planets have made similar transformations, albeit few have been as enslaved as this one, but they did do it.

"Earth's people have one big advantage, they have millions of brothers and sisters from an armada of starships just waiting to add their assistance. This is in addition to those from other star civilizations like Ethete, Ajax, me, and millions like us who are 'visitors' on this planet.

"In light of what I saw this morning, I'm mulling over specifically how next to proceed." Sarah kissed him again. As she bounded off, she added, "I'm going to check with those who see the forest, not just trees."

THREE

"He's not expected to live out the night." The security man had explained that he was speaking from the hallway outside a private hospital room. Joseph Randolph, a member of the Board of Directors of several major corporations had been the victim of an assault as he walked from a Broadway play.

"Get him out of there," Grant Clever shouted at the security man. He was speaking from his home in Chevy Chase, Maryland.

Moments after an ambulance had brought Joseph Randolph to the emergency entrance of St. Luke's - Roosevelt Hospital, Randolph's regular physician had arrived, along with two security men in black uniforms. After a brief conversation, Randolph had been hustled off to the private room in which he now lay. His physician had rejected the idea of an operation as the emergency room doctor recommended; instead he had produced papers and ordered morphine. The hospital listed the patient's condition as critical.

Clever's supposedly ultra secure telephone line had been tapped with a sophisticated device that transmitted all conversations via a satellite link to Warren Ophir, two thousand miles away. Ophir overheard the conversation and smiled to himself; the death of Randolph simplified his life. Ophir had been alerted to events by one of his own agents, the one who had engaged the services of the attacker.

Warren Ophir continued to listen as Clever received a second phone call, an account from Randolph's attacker. As previously arranged, Randolph's companion for the night, a beautiful young socialite, had lured him to the dark side street. She had been paid $50,000; the attacker had been similarly compensated.

When the conversation ended, Ophir put down his headphone

24

and clicked off the recording device. He stood, aided by his cane, and stretched his back and legs. Comforted by this latest piece of news, he walked from the security center.

A week earlier, Ophir had overheard another conversation involving Grant Clever. In it a different security man reported that Oliver Vanderbush, the Vice President of Entertainment for a major television network and another World League Board member, had died shortly after an automobile accident. His body had been spirited away by a paramedic team that arrived on the scene moments after the crash.

"So, as far as you can tell, there were no aliens involved?" Carlton Boyle asked as he seated himself on one of the sofas in the Oval office.

"Mr. President, I won't know for sure until I can get into the bowels of that site," Sam Wellborn replied. "It's too hot right now for anything but a robot probe, and a robot just can't climb over some of the rubble -- but, from what I can see, it looks like a high tech manufacturing facility. All the corpses appear to be human. Until we can excavate the site, we just can't be certain.

"Keep in mind that much of it was vaporized. Some of the blast came out openings in the side of the canyon wall. That accounts for the radiation leaks into the atmosphere. Good thing it was small, or we'd have radiation all over the western states."

Sam Wellborn was seated on one of the sofas in the Oval Office. A man of fifty-six, Sam wore his curly brown hair very short and well groomed. This morning he was dressed in a wrinkled blue suit with white shirt and yellow tie. His eyes bore the marks of someone who had flown much of the night on a military transport out of Hill Air Force Base in northern Utah. Although he was a Special Assistant to the President of the United States of America, keeping a low profile served him well. To the crew of the plane he was just another bureaucrat who needed a lift.

"So if this is not the work of aliens," the President asked, "how does somebody get their hands on a nuclear bomb? Can I believe our military when they say this facility was not one of ours? Some of them buy the alien story; others are not convinced. With no hard evidence, most of them are going along with the terrorist theory as reported by newspapers and television."

"Mr. President, I just don't have good answers yet. I'll let you know as soon as I do."

Sam knew the President wanted to get clarity on the explosion. Without a definitive answer the public continued to see it as a fearful mystery. Coupled with the tsunami it had slowed the country's economy as people waited to see if Carlton Boyle was going to take charge of things.

"I think it's a good idea to wait until we're absolutely sure what really occurred before beginning any campaign to change the story," the President said. Now that the public had latched onto the story of a terrorist plot, if it turned out to be something different, what were they going to believe? What Sam did not say was that delay meant the idea of a terrorist incident would lodge itself ever deeper in the public's psyche.

Sam had never questioned his loyalty to Carlton Boyle. It was a respect and admiration based on years of close association. Sam was the President's task man; whenever Boyle needed someone to oversee a special project, he called Sam. This had begun during the years that Boyle was Governor of the State of Washington and had continued since he became President. When the nuclear explosion in Utah had occurred, a few short weeks after his inauguration, the President had immediately sent Sam to investigate. Sam had been in Utah when the tsunami hit the coast of the Northwest. After he received reports that the President had been lost, it was Sam Wellborn who had kept the search going until they had found the President's sanctuary. Sam had been on the spot the day Carlton Boyle emerged from the cave where he had ridden out the tsunami.

The President leaned onto the back of the sofa opposite Sam and glanced at the clock. His face showed signs of someone who had not slept well. Deep wrinkles lined a brow under a full head of brown hair parted on the right. His brown eyebrows capped his glasses. The dark circles under the eyes were those of someone who bore a heavy burden.

Yet there was something strange about this man Sam had known so long. He could not put his finger on it.

"Something I can help with Mr. President?" Sam sensed that Boyle was on the verge of disclosing something. This had been their habit; confidences were regularly exchanged between the two old friends. Sam had a Top Secret security clearance and thought he knew most of the President's closely guarded secrets. Rather than give him an official office within the administration, it had served both men to retain Sam as the President's Special Assistant. Their meetings were generally not known by anyone beyond the President's close circle and were never on the daily agenda.

"Not right now, Sam, maybe later."

"How about a walk?" Since everything that transpired in the Oval Office was recorded, it had been their custom to walk outside the White House whenever they wished to discuss something they did not want some historian to learn about it.

The President blinked a couple of times and said, "Uh, not right now Sam, I need to focus on other things."

Carlton Boyle rose from the sofa and put on his suit jacket. This was his indication that their meeting was over. Sam noted that the President's eyes had a far away look to them, as if he were struggling to recall something. The best Sam could come up with was to wait for another opportunity to delve further into whatever was troubling him.

The President blinked several more times. The far away look disappeared, and he said, "The CIA has convinced me that the radicals in the Middle East are celebrating our economic collapse. They see the revolving door of the Presidency as a sign of weakness."

"You have a lot on your plate," Sam Wellborn addressed his old friend. "A lot more than most Presidents."

"Sam, my Natural Disaster Preparedness Task Force is due to meet right after lunch. I want you to chair that meeting.

"Our country can't survive another disaster like that tsunami, or the exaggerated casualty estimates. Look at what it's done to our economy.

"Tell this group what you observed out west. Share your impressions with them; take them into your confidence; become part of the group. Mold it in whatever way you want -- add to, subtract from. Then report back to me. I'm anxious to hear any new ideas they might come up with. Not only can we not afford the loss of life and property, this country can not survive another coup."

"Will do, Mr. President. What about my investigation of the Utah explosion?"

"I want you to drop it. I'll keep you posted on any military or intelligence reports. You're always talking to me about manifesting things; well put that skill to work. Manifest something out of this Task Force."

"So you are taking me off the Utah explosion?"

"Yes, for now. Oh, and I asked Gordon Moore to sit in. I'm not quite sure what to do with him, so he's yours."

"I thought he was running your amnesty program."

"He was, is. We just haven't had as many people turn themselves in as I'd hoped. Seems like it's run its course."

"Mr. President, why are you doing this? I told you I'd get answers as soon as they're available."

"Sam, I want the military to handle this. They know all about nuclear explosions."

Sam was pissed, but he decided not to push things further. He knew what it was like when Carlton Boyle made up his mind.

The President had not mentioned this task force job when he had recalled Sam to Washington. On the surface it sounded pretty dull after overseeing the investigation of a nuclear explosion. He had not met the members of the task force, probably a bunch of academics, however he already knew he intended to make it into something more than just another government study. Sam Wellborn also knew he was going to find some way to keep his hand in the Utah investigation.

Sensing that Sam was not happy, the President said, "Sam, do what I'm asking because you know we both love this country. It's the greatest country in the world; let's keep it that way. No more unscheduled turnovers at the top, no more destruction from tsunamis. What I'm proposing will be of great assistance to me."

"Mr. President, I'll do as you request." Sam knew Carlton Boyle was right. Sam Wellborn did love the United States of America and would do whatever was required to keep it a great country.

A knock on the door interrupted their conversation. It signaled the President's next meeting was ready to begin.

Stepping through the doorway, Sam nodded to Janet Overton, the Secretary of Commerce; she was one of the few Cabinet level officials Boyle had retained when he resumed the Presidency. Three Asians in dark suits with white shirts accompanied the Secretary; she also was dressed in a dark business suit. Sam took a few steps down the corridor that led to his office.

When the door shut on Overton and her guests, Sam turned to the President's personal secretary. "Sally, who were the people who were in with the President -- before I met with him? I only recognized a couple of them."

Earlier, as Sam had waited in the outer office, he had counted six men coming out of a meeting with the President. Sam immediately recognized one of them. Grant Clever was a large man, thinning on top; he walked with a slight limp. Their eyes met briefly as Clever passed by. He recalled that the man was a prominent cabinet-level official from two administrations ago. He also identified Admiral Justin Ridgway, the Secretary of the Navy. He had talked with the Admiral at a diplomatic reception. The others he did not know. All six had passed by without acknowledging him.

Normally Sam moved about the White House with a minimum of interference. He had an office in an unobtrusive corner of a lower floor next to his assistant, Tiffany Wheeler, who anchored his far-flung efforts on behalf of the President. The people who controlled access to the President, including Sally O'Hara and the Secret Service, knew that Sam Wellborn had an unofficial, but very special relationship with the President.

This was the first time Sam had been back at the White House since Carlton Boyle had reassumed the Presidency. He had been preoccupied with the nuclear explosion. Upon entering the White House this morning, he sensed a difference. He had commented to Tiffany on it. She had replied that there were new security procedures surrounding the President. Sam had written it off as reactions to the demise of Richard Tyler and the reemergence of Carlton Boyle. Now he was not so sure.

Sam had gotten to know Sally O'Hara, the President's secretary, as soon as Carlton Boyle was sworn in. They had shared a couple of lunches when Sam was in and Boyle was out.

"You won't find much on them -- I checked. The ones from DC are Grant Clever, Henry Bustamonte, and Justin Ridgway. Their files have been redacted. The one in the expensive suit is a guy from New York, Wall Street type. His name is Jonathan Olson. Bustamonte had me check on an airline reservation for him one day.

"The skinny one is Jeremiah Goldman, always wears a sport coat. He's a psychiatrist over at George Washington University Hospital. The sixth guy is new; I don't know him, tags along behind the others. My guess is they're interviewing Vice Presidential candidates."

"Can I assume the Secret Service vetted them?" Sam asked.

"We've instituted some new security measures that bypass the Secret Service. The President is still trying to sort out who was part of Tyler's inside group."

"What about you?"

"I just keep my head down and do my job. Tyler hardly used me for anything. I was so happy when the President returned. I will tell you this, that group meets with the President every day at 8:45 AM. They're in there right after the daily briefing."

"Bet you could tell me some good stuff about the Tyler days, eh?"

"Oh, yeah, buy me lunch sometime," Sally smiled. Her phone rang, and Sam walked away.

FOUR

At 1:30 PM, Sam walked into a conference room on the floor below the Oval Office. Members of Carlton Boyle's hastily assembled task force were seated around a large cherry wood table in a room with dark paneling and a high ceiling. Each had been asked to bring a recommendation for future action.

According to Sam's briefing materials, this group had come into being immediately after Carlton Boyle returned to Washington. Spanning a variety of disciplines, they were to give the President independent viewpoints on events surrounding the tsunami and how to prepare for the possible occurrence of another.

Sam held the door for Tiffany Wheeler, the slim brunette who had worked with him as an administrative assistant during the presidential campaign. This morning she looked quite attractive in a blue skirt with matching jacket, and a white blouse with red scarf.

Sam had been a key player on the nominee's strategy team; Tiffany had managed Sam's flow of polls and surveys, set up meetings, and kept him informed. He had come to respect her for her keen insight as well as her willingness to help out. He particularly liked her upbeat attitude; it had carried them through some difficult times during the campaign.

Since moving into the White House, Tiffany had managed to garner respect among its high-energy staff, despite the fact that her boss was almost invisible. She had succeeded in keeping Sam appraised of what was happening around the White House, except when Richard Tyler had taken over. During that time she had fled to her parents' retirement home in Florida.

Sam had asked her to take notes on this meeting, which, like all meetings in the White House, was being recorded. She carried a three-ring binder filled with background information on each participant. Most of them knew each other, having worked for years in the fields of environmental impact, seismology, and tsunamis. Reviewing their names and credentials, Sam felt like a real outsider. As he entered the room, he queried himself, "Why did the President ask me, of all people, to head this up?"

Julie Tulagi, PhD, a honey haired bundle of energy dressed in a dark business suit, was a specialist from the National Oceanic and Atmospheric Agency in Boulder, Colorado. She had been speaking out on global warming for many years.

John MacDonald was from the United States Geological Service's National Earthquake Center in Golden, Colorado. A tall thin man, he wore a gray suit with a yellow shirt and red tie. He was best known for his research on a connection between global warming and earthquakes.

Marcus Westhuizen, PhD, from the Woods Hole Oceanographic Institute in Massachusetts, was an expert on glacier melt, ocean currents, and their impact on weather. A large bear of a man with a full beard, he was dressed in a blue blazer two sizes too small for his frame, with a white shirt and stripped tie. He had evidently spilled coffee on the front of his shirt.

William Cortland, PhD, a short rotund man with a mop of dark hair, was from the National Oceanic and Atmospheric Administration's Center for Tsunami Research. He had been visiting in Washington, DC, at the time the tsunami wiped out his home on the coast of Washington State. He wore a rumpled tan suit and a plaid tie that looked like he had rescued it from a recycling store.

Guido Sproule a specialist in tsunami warning systems had flown back from Japan where he had been installing a piece of early warning technology. He ran an electronics company in Phoenix, Arizona that specialized in these systems. Sproule, who wore the tan of a man who enjoyed Arizona's broiling summers, was dressed in a brown jacket and blue slacks. He wore a bolo tie with a turquoise clasp.

Dr. Gordon Moore, M.D., a tall well-built man with a ruddy complexion, wore a dark blue pin stripped suit with a white shirt and red tie. Moore had been in the papers since accepting the job to ramrod the President's amnesty program. Seated at the far end of the table, he looked as uncomfortable as Sam felt.

Sam introduced himself to each person. Then he grabbed a glass of water and took a seat about midway down one side of the table.

A moment after Sam was seated, the President appeared. Everyone stood. Carlton Boyle walked to each and shook hands, welcoming them to the White House. Then he motioned them to be seated.

"I must attend to an, an emergency," he said, still standing. "I've asked Sam Wellborn to chair this meeting and to join this force. If I can rejoin, I will, but please get going. Thank you much for coming. I assure you, I'd much rather being doing this than that I have to do." With these brief remarks he turned and left.

Sam noted the minor errors in the President's otherwise smooth speech. He glanced at Tiffany. She raised an eyebrow to indicate that she too had noted the strangeness.

Glancing around the table, Sam was struck by the lack of anyone from a major corporation, the financial world, or any representative of the Environmental Protection Agency, Homeland Security, Justice, or Treasury.

"Ladies and Gentlemen, let's get right to it," Sam said after the waft of the President had vanished. "The President is seeking your advice. The product of this task force will be short, pointed, and direct recommendations to the President on coping with disasters such as we have had on the West Coast. I'm going to let you introduce yourselves as we each take about ten minutes to make introductory remarks. Since I don't know any of you personally, let me start. I am a Special Assistant to the President."

Sam went on to briefly outline his career and his connection to Carlton Boyle when he was Governor of the State of Washington. He hinted at several special assignments since Boyle had been elected President. This was a hastily composed speech; he hoped it was good enough to get the others' full cooperation. He could not resist throwing in a comment about his investigation of the Utah nuclear explosion.

As he listened to them introduce themselves, he realized that on one level, he was pleased that Carlton Boyle had trusted him to chair this task force. It provided a nice distraction from his other concerns, and the intent of the group was important in that it demonstrated the President's commitment to a better world. It was this commitment that had cemented his loyalty to Boyle. However, he sensed that the President now was more interested in preventing a misdirection of the government than he was in preventing another "natural" disaster.

On another level, Sam was much more interested in finding out more about the group of people who were meeting with the President every day, and whether they were responsible for the changes in his old friend, and his own abrupt reassignment. He was not about to forget the mystery surrounding the nuclear detonation. His personal opinion was that blaming it on terrorists was nonsense.

When they had each finished, and they had taken a quick break, Sam said, "As the President has directed, this task force will be focusing on the tsunami that devastated our West Coast. The President believes that the future of our great country may well rest with the advice this group provides. As you might suspect, we have those within our government, and within other governments, those who have their own opinions and agendas on dealing with these disasters. But the major tsunami that had been predicted for so long did finally happen. I have seen the devastation first-hand and can tell you it is almost beyond comprehension.

"I would like to believe we stand today at the threshold of a new era. Can we learn from the events of three weeks ago? How can we make ourselves secure from such an event in the future? The task is huge, and we may not have the luxury of time. Can we really predict when another tsunami might strike our shores? Can we look behind the predicting and find the causes? Can we do anything to prepare people? We are a great country; we have vast resources that we can bring to this discussion. What should they be?

"Our job today is to outline what needs to be done without considering the constraints of our current technology, institutions, or funding, and to determine how we go about doing it. I want everyone to have his or her say; we'll stay here as long as necessary.

"I would like to add one additional point. The early casualty estimates from the tsunami did irreparable harm to our economy. I know that two of you were close to those estimates, and that you objected at the time. That is why you are here today. Having seen the great harm their publication did, we must find ways to make sure it does not happen again."

"With that introduction, I would like Julie to begin." Not quite knowing what to expect, Sam took a deep breath and sat back with a yellow pad on his lap. He planned to have an initial summary on the President's desk the next day. Getting back to the nuclear explosion called to him.

The group discussion went on well into the dinner hour. At that point Sam adjourned the meeting until the following day. So far he had seen data and a lot of posturing; he had not seen much in the way of recommendations. He gave them an assignment: Each was to come back tomorrow with something concrete to give the President.

On the way to his suburban Virginia home, Sam received an urgent message from his wife. He arrived to find a patrol car in the driveway and his wife, Maggie, in a tizzy. While she was out to dinner with friends, someone had broken into the house by bashing in the front door. After touring the house with an officer, she had decided that nothing appeared to be missing.

Upon inquiring, Maggie said that she had not seen the security patrol that Sam had put in place after he had been beaten and drugged in their driveway a few weeks ago. Sam called the office of the security firm only to find they were no longer in business.

As soon as the officers left, Maggie began complaining that she no longer felt safe in the house; she blamed Sam for failing to put a more secure lock on their front door. Maggie went to bed that night without further conversation.

Sam made a mental note to talk to Chuck Brown at the FBI who had recommended the security firm. Even with the craziness surrounding Richard Tyler, someone should have notified him of the lapse. He checked all the doors and windows before retiring for the night. He also checked to be sure his revolver in the nightstand was loaded.

The Natural Disaster Preparedness Task Force resumed the next morning over coffee and cinnamon rolls. After a restless sleep in his own bed, Sam felt very tired, certainly not what he would have desired as the task master for this group. Maggie was still in bed when he left the house at 6:45 AM.

He polled everyone for his or her recommendation. To Sam's frustration, he got only extensions of the current thinking and promises to do a better job, nothing radically new. Gordon Moore indicated that he wished to speak.

"Yes, sir, Dr. Moore, what have you got for us?"

Dr. Gordon Moore sat at one end of the table. When his turn had come to introduce himself, he had focused mainly on his medical background. He also had stated that he was not quite sure why the President had asked him to be part of this task force. He had remained silent, as discussion had dragged on yesterday. Sam had been surprised when Moore showed up the second day.

"As I said yesterday, I've been heading up the President's amnesty program," Moore said. "At first, I wasn't at all sure how my work was going to fit into this group's discussion, but if you will bear with me, I think I'm beginning to see a connection. And believe me, it is not a connection I would ever have suspected, nor one I would, even now, choose to make.

"The number coming forward is gratifying, but it is tailing off. I find it amazing that some of these people have been holding on to their piece of some secret or another their entire careers, afraid to say anything.

"What I've gleaned so far pretty much supports various conspiracy theories you might have heard about -- with the exception that much of the shadow government isn't really within the government; it is in the hands of private corporations. Even things like intelligence and military have been privatized to keep them away from oversight."

As Sam listened to Moore's revelations, from the men and women who were taking advantage of the amnesty program, he realized that they confirmed some of the rumors and theories he had heard over the years. Heretofore he had routinely dismissed all such rumors as nonsense.

Gordon Moore was still speaking, obviously eager for an audience. "The bad news is that the men and women coming to me are mostly junior officers, lower level employees -- no senior officers, not one in a current position of power. I've been told that anyone above a certain level has been so thoroughly conditioned and threatened, that even with the amnesty program, they are afraid.

"Now for the connection to today's discussion, one man has been talking about his involvement with weather modification. It seems this was begun by the Soviets; secret projects within our government have been catching up ever since. Since the end of the Cold War, both sides have continued their developments. More importantly, this man believes that it has been used to deliberately destroy the environment -- to instill fear, but also to give people around the world another enemy. Maybe, just maybe, one of these programs resulted in the destruction you all are gathered here to talk about."

Sam had to bite his tongue to keep from interrupting Moore. The good doctor was really reaching if he thought the government of the United States was attempting to destroy the environment. And the whole subject of fear mongering was equally ridiculous. America had lots of enemies, lots of people who were jealous of its lifestyle, its position in the world.

When Sam once again focused on Moore, he was saying, "But there is more. Another man has told me that his organization knew about the tsunami before it hit. He was part of a surveillance program that monitored communications within and between government agencies. He overheard a conversation in which someone instructed someone else not to take any action. He took the information to his superior, but was instructed not to relay any information to anyone who could take action to warn people along the coast of Oregon and Washington."

Sam was almost livid. He did not want to hear more criticism of his country. He had seen the way people lived in other countries. Americans had it so good. How could they bite the hand that fed them? How could a man who reported to the President be saying stuff like this?

As they were breaking for lunch, Moore cornered Sam in the hall. Sam tried to maneuver around him, but Moore was intent. "One of my insiders mentioned that Utah site you were working on, said it was being used to manufacture alien reproduction vehicles."

"Alien reproduction vehicles?"

"Yeah, we've been reverse engineering ET craft for decades. Hard to tell how much we've accomplished."

"So, who's this we?"

"The shadow government. Sam, I've learned a lot, from the people who came forward, about the government behind the government, and what they are up to."

"I don't think there's anything to this business about a shadow government," Sam said.

"Let me show you what I have. Maybe I can change your mind."

Sam nodded, more to get Moore on his way than out of real interest. "Maybe we can get together after I wring a few recommendations out of this group." He added to himself, "That guy is going to have to show me a whole bunch to change my mind about a shadow government."

FIVE

That same evening the residents of Harmony Center prepared to celebrate. Government funded repairs, stemming from the rogue INS raid of the prior year, were now complete, as were certain upgrades. For the foreseeable future, there would be no workmen interrupting the quiet of their desert retreat. In celebration, Harmony was opening its doors to its neighbors and to the families of those who staffed it.

Of immediate concern to Ethete Johnson, John deBeque, Sarah Smith and Ryan Drake, was whether fallout from the nuclear explosion had drifted to their location; Harmony was only a few miles south of the Utah border. Official reports were sketchy, but they indicated that a large area of Utah was under quarantine.

After Ryan and Sarah had emerged from the wrath of the tsunami, and shying from the publicity of having rescued the President of the United States, they had quietly slipped back to Harmony Center. One of the upgrades, that Ryan had insisted on as a part of its reconstruction, was a small satellite dish so that the facility could receive information from the outside world. He sat in the corner of Harmony's great room that had been arranged for John deBeque and him. The satellite setup also supplied a telephone link that they had found useful, but only when someone was at the computer to receive the call. They had not installed a television receiver, the third piece of the satellite package.

John deBeque was using his computer hookup to design a web site for their initiative on planetary transformation. He was also assisting Ethete who was pursuing an obscure thread as to exactly how Earth religions had been distorted into instruments of control.

As Ryan sat reading printouts -- he insisted that it was too hard to read off his computer's screen -- Sarah stood behind him. John and

Ethete had rushed to Kayenta when Sarah had received a dim and somewhat garbled telepathic message that Ajax Johnson, her brother, was there and needed a ride.

Singing Bird, and her husband, Johnny Black Raven, were putting the finishing touches on Harmony's long dining table. The table was set for thirty.

Checking the time, Ryan put away his papers, and went off to check on the air handling system. While it had been rebuilt as a part of Harmony's reconstruction, Sarah continued to tell him that it was not delivering clean air. Cooling of the underground facility depended on capturing the earth's cool temperatures through an elaborate system of underground pipes and heat exchangers. For heating it captured air from the geodesic dome.

As had become his daily routine, Ryan removed the cover from the electrostatic filter unit. The filters were clogged again, as they had been every time he had checked them. The debris gave off a faint smell that he could not identify. It was clearly not normal for them to clog every day, but he was glad the gunk was not getting through. If he were anywhere near Boulder, Colorado, he could have someone at his old company, Sanitas Technologies, analyze it. Without proper instruments he could not track down the nature of the problem. He washed the filters and returned to the dining area.

Not long thereafter, Navajo women, children, and men began to wander into Harmony's great room; Sarah greeted each adult or child by name and pointed to seats around the table, many of the children were coughing, some had drippy noses. This was the first time most of them had seen the inside of this facility since its initial construction.

Ryan's college chum Ben Tsotsie, and three of the crew from his nearby dig, wandered in. All three were coughing. Ben gave hugs to Sarah and Ryan before finding a place a few seats away.

"Are you okay?" Ryan asked stepping over to the archeologist.

"It's the gray air," Ben replied, "seems like it gets worse every year. No more blue skies, just gray."

"Our filters are picking up all kinds of strange particles."

"Yeah, that stuff the airplanes are spraying is not healthy. Some people say it's to make rain, but I don't believe that."

"When did it start?"

"Several years ago, before I began to dig, before Harmony Center. I remember when me and my men would walk down here in the evenings to look at the big hole, wondering what was going to be built. We'd look up at the gray sky and complain. The next morning the sky would be almost blue. Then the planes would come over and make their X's, and by noon it would be gray again. It was not many months before everyone was coughing. Do you know what they are spraying?"

"No, but I'm going to find out."

Ryan took a seat around the corner from Sarah who sat at the head of the table. When everyone was settled, she asked for silence so that each person could give gratitude. Then two Navajo teenage girls brought heaping platters of food to the table.

Ryan helped himself to salad, chili rellenos, cheese enchiladas, re-fried beans, rice, and tortillas. There were also green beans and a green salad, both from their garden under the geodesic dome. Singing Bird refilled his iced tea and patted him on the shoulder; a grandmother with ten grandchildren, she had taken a liking to this white man.

As Ryan ate, Sarah chatted with Maria Tomichi, the mother of George Tomichi, the man who had managed the garden under their geodesic dome. Tomichi had been killed in the rogue INS raid. His mother had received compensation from the government, but his loss was still felt by all. They had been unable to find anyone with a similar dedication to or understanding of organic gardening.

"Anything interesting in the news?" Ben asked. The men at his camp, a mile up the road, had few conveniences. Their news of the outside world came from the Navajo Times, when they made their weekly trip to Kayenta.

Mindful of the others at the table, Ryan raised his voice and said, "There's the new Vice President, John Malm, most recently a partner in a Wall Street firm -- no political experience. Hard to tell what's really going on with that appointment." Ryan flashed back to the pictioning Sarah had given him of the people in the Oval Office. He could not be sure if the picture on the internet was that of the silent man she had seen that day.

He quickly continued, "I've been interested in that nuclear explosion north of us." Ryan gestured in the direction of the north wall of the large underground room. "It's hard to tell from published reports, but as far as I can tell, what little radiation escaped from the explosion is drifting to the northeast. I am guessing we are safe."

Several people who had been listening to his remarks murmured thanks.

Ryan continued. "One early report said that they found remains of an ET saucer, but now the media is blaming it on terrorists."

Ben spoke up, "My cousin who lives up that direction says it was a military base. Lots of barbed wire and guard dogs. The guards shot over the heads of my people when they came close. Now they want people to think it was some sort of a base for terrorists. We know better."

Ryan said, "I think you might be right. Anybody else have an opinion?"

One of Ben's workers and Singing Bird's grandson, Jimmy Black Raven, said, "My wife's cousin is married to a Ute. He hunts up in that area. He has seen flying saucers many times. Zoom. Zoom." He made a swishing motion with his left hand. "They make no noise."

No one else asked anything. This did not surprise Ryan, as the Navajo were somewhat reserved, plus most of this group did not know him well enough to open up. Ben was cut from a different cloth than the average reservation Navajo. He had been to college at Arizona State University, which is where he had met Ryan. He was also the leader of a nearby archeological dig; most of the people around the table knew him, some were related. If anything, he had a larger standing with the locals than Ryan, who was seen as a latecomer and an outsider. Most of the locals were still in awe of Sarah.

'Do not be discouraged by their lack of response,' communicated the voice in Ryan's head. *'They are weary of speaking in a group, particularly when the Star Woman is present. Many of them know the truth of what Ben Tsotsie and Black Raven have said.'*

"I have seen many objects in the sky near my home. I have read about others. What are they?" A Navajo woman seated a few places away asked. Ryan thought her name was Joyce; she addressed the question to Sarah. He had noticed the two of them in long conversations.

"Many of them are the ships of your brothers and sisters from distant star systems," Sarah replied. "They come here to awaken Earth-humans."

"I am already awake," the woman insisted.

"But many are not."

At the end of the meal, Singing Bird served her delicious sopaipillas. Ryan took a bite of one, closing his eyes to get the full impact of the fried delicacy with gooey honey.

After the dishes had been cleared, Sarah stood, looking around the long table until she was sure he had everyone's attention. "Thank you all for coming to help us celebrate."

After further words of welcome, she said, "I want to take a few minutes this evening to discuss things from my perspective as a visitor to your planet. Prior to observing conditions among the people of this planet, I had always thought of slavery as imprisonment or a slave labor camp -- although I had never been to such a place. Now, after residing on this planet, I have a completely new concept: fear based slavery.

"On this planet, fear reigns so strongly that all are enslaved by it. Those who rule this planet understand fear and have nurtured it to their advantage. Daily, they amplify it utilizing a variety of measures that come to you through the television and in newspapers, through movies and books. These overlords feed their own darkness from the negative energy generated by Earth's people.

"At the same time they wish you to believe that you are free. In many ways you are. You are free to think and believe as you wish. You are free to project whatever energy you desire. It is the energy of each of you that can be used to dispel the fear of enslavement." She motioned to those around the table.

"Those who rule have twisted each of your institutions to their ends -- governments, corporations, education, healthcare. They all started with a noble mission: to provide a needed service or to produce a worthwhile product. Everything goes along fine, until an institution has achieved a measure of success. Then those who wish to control infiltrate and take over. After that, decisions are made for their benefit, rather than serving those for whom the institution was intended. Money, threats, physical force, and various forms of mind control are used to accomplish this. Thus they use your imaginations and energies to create new things to their advantage.

"Identical procedures have been enacted in every other country. Sometimes it is done as a dictatorship; other times it goes under the guise of democracy. In short, those who rule have, in one way or another, enslaved all of Earth's peoples."

The people at the table hung on every word from the star woman. Each of the adults, even the men who temporarily worked at Ben's camp, had experienced at least one genuine conversation with Sarah. She had also played with each of the children. Among these simple people she had created a genuine community. It had enabled her to learn of life on this dense planet; it had afforded them the opportunity to learn of life on another planet.

One woman spoke up, "We know the ways of white men." Others nodded.

Sensing that Ryan was about to say something, Sarah said, "Let me finish. The ultimate unkind twist they have forced upon modern societies is to create a dependence on burning hydrocarbons. From the generation of electricity to powering automobiles, modern civilization is a hydrocarbon-based civilization."

She motioned to those at the table. "How many of you do not use electricity?"

Several adults raised a hand. Many of the older Navajos lived without electricity.

"How many use gasoline or diesel?"

Most hands shot up.

"As things stand today, you have no alternatives. However, of all people, you of Navajo ancestry," she gestured again to those around the table, "should not have made yourselves dependent on outsiders."

More heads nodded.

"What has happened on this planet is the opposite of conditions on my home planet. There, love is the basis for decision-making, not fear. There, the leaders function in the best interests of all people. They are not rewarded for what they can achieve for themselves. There, we have universal wealth, and free energy for all. There we do not burn hydrocarbons.

"But we must not condemn those who oppress us. Just like you, their souls volunteered to incarnate in their bodies to act out their roles in this time and place, perhaps to balance out some past karma. In past lives they may actually have been one of your people. With their dark actions, they are giving you the opportunity to choose a path, choose between light and dark.

"Now let us see how we each can use our individual energies to make a difference..."

At that moment, one of the large double doors from the stairway leading to the outside banged open and the bedraggled figure of a man stumbled into the room. He wore a wool ski hat and had a heavy poncho draped over his shoulders. A purple bruise surrounded one eye; his left cheek showed the red scab of an ugly gash.

Ryan and Sarah rushed to his side.

"Looks like I'm late for the celebration," he said.

Ryan grabbed Ajax Johnson's arm to steady him. He helped him to the chair he had been occupying. "You look like you've been through hell," Ryan said.

Sarah gave her brother a hug and kiss. "I am so happy to see you. We were very worried."

"Try doing anything when you've lost your ID," her brother said.

"I've been hitching rides since I got to Arizona." He patted Sarah's hand, "After I contacted you, I found a ride from Kayenta to here."

"You missed Ethete and John deBeque," Sarah said. "They went to find you. I'll let Ethete know you are here."

Ignoring her comment, Ajax coughed and continued, "You can't imagine some of the places I've been the last few days. I couldn't be sure I'd find you here. I saw a newspaper with your picture in it, rescuing President Boyle and all." He tried to smile, but the effort was too much.

Singing Bird set a steaming cup of black coffee in front of the former football star. He had resided at Harmony just long enough for her to learn what he liked to drink.

Johnny set down a heaping plate of enchiladas, chili rellenos, beans, and rice. Singing Bird stood ready with a refill on the coffee. "Decaf," she announced.

Conversation died as he ate. The Navajo families took this as their clue and began to drift off. A couple of the women went into the kitchen to help Singing Bird.

SIX

After Ajax had finished off the food and his second cup of coffee, Sarah said, "Tell us about it."

Ajax pulled off his ski hat to reveal more bruises, and the scab of a deep gash beneath the light blonde stubble that covered his formerly bald head. He said, "My gig in Gallup went real well. All the reporters from here followed me, and a few more showed up. Funny though, nothing made it into the papers or onto the TV."

He took a sip of coffee and continued. "Well, after my gig, I headed to out California nice and slow -- to encourage the reporters and anyone else to follow. When I found an open stretch of road west of Holbrook, I left them in the dust. I got as far as Twentynine Palms, jumping from the Interstate to back roads after John deBeque made his announcements about Ernest Steiger and the media affiliates. Anyway, I found a nice little motel and checked in -- only two hundred a night. It was fun to watch the television anchors respond to John's material. They stumbled all over themselves trying to explain how they had never been compromised and how the networks were not under anybody's control."

"The day of the tsunami we had a brief blackout, nothing more. The following morning a couple of military police knocked on the door of my motel room, guns drawn. They handcuffed me and shoved me into their car. One of them put a hood over my head -- guess they were worried about what I was going to see. They picked up one other guy along the way -- shoved him in the back seat next to me and told us to be quiet.

"When we arrived at this camp out in the desert, they locked us into a big wire cage. There were lots of other men and women -- no privacy whatsoever -- just cots and holes in the ground. All they gave

44

us was a single blanket; it got real cold at night. We figured out that we'd been tagged by the American ID card that everyone has to show when they check into a hotel."

Ajax paused as a coughing fit overcame him. When he regained his breath, he continued, "None of the guards said anything. It was like they really didn't want to be doing this. They brought us food and water, then went away.

"After two days, they unlocked our cages and herded us all onto buses. They dumped me back in Twentynine Palms -- turns out, this concentration camp was only a few miles away. My Corvette was still parked in front of my motel room -- just like nothing had happened. I stumbled inside and slept for twenty-four hours. I contacted our allies and asked what I should do. They told me to come to Harmony Center."

The doors to the great room swung open and Ethete and John deBeque walked in. Ethete ran to Ajax and gave him a hug. With excited words, she said, "I'm so glad you're okay. We went to Kayenta, but didn't find you. Sarah communicated and told me you had made it here."

"He was just telling us his story," Ryan said to John deBeque.

When the two newcomers had settled into places at the table, Ajax brought them up to speed. "As I was saying, I packed up and drove east. When I got to Needles I found out that they were turning back everybody who didn't have an Arizona driver's license. Seems there were lots of people from California who were worried about another tsunami. They were searching every vehicle to make sure nobody slipped through -- like it was the border for a different country. All I had was my California driver's license, and my American ID, so I figured I wouldn't be getting to Harmony via the Interstate.

"California had set up a tent city just outside Needles, barbed wire and everything. It seemed that Arizona had informed California years ago that, in the event of any disaster, they would not be taking refugees.

"I heard there was very little in the way of food or water at the camp, just lots and lots of people milling around, wondering what to do next. I also heard they were worried about plague and that was why Arizona was keeping everyone out.

"So I drove north along the Colorado River, looking for an out-of-the-way place to cross into Arizona, thinking if I got away from the Interstate I'd be better off. Pretty soon I came to the Nevada border. There weren't as many people here, and only a few guards, but the same story. A big sign was posted: NEVADA RESIDENTS ONLY. But I watched as fancy cars with California plates drove up and passed money to the border guards. With my Corvette, I drove up and acted like I knew where I was going. Cost me a hundred.

"Well it's not that far from the border to Laughlin. I drove into town to find the casinos in full operation, lots of cars with California plates in the parking lots. I stopped one place; people were drinking, smoking, and playing the slot machines and tables -- like absolutely nothing had changed.

"When I drove north of town to catch the bridge over the Colorado River to Arizona, I found the road blocked and more signs up. So, I turned around, went into one of the casinos, had a nice meal, and looked east across the river."

"I asked my waitress where she was from. She said Arizona. I asked how the casinos were managing to keep going with the border to Arizona closed. 'Well, mister, you see the bosses here want to keep things going, ya know, raking in the cash. You see over there. The hired help, like me, we live over there. People from Arizona, they come and go. Nothing's going to shut this place down. Anything else I can get you?'

"'How do you get across to Arizona?'

"'See those sightseeing boats? The authorities over in Bullhead City kinda close their eyes when they see folks bein' dropped off.'

"'So what would it take to get me across?'

"'Money, honey. Money, and knowing the right person.' After she negotiated me up to two hundred bucks, she wrote down the name of the captain of one of the boats.

"I went across late that night," Ajax said. "Paid another three hundred bucks to the skipper and he delivered me along with the maintenance, housekeeping, and food service people. I was real bummed-out having to leave my Corvette, but I gave the parking attendant at the hotel a wad of cash to look out after it.

"When I got to the Arizona side, there was a uniformed policeman checking everyone's driver's license and American ID. He had one of those little machines that reads them. When he scanned mine, the machine beeped, and he scowled.

"He was all set to force me back on the boat when a golden globe appeared between us, like one of the small spheres you told me about." He motioned to Sarah and grinned. "He got this dazed look and went to check the next person in line. After that no one asked me for anything."

"What's this golden globe thing you're talking about?" John de-Beque asked.

Sarah explained that globes, or orbs, about six to eight inches in diameter had helped Ryan and her on several occasions. They were from one of her non-human friends. They could cloud the consciousness of someone who was impeding progress; they were also intelligent enough to act as guides and guards.

"I hitched a ride east on a semi, but the bastard pulled a gun on me when we got to a rest area. He marched me out behind the restrooms where he and two of his buddies worked me over real good.

"One of them even said, 'Hey you kinda look like that football player fella. Well, football player, guess you ain't so tough after all.' That was before he hit me on the head with a tire iron. After I passed out, they took my wallet and my watch.

"So there I was, without any money, credit cards, or ID, and I'm stumbling around in a daze, all bloody. Try hitching in that shape, especially when everybody's paranoid about everything.

"It was so ugly. Slept in a lot of restrooms. Do you know how bad those places stink? I didn't have to lock myself in because one of those globes stood watch at the door. And each morning and evening I was led to someone in the rest area who would share food with me. Three days of that. and I arrived in Kayenta."

"Why didn't you communicate with me?" Sarah asked. We could have come and found you.

"I kept trying. I guess the knock on the head did something. I'm dizzy most of the time." The bald headed football star took one last bite of enchilada and slumped into his chair.

"Quite a story," Ryan said, patting Ajax on the arm. "We're glad you made it here."

"Let's help him to his room," Sarah said. "He needs sleep."

"And we will begin energy work," Ethete said. "I am particularly worried about that gash on his head."

As they were settling Ajax into bed, a giant white-haired man suddenly appeared in the room. He acknowledged each of the four standing around Ajax's bed with a hug and "It's good to see you again." Dr. Victor Adamson had not been at Harmony Center since Sarah and Ryan had returned. The designer of Harmony Center, he had been overseeing its reconstruction, but the crew told Ryan and Sarah that he had been called away.

Then he leaned over the bed of the barely awake man and said, "You've had a rough time of it, Ajax. I'm sorry I was unable to be of more help. Unfortunately, I was taking care of pressing problems below."

"I appreciate the help you sent," Ajax mumbled. "It kept me out of even more trouble, but next time send one that can smell."

"Get well soon." Dr. Adamson turned and motioned for the others to follow him.

As they strolled back to the great room, Sarah said, "What are the problems below?"

"Agents of the cabal were tunneling deep into the Earth's crust, attempting to intrude into our civilization. We dissuaded them with some sulfur-laden air. They believed they had drilled into hell," he chuckled, "but I expect they will try again."

"Below?" John deBeque asked.

"When Atlantis and Lemuria were destroyed, some of their residents escaped deep into Earth," Sarah said. "They created advanced civilizations that most surface dwellers are unaware of."

"Let me interrupt, to issue an invitation," Dr. Adamson said. "The Earth representatives will meet soon. The presence of all four of you is requested. I will inform you of the time. Now I must turn to my duties elsewhere." With that brief conversation he vanished as quickly as he had appeared.

SEVEN

"It's time we talked," Carlton Boyle said under his breath. He and Sam Wellborn were standing in the hallway leading to the Oval Office; the President had asked Sam to straighten his tie.

"Sure, Mr. President," Sam replied in a whisper. "When?"

"Come on, I need some exercise." The President grabbed Sam's arm and tugged him along. His old friend led him to the White House swimming pool; two Secret Service agents trailed a few steps behind. When they arrived at the pool, an attendant pointed Sam to a changing room.

Earlier Sally O'Hara had called to ask Sam to come to the Oval Office at 11:00 AM. Sam had assumed the President wanted to get the latest about the Natural Disaster Preparedness Task Force. Sam had met with that group yesterday for a third session; the prior day, he had sent the members off to a different conference room to meet among themselves to hash out a set of recommendations. He had been disappointed when they reconvened. Nothing new had been presented, just the same old strategy of more ocean floor sensors, better communications among the various agencies, more money spent to research the true causes of tsunamis, etc. He was not looking forward to reporting to the President. Now Sam was taken back. After the cold shoulder treatment he had received at their last meeting, Sam was not expecting whispered words.

When Sam entered the tiled pool area in White House swimming trunks, music was blasting as the President thrashed about like a novice. He found this a little strange as they had both been champion swimmers in college, in fact that was how they had first met.

Sam plunged into the pool and swam to its far end. He turned around and did a lazy backstroke to Boyle's side. "You look like a drowning man."

"Care to thrash around with me for a while?" The words echoed off the white tile walls of the room.

"Sure thing." Sam got the hint and began to slap the water as Boyle was doing.

"They're watching me all the time," Carlton Boyle said, his voice lowered. He raised his eyes to the Secret Service agents standing on the rim of the pool.

Sam paused, dumfounded. "Isn't that what the Secret Service is supposed to do?"

"Keep moving around. It interrupts their listening devices."

Sam did as requested, sinking under the water and emerging with a great deal of thrashing about. "You mean they're keeping tabs on you?"

"Watching my every move."

"But you're..."

The President cut him off. "They're not really Secret Service agents."

Sam had no words to express the sinking feeling that came over him. This could not be happening. They chatted for a few minutes about how the President was feeling isolated, then Sam asked, "How's Margaret handling things?" Newspaper reports had told the nation that the First Lady had become ill shortly after the President's return from Oregon.

"Thanks for asking, she's drinking and taking drugs. Started when she thought I was dead. In fact, that's what I wanted to talk to you about." Boyle nodded toward the suited man. "Margaret has one with her all the time. If I screw up, they'll kill her."

"I don't believe what I'm hearing."

"Even told me how they'd do it: lethal injection."

Sam glanced up at one of the suited men standing at the edge of the pool. He slapped the water again and asked, "What can I do?"

"Get her away from here." The President pleaded with his eyes. "Just get her somewhere safe."

"I'll get to work on it."

As Sam watched the President climb out of the pool, he felt like a character out of a plot from a cheap novel. But he had known Carlton Boyle a long time and trusted the words he had just heard. The President had just entrusted him with something that was huge. Who could possibly be pulling the strings behind this? Stunned, Sam watched the Secret Service agents accompany the President to the changing room;

he was left alone in the pool.

This could not be happening. In Sam's America, the President of the United States was above being threatened. What did they want? Sam swam three laps before getting out.

In a locker room deserted except for the attendant, he showered and dressed. Sam concluded that the man he had been with in the pool was not the same one he had known these past few years. What had happened to him?

As he was making his way back to his office, lost in thought, he bumped head-on into one of the suited men who had been with the President at the pool.

"Excuse me sir, I think you left this in the dressing room." The agent affixed his White House photo ID to his suit vest pocket. "Can't have anyone running around these halls without one of these."

"Thank you, uh agent?"

"Crowley, sir, Marcus Crowley."

"Crowley, huh. I'll remember that name." Sam surmised that since he was not regimented to White House procedures, he had simply failed to notice that his ID was not in place. Or had he?

He went to his office, stripped off the coat, and hung it on a side chair. Then he stepped next door to Tiffany Wheeler's office. Before she could greet him, he put his finger to his lips. Then he motioned for her to follow him down the hall toward the cafeteria.

"What's going on?" Tiffany asked.

"Walk like nothing's unusual." Sam took a deep breath, then whispered, "I want a list of alcohol rehabilitation facilities, something out west."

Tiffany looked at her boss, started to say something, but then stopped. They had been through enough together to know that he would explain everything in due time.

They got two coffees and went their separate ways. Before going back to his office, Sam used his cell phone to set up two appointments.

At 8:30 AM the next morning, Sam Wellborn strategically placed himself so that he was chatting with Sally O'Hara near the Oval Office. Two Secret Service agents stood guard outside the door leading into it, another two were in the hallway leading here. The people who had attended the President's daily briefing marched out of the Oval office heading their respective directions. Two of them stopped to say hello to Sam.

At 8:44 AM, the President's mysterious morning visitors arrived; two Secret Service agents accompanied them. They did not wait to be announced, nor did they acknowledge Sally or Sam. The Secret Service agents stationed outside the door of the Oval office quickly wandered off. Henry Bustamonte opened the door into the President's inner sanctum and calmly marched in; the others followed. The Secret Service agents who had accompanied the group positioned themselves outside the door as soon as the six entered.

"It's like this every day," Sally whispered.

"I think we need to have lunch," Sam said.

"I'm free tomorrow, the President's going to Camp David this afternoon."

"Okay, meet you at the usual place. Noon?"

"Eleven thirty, I want a good table."

EIGHT

The Boeing 757 landed at Denver International Airport at 3:46 AM the next morning. It taxied until it reached buildings normally handling cargo in and out of the city. A corner of one of these was used as a receiving area for visiting dignitaries who wished to avoid the passenger terminal.

After the engines were shut down, security personnel wheeled a set of stairs to the side of the plane. Secret Service agents in dark suits and security personnel in black uniforms greeted it.

Jose Alvarez, a janitor working in an adjacent building, paused to watch this somewhat unusual scene. The last passenger flight out of the airport, a delayed plane to San Francisco, had departed at 11:50 PM. Except for maintenance personnel the cargo buildings had been closed since 9:00 PM.

Jose had not understood the directions from his supervisor that everyone was to go home early. So he had gone about his regularly scheduled job of carting trash to the big dumpster outside.

When he saw the first one emerge from the jet way, he covered his mouth to stifle a scream. The devil itself had shown up. Jose trembled and fell to his knees. "Sweet mother of Jesus," he mumbled.

Inching himself up to peer over the trash bin, he continued to watch the amazing scene. More of the devils came down the ramp.

A sleepy Henry Bustamonte, oblivious to the fact that someone was watching, emerged from the door and staggered down the stairs. His administrative assistant, Josh, a young man with a black computer case slung over his shoulder, followed him. Both wore dark suits, white shirts, and red ties. Bustamonte spoke briefly to one of the Secret Service agents and then headed for the entrance to the building. Due

53

to his preoccupation with Carlton Boyle, this was his first trip to this destination.

The President's Chief of Staff waited patiently until Grant Clever joined him at the doorway. Focused on the very attractive young woman on his arm, Clever did not acknowledge the security personnel who facilitated his arrival. Clever and Bustamonte entered the waiting area together.

Jonathan Olson, carrying a heavy briefcase, arrived next in the waiting area. On the flight he had told Bustamonte that he and his people were transferring the control algorithms for the League's debt and derivatives operations to their new super secure site. As usual he wore a dark blue pin stripped suit with a white shirt and red and blue club tie.

"On the dirt, spread 'em." A gruff voice announced. Jose had heard words like this before; he complied without hesitation. His hands were roughly secured behind him. A second after he felt the prick of the needle in his neck, everything went blank.

After identifications were checked against a printed list, Bustamonte and the others went through double doors to a freight elevator on which a special control panel door was open. The elevator whisked them down to a level that was well below that used by the underground trains that served the main terminal and the three concourses of DIA.

Bustamonte walked down a short well-lighted hallway and stepped through a doorway into a large cylinder with airline-style seats, two on each side of the windowless tube. No door for a conductor or engineer was visible at the blunt forward wall of the compartment. When all were onboard, the doors closed securely, and the cabin was pressurized. With barely a hint of forward motion, the tram accelerated. There was virtually no sound associated with their trip except quiet conversation, which given the early hour was limited.

In fourteen minutes he felt the car decelerate. In another moment, the doors opened. He walked onto a platform and turned to look at the exterior of the streamlined tram that had sped him from the Denver airport. It was about fifty feet long with a pointed nose and sleek metal skin. Its rear end appeared to be encapsulated by a dark skirt. On the flight he had explained to Josh that these levitated monorails traveled in a vacuum to increase their speed. What he did not tell Josh was that this was a one-way trip and that the young man would be remaining in Colorado.

Similar cylinders were pulled up around this hub, like the spokes of a wheel. Its ceiling and the tunnels coming into it glistened as if they were made of glass. The scene looked a bit like a train station but without the smells associated with diesel or electricity. A security man in a red uniform scanned his retina, when it read positive, he directed him to an escalator.

The escalator took him up into what looked like the well-lighted lobby of a modern office building with a thirty-foot ceiling. Large plants were positioned around its perimeter; flower boxes were interspersed among them. There were video cameras positioned at various angles. Bustamonte was quite sure he was being compared against images in a data bank.

People in uniforms of blue, green, and red hurried about. Red ropes funneled arriving passengers to the reception desk. Although he had visited other underground installations, this was his first to their newly constructed headquarters.

"About time," Warren Ophir said. He was standing next to the polished wood reception counter, behind which sat three attractive young women in green blazers. A large sign behind the counter read, WORLD LEAGUE. A gold pyramid thrust itself, at an upward angle, from the wall above the name. Beneath the pyramid were the words, RIDING THE WAVE OF EVOLUTION.

"Come on, I'll walk you to your office." Ophir pointed to a bank of wood-paneled elevators. "Just like in the big city -- except these go down, not up. I'll have one of my people show your assistant where to put your bags."

"Most people I run into think you died in that nuclear explosion." This was the first time Bustamonte had seen Ophir since Boyle's first presidency.

"I like it that way," Ophir chuckled. "That nuclear thing was that crazy German's idea. Can you believe he blew himself up with a nuke?" He laughed. "Watched the whole thing by picture phone from my DC office. Damn, I'm glad I refused his invitation to be there."

"He reported to you, right?"

"Yes."

"You okayed it, right?"

"Yes."

"Do you have any idea how much that has cost us? Those ARVs were to deliver the EMPs."

"Yeah, I know. It's the end of plan A. So, what's plan B?"

"You'll hear about it soon enough," Bustamonte replied, "but not from me."

Ophir stared at the heavy-set man. He gripped the gold engraved head of his cane, thinking he could kill the other man with a single well-placed blow.

Bustamonte stared back, refusing to give an inch.

After what seemed like a long time, Ophir motioned him to the elevator door. "Come on; I'll show you around. Show this man some identification." He paused in front of one of the elevators with his own ID badge extended.

"But you know me."

"Rules are rules. They apply to everybody, even me. Not everyone gets to ride every elevator to every floor, not even you. By the way, red uniforms indicate security; don't mess with them."

Bustamonte dug into the pocket of his suit coat to find a holograpically encoded identification badge with his picture. He extended it to the security man who had an Uzi slung over his shoulder plus a belt with a 9mm automatic.

On the elevator, Ophir used the foot of his cane to punch the button for the sixth floor. When they alighted, another guard checked their identifications.

They walked through a large brightly lighted corridor, doors on either side. Except for a slight bend, it could have been the hallway of any modern office building.

"This used to be the tunnel of a gold mine." Ophir pointed to the ceiling. "Those old miners would chase a vein for miles. We walled off most of the side tunnels; use others for disposal of trash.

"Overbearing rock was stable so the construction crew simply fused a layer of rock as support. We didn't want to disturb the appearance of the ranch house by tearing the mountain apart. It's the same process they use to create the tunnels for the monorail."

When the lights flickered briefly, they halted. A moment later Ophir's cell phone rang. "I'll be down later," he said after a brief conversation. The lighting was now steady.

"The energy units that supply our electricity are acting up," he said to Bustamonte. "This is the beta installation for our scaled up free energy model. Our guys have gotten pretty good at making small units, but stringing enough of them together to power this place has proven to be challenging. But at least we are isolated from the oil crisis." He chuckled. Warren Ophir knew full well that the World league had created the crisis. "And, yes, cell phones work down here, powered by an energy unit all their own; we took care of that in the initial design, while we were shielding the entire facility against non-physical intrusions."

"What about the air?"

"Re-circulated, like on a submarine, another set of energy units." He went on to explain how outside air was brought in, filtered, and distributed to all nine levels of the underground facility. "In total there are two hundred and nineteen different rooms. In the event of problems on the surface, like the strange weather we've been having, this facility could operate self-contained for over six months.

"In case you are interested, they found a small amount of gold as they were constructing things. We are now processing it during times of low electricity usage. I'm sure you will find it quite pure."

In about seventy-five feet, Ophir paused before an oak door; the name on it, in gold letters, read HENRY BUSTAMONTE. Inside was a large office suite with a secretary's work area including wood veneer file cabinets, and a small conference room. Bustamonte's office was twenty by twenty. At its center was the cherry wood desk he had selected. Several comfortable leather chairs surrounded it. Behind the desk was a credenza with computer display. The only thing missing was a window. Classical paintings, from Bustamonte's private collection, hung on the walls.

"I'd say you were pretty well set." Ophir plopped down in one of the chairs opposite the desk and watched Bustamonte, while fingering the engraved gold top of his cane. The President's Chief of Staff walked around the room examining each corner, adjusting the position of one of the chairs; then he sat in the leather chair behind the desk.

"Pretty nice," Bustamonte said, "yeah, pretty damn nice. If I'm going to be spending time here, might as well be comfortable."

"So what's happening?" Ophir asked. "Underground, we don't get much real news."

Bustamonte spent the next few minutes giving Warren Ophir a rundown on the happenings in Washington that had not made the newspapers or television. The World League did not commit much to paper and transmitted little news via its computer network. They had recently moved their data management and worldwide communications center from outside Washington, DC to this secure location, hundreds of feet under an innocent looking mountain to the west of Denver, Colorado.

"And the League?" Ophir asked. His dark brown hair had recently been styled. Dark eyes betrayed little of his thoughts or emotions.

"Uh, I think you'd better get that from Clever. You know how he is."

"How about a hint or two?" This was the first time in his professional career that Warren Ophir had not had the ability to wander around Washington, DC, or any other city he chose. For over two weeks, he had been stuck in this hole, depending on what outsiders told him in the way of hard news. Of course, there were the hidden microphones and cameras he and his men had long ago planted, but they did not give a complete picture. He did not bother with news from the internet, television, or radio.

Richard Tyler, who perceived Ophir as a threat to his grab for power, had arrested a number of the intelligence affiliates. Ophir joined his operatives in Columbia and sent out a stand-down message to intelligence affiliates worldwide. When Carlton Boyle came back, Ophir had remained out of the country until he saw how things were going to shake out. Just over two weeks ago, he had received a message from Grant Clever informing him that they were back on track and inviting him to this facility. Ophir had immediately begun contacting his affiliates.

Just last week, Ophir had found a way to circumvent the strict communications monitoring protocol of this super secure facility. Now he could piggyback instruction to his affiliates on other data traffic. But somehow Clever had gotten wind of it; they were to meet later today to discuss things.

"Kingman's still in jail," Bustamonte laughed. "Seems some crusading prosecutor and a Federal judge ganged up on him. Looks like we'll have to let it go to trial, just to make people think that one of the bad guys was apprehended and that the justice system is functioning. Delta won't say anything. Boyle will pardon him in a few months. Clever's anxious to keep Kingman out of the action. I'm guessing you know about Vanderbush and Randolph."

Ophir nodded. "What about your charge?"

"He does exactly what I tell him to do," Bustamonte grinned. "Nobody has figured things out."

"That's great. Why'd it take you so long to move on him?"

"Well, you know, Boyle wasn't expected to win. We thought we had it sufficiently slanted. Then, we couldn't get started until he took office and we saw how he was going to behave. We were all set when he made that surprise trip to check-up on construction at his family's ranch. When the tsunami hit, we wound up with our man Tyler. Everybody thought we were home free until Kingman and he went ballistic with their dictator thing. After Boyle resurrected, we put the original plan into effect; it only took a couple of days."

"What about his wife? Has she figured things out yet?"

"Tyler drugged her and locked her up in the private quarters of the White House." Bustamonte chuckled, "Now she's hooked on the stuff, along with alcohol. We're working on a way to maneuver her out of the picture, make it look nice and natural for everybody."

Bustamonte looked at the former secret intelligence czar. He knew he had to manage this man just right, just like he managed other dangerous people. He had worked at the Defense Intelligence Agency with Ophir. They had become quite friendly, but Bustamonte had never come to trust Ophir. Then their paths had parted, and Ophir had gone on to become the overseer of the intelligence affiliates, an arm of the World League.

In reality, Bustamonte knew that the intelligence affiliates were Warren Ophir's fiefdom; its members owed loyalty to him before anyone or anything else. The other members of the World League's Board had long ago concluded that Ophir's spooks awaited their master's directions. And the security in this place, he had to talk to Grant about it. How had they allowed Ophir to design it?

After Carlton Boyle's resurrection and Richard Tyler's suicide, there had been a rearrangement of the leadership of the World league. In a dramatic struggle, in which several members of the League had been assassinated, Grant Clever had replaced Delta Kingman as Chairman. Although he had just proclaimed otherwise, Bustamonte was quite sure that Kingman would never get out of jail alive.

"Going back to our previous conversation," Ophir said, "so how are we going to create EMPs now?"

"We can still use scalar. We just won't be able to do as much."

"Changing the subject, Boyle's amnesty program really hurt us," Bustamonte said. "Some people took the opportunity to talk. We've diverted the whole process, but there are one or two items that need damage control. Maybe some of your people could help out."

"Sure, let me know," Warren Ophir said as he stood to leave. He immediately regretted the words. No sense in emphasizing that he was in touch with all his old connections.

At 11:25 that same day, Sam sat at Fu Kee, a Chinese restaurant in Washington, DC, that both Sally O'Hara and he frequented. As he waited, he thought about his encounter with Carlton Boyle in the pool. There was something about the man that did not seem right. Was it possible the President was taking a prescription drug that was making him appear different?

Putting these thoughts aside, he motioned Sally to the table as she came in the door.

"What you saw this morning has happened every day since the President got back from the tsunami," Sally said. They had ordered lunch specials and were sipping Chinese tea.

"Did it just start all of a sudden?"

"Let me see if I can remember." Sally took a sip of water, as she searched her memory. "Okay, here goes, it started a few days later. The third day he was back, Grant Clever had an appointment with him. That was the day before he went to George Washington University Hospital for his debilitating headache. The day after he came back from that, the whole group traipses in, just like this morning."

"Did Clever meet with him alone that first time?" Sam asked.

"Now let me think." She paused, took a sip of tea, and then looked up at Sam. "He brought that other man with him, Goldman, the skinny one with the van dyke. That was it; yes I'm sure I remember it clearly now. They stood in front of my desk the whole time they were waiting for the President, didn't say a word to me."

"Why didn't the Secret Service vet these guys?"

Sally looked around the room, studying faces. They had chosen a booth in a back corner. She sat with her back to the wall. Sam had insisted that she put her purse on the seat of the booth and cover it with her heavy coat.

"There are new faces, Sam, guys that don't fit the mold, if you know what I mean. No women in the white house Secret Service any more. The First Lady has two men who take care of her. She used to have women, but no more. I know you remember James Batcher, former head of White House security; well, I haven't seen him since the day after the President returned from the hospital. I heard that he'd gotten sick, but I don't really know. You see, they don't tell me as much as they used to. Even the President doesn't confide in me so much any more."

They paused their conversation as the waitress brought their luncheon specials. Sally's was Kung Pao chicken, Sam's was shrimp in garlic sauce.

"What about his new Chief of Staff, Henry Bustamonte. How do you get on with him?" Sam asked after they had sampled the food.

"He and I don't see eye to eye." Sally's response was terse. "His secretary controls all the President's appointments. All I do is type up the

President's correspondence, just type and file, type and file. It's not like when President Boyle was first sworn in. Did you know he specifically asked me to stay on; told me he wanted my experience? He seemed a lot happier before the tsunami. I guess all those new security measures are necessary, with the terrorists and all, but I've been the secretary to Presidents for thirteen years."

"What security measures are you talking about?" Sam asked.

"Oh, the ones where they sweep my office each day to be sure there are no listening devices. And then I have a personal escort whenever I'm in the building. He walked me to the gate when I left to have lunch just now. Wanted to know who I was meeting and when I'd be back. I told a little white lie, said I was going to meet my cousin. Oh, and I've been told that they record every conversation in every office, every telephone call too."

They chatted for another forty-five minutes. Sam became increasingly weary of Sally's remarks. It was she, after all, who had called him to meet with the President two days ago, not Bustamonte's secretary. And there was one more little thing; Sally never ordered spicy Chinese food, claiming it bothered her stomach, yet she had devoured her lunch today. Like the President, she seemed different. However, when they separated in front of the restaurant, he dismissed his concerns; it would not serve anyone's best interests if he became paranoid.

NINE

Sam Wellborn had agreed to meet with Dr. Gordon Moore only after the doctor had badgered Tiffany for the fourth time. Sam had told Tiffany he had more important things to do than listen to the good doctor rave about a secret government. All that had changed after his talk with President Boyle in the swimming pool.

The two men had arranged to meet at the Blue Sea Grill in Baltimore, Maryland. After what Sam had learned from Sally O'Hara, he was fairly sure his every move was being watched. Although he was reluctant to do so, he allowed Metro security to scan his American ID as be boarded. He took the Red Line to Rockville, Maryland, where he hired a taxi to Baltimore. Given the high price of gasoline, the cab had cost a small fortune. It took him an hour to walk the last mile, weaving in and out of stores along the way.

He waited near the door until Moore arrived. At Sam's urging, they both shed their overcoats and suit coats, hanging them on the rack near the door.

"Did you follow my instructions?" he asked Gordon Moore when they were seated.

"I did as you suggested. I don't believe I was followed."

"Good." As they glanced at menus, Sam remarked, "I've heard that your amnesty program was getting to the heart of some sensitive information. But just when it was about to produce something really juicy, one of your witnesses died. Now I've been told it's drying up."

"I have that sense too," Moore said.

"The top people whom it was intended to bring into the open are scared. What you are now getting are people carrying deliberate misinformation."

"And exactly how do you know this?"

"Gordon, I know a lot more people around Washington than you do. I've been in the political game a long time. I am one of the few people this President really trusts."

"That last part I figured out. What I haven't figured out is why you're heading up the Natural Disaster Preparedness Task Force."

"I haven't either." What Sam did not say was that he had figured out that the President had been told to stop him from investigating the Utah explosion. Why he was not yet sure, but he suspected it was because he was getting close to the truth. But then he was not sure about a lot of things right now, or a lot of people, which was why he was meeting with Moore at this out-of-the-way restaurant.

What was even more maddening was that he loved his country, loved how Americans had crawled to the top of the world heap. He had visited other countries and was always grateful to come home. But right now, Sam was not sure whether he could trust his old values, whether he could trust anyone.

They both ordered crab cakes. Sam ordered a Caesar salad; Moore ordered chowder. Sam guessed the tab was going to be well over a hundred dollars, but he shrugged it off as he planned to use his government credit card.

"I'd like to know what you can tell me about weather control," Sam said as he picked at his salad. "And that comment you made about people knowing about the tsunami and not warning the public."

"Where should I start?"

"Wherever you'd like."

Moore hesitated, then said, "And then I want you to tell me what you know about the government's cover-up of ETs. And anything you know about Sarah Smith."

Sam had not expected this. Trying not to show surprise, he continued to munch on his salad.

Moore read Sam's face and said, "I hadn't put it all together until you showed up at the first meeting of the Task Force with your assistant Tiffany. You see I was at Peter Jones' presentation in Denver, the one where he openly declared he was from another planet, and showed everybody that he did not have a navel. I saw Tiffany deliver certain photos to Ryan Drake that night; photos he later passed around to the audience. So yeah, I know that you know."

Sam smiled. Dr. Gordon Moore was sharper than he had given him credit for. "Guess I'll have to watch my step from now on. I wonder who else has made that connection? Okay, I'll tell you what I know -- which isn't much. However, since I'm buying, what did you find out about weather modification?"

Moore laid out what he had discovered from three people who had come forward under the amnesty program, one man and two women, all from the Air Force. "The U.S. project began in response to the Soviet's program. After almost fifty years, the U.S. is able to control weather patterns -- to increase or decrease the severity of hurricanes -- and this technology has been used in more than one instance. The technology is not yet one hundred percent, but more research is under-way to improve it.

"What people call chemtrails are part of this weather modification program. These chemtrails are also used to modify the atmosphere to enhance radio communications. All three of these amnesty-seekers had been told that the Russians were continuing their program."

Over Maryland crab cakes, Moore talked about a conversation that a secretary from the National Oceanic and Atmospheric Administration had relayed to him. "She overheard her boss tell two different people that they were not to alert people along the West Coast to the likelihood of a massive tsunami. This warning had been derived from NOAA's undersea sensors." The woman had died in an automobile accident before Moore was able to have further conversations with her.

When Gordon Moore finished his entree, he sat for a moment star-ing at Sam. "I know you're interested in what I know about that Utah explosion." He paused gathering his thoughts. "What I've learned is almost beyond belief, but I have now heard it often enough to believe it. It goes to the very heart of a secret government conspiracy, which until I heard this stuff -- well, let's just say I was skeptical."

"I'm still skeptical," Sam said. "This is not some two-bit country in Africa, we're talking about the United States of America."

"I know," Moore said. "And it's because I know, and am now convinced, that I'm worried about my safety and the safety of my fam-ily. If this stuff is true, it will shake the very foundation of America. It's why I agreed to meet you way out here and follow your security precautions."

Sam leaned forward over his plate, elbows on the table. "I'd like to hear what you have."

Moore took a very deep breath.

"Can I get you gentlemen something else," the waitress inter-rupted.

"Two coffees," Sam replied without taking his eyes off Moore. She asked if she could clean off their dishes. As she was doing that, both Moore and he searched the room for anyone who showed a particular interest in their conversation.

"Okay, here goes," Moore said. "I have talked to four different people, one Air Force, one Navy -- not the same ones as with the weather projects. A private company employed the other two. All their stories are consistent -- if I piece them together. I interviewed them separately; no one of them had the complete picture."

Moore took a deep breath. "I've been looking for someone to talk with -- this is too important to keep to myself. I tried to talk to the President the other day, but he didn't have time to listen." He shook his head and took another deep breath. "As I told you a few days ago, that facility in Utah was built to manufacture alien reproduction vehicles."

Moore nervously sipped on his coffee. "Our government, and other governments too, have captured ET craft -- after they crashed, sometimes after we shot them down. The Germans had projects during World War II to reverse-engineer these craft. Well, after fifty years, and no telling how many billions, we have done it. We have made copies of ET craft." He paused for emphasis. "They're these so called alien reproduction vehicles. That facility in Utah was set up to manufacture them. It wasn't an alien facility, or a terrorist one either; it was a facility to manufacture alien vehicles."

"Whose facility?" Sam looked at Moore skeptically.

"Don't know.

"Don't know? What did these people say?"

"They don't know. The only name that came up was Günter Von Hedemann. He was the top guy at the facility, but nothing about who he worked for. I've tried to find something on him, but no luck."

"I'll have Tiffany give it a try. She's really good at this kind of thing, knows how to work the computers at the library." Sam scratched the name down, showing it to Moore to check the spelling.

"The only person anybody ever saw that seemed to be over Von Hedemann was some shadowy guy who came around about once a month. He wore a black suit and walked with a cane. Nobody knew his name. They were all too afraid to ask questions -- scared of the security force. One misstep, and you were never seen again."

"You said there were two who worked for private industry?"

"Yes. They told me they worked for a LNR Corporation, at least that was the name they saw on the paperwork. Turned out they were pretty lucky. They were away from the facility, taking delivery of a special piece of equipment, the day the explosion happened. They didn't know what to do, so they hid out until the amnesty program was announced. I may be the only person who knows where to find them."

"I'll have Tiffany check out this LNR." Sam made another note, then returned to sipping his coffee and studying Moore. "How does someone get enough money together to create a manufacturing facility like that without a lot of people knowing about it?"

"That's part of what's been bothering me too. But wait, there's more. And the Air Force and Navy men both agree on this point. The purpose of manufacturing these ARVs was to stage an attack."

"An attack?"

"Yeah, an alien invasion."

"For what purpose?"

"You willing to engage in a little speculation?" Moore asked as he sat down his coffee.

Sam said nothing. He was busy putting pieces in place.

Without waiting, Moore said, "I think the plan was to use the fear engendered by such an attack to keep this secret government in control. And not just here in America -- everywhere else too."

"Was?" Sam asked. "Do you really think the explosion was the end of their plan?"

"I'm guessing it put a real crimp in it," Moore said.

"Wonder what happened?" Sam thought back to the Utah site where a blast had ripped open a huge crater and incinerated almost everything.

"My guess is that somebody screwed up," Moore said.

Sam sat back in his chair. The people who had Boyle under their thumb were already in control. The explosion in Utah had not ended anything.

"I've seen lots of reports about UFOs," Moore said. "I'm wondering if the shadow government has a few ARVs still flying."

"My sources tell me they are not from this planet," Sam said. "I think they're friendly, just trying to wake people up."

He recalled his meeting with Sarah Smith when she had pictioned her home planet for him. After that he was pretty sure that she and her kind were not going to invade Earth. That, in fact, they were here to help things. As he understood it from Sarah, showing their craft was just phase one.

The whole alien invasion thing had to be a psychological play.

Over the years Sam had seen some of the movies about alien invaders. These depicted something quite different than what Sarah had shown him. Was there any truth to them? Could whoever was behind the Utah site still fake an alien attack, or had all their craft been destroyed in the explosion? Sure there had been a few favorable movies, but the evil alien ones got the best crowds.

They talked for another hour. At the end of it Sam was finally willing to entertain the unbelievable proposition that there might be a secret government behind the duly elected one. How else could he explain what Carlton Boyle had told him, what Moore was telling him?

Sam also knew from his own experience that some of the top people in the government were involved in drugs, sex, and bribes. It was not a pretty picture, but it did not diminish his view that America was a great country.

"I'd like to talk to your people," Sam said.

"I'd have to check with them. For their safety, I've kept their names and locations to myself." Moore played with his empty coffee cup. "My wife has a key to our safety deposit box at Wells Fargo in Boulder -- just in case..." Moore did not complete his thought.

Sam looked at the extremely nervous person across from him and said, "My suggestion for you is this: Find someone at the New York Times or Washington Post to give this to. Or go to someone in the alternative media. Get them started on their own investigation."

"I have one more thing you might be interested in," Moore said as they got up from the table.

"Shoot."

"A man, who had worked for both private contractors and for the Navy, told me about the scalar weapons they had been developing. At the time he left the project, they were focused on disabling an enemy by creating an electromagnetic pulse that would wipe out his electrical and electronic equipment.

"He tried to explain it." Moore shook his head. "Standing waves, or something like that. I've got it in my notes -- just another tidbit for you, in exchange for today's over-priced lunch."

The two men departed the restaurant, taking different routes.

TEN

That afternoon, Ryan Drake received a message in his personal email from Tiffany Wheeler. It asked him to call Sam Wellborn. The email also asked about Sarah's whereabouts.

In light of Sarah's recent experience with Carlton Boyle, the request seemed out of place, particularly since Ryan and Sarah knew both Tiffany and Sam Wellborn were very close to the President. Yet Tiffany had couriered copies of top-secret government archives about the Roswell crash to Ryan, information that Ryan had later distributed to the audience at Peter's disclosure. Sam had taken a risk in doing that, now Ryan was being asked to take a risk in reconnecting with his childhood friend, despite what Sarah had recently experienced.

After glancing at the email, Sarah said, "I'm going to drop in on Tiffany." She closed her eyes and willed her etheric body to travel.

Tiffany Wheeler was in her office at the White House. Sarah watched as she cleared her desk and stuffed documents into file drawers. She carefully placed a small, framed photo in the top drawer of her desk. Sarah saw that it was a picture of her boss, Sam Wellborn. Sarah had met Sam when Tiffany and he had come to Boulder to interview her. She had pictioned her home planet for both of them. Tiffany checked around one last time before locking the office door behind her.

Sarah took time to glance about the office. The pictures on her desk were of her family set against what Sarah surmised was Tiffany's parents' home in some place with palm trees and lush vegetation. Sarah gathered that she had a younger brother. Everyone's energy said that they were in good health.

On one wall of the office were pictures of a house set among trees. In one of the pictures the trees were covered with white and pink blossoms. In another, Tiffany was posed on the front porch of the house. The energy of these pictures was peaceful and grounded.

On the wall facing her desk was a picture of Sam Wellborn and Tiffany, arms around each other's backs, at a political rally for President Carlton Boyle. The energy of this picture was loving. Coupling it with the photo of Sam that Tiffany had so carefully placed in her desk, Sarah surmised that Tiffany Wheeler was in love with her boss.

She was about to withdraw when a key was inserted into the lock and the door opened. Two men in suits walked in.

"So what are we looking for again?" The taller of the two asked.

"Go through her desk; see what turns up. Keep an eye out for anything from Wellborn about his investigation in Utah. I'll go through the file cabinet. Don't make a mess."

"Gotcha."

As Sarah watched, the two men carefully searched every folder in every drawer. They were careful to put things back exactly as they had found them. The taller man stooped to check the discarded papers in the wastebasket.

"I think I got something here." He smoothed out a wadded single sheet of white paper.

The shorter man came to his side. They both stared at the paper.

Sarah adjusted her perspective so that she could look over their shoulders. The paper appeared to be the cover sheet to a report entitled, "Report to the President, Utah Nuclear Detonation." Sam Wellborn's name was the only one listed as the author.

"I think the boss is going to be very interested in this. Good work." He folded the paper in thirds and placed it in his jacket pocket. "Let's just say housekeeping came early today." He laughed as he stuffed the rest of the trash back into the receptacle.

"Where's her computer; the rest of it must be there."

"She always takes her laptop home with her."

The two continued searching for another ten minutes, then made sure everything was as Tiffany had left it. They let themselves out, seemingly unconcerned that they had just rifled the office of the assistant to a very senior official, an office very near the seat of executive power of the government of the United States of America.

Sarah returned to where Ryan sat at his computer and shared what she had seen and heard.

"I'm going to call Sam," Ryan said. "There's a bunch of things that don't make sense."

"And I'm going to pay a visit to Tiffany at her house."

When Sam walked into his office the following morning, there was a message from Tiffany that she needed to talk to him. He walked next door to her office.

"What's up?"

Tiffany stood up from a desk littered with papers and files. She was wearing a beige skirt under a blue blazer. Her face wore a frown.

"Julie Tulagi called. She wants to meet you for a private chat, something about no progress and wanting to go back to Boulder. Can you hustle over to the Hyatt?"

Sam bristled. Who did Tulagi think she was anyway? He outranked her in almost every way. She should be coming to meet him.

Tiffany put her arm through his. "I'm going with you -- now." She gave him a little tug and they went off down the hall.

"Nice outfit, by the way." She pointed to Sam's blue blazer, beneath which he wore a white shirt and red tie. Sam had on beige trousers. The two of them looked like an advertisement for navy blue and beige fashions.

"Okay, so what's going on?" Sam asked as soon as they had exited the grounds of the White House.

Tiffany pointed to his temporary ID.

"I'm clean," Sam said. "A friend of mine at the FBI took care of everything."

"So what was it?"

"A small transmitter pasted to the back of my regular ID badge, range three hundred feet. Stupid me, I forget my ID today; had to stop and get this one."

"Tipping who off? And what does this have to do with alcohol treatment facilities?" Tiffany led him into a Starbucks.

"I though we were going to the Hyatt to meet Julie Tulagi," Sam said.

"Order some coffee; we need to talk."

"No Tulagi?"

"Tulagi has already gone back to Boulder, but that's not what we're here for. I want some answers from you, then I'll tell you what I found out."

After receiving Tiffany's latte and Sam's espresso, they sat at a small table in the back of the shop. Sam insisted that Tiffany place her purse and coat on the chair of a nearby table.

"You go first," Sam said. He checked around to see if they might be overheard. He judged the music to be loud enough to drown out their conversation.

"Then you'll give me answers?" Tiffany asked.

"As best I can."

"Ryan Drake replied to my email," Tiffany said. "He's in Arizona. You can call him at this number, but it's one of those Internet satellite phones, not very good reception." She handed Sam a slip of white paper. "Also told him it was okay to call you on your cell phone."

"That's all?"

Tiffany hesitated. "Sarah Smith came to visit me last night."

"She's in town?"

"She showed up in my bedroom just after I pulled up the covers. She was so real I could have sworn it was the real her, really spooked me. She explained that it was her visage, that she was in Arizona."

"How does she do that?

"I don't know. You'll have to ask her. Anyway, she said that she had watched as two men searched my office, right after I left yesterday. They took a sheet of paper; it was the title sheet to your unsolicited report to the President. I've been working on it at home, but I took it there to get it printed out."

Sam shook his head. "Why would they want that?" He slumped back in his chair. He stared at the ceiling for a long time. Then he said, "This is what I know for sure, the rest is speculation. Keep in mind that I still believe this is the greatest country on the planet. However, I've learned some things that most people have no idea about. It doesn't diminish how I feel about this country, but it makes me uneasy to be so close to something dark."

"Something dark?"

"That's the only way I can see it right now. It's dark, dark intrigue, dark power. And I know in my gut that I've just scratched the surface." Sam told her what the President had said and described the strange way he had been acting.

At the end, Sam said, "I think the first step is to get Margaret out of the White House and into a treatment center. Once she's out of there, we stand a chance of helping the President. Getting her someplace safe, where they can't touch her, won't be easy. She's too well known to just hang out some place without the press knowing its location. Work on finding her a very private treatment center.

"I need to talk with Ryan Drake; he's certainly outside this craziness.

And I'm going to identify some other people who're not part of this."

Tiffany said as they walked out, "And you really do need to talk to Julie Tulagi. She has some recommendations."

Tiffany went back to straighten out her office. They had decided that she could be of more assistance if she were not working inside the White House. Sam would set her up in a rented office, get her a secure phone, and pay her salary. In the meantime, they had to assume that every conversation might be monitored. They agreed that he would officially dismiss her that afternoon.

Ryan Drake's call to Sam came as the President's Special Assistant was being driven home. "Good to hear from you." Sam looked up to make sure the glass between him and the driver was closed. "What's that delay I'm hearing?"

"Satellite telephone," Ryan said. "One of the disadvantages of living out in the bush is the lack of hard-wired telephone service. Before I installed this satellite system there was no telephone at all."

"We need to meet."

Ryan told Sam where he was, and that he and Sarah had no plans to leave Harmony. Sam explained that he was tied down in Washington. They went back and forth for ten minutes, and then decided they would have to work by long distance.

Ryan asked, "What about the secure line the President provided for Sarah? It seems to work better than this."

Sam's words came back, "Not unless we want to be recorded."

"I'll get to a pay phone. What time can I call you tomorrow?" Ryan asked.

"In the afternoon, my time. I'll email you a number."

The next day, Tiffany called Sam's secure White House line from her home in Virginia. She had moved her personal things out of the office next to his.

"I'm looking for an office in Virginia," she said when he answered. "Moving my things was so traumatic. The guards searched through every piece of paper, examined every picture, every small knickknack. After I told them I was leaving my job, they physically searched me and made me empty my purse.

"I did find several places for the lady, one looks particularly good."

"Let's get together so you can tell me about it."

In a secure facility, miles from the center of Washington DC, Sam and Tiffany's conversation was recorded from a tap on Tiffany's home phone, a tap recently placed on the phones of everyone who worked in the White House. By prior arrangement, it was tagged and forwarded to a young woman who worked for a private security company. She immediately placed a phone call.

The man listened for a moment and then placed a second call. "As you suspected, they are continuing to meet. Do you want me to follow the girl or the guy?"

He waited as the person on the other end conferred with someone.

"Understand, I'll take the girl," he responded to the person on the other end. "Oh, by the way that other matter has been handled."

There was a pause in the conversation as someone on the other end said something indistinguishable. "Yeah, I'm well aware of the need to find ways to circumvent the scramblers that Wellborn is using. Hey, remember we're the ones who developed them in the first place. And, yes, we are working on it. I'll let you know when we have something."

"Traffic lights are out all over the city," Sam's driver, a new man employed by the limousine service, said into the speaker connected to the rear compartment. They had been stalled in morning traffic for twenty minutes.

Spotting a small coffee shop Sam said, "I'll walk from here."

"Kinda messy out there." The driver pointed to the slushy street and began maneuvering to pull to the curb. "I can wait to drive you to the White House."

Sam, bundled in a full-length dark blue cashmere coat and black gloves, responded, "No need. I'll catch you late afternoon, at the White House, thanks." He pulled open the door, stepped out into a puddle of ice water, and then headed for the door of the coffee shop.

After purchasing the Washington Post, he threw it and his overcoat on a chair and went off to order a double espresso.

He skimmed an article about the Utah explosion. The media was trumpeting it as a terrorist plot gone wrong. From a conversation of three days ago with an army colonel that he had befriended when he was investigating the site, Sam had confirmed that this conclusion was not warranted.

LIGHTS OUT AT ARUNDEL MILLS. The shopping center that

opened in 2007 had been plagued with electrical problems during the last six months. The latest, affecting the surrounding residential and commercial area as well, had lasted for five hours. Other shopping malls across the country had also experienced power outages due to a lack of electrical generating capacity. With oil prices skyrocketing, and claiming that they had new scrubber technology to protect the environment, public utilities across the country were building coal-fired plants to increase capacity. In the meantime, rolling brownouts and service disruptions were the norm.

An article in the business section reported that the U.S. Treasury Department, in an unprecedented move, had taken control of United Bank. Amidst problems with FDIC insurance, this move was intended to buoy confidence in the banking system's ability to meet the demands of individual depositors across the country. The article stated that individuals would immediately be allowed to withdraw 33% of their United Bank balance. The remainder could be withdrawn over the next ninety days. As an inducement to stave off wholesale withdrawals, the Treasury would guarantee 5% annual interest payments on all balances at United Bank. The article said that people were lined up to withdraw funds at every one of United Bank's branches in fifteen states.

He barely caught the headline of the small article. It was on the third page of the second section. AMNESTY DOCTOR DIES. The article told how Dr. Gordon Moore had been involved in a fatal car crash the previous evening. He was alone in the car when he had apparently lost control and plunged over a steep embankment. He was survived by a wife and two children. The article talked about Moore's work to implement the President's amnesty program and how it had allowed many people to come forth to share their stories of government waste and cost overruns.

ELEVEN

At Harmony Center, hidden away on the Navajo Reservation, time passed slowly for Ryan Drake. He sat in the corner of the great room in front of his computer. This morning, like most days, he was sipping chai and scanning the internet and emails. John deBeque was a few feet away working on their new web site; they had decided to name it "Civilization of Light."

What Ryan gleaned from the internet confirmed how much things were changing in the world outside; he itched to get a firsthand look at it. To him it appeared that the infrastructure of the world was coming apart. Harmony's underground facility was an oasis amidst economic and political chaos.

He reflected on the fact that Navajos referred to themselves as the "Dinah," and their lands as the "Navajo Nation" because, according to the treaty with the United States, their territory was a separate sovereignty. White men continued to call it the reservation or the "res." He was not quite sure why this was important, but something within urged him to focus on that distinction. In recent years, the Navajos, along with other Native Americans, had been successful in asserting their rights over their lands and peoples.

Ryan glanced at an article on the Consumer Price Index. It showed a 5% rise over the past year. Based on his first-hand experience, this index, published monthly by the U.S. government, had to be a lie. He had first become aware of escalating prices when he had driven the pickup to Kayenta. When he had gone to buy gasoline, the ten-dollar a gallon price had hit him. With no other choice he had tried to pump a full tank of the high-priced stuff using the credit card they kept in the pickup. The pump shut off at $75.00; he had to restart everything a second time. Then he learned that the Navajos who worked at Harmony had cut their driving to a minimum and were carpooling.

When he looked more closely, he found that prices for gasoline and food were double from what he remembered as of six months ago, the time before he had met Sarah Smith, before he became aware of the cosmic paradigm. With the excitement attendant to those discoveries, he had not paid attention to much else.

Ryan's reaction was to install a tank and gas pump at Harmony. It now supplied both their vehicles and those of their small staff. They had also purchased an electric vehicle that they recharged from Harmony Center's ample supply. It had a range of one hundred miles, more than enough to travel to Kayenta and back, but not enough to travel outside the Navajo Nation.

When he had checked the value of the dollar against the price of gold and against other currencies, he was astounded to find the price of gold at three thousand six hundred and fifteen dollars an ounce and that the dollar was down to thirty percent of what it had been six months prior.

Ryan saw the economy as tilted on the abyss. Almost anything could throw the U.S. into a meltdown like Germany or Argentina had experienced. If that happened, it was anyone's guess what would happen around the world, let alone to people with home mortgages, little savings, and high credit card debt.

Some countries were headed back to precious metals-backed currencies. Switzerland, which had been the last to move away from doing so, had reconnected its franc to gold. With many investors holding Swiss francs, it had proven traumatic, escalating the world price of gold to its current level. The first step in the process was distributing the horde of francs that the Swiss central bank had amassed. Large checks were sent to ordinary citizens monthly. The wealthy had screamed foul, but demands by ordinary Swiss citizens had made the scheme work. Once the gap between rich and poor became less, the reconnection to gold was made. This had been accomplished with minimum inflation. Speculation was that connecting the dollar to precious metals would raise the price of gold to astronomical levels.

Ryan followed the price of TTT Instrumentation, the company to which he had sold his company, Sanitas Technologies. TTT was trading down from where it had been when they closed the acquisition. Fortunately, he had negotiated a cash deal for Sanitas' major shareholders, including himself. He had received a few shares for consulting with

TTT; his former employees had received stock options as inducements to stay on.

When he had chatted with Carlton Boyle in the cave in Oregon, they had discussed the world of business. Boyle had admitted that despite the fact that many multi-national corporations functioned beyond the control of any government, the U.S. had used its military, or the threat thereof, on behalf of these firms. He also commented that multi-nationals were in the process of systematically privatizing public services in the United States, and throughout the rest of the world. It had started with central banks and now encompassed corporate management of everything from water to prisons to the military. The result of all this had been to concentrate more wealth and power in the hands of the managers and owners of the multi-nationals.

This was new information to Ryan who had been involved in the world of business as an entrepreneur and CEO of a small company. His major exposure to the multi-nationals had been as customers or competitors. That private corporations would even want to run public services was a new concept for Ryan. He had told the President that he was not sure how they could make money doing that. Boyle had pointed out that the costs for the services always went up after they were privatized. He also told Ryan that private security firms were now deeply involved in the intelligence business.

Boyle had said that he considered it his mission to return these essential services to direct control of governments or place them in the hands of not-for-profit or profit-sharing entities, all of whom would operate in the best interests of those they served, not those who ran the entities and their shareholders. In light of Sarah's recent experience in the Oval Office, Ryan felt it was unlikely the President would carry out this program.

Since Ryan was no longer involved in the business world, he now looked back on his experience there in a new light, saw that competition and profit were not necessarily good motivators, as was assumed by the majority of people in that world.

At the same time, he knew from personal experience that most corporations provided valuable products and services. He also knew many men and women who were not necessarily driven by greed or the need to control; they simply went about their jobs while a dysfunctional system engulfed them.

What kind of a system could be implemented to retain the goods and services while avoiding the greed-based tenants of capitalism? How could the good men and women be marshaled to provide what people needed and wanted without destroying the environment, without consuming vast quantities of oil, without exploiting people, and without the enslaving all of mankind?

With an economy in the tank, Ryan had become concerned about the investments he had made with the cash he had received from the sale of his former company, Sanitas Technologies. The stockbroker who had placed these funds for him had died in an ice climbing accident; he needed papers from a safety deposit box in Boulder to prove his ownership to the man's successor, and to gain on-line access to the investments. He shook his head in disbelief that he had totally neglected his personal situation for the past six months.

In addition to the economic situation, the news was full of threats by terrorists. One of the most persistent was the Utah explosion. There was no hard news, just a constant rehashing of a terrorist plot. He passed several pages to John deBeque who was huddled with Ethete.

John had grown a beard since he had the published pages from Ernest Steiger's diary three and a half weeks ago, pages that had unmasked the activities of the media affiliates, and had cost several publishers and editors their jobs. Despite his youth, the beard had grown out mostly grey. He had also stopped using hair coloring, so the sprinkling of gray hairs on his head matched those in his beard. When he donned horn-rimmed glasses, the overall effect was to age him twenty years. The picture on his Arizona driver's license and American ID looked very little like the former front man for the media affiliates. Each day he grew more confident that none of his old associates would recognize him.

Ethete had completely recovered from the effects of her drug binge. She was back to looking like the Hollywood model that had posed for the pictures in her Solano Beach condominium. It was easy to see how her dark hair, delicate nose and mouth, and flawless skin had attracted lots of attention. Her intense gray eyes and longer fingers were the only outward marks of her off-planet origins.

Ryan had observed that Sarah and Ethete had become very close, spending hours in quiet meditation. They seemed to amplify each other's energy. A remarkable transformation had taken place; they both seemed lighter, both ate less, both seemed healthier, more energetic. Sarah had told him that she was finally overcoming Earth's incredible density, a density imposed on the planet by the fearful humans who occupied her surface.

Looking back at the papers spread before him, Ryan said, "So how do they do this?" His question was directed at John deBeque.

"Do what?" deBeque looked up from the pages he was reading with Ethete.

"Manage to get certain articles on the front page day after day."

"Mostly it's about what doesn't get published or reported," deBeque replied. "Only a portion of the news finds its way into print or onto the airwaves, even less in the case of international. What makes it to the public is carefully managed. My old job at the media affiliates was to manage what got printed, not what got left out. Some of the ways that news comes to light is not too pretty: Careers have been jeopardized. People have been threatened."

John stood and paced like a college professor in a classroom. "Before I tell you about the specifics, let me tell you how I was part of the mind control apparatus. That's how people in my organization, the media affiliates, saw themselves: mind control specialists. You see it's all about beliefs. Peoples' beliefs determine their actions. Control the beliefs; control the people. My job was managing beliefs.

"Where do people's beliefs come from? Parents are the most important. At the very least they lay the foundation on which everything else is built. After parents, religion plays the biggest role, and after religion it's history."

"I see the religion part of it, but what's history have to do with mind control?" Ryan asked.

John paused to take in Ryan's query. "Who you believe you are is determined by what you are told about where you came from, your ancestors, and the history of your country, your society, even the town in which you live. What I understand about myself is a whole lot different if I grew up in a village in Austria versus a town in the U.S. Keep in mind, it's all about beliefs, beliefs of who I am."

"And the energy your beliefs cause you to transmit," Ethete added.

"Okay, and the energy." John bowed to Ethete. "Here's how it works from my perspective. Certain people in the media are in league with the established powers, others are just lazy. Many times they will take whatever they get and treat it as their own, without further investigation -- assuming they believe it's from a reliable source. Once we convinced them that we were trustworthy, by supplying a little insider news, our job was easy. I simply came up with a new slant to any story, and had my people dig up an obscure fact or interview to make it look like it was something new. If my handler, Ernest Steiger or after him, Warren

Ophir, told me to keep feeding the media a particular line, I'd find ways to do it. It's amazing how many ways you can find to slice bologna.

"Television requires a different approach, because it has a narrower window of attention. There we sought out people with an affinity for the story we wanted to promote. We gave them an exclusive on it along with our research. As soon as one of them jumped on it, we had a winner. After a few years we learned who we could count on. After that we just kept feeding them tidbits to keep the story alive, or create a new version."

"So why a particular story?" Ryan asked.

"Go back to beliefs, that's what managing the news is all about. As an example, if people get it into their heads that the nuclear explosion in Utah was the work of terrorists, no matter what comes out next, most people will continue with their original belief -- after all it's been reinforced over and over. It's all about hammering on the key belief."

"So, what kind of a job are they doing without you?"

"Let me show you." John grabbed a sheet from Ryan's pile of stories. Look at this phrasing, 'The government's investigation has not unearthed any information to disprove that this was anything other than a terrorist base.' This was most likely done by Alan Lufkin, one of my better guys. He likes to phrase things that way. It takes the reader for a ride by getting them to assume the terrorist theory is true, then reinforcing that theory by pointing to a credible investigation, or in this case a lack thereof. Watch closely, tomorrow you'll most likely see the same idea using different words. I've been watching this particular story; it's stuck around a long time. I think they're teeing things up for something big.

"I look back on what I was doing and say, 'How could I have been so naïve?' I guess I had to leave it behind to see it for what it was?" John deBeque sat back down next to Ethete.

"That's what it was like for me too," Ryan smiled as he recalled his days as a CEO. "You mentioned a name I hadn't heard before, Warren Ophir. Tell me about him."

"Actually don't know much. He's some kind of a spook. Gave me the creeps. I always felt like he was ready to pull out a gun and blow me away. I only visited him once at his office, if indeed it was his office. We usually met in the back seat of his limo. But he did have good stuff, from way deep in off-the-record projects. We did some great leaking."

"You know, John, what's coming together for me is something much deeper than the media affiliates," Ryan said, "I'm beginning to see how much of everything I thought was true is a lie, is a deliberate fabrication. The media is just the instrument, not the heart of the problem. I'm trying to figure out how far back in history this all originated. Is this just modern stuff, or has it been going on all along?"

"As far as I can tell," deBeque said, "the history we all studied in school has been rewritten to support the idea that our modern society is the pinnacle of civilization. After my experience with the media affiliates, I'm not so sure. I found a book in the library here." He pointed to a volume on a side table. "It's translations of ancient cuneiform writings that indicate that people way back then knew about people from other planets. They were led to believe that the beings were gods."

"And I'll bet they were told to subject themselves to these gods," Ethete chimed in.

"Makes sense, they had a lot more technology than the people of that time."

"So how do we keep that from happening again?" Ryan asked.

"That's my job," Ethete said, "mine and the millions of other humans from off planet. If we can come across like ordinary Earth-humans, then the chances are we won't be mistaken for gods. That was the idea behind me becoming a movie star and Ajax being a football star."

"And you really thought that was going to work?"

"Except for my drug addiction, and even that worked out okay. Is that what you would expect from a goddess? Look at Ajax's injuries, shouldn't a god be able to prevent something like those happening?"

Ryan turned his head to the sounds of people approaching. Ajax, accompanied by Sarah, shuffled into the great room. The ex-jock was dressed in the steel blue warm-up outfit he had kept from his days as a professional football player. This was the first time he had been out of his room since he had returned. After quick greetings they settled into chairs at the long table in the middle of the room.

Waiting until they had obtained coffee or tea from the kitchen, Ryan said, "John was just teaching me about mind control. I hadn't appreciated what an expert we had among us."

"I could have told you," Ethete said, smiling at deBeque.

Ryan went into the kitchen to get another cup of chai while Ethete and John deBeque moved to the long table to chat with Ajax.

When he returned he said, "It's becoming clear to me that we should not be hiding away in the Arizona desert. If we're to find out what's really going on out there, we're going to have to get in the thick of it."

Ryan had told everyone yesterday that he was not at all sure what he was going to do when he left Harmony, but he was anxious to get going on something. Sarah and he had discussed the difference between doing and being. Ryan said that he was still not sure he saw himself as a "be-er." He felt the need to get to Boulder to check on reconstruction at his mountain house, the new Phantian Learning Center. When Sarah had viewed it a few days earlier, she reported that work was progressing.

John deBeque also was ready to do something, although he was sure he was a marked man. His current appearance gave him the ability to travel unnoticed, but as soon as he went public, he was sure he would be hunted down as a traitor. Nonetheless, he was ready for something. Like Ryan, he had not been far away from Harmony; instead he had devoted himself to creating the new website.

The five discussed things over breakfast. In the end, Ryan decided to make a trip to Boulder. Ajax, still not well enough to travel, would stay put for now, as would John deBeque, Sarah, and Ethete.

At 2:00 PM, Ryan left for Kayenta to make his call to Sam Wellborn.

TWELVE

The following morning, Sarah, Ethete, John deBeque, and Ryan headed out after breakfast. Each carried a small daypack and two water bottles. Looking like a group of desperados, each wore a bandana over their mouths to help filter the particle-laden air.

The idea for a hike had started when Ryan convinced John deBeque to join him, "to see the wonders of the Arizona desert," before Ryan took off for Colorado the following day, before the next chapter of their adventure caught them up in another whirlwind. Ryan had also become concerned that John deBeque was not getting enough exercise.

Since returning to Harmony, the two men had spent long hours constructing the Civilization of Light web site. Now it was up and running with videos of Peter Jones, Sarah, Dr. Adamson, and Ryan. In addition it contained essays composed by Sarah, Ethete, and Ajax. John deBeque had composed the first "Civilization of Light Newsletter." It had been sent to people across the country; in it was an invitation to become involved in creating Earth's new civilization. Search engines had found the site and visits were escalating.

Sarah wanted to revisit Fortress Mesa, so she joined them. Ethete, staying close to John, had decided to come along. Ajax was still not well enough for a strenuous hike.

"What do you remember about the last time we climbed Fortress Mesa?" Sarah asked. She slipped her hand into Ryan's, matching him stride for stride as they walked up the road toward the foot of the mesa.

"That I fell in love with a beautiful woman?"

"And?"

"That she turned out to be from another planet."

83

They looked at each other and chuckled, the way in which only those who are intimate can do. Sarah and he had made love last night. Since their first time, their lovemaking had taken on an increasingly spiritual aura. They enjoyed each other physically, but it was the joining of their etheric bodies that caused them to turn to each other again and again.

They took a short detour from the road to chat with Ben Tsotsie and his men. The three diggers had just finished breakfast and were preparing for a day unearthing artifacts. Ben's crew was down to two; his research grant had been trimmed. The media was blaming a faltering economy for budget cuts at state and national levels.

"I'm just happy to be digging," he told them. "Found a chard yesterday that looks like it could be Oriental. I looked everywhere, but couldn't find the 'Made in China' label," he laughed.

It was that easy humor and his casual manner that had attracted Ryan to the Navajo when they were students at Arizona State University. They had remained friends thereafter. It was Ben who had enticed Ryan to this archeological excavation, and then set up his introduction to Sarah Smith.

"How could it possibly be Oriental?" Ryan asked. "How far back in history are you, a week ago?"

"In this particular strata, a hundred years before your European ancestors invaded," Ben smiled.

After a few more light-hearted moments, the foursome headed out. The last time Ryan had come this way, it had been dark, and as part of a small expedition led by Cody Tsotsie, Ben's cousin, he had been helping Sarah and Peter Jones flee from the INS.

In a half-mile they arrived at an old mine; its tunnel into the side of the mesa was a bit farther up the slope of the mesa. Ryan led them across rocky tailings that had been leached of precious metals.

They hiked in silence, each enjoying the desert in his or her own way. Ryan particularly enjoyed its dry air; after growing up in the humidity of St. Louis, it was a real treat. From a low of forty, last night, the temperature was already up to about sixty and would probably top out at seventy-five by noon. The only sound that disturbed the wonderful silence was the crunching of his boots on the brown sand that passed for soil and an occasional scraping of his pants on clumps of ts'ah, sagebrush. Smells were of sage, and an occasional whiff of Sarah's tea tree lotion. It had been that lotion that had first signaled to him that she was somehow different. Only after he had learned that she was from

Phantia, light years away, did he understand just how different.

For the next mile they traveled across a treeless terrain of exposed ruddy sandstone. Tufts of grass clung to life in shallow pockets of dirt; they glistened from the moisture of rain from yesterday. Ryan envisioned an ancient beach, water lapping against the shoreline eon after eon, building soft, gentle folds and domes. He could almost see and hear the waves against the sand of the beach. Then the compression of the sand into rock by heat and other layers atop, and after that erosion from wind and rain exposed the sandstone once again.

At the southwestern slope of Fortress Mesa, with Harmony Center well out of sight, they reached a scattering of trees and bushes. Ryan found the gulley up which Cody Tsotsie had led them. They paused only long enough to drink. "We need to get to the top before it gets too hot," Ryan said.

"Too hot, I'm already burning up," John deBeque complained.

"A little exercise is good for you." Ryan waved them onward. The route wound through huge fragments that had cleaved off the rock face. At the head of the group, Ryan trudged upward in the soft sand of the ravine that cut into the sheer side of Fortress Mesa. They were now five hundred feet from the top.

As Ryan maneuvered around large rocks, he often came away with a fistful of the soft sandstone. He sank into the sandy soil; dirt slid to the toes of his socks. Despite his hiking boots, his feet twisted sideways. He felt rocks through the sides of his boots.

Behind him he heard a yelp and the sounds of someone falling. Turning he saw John deBeque plastered against a boulder like a swatted fly. He had stopped his descent, but it had probably cost him a bruised shoulder. Ethete was at his side, examining his wrist.

Ryan climbed down to investigate. John's hand was bloody, but nothing was broken. After a brief rest, they continued up the mesa.

Ethete encouraged the young man upward. Sarah came to his side. Smiling, he wrapped his good arm around her waist.

Scraggly junipers clung to either side of the ravine, finding just enough nourishment and water to survive in the rugged climate. Higher up, layers of the cap rock were clearly defined in hues of yellow and red. Ryan fell to one knee as he maneuvered under the branch of a tree.

When the four of them finally struggled to the top, everyone was breathing hard. They stopped for water.

Then they began hiking through the piñon and juniper forest on top of the mesa. A short distance through the trees they found where

Sarah, Peter, Cody, and Ryan had camped that first night. It had been so much easier than staggering along in the dark. Last time Ryan had spent most of his time assisting Peter Jones who had stumbled almost every step of the way. He was to learn later that Peter had suffered an injury while transporting from Phantia to Earth.

"I'm ready for lunch," John deBeque said. He was favoring the arm that had been mashed against the rock when he slipped. The palm of his hand exhibited a bloody raspberry where it had scraped against the rock. "This is more exercise than I've had in a month."

"Clears the mind," Ryan said,

"I'm not sure my body can handle much more." John deBeque motioned to his arm as he plopped himself onto a large rock.

"Let's see if we can help," Sarah said.

Sarah and Ethete stood next to the young man, gently placing their hands on him. Ethete held his injured hand in one of hers; her other hand went on his shoulder. When Sarah's hands were positioned, the two Phantians closed their eyes. Ryan sat down on the stump of a tree that hunters had cut for firewood.

After a few minutes, the two women opened their eyes and removed their hands. "How does your arm feel now?" Ethete asked.

John deBeque stretched out his arm and wriggled his hand. "My wrist feels as good as new, and my shoulder doesn't hurt any more." Examining the palm of his hand, he said, "It's almost healed. How did you do that?"

"We interacted with you at the quantum level," Ethete said. "It was fairly easy to suggest to your shoulder and wrist that they go back to where they had been before you were injured. Your scraped hand was somewhat reluctant, so we let it go for now."

"We can teach you to heal yourself, and others," Sarah said, "through accessing energy at the quantum level, where there is no time. This is how mankind will ultimately change itself: By remembering a time when they were not fearful, reliving it, and adopting it as the way in which they wish to now live. In some cases this will mean remembering life before recorded history."

"Or maybe life on another planet," Ethete added.

"When enough Earth-humans have done this, the energy of all will coalesce with what your scientists call morphic resonance."

"Say that again," Ryan said. He had been standing back, now he came closer.

"Morphic resonance," Sarah turned to him and repeated the

words slowly.

Ryan looked at John deBeque.

The young man shrugged.

"You might call it the hundredth monkey effect," Sarah smiled.

Ryan and John deBeque laughed and gave each other a thumbs up.

Unperturbed by their antics, Sarah continued, "It is but one technique to help people change; some have already adopted it. They may not think of it as I describe but that is the way in which they behave. We call them lightworkers, because they operate from a place of love.

"Contact experiences with their brothers and sisters from other star civilizations or with celestials, or near-death experiences, have awakened many. They have been shown an alternative to the current consensual paradigm, shown that it is not the highest way to live. Others see through the lies of the media and have simply become tired of behaving on the basis of fear. And finally, some others have experienced lives so horrible that they choose to live from a basis of love."

"Consensual paradigm?" Ryan asked.

"Things on this planet require the consent of everyone incarnated here, consent for that which is good, consent for that which is not, consent for that which is, thus, a consensual paradigm. Until the people of Earth decide to change things, it will continue. Keep in mind all is energy. The consent is for the quantum to organize the physical into what you call reality -- 'this is the way things are.' It is the same throughout the universe."

"I can see we're going to have to discuss this quantum and morphic resonance stuff some more," Ryan commented.

Sarah persisted, "If we can get enough people behaving in a new way, then morphic resonance will take over and the whole of society will behave the way in which those with insight behave. And yes, we will discuss it at greater length, just go with me for now."

"Okay, forget the details, just explain how will we get enough people headed the right way to create the hundredth monkey effect."

"Sadly, we may have to wait until conditions deteriorate enough that people are ready to look for a better way," Sarah said, "right now most of them are pretty comfortable."

John deBeque said, "Thank you, again." He reached out to embrace the two women. "I also need to think about this resonance thing some more, but I think I've got the general idea."

"When you feel it in your heart, you will know you truly have it,"

Sarah said.

"How about my stomach? I'm ready for food."

As the others prepared lunch, Ryan walked to the rim of Fortress Mesa. Enveloped by the marvelous silence, he listened to the sounds his boots made as he crunched the ground cover, or broke an occasional twig. In the city a constant hum pervaded everything, sometimes near, sometimes distant, always present. In the wilderness it was always quiet.

The cliff on which he stood was a thousand feet above the barrenness below. He imagined a giant slab of cap rock crashing down the slope of the Mesa, splintering into a thousand chunks. To his back was the piñon forest; in front, space.

Miles away, he saw the sandstone cliffs of another mesa and towering buttes in the distance beyond that. For as far as he could see, there were no roads, buildings, or power lines, only shades of brown and red.

Overhead, barely visible through wispy clouds, a shiny speck winged its way westward -- probably the Denver to Los Angeles flight. He had not flown since they returned from Oregon. From the air, trees marked higher elevations, dark canyons dug into the desert's smooth surface. From thirty-eight thousand feet, mesas looked like sculptures formed by some giant hand.

The white man had forced the Navajos onto this stark land. The largest tribe in America controlled an area the size of West Virginia. Dependent on government handouts, many lived without electricity, most without phones or paved roads. With the rising price of food, and no adjustment for inflation, many Navajos were at the subsistence level.

In recent months the tribe had finally obtained a Supreme Court ruling that granted them ownership rights over these lands. Now it was truly the Navajo Nation, a separate entity within the boundary of the United States of America. The only anomaly was the lands of the Hopi that rested within the new nation. This was a source of continued negotiations. Now that they were free of outside interference in tribal affairs, many of them were turning back to their historical traditions.

Could Sarah, and other visitors like her, really help a whole planet move from its deep-seated fear? How many Earth-humans would have to see beyond the fear-based consensual paradigm to make that happen? What percentage was necessary to trigger morphic resonance?

Ryan wandered along the edge of the mesa, rocks, visible in daylight, displayed orange, green, and gray lichen, tse'laad -- a sure sign of a milder climate than the desert floor. Red wild flowers, 'azee'haajinii, Indian paintbrush, dotted the landscape. While he saw no deer, their scat was everywhere. Animals like these would not survive the hot summers on the desert floor, yet they appeared to thrive at this higher elevation.

Ryan's tranquility was disturbed by a sense of foreboding. What lay ahead in Boulder? Did his spirit guides see something they were telegraphing to him?

Piñon nuts were scattered on the ground -- in the store in Kayenta, a small bag cost $6.00. He squatted to gather a few, cracking one between his teeth. Sweetness flooded his mouth; he cracked another as he wandered along.

Not too many years ago, people had fed themselves off the land. Undeveloped areas, like the top of this mesa, were fast disappearing, overrun by encroaching civilization. Still uneasy Ryan wandered back to the others.

Lunch was spread out on a plaid tablecloth. He approached Sarah and wrapped his arms around her middle.

"I'm going to miss you," she said, covering his hands with hers.

"Being apart is going to be different," he said as they took their places on the ground.

"Don't be gone too long."

"Just a few days."

After sliding their bandanas down around their necks, they ate in silence, enjoying each other and the tranquility of their surrounding.

"I understand now why you feel this place is special," John deBeque said, "but what really happened the last time you were here?"

THIRTEEN

It was still dark the next morning when Ryan Drake hoisted his backpack onto one shoulder and grabbed a mug of chai. Sarah climbed the long stairway to the ground-level hogan with him. This would be the first time they had been apart since he had rescued her from Ernest Steiger's mansion on Lake Michigan several months ago. After a long kiss, and a promise to stay in close touch, he turned the Ford pick-up toward the front gate.

As he was turning onto the highway that led to Kayenta, Ryan glanced back toward Harmony Center. It was dwarfed by Fortress Mesa, a thousand-foot cliff silhouetted against the night sky. Now, as he drove north, he recalled how he had first learned that Sarah was not from Earth, and how she had given him his first vision of another planet. It had been a startling experience, but one he would not have traded for anything.

Five months ago, when they were about half way across the mesa, they paused to give Peter, whom he had been told was partially impaired, a rest. Using a wind-sculpted rock as a pillow, Ryan had fallen asleep.

Peter and Sarah had awakened him, saying they wanted to talk. This is how it had begun, very innocently at first, and then Sarah had announced that Peter and she were from some place called Phantia.

"Never heard of it," he had said.

"It is... another planet."

"Sure. Come on, Sarah. Give it to me straight." He recalled that he could not resist a small laugh.

"We are from a planet named Phantia. It is a different world, many light years away."

"Fine. So tell me, where are you really from?" He had trouble getting the words out in a polite tone. This whole thing was degenerating into nonsense; he had little patience with fools.

"Phantia," Sarah said again, pronouncing it like fan-cha. She checked to make sure he heard the word. "Ryan, we are from a different world."

His eyes confirmed that she was the same person he had met a week ago, been with for the past two days -- maybe some radical ideas, but otherwise pretty normal. Her words did not compute.

"I knew those crazy ideas had to come from somewhere," he had said with a smile. "But, I'm not buying you're from another planet. No way."

"We traveled trillions of miles to get here." Sarah spoke patiently, as if she were a teacher giving him a geography lesson. "We arrived at Harmony a year ago and are just now becoming acclimated to your planet."

"You're kidding, right?" His head tilted left. This happened in the movies, in sci-fi books. He could not be out here with aliens. His heart raced. "Listen, I've been around, you know. I have traveled all over the world. Met weirder people than you two. I wouldn't have gotten very far if I'd believed stuff like this." He folded his arms across his chest.

In a calm and measured voice, Sarah said, "What I have told you is true. We are not from Earth. We are from Phantia."

She had gone on to point out her larger than normal eyes. Then she asked him to take her hand. Her skin was like that of a teenage girl, trimmed and natural looking nails, few wrinkles. Fine blonde hair covered the back of her hand. Her fingers were slightly longer than his, slightly thinner -- different, but not the hand of a person from billions of miles away.

"OK. Your hand's a little different," he admitted. "Does that prove you're not from Earth?"

"Close your eyes." She clasped his hand more tightly. "Do not open them until I tell you to." Seeing his reluctance, she said again, "Go ahead. Close your eyes and relax."

At first nothing happened, just a beautiful woman holding his hand.

Then, in his mind's eye he was at the entrance to Harmony, the two ruddy beehives, the geodesic dome, the impressive facade of Fortress Mesa close behind. Unlike a projected picture this view engaged his peripheral vision; he was able to step within it and glance from side to side. With sudden perceptiveness he understood that he was seeing Harmony through the eyes of another, through Sarah's eyes. Moreover he was able to feel her sense of wonderment at seeing her new home for the first time, wonderment at standing on the surface of a different planet. The realization shocked him, but a sense of calm comforted him. He resolved to follow her lead and squeezed her hand.

The scene changed. He saw Harmony as if he were suspended from a hot air balloon. The scene had a greenish hue as if he were seeing it through night vision goggles like those he had used in Vietnam. In his mind's eye he glanced about for support, something to hold onto, and tightened his grip on Sarah's hand. He felt her steadiness and relaxed his grasp. He noticed a white-haired man standing before the large hogan, eyes shaded by his raised hand as he looked upward. He felt Sarah's apprehension as she first viewed the bleak desert of her new home.

The scene changed again, and he saw the curvature of the planet. He saw it unassisted, as if from an orbiting platform in the full light of day. The continent of North America lay beneath him; the immense globe filled his peripheral vision. Harmony was an indistinct spot somewhere in the beige desert of the Southwest. Thick clouds covered the Midwest; the California coastline touched the radiant blue of the Pacific; the vastness of Canada lay to the north. Like an astronaut seeing his home planet from space, a sense of awe and wonderment filled him. He wished that everyone could have this vision of oneness, land without boundaries, pristine waters, nature untouched by the hand of man.

The globe began to rotate. He viewed the broad expanse of the Pacific, the breadth of Asia, the coastline of Europe, and back to the North American Continent. The planet's beauty startled him. To the casual observer, this celestial gem did not reveal congested cities, or man's steady replacement of the natural with concrete, asphalt, and garbage. Despite his great height and no apparent support, he had no fear of falling. Ryan felt the reassuring grip of Sarah's hand.

Earth as a tiny sphere, blue water, green and brown land, patchy white clouds. A view of the sun surrounded by a starry backdrop. While successive views played across his mind's eye, Ryan felt exhilaration. Earth bound humans could but imagine the view presented to him. Yet here he was, traveling away from Earth as if aboard a spacecraft. His home planet receded into the background and disappeared amongst the fantastic brilliance of the stars.

He saw view after view of star-studded space. Individual stars displayed different intensities and hues, giant red, tiny white. The constellations first appeared as from Earth, and then shifted into un-recognized configurations. He had the sensation of motion, but vast distances impeded measurement. Nearby points of light reminded him of cabin lights piercing the darkness of a mountainside. In the distance, the Milky Way, undistorted by atmospheric interference, became a sea of individual suns.

The immensity of the universe struck home, as it had impressed Sarah when first she traversed these vast distances. He could feel her sense of awe and, for the first time, truly appreciate the vast distances between even the nearest stars. Having seen this, he knew he would never again believe that mere chance or blind evolution could create anything so incredible.

His home planet reappeared, blue water, green and brown land, and patchy white clouds. Ryan looked for familiar shapes, but the contours of the oceans and continents were unrecognizable. Then they settled onto the surface of Earth's twin, amid a verdant landscape of rolling emerald hills.

Eyes moist and hands trembling, Sarah knelt and touched the ground of her beloved home planet for the last time. Then she turned and waved to her children. Ryan felt her emotions as she stood on the rim of her grave -- life, as she had known it, was ending as surely as if she were dying. She joined her team in their white robes and entered the craft that would take them to the interstellar transport that waited in orbit.

He glimpsed a sleek craft on an expanse of concrete, obscured by a crowded amphitheater. The companion who held his hand was the center of applause. A young blonde woman in her twenties hugged her with both arms. He felt Sarah's love; understood that this was a daughter she had left behind on Phantia. A small child clung to her leg and cried out in strange words. He felt Sarah's attachment and anguish in his own heart.

Distinguished bald men and blonde haired women addressed his companion and the others in white robes. He recognized Peter Jones standing straight and proud to his right. Others he would come to know as Ajax and Ethete stood on either side. A shimmering figure appeared and addressed the crowd. Ryan sensed that all the humans in the crowd saw and heard what he knew was a celestial personality. He understood that without Sarah's skill he would not be able to see the celestial, but knew that most people on Phantia possessed her same skill.

He remembered feeling Sarah's hand relax and pull away. He

opened his eyes. He was back amid the piñon trees and sandstone of Fortress Mesa. He looked at the two from another star system.

They were from a different planet.

He had visited there, seen others like Sarah and Peter. But what he most remembered was that it was so beautiful and peaceful there.

At last he had asked, "What do you want from me?"

"We want you to help us reach out to the others of your world," Peter had said.

"To tell them what you now know to be true," Sarah had said. "To help us transform this world into the beautiful place it can become when truth and love are substituted for violence, greed, and power."

FOURTEEN

Now as he drove into Kayenta, Ryan smiled at this recollection. He had learned so much more about the larger picture since his first time on top of that mesa. Now his life was in a delicate equilibrium born of existing in the lighter density fostered by Sarah and the other Phantians, then abruptly descending into the consensual paradigm that defined this 3rd dimensional planet. Where he was now headed was clearly consensual paradigm territory.

Despite everything that had happened over the past few days -- Carlton Boyle rejecting Sarah, the rifling of Tiffany's desk, Sam's urgent request to meet, and his premonition about going to Boulder -- he felt no foreboding this morning. It was as if the new sense of who he was had infused his body, mind, and soul with a new confidence. It was somewhat like the confidence he had experienced as the head of a successful company, but it came from a different place. Surprisingly, this did not give him a sense of importance, rather he felt humbled and awed by the whole thing. It gave him a determination to carry things through the right way. It was a confidence born of sampling life in the lighter density.

He stopped in Kayenta hoping for a second cup of chai. It was early morning; few of the businesses had their exterior lights on; the service station at the intersection of the main highways was closed. Looking farther north toward the Utah border, he saw that none of the town's streetlights were on.

Finding the lone coffee shop closed, he settled for an iced tea at the other service station. It cost four dollars. Ryan felt to make sure he had his wallet with its emergency money; he always carried a few hundred dollars.

Dawn was creeping into the sky as Ryan Drake turned the pickup east onto US 160. The grayness pushed the night westward over his head. The morning ritual of pink and orange splendor began. The sun edged its way above the horizon, and then with a blast of golden fury thrust itself into the morning sky. He donned sunglasses.

A half-hour east of the town, he saw the giant stickmen marching across the desert before him. Erect and in perfect formation, they towered over the landscape as they engaged in a gigantic tug-a-war pulling at the lines with their broad arms. They paraded alongside the highway as far as he could see, then they disappeared into a valley.

Ryan marveled at the grid, delivering electricity to distant locations. Yet he calculated that if a single stickman were to falter, the whole scheme would crumble. And if a number of stickmen in different locations were to stumble, the entire electrical grid for the United States could go down. If some terrorist organization wanted to wreck havoc, this was America's vulnerability. As Sarah had pointed out in her recent talk, people were wedded to electricity.

His first thought was that it was some sort of an airplane; then he realized it was much too large for that. The huge craft was slowly lowering itself into the valley that lay a couple of miles to the north of the highway. He estimated that it could be as much as a quarter-mile in diameter. At first he thought it was sunlight glinting off the craft, then he realized it glowed with a light of its own. Ryan glanced away as he pulled to the side of the road. When he glanced back, it had disappeared.

"So what was that?" he mused.

'You will come to know,' the voice in his head responded.

At the Colorado border, the guards asked him to show his driver's license. Since it was from Colorado, he expected to pass through with no questions. He would deal with getting back into Arizona in a few days. They scanned his American ID. When the machine responded, the man raised an eyebrow, but passed the ID and driver's license back to him without comment.

Still on US 160, Ryan noted how light the traffic was on the main street of Cortez. Not many cars were parked on either side of the street. Only a few small neon signs were lighted: OPEN at a café, VACANCY at a motel, and BUDWEISER at a tavern. The signs at City Market, the town's supermarket, shone brightly.

He picked up a radio broadcast, "The United Nations Special Committee on World Hunger estimates that over five hundred million people have now died as a result of escalating food prices. Industrialized countries have pledged additional aid, but relief efforts are being hampered by the high cost of fuel. Worldwide grain harvests are down by thirty percent due to a combination of weather and fuel costs."

Ryan wondered why this was happening.

'These are the winnowing times,' the answer came to him.

"They knew ahead of time they were going to starve?"

'Many came to this planet to experience the density of living on its surface, if but for a short time.'

"Why?"

'Earth is a transitioning sphere. The darkness will not persist for long.'

Ryan felt like a man stretched to the limit with a foot on either side of a deep chasm; the sides of the chasm were too far apart to get both feet together on one side or the other. One foot was connected to the physical world in which he had operated for many years. The other foot gently held him in a higher dimension that contained the truth behind the physical world, the reality of his brothers and sisters from distant planets, and his connection to the voices that gave him insights.

As he skirted the southern end of the San Juan Mountains, and later as he traversed Wolf Creek Pass, Ryan noted snow only at the higher elevations. Alongside the highway, he saw green grass and the budding of aspen trees; this usually did not start until late May. Encouraged by the warmer temperatures of the past few years, pine beetles had wiped out large swathes of pine forest. Patches of ugly brown sticks had replaced formerly green hillsides.

The latest announcement, which he had seen on the internet, had reported that scientists now calculated that Earth's temperature had risen by an average of four degrees over the past fifty years. It was becoming evident that earlier contentions about a change of this magnitude had been suppressed. Extreme weather was being reported from all corners of the globe.

A relentless wind buffeted his vehicle. In the last few months, everyone had commented on the fierce wind. Now it was always there, day and night. It was as though the planet was scouring itself in preparation for donning a new garment. Ryan hoped it would dissipate the gray haze that despoiled the blue sky.

When he had stopped for lunch at Del Norte he noted vacant storefronts; a few had been boarded up. He grabbed a sandwich at The Natural Connection; it cost thirteen dollars.

As he sat munching his expensive sandwich, he noticed a discarded paper on the chair next to him. On its front page was a large grainy picture of a saucer-shaped craft. The caption beneath the photo read: SAUCER VISITS SAND DUNES. The accompanying story told how a tourist had snapped the picture when the craft had suddenly burst out of the side of Mount Blanca.

A headline on the lower half of the front page caught his eye: RE-FINERY TORCHED. He scanned it as he finished his food. Terrorists had attacked and disabled one of the world's largest refineries, the fourth largest source of gasoline and other refined products for the United States. It was predicted that this would exacerbate an already tight gasoline market. A few years earlier, two U.S. oil companies had convinced the government of Nigeria to build the massive refinery as a means of improving that country's share of revenues from oil production, and as a means of moving more of the oil companies' profits off shore. High gasoline prices were blamed on the refinery fire.

After lunch he had trouble finding fuel for the pickup, and when he did, it was thirteen dollars and forty-nine cents a gallon. His most recent purchase of five hundred gallons for the tank at Harmony had been at nine ninety-five.

Intent on making it to Boulder before dark, he tore through the San Luis Valley on gun barrel-straight US 285 north of the town at nine miles over the speed limit. Fierce side wind caused him to grip the steering wheel with both hands, fighting to keep the pickup on the roadway. There was little traffic, passenger cars or eighteen-wheelers; it was testimony to the effects of the high price of fuel.

'Open yourself to the larger reality.' Ryan heard the words in his head. Was this a communication from Sarah?

'Who is this?'

'We are the Wise.'

He concentrated, and said in a speaking voice, "What do you want?"

'You will be challenged in the coming days. Do not forget what you know and who you really are.'

The intermittent conversation continued for the next hundred and fifty miles until he reached Bailey. There it abruptly halted.

When he drove out of Turkey Creek Canyon, west of Denver, he was startled to see the city so clear. He turned north on CO 470, which would have been part of the Interstate Highway System except that Richard Lamm, the governor at that time, was attempting to control urban sprawl. So it became a limited access parkway instead.

During the fifty-five minute drive north through Golden, Ryan kept glancing east. The brown haze that usually marked the Denver Metropolitan area was almost absent, as was traffic on CO 93.

When he dropped down into Boulder, the air there also was unusually clear. Driving down Broadway, he encountered hundreds of bicycles, some towing two-wheeled carts. New signs read: RIGHT HAND LANE RESERVED NO POWERED VEHICLES. He followed an electric powered golf cart for three blocks until it turned off into the shopping center at Balsam Street.

As Ryan Drake approached the burned-out shell of his house west of Boulder, he could see that the place was deserted. He thought about the news conference he had conducted two months ago on the grassy knoll in front of the house. Both Peter Jones and Sarah Smith had talked about their extraterrestrial origins here; that was before Peter's car had been forced off the road and Peter had transitioned.

He saw signs of reconstruction on the house: a new half finished roof, several new windows, a pile of construction material, and a large dumpster filled with scrap. The exterior logs had been refinished to eliminate burn marks. Looking through windows on the front side, he saw that the remnants of the home's burned interior had all been hauled away, and the job of refinishing the inside walls had begun, but it was evident that no one had worked here in the last couple of days.

Ryan thought back to those moments, only weeks ago, when he had walked into the booby trap that had caused the fire. The first thing he had noticed that day was the boulder, he could not compute why it was laying on the expensive blue and white Navajo rug. Chunks of black mortar still clung to it. He guessed that someone had pried it loose from the moss rock fireplace and it had rolled onto the carpet.

Then his eyes had been drawn to the three chocolate leather sofas in the center of the great room. Long slits had opened their armrests, backs, and seat cushions. Someone had methodically pulled out the white polyester stuffing; tufts of it were everywhere. The sofas hung on their frames like deflated brown dirigibles.

While he had paused on the ceramic tile of the foyer of his mountain home, the buzzing of the security system had attracted his attention. He knew he had only thirty seconds to punch in the disarm code, thirty seconds before it would sound an alarm at the monitoring company who would, in turn, alert the Boulder County Sheriff. In a stupor from the twelve-hour drive from Scottsdale, Arizona, he had started to take another step, but halted. Sarah's words had given him pause.

As they had waited for the wrought iron gate across his driveway to open, she had said, "Something is wrong with your house."

Ryan had seen nothing other than tiny red flashes; at the time he had dismissed them as weariness from the long drive. He blinked a couple of times and the reflections disappeared. Disregarding her warning, he had pulled his Jeep around the circular driveway to the front of the house. Unloading here meant fewer steps than lugging their belongings from the garage.

"Ryan, be careful." Sarah had grabbed his arm as he had reached to open the driver's door. The only other time he had seen that look in her eyes was when the Immigration and Naturalization Service had chased them across Fortress Mesa, when she had been afraid of being captured and prematurely exposed. He had seen nothing like it during the past six weeks.

He had ignored her concern, walked the short distance from the Jeep to the front door, and opened the house.

Now, he stood transfixed.

His home had been ransacked.

The security system beckoned him -- he had twenty seconds before the alarm sounded.

The destruction around him produced a sinking feeling. He and his ex-wife, Vicki, had spent so much time and effort constructing and furnishing this house, the myriad details, long hours, and, yes, bitter disagreements. "This is our dream home," she had said when at last it was finished, six years ago.

How had intruders bypassed the house's security system? Why hadn't the Sheriff's Department already responded to the break-in? Why would intruders bother to reset the security system?

Ryan took in the assaults to the house and its furnishings. Two ficus trees, that had formerly framed his floor-to-ceiling picture window, lay on their sides. Their root balls had been exposed, crushed open to reveal anything secreted there. Next to the glass wall, the baseboard molding had been torn away, the interior of the wall probed with something that had dislodged clumps of pink insulation.

What had saved him was a whiff of the unmistakable odor of propane.

He bolted out the door.

Seconds later, the house was engulfed in flames.

Now, when he dialed the contractor who was in charge of the reconstruction, his secretary said he was at another job site. Jim Archer answered his cell phone on the third ring, "Archer here."

"This is Ryan Drake."

"Been wondering when you'd call. That last check of yours bounced all the way to Kansas. I'm out big bucks with my subs."

Rather than bristle at the implications of Archer's words, Ryan said, "I don't understand what's going on. I thought I had plenty of money in that account."

"Get me a cashier's check, then I'll go back to work. Oh, and just so you know, I put a mechanic's lien on the property."

Ryan took a deep breath before he said, "Jim, I'll get it straightened out, and I'll get you your money." After glancing at his watch, Ryan said, "Be back to you tomorrow."

"Don't bother to call me unless you got real money." Archer abruptly disconnected.

Before he jumped into the pickup, Ryan walked around the rear of the house. Walking carefully to avoid the holes that the invaders had dug as they searched for copies of Steiger's diary, he saw several ponderosa trees still bore the marks where the fire had singed them. The sliding glass doors, leading to the indoor pool, had been replaced and were securely locked. The swimming pool had blackened pieces of wood in the dirty water at its bottom. He recalled when Sarah had emerged naked from that swimming pool; he had seen for the first time that she did not have a navel.

FIFTEEN

At Harmony Center, Sarah Smith continued to be troubled by her recent telephone conversation with the President. Determined to delve deeper, she went into a quiescent state and directed her etheric body to find him.

She found Carlton Boyle sitting behind the desk in the Oval Office. He was alone.

She watched as he thumbed through a stack of papers, applying his signature to several. She noted that his hand moved a bit slower than she would have thought normal.

A moment later Boyle stood. He gripped the edge of the desk to steady himself. Taking a few steps toward the window behind his chair, he looked out.

Sarah looked out to see what it was that the President was seeing. It was not the landscape of the White House; it appeared to be a picture behind the window frame. She examined it more closely. Yes, it was a picture, attached to the window. She went behind it and was startled to see that the exterior wall of the White house was bare wood, and that the Oval Office was like a set for a stage production.

She moved around the set. On the far side she saw a room attached to it, a room in which an observer could gaze into the set of the Oval Office through a one-way mirror. No one was in the room.

Outside the entrance to the Oval Office, a woman sat at a desk. Sarah watched as the woman rose and took more papers for the President's signature. She too moved as if she were in a daze.

Confused, Sarah willed herself to visit the real Oval Office. In an instant she was standing near the desk. No one was there. She turned to look out the window. She saw a gardener pulling weeds among the shrubbery. Farther out she saw moving vehicles on the other side of the wrought iron fence that surrounded the grounds of the White House.

Moving to the outer office, she saw a woman whom she assumed was the secretary to the President. The woman looked identical to the one she had just viewed on the stage set.

"Time for dinner," Ethete said sticking her head through the doorway into Sarah's room.

By the time the words registered, Sarah was back in her body at Harmony. She opened her eyes and joined Ethete in the hallway.

"I just viewed two Oval Offices," Sarah said. She went on to tell Ethete about the out of body travel she had just experienced.

"After we eat, I'll go back there with you," Ethete said.

The day after he had visited the reconstruction of his mountain house, Ryan Drake presented himself at the President's office at the Bank of the Rockies in Boulder. Rather than knocking on Edmund McCain's door, as would have been his CEO behavior, he waited until a secretary properly announced him.

He had known McCain since the early days of Sanitas Technologies, before McCain became President of the Bank. They had an uneasy relationship, saying hello at the health club and at social functions. Ryan suspected the banker liked to feel that he had an edge over a mere CEO. With Ryan completely out of the world of business, McCain would probably try to apply that air of superiority even more.

After shaking hands and exchanging remarks about the current state of business, Ryan said, "Ed, my checking account had a hundred thousand the last time I looked at it. Check it out will you."

"Have we been down this road before?" McCain asked over his reading glasses. He turned to his computer screen and typed characters to bring up Ryan's account.

Ryan had indeed been in this situation before. Last time, it was Sanitas' bank account that had been emptied, as well as his own. Last time the money had been recovered; he could only hope that would be the case this time.

"Just over two thousand," McCain announced. "Looks like you made two large withdrawals within the past week, wire transfers to Banco Panama."

Ryan sighed. This was déjà vu. The last time it had been Ernest Steiger's people. Since the former head of the media affiliates was dead, who was behind it this time was anybody's guess.

"Like last time, Ed, you'll find I didn't authorize the wires."

McCain said, "Check with me tomorrow."

A knot formed in Ryan's stomach. He reached for the roll of antacids he habitually kept in his pocket. They were not there. In the higher density of Harmony Center he had no need for them. The gnawing grew worse.

He slowly walked out of the building and turned down a side street toward his car. A panhandler asked him for money. He gave the man a five-dollar bill, the last one he had.

"Things will turn out for the best," the toothless beggar said to Ryan. "Those who are working with you," he motioned upward, "will look out for you. Do not be afraid, or blame yourself. There are larger forces at work here."

"Who are you?" Ryan asked.

"One who knows," the man replied as he shuffled away.

Ryan turned toward where he had parked his car. Unlike times past, he had experienced no trouble finding a parking place on the street. The city, however, was still exacting a hefty fee from the few automobiles. When he glanced back over his shoulder, the man had disappeared. A feeling of larger forces at work buoyed him.

Rather than move his car, he walked the six blocks to the Boulder Post Office, at 14th and Walnut streets, where he checked his mailbox. In the chaos of meeting people from other star civilizations, fending off personal attacks, rescuing Sarah from kidnapping, and sheltering the President from the tsunami, mail had been far from his mind. Only since Sarah and he had returned to the quiet of Harmony Center had he given his bills and investments a second thought. He exchanged the orange slip in the box for a white post office basket of letters, bills, and flyers that he took to his hotel room.

It took a long time to methodically sort through months of documents. In the basket he found account statements that showed his investments disappearing. Four bank accounts had been frozen because banks had insufficient assets; one of the banks had since declared bankruptcy. The Department of Homeland Security had frozen one investment account manager because it was accused of money laundering. The FBI and SEC were investigating other losses, the results of embezzlement. Six reported that trading losses in commodities and forex had wiped them out.

To top it all off, he found a letter from the IRS demanding an additional payment of $76,512 on the stock he had received from Sanitas.

Ryan leaned against the headboard; the bed in his hotel room was blanketed with bad news.

He had carefully concealed all of the money he had received from the sale of Sanitas in bank and brokerage accounts in the U.S. and around the world. All that money had been frozen or had disappeared. Except for three money market accounts, worth about sixty six thousand dollars combined, plus whatever he could retrieve from Panama, he was busted. He owed Asher thirty-six thousand for work on the reconstruction. The proverbial rug had been pulled out from under him. How had all his investments crashed at the same time?

He called Jim Archer's cell phone. "I'll get you a check for what you've done so far. When I get more funds, I'll let you know." Archer said he was sorry that he had blown up yesterday, that he had really been looking forward to working on the house, and that he hoped that Ryan would call him to get back to work on it.

Ryan ordered room service and ate alone that night, too dejected to call any of his friends or former business associates. He was unable to call Sarah whenever he wished because the satellite telephone rang on his computer. She was not scheduled to turn it on until morning. He missed sharing things with her, missed having her next to him as he fell asleep.

He tried connecting with her mind-to-mind, but he was so agitated that it did not work. He tried meditating to no avail; he could not quiet his body. He took a shower to relax. Nothing seemed to help. His mind was a flurry of dark images and exaggerated possibilities.

He turned on the television, a habit from his traveling days. Flicking through the channels, he found three reports on the tuberculosis pandemic sweeping Africa and Asia. As much as thirty percent of the population of some countries had been infected, the death rate was over sixty percent. At the request of the Center for Disease Control, immigration authorities were restricting entry into the United States and Canada for anyone who had traveled to those regions. Only after a screening in the country of origin, a screening that could take up to five days, were people traveling from those regions being admitted. Relief efforts by the United Nations had been stressed beyond capacity.

Another of the all news channels was tracking the financial plight of the economy. One particularly poignant shot showed people lined up at a branch bank in Newark, New Jersey. "I've been here for two days," one man said. He pointed to a sleeping bag and ice chest.

The station had begun to keep a tally on bank failures around the world. The chart showed how the chaos had spread to virtually every country. Central banks in Poland, Macedonia, and Egypt had declared bankruptcy. Since this had never happened before, international monetary authorities were at a loss.

Ryan turned on an old James Garner movie and relaxed one notch. Contemplating a crumbling civilization, he fell into restless slumber. He awakened at 2:54 AM, his mind reeling with the implications of his financial situation, his stomach in knots.

After tossing and turning with no further sleep, he got up at 5:47 AM and showered. Too agitated to meditate, he drove to downtown Boulder and parked on a side street. On the way through a residential neighborhood, he noted that about one out of three houses had a "FOR SALE" sign on the front lawn.

He wandered west on Pine, passing a church where dirt had replaced grass and shrubbery had over-grown the sidewalk. Windows had been boarded up. A man in ragged clothing was huddled near its front door. The weather was balmy for this time of year, but the brisk wind intruded through his windbreaker.

Ryan reflected on how much Boulder had changed. He had initially visited here twenty years ago, then settled here ten years ago with the founding of Sanitas Technologies. In those earlier days, Boulder had been funky, small, independently owned shops had dotted the Mall and the side streets. Well-known retailers had replaced those funky shops. Now as he wandered east on Walnut, searching for a morning cup of chai, everything had changed. Modern, multi-storied glass and granite buildings had replaced the older structures, expensive condominiums on top of ground floor retail space.

He turned into the Pearl Street Mall, deserted at this early hour except for a few people hurrying to morning appointments. They clutched at hats and clothing as wind gusts whipped at them. A whirl of dust filled the air; Ryan turned from it.

Kiosks, fewer than he remembered, dotted the Mall along with newspaper machines. TERRORIST BATTLE. The headline, on the front page of the Boulder Daily Camera, jumped at him. Ryan inserted coins then stuffed the paper under his arm. Given his desperate financial situation, the last thing he wanted to deal with this morning was the subject of terrorist anything.

He paused to reflect on the fear and turmoil that surrounded him since he came to Boulder. This lower density paradigm was all about fear, and people's reaction to it. The contrast with the lighter density of Harmony Center was dramatic. It was as if he had stepped into a different reality, a reality that coexisted on the same planet.

He walked on, a lone squirrel searched for food among the fallen needles of the pine trees. The grass in front of the Boulder County Court House was green, testimony to the mild winter. He walked west, passing the BOULDER CAFÉ on the right, WELLS FARGO BANK on the left. From published reports it had, thus far, avoided the problems of other big banks. PEPPERCORN a few doors down on the right was where his former wife, Vicki, had spent their spare money on implements for the kitchen. Some storefronts were vacant, unheard of on the Pearl Street Mall, one of the most successful in America. He paused to glance at the bronze statue of the young girl on the swing, across from BEN AND JERRY'S. The walk light at Broadway was counting down as he stepped to cross.

A man in a suit was chaining his bicycle to the rack on the west side of Broadway. It was the third bike rack he had seen in two blocks.

He passed the BOULDER BOOK STORE, pausing to glance at the window display. One of the books caught his attention, TRILLION; it promised insights into the larger reality. The others were popular offerings that trapped people by rehashing the consensual paradigm.

TOM'S HAMBURGER CAFE was on the next corner, but not open for business. He had met there with a fellow entrepreneur to advise him against starting a new airline. The man had gone ahead anyway, and been quite successful. PASTA JAY'S was at the end of the block. He liked the lasagna and did not mind that they included anchovies in the sauce, something that had caused the local vegetarians to boycott the establishment. He passed MASTER GOLDSMITH where he had bought a ring for Vicki. The store went by a different name in those earlier days.

Across 9th Street, the lights inside UNIVERSITY BICYCLES were ablaze, small wonder with the number of bikes everywhere. Ryan turned back down the Mall. He passed JAX FISH HOUSE where he liked to go for broiled salmon. TRIDENT BOOKSELLER was just opening for the morning coffee crowd. In no mood to encounter an old friend, Ryan decided not to enter.

Farther east the building of the Boulder Daily Camera dominated the block. The paper had given his company, Sanitas Technologies, lots of good press for its innovative approaches in measuring pollutants and setting up a worldwide monitoring system. Ryan was proud of his company's accomplishments, but they paled in light of what he had learned about the secret government, paled in light of the battle for the energy of the humans of this planet. A newspaper conglomerate owned the Camera.

Ryan continued east on the mall, crossing Broadway again. Pushed by the west wind, he continued east four blocks until he reached the bronze sculpture of the elk in the middle of the Mall. Something about these majestic animals had always thrilled him. They had wandered through the property surrounding his mountain home until he had put up a security fence.

Men, employed by Ernest Steiger, had neutralized that fence, invaded his property, and had kidnapped Sarah. He also remembered rescuing her from Steiger's mansion on Lake Michigan, and discovering that mind control was being practiced by Steiger's media affiliates. Even though these events had taken place months ago they seemed like yesterday. He walked up to the elk and touched its cold chest.

Finally exhausted, he walked north on 14th Street to Lucile's. There were only a few patrons at the normally crowded tables the proprietor of this Cajun restaurant had squeezed into the renovated house on 14th Street. He ordered Eggs New Orleans, grits, a huge biscuit, and a cup of spiced tea. Prices were double what he remembered.

TERRORIST BATTLE, the article on the front page of the Boulder Daily Camera, written by an investigative reporter, was all about clandestine battles between terrorists and government agents. Although it challenged commonly held plausibility, had been repeatedly denied by government agencies, and was a mainstay of novels, in reality covert agencies of the developed countries had been engaged in an active war for over twenty years. The most recent battle had ended with the U.S. military destroying a terrorist base in Utah with a small nuclear device. "It was our final recourse," an unnamed military official was quoted. The final line in the article stated that the truth was finally out.

As he read the words, Ryan spilled a chunk of biscuit and raspberry jam on his lap. Who among John deBeque's old employees at the media affiliates had come up with this tall tale?

The second article on the front page was all about another major bank that had been taken over by the authorities, the fifth in the last six months. This bank, the largest to date, had branches throughout Colorado. With all that had transpired over the last few months, the problems in the banking world had eluded Ryan. Now it hit him square on; the entire economy was slowly imploding. It was not just about his personal finances; this was hitting everyone, and hitting hard. A small picture showed people lined up to withdraw funds from one of the bank's branches in Denver.

A small article in the lower right hand corner caught his eye. It reported that the number of cases of mycobacterium tuberculosis, an easily transmitted disease that had been eradicated in the U.S., had skyrocketed in the eastern States. Internationally more than three hundred twenty-five million people had died from the disease. Due to stressed immune systems, it had reached catastrophic proportions among people in sub-Saharan Africa and Bangladesh. No reported cures had been announced.

The World Health Organization, an agency of the United Nations, estimated that as much as thirty percent of the population of certain countries was infected. Adding this to the HIV/AIDS pandemic that had swept South Africa, Swaziland, China, and other Southeast Asia countries, and the number of deaths was already ten times those attributed to the Black Death.

Hospitals throughout Colorado were overflowing with TB patients; clinics and hotels were being turned into care centers. People from the eastern U.S. were flocking to Colorado's drier climate. This outbreak was attributed to the multidrug-resistant strains of tuberculosis that had come into the U.S. from abroad. Due to its resurgence, Congress was demanding even tighter border security.

An article on page six stated that in many areas of the U.S. seventy percent of children were being diagnosed with asthma or similar respiratory diseases; this was up from six to eight percent ten years prior. The article offered no explanation for the problem.

Ryan reflected on his conversations with Sarah about the quality of air in Harmony's facility. She had received information from off-planet observers that ions of aluminum and barium were being added to the atmosphere to enhance low frequency broadcasts directed at all parts of the planet; some broadcasts were legitimate military applications, some was used to induce fear. There were also certain biological agents in the mixture. These attacked people's immune systems exacerbating various health problems. The diminished energy of people with health problems allowed the dark energies of fear, anger, and violence, which these broadcasts carried, to more easily infiltrate their psyches. Ryan saw it as a vicious spiral.

In his old role as the CEO of a company that manufactured instruments for measuring air quality he would have seen a new market. Now he saw human suffering and wanted to know why. His personal financial situation took on a diminished perspective.

When he went to pay the check, Ryan noticed a small sign near the register: WE ACCEPT SILVER COINS: QUARTER = $11.50 DIME = $4.50. The logo on the placard read: REAL MONEY ASSOCIATION. He had noticed similar signs in retailers on the Mall, but had not paid attention until now. He returned to the paper on his table to check the price of gold and silver. A chart showed their twofold increase over the past year. He glanced at the stock market charts; every one of them had descended to levels not seen in over fifty years.

Again Ryan was struck by the fact that the American economy was imploding. History showed that every economy that had printed money without solid backing had melted down sooner or later. This was particularly true in the case of certain unpopular adventures, such as wars, that were funded by printing money rather than taxing people. Given people's lack of confidence in the dollar, it would take almost nothing to throw the entire world into a depression. What would happen to people with little savings and huge credit card balances? What would be the proverbial straw?

He returned to his room and began to meditate the way Sarah had shown him. After an hour, he had settled his chattering mind. When he felt his body relax, he returned to that powerful center of love from which he knew all would be okay, from which he now wished to function. A while later, he heard the words of the toothless beggar, "Do not be afraid, or blame yourself. There are larger forces at work here."

After another hour he felt renewed. There was a part of him that wanted to flee back to Harmony Center. There was always enough food, it was warm and cozy, and he would have no further need of money. He was missing Sarah with her optimistic insights. He made a note to ask her where they got the money to operate Harmony.

From a pay phone in the lobby of the hotel, he called Sarah at their agreed upon time and told her of his financial plight. She assured him that she had enough money to see her mission through. They concluded that renovations to his former house in Boulder would not go forward.

He asked her to have John deBeque look at the terrorist battle news story, and get back to him with any insights.

"When are you returning?"

He could tell by the tone of her voice that something had changed. "Since I'm here, I'd like to stick around a couple more days."

'Ryan, something has occurred that you need to be part of.' Sarah

110

switched to mind-to-mind communication. *'It is most important.'*

'I will communicate with you after I talk with Sam.'

'This has to do with Sam and the President.'

'Can you tell me more?'

'When you return, first determine what Sam knows and where he is headed.'

Ryan looked at the phone in his hand and hung it up. Why waste money when he could communicate with Sarah directly? As yet he had not yet figured out how to make this happen without initiating it by making the phone call first.

SIXTEEN

At 10:30 AM, Ryan arrived at Book Ends, next to the Boulder Book Store on the Pearl Street Mall. The normally busy rendezvous was almost deserted. At Sam's urging, Ryan had taken a circuitous route from his hotel to the coffee shop. He arrived early and ordered a chai. He thought back to his communication with Sarah and wondered what she had discovered.

Sam walked in the door a few minutes later. He had arrived late the night before on a flight from Washington. He was staying at the St. Julian, a few blocks away; he too had taken a circuitous route to their meeting, walking west on Canyon. He then cut north two blocks to connect with Pearl Street. When Sam's espresso was ready, they found a small table near the window.

Ryan and Sam had grown up in the same neighborhood and had gone to school together, until Ryan's father sent him off to boarding school. While they sipped on their drinks, they caught up on old friends and family. Ryan talked about his two children, Danielle and Darren, and how they were doing. Sam had two children about the same age: one was a doctor, the other a mother of three boys. Both lived in New York City.

"I had a bitch of a time getting here," Sam said. "Good thing I have a government ID." He went on to relay his experiences with finding a suitable flight, because the airlines had cut back so much. Then he had problems with security because airport security insisted on opening and searching everyone's luggage, checked and carry-on. Then the fees at the rental car agency had skyrocketed and the car they gave him was in such bad shape that he had returned it for another, more expensive model.

"I thought the government was supposed to take care of stuff like that," Ryan jabbed at his old friend.

"Hey, don't bust me, I'm just a dedicated government employee working overtime."

Ryan put Sam's experience into his model of an economy spinning out of control while the government in Washington seemed paralyzed. His inner voice had repeatedly pointed out that such institutions would crumble in order to allow new ways of organizing human affairs. Sarah had talked about it in terms of energies: "When victimization from fear gives way to the power of love, mankind will construct a new civilization."

"How is Sarah?" Sam asked, almost as if he were reading Ryan's thoughts. "I understand you were with her in Arizona."

Ryan replied, "Sarah is good. She sends her best."

Sam explained that he had sought out Ryan because he wanted someone totally disconnected from Washington to whom he could talk. He took a long sip of his espresso -- one of the things upon which he and Ryan had previously agreed. Sam pointed to Ryan's tea and raised an eyebrow.

"I've changed my eating habits, drinking too," Ryan replied. "Sarah convinced me to look at what I was putting into my body. I've found I like this; my stomach likes it a whole lot better."

Sam shook his head and took another sip of his espresso. "After you hear what I have to say, you may go back to coffee. Ryan, what I'm about to tell you must be kept strictly confidential. And please don't take it as a condemnation of our whole political system."

Although he was skeptical about Sam's last remark, Ryan nodded for him to continue. "May I tell Sarah and the others at Harmony?"

Sam hesitated for a moment then replied, "Of course."

Then in hushed tones, Sam proceeded to tell Ryan about his conversations with Carlton Boyle, and the people who seemed to have control over the President. Then he launched into telling Ryan about the Utah nuclear explosion he had been investigating. "I'm sure this gang decided I was getting too close to the truth and told the President to sideline me." Sam also relayed what he had learned from Tiffany, from Dr. Gordon Moore, and about Moore's death. Ryan listened as his old friend filled in gaps in what he already knew.

"I assume you know that Sarah visited Tiffany?" Sam asked.

"Yes." Then Ryan said, "When we lay this all out, you're going to be amazed at how our information dovetails. So, you believe it's possible that this group really is calling the shots? An American President under someone else's thumb. Is it possible to do all this just by threatening the First Lady?"

"No, I think there's more going on than that. He doesn't look well. Seems lethargic -- not like himself at all."

"What about other people in Washington?"

"I'm not sure I understand what you're asking."

"Are they acting funny also? Maybe it's the water." Ryan smiled and raised a hand like a youngster to ward off physical assault by a younger brother. Then he continued, "Seriously, let's make a list of what you know, then I'll add what I've found out." Ryan pulled a small notebook from his pocket.

He checked around the coffee shop. Several couples, lost in conversation, leaned over distant tables, sipping beverages and eating pastries. Behind him, at the farthest end of the room, Ryan noted two men at separate tables. The two had arrived just after Sam had entered. The sports section of the Boulder Camera covered the face of the one who wore a blue sweat suit. The second man in a brown leather jacket, eyes closed, kept time to the beat from what appeared to be an iPod. At a nearby table, a young woman was engrossed in her laptop. Receiving a strong intuition to guard their conversation, Ryan scooted his chair closer to Sam's.

"Number one," he said. He deliberately kept his voice soft and focused away from the other drinkers. "We know that people are controlling the President. We don't know how much or for what purpose. Number two, we don't know who is involved."

Sam corrected him, "We know who some of them are."

"Okay, but we don't know them all."

Sam shrugged.

"Okay, we leave it as a question. Number three, we know that some members of the Secret Service are involved," Ryan said. "Number four, you suspect the President pulled you off the job of investigating the Utah explosion for some unstated reason. Number five, we know somebody is interested enough in you to rifle Tiffany's office. Number six is one you haven't mentioned, but I'm sure it needs to be on the list: you need to keep your job as Special Assistant to the President. Otherwise you lose your ability to help Carlton Boyle, and I'm sure you like the paycheck." Ryan flashed to his own depleted financial situation.

"Whew, when you put it like that, it seems pretty daunting," Sam said. "And I can tell by that grin that you know more. So what can you add?"

"Sam, I want to take you back a couple of months to all the stuff I gave you about Senators and Congressman who had been compromised, and about the media affiliates. You remember?"

"Oh, yeah." Sam said. "Want another?" He held up his empty cup.

Ryan replied with the palm of his hand.

The man with the iPod looked up as Sam walked to the counter.

When Sam returned with his fresh espresso, Ryan said, "I think I understand what you've told me so far, but let me ask a couple of questions. First, who is this Chuck Brown?"

Sam quickly responded, "The Director of the FBI and a friend. I believe I can trust him." He took a sip from his ceramic cup.

"With your life? Remember that fake alien Sarah and I captured? We turned him over to the FBI. I haven't seen or heard anything after that."

"Yeah, I remember. Brown got out-maneuvered on that one."

"He told you that?"

"Yeah, I asked him and that's what he said."

Ryan shook his head. "So how does the head of the FBI get out-maneuvered? And what happened to my fake alien?" He felt his ire rise, took a deep breath, and settled back in his chair.

"I don't know, but I'll ask him again, okay. You got me on that one."

"Did you ever meet Jake Ashton, FBI?" Ryan asked.

"No, I don't recognize that name."

"Ask Chuck Brown about him. I want to know Brown's reaction."

"So you trust this Jake Ashton?"

"Yeah. He was the one I handed the fake alien to. When the Tyler crowd came after him, he disappeared. And while you're at it, try to track down Glenn Koslowski and Tony Santori, two of the President's Secret Service agents. They were with us in that cave in Oregon. Ryan tore out a page from the notebook with their names on it.

"I'll see what I can do," Sam said stuffing the paper in his shirt pocket. "You pose a good question. So, how do I know who to trust? If the cabal is controlling the President and has infiltrated the Secret Service, they sure as hell have people in other slots."

"I've got some pretty powerful allies." Ryan cocked his head upward. "I think I can get them to check people out for us."

"For us? Sounds like you're ready to join up," Sam said.

"Let's see where this all leads us, then I'll decide. Just for the record, I feel everything you've told me is connected to the Ernest Steiger stuff," Ryan said, "and to what and who was behind it -- and still is behind it. The media is the single most influential force in this country, maybe the world. Whoever controls it, controls the people. Now, let me tell you what Sarah and I have learned."

Ryan went on to tell Sam about Sarah's visioning of the Oval Office and the people there.

"That fits," Sam said. He had a frustrated look on his face. "Wish I knew where they got the balls to treat the President like they owned him."

"I feel it's the same gang that welcomed Tyler," Ryan said. "The same ones who were mixed up with the media affiliates. They're still in business."

"You might be right. I asked Chuck Brown to check on them. So far nothing."

"I do have a name that John deBeque gave me, Warren Ophir. Have Brown check him out."

Ryan hesitated. A man in his late thirties entered the shop and went straight to the counter. He was big and, under his leather jacket, appeared to be quite muscular. After he received his drink, he sat down at the iPod man's table.

Ryan continued in a lower voice, "This cabal I'm talking about has some really powerful off-planet entities calling the shots. That's where they get the balls to take over the Presidency."

"Off-planet entities?"

Ryan told Sam what he had learned from Sarah about the off planet beings who had come to Earth hundreds of thousands of years ago and enslaved primitive people, our ancestors. They had set themselves up as gods and created religions to make the people believe they were inferior. In Ryan's opinion, most religions were extensions of the old ones -- cleverly twisted to appear new, cleverly designed to continue the enslavement. I don't know about you, but I grew up believing I was a sinner."

"Yeah, me too. Didn't stop me from getting into trouble," Sam chuckled, "but sure made me feel guilty. Mea culpa." Sam pounded his breast with his fist.

"Most religions put people in a position of feeling 'less than.' This is what enables the unscrupulous to dominate them." Ryan shook his head in disgust. "I'm coming to see religions at the heart of all this fear stuff, along with a few other hidden agendas."

"I see where you're headed," Sam said. "It doesn't work for me, but I hear you. Just so you know, I still go to church."

Ryan gave a nod of acknowledgement then continued, "I don't understand all of it, but it seems that this whole thing works by engendering fear. The fear that debilitates people is the same fear that feeds those who are attuned to the dark. Believe it or not, the off-planet entities actually feed on it -- like a vampire feeds on blood. The problem with fear is that, after a while people become immune to whatever gave them the fear, so the ones who are creating the fear have to ratchet it up a little higher. Terrorist threats, followed by terrorist battles, are a good example.

"The men behind the scenes, like Ernest Steiger, see people waking up to their schemes -- people don't trust the media like they used to. These men, and their off-planet allies, see the institutions they had so cleverly twisted to their use beginning to display vulnerabilities -- people are less willing to tolerate the gap between rich and poor. This cabal is afraid of people like you who are intent on finding the truth -- which explains why the President sidelined you."

"Give me an example of someone who feeds on fear," Sam said. He had been looking at Ryan skeptically.

"All right." He wanted to help Sam understand the things he had learned from Sarah. "There is this young man I've spoken of, John deBeque, who was Ernest Steiger's point man. His job was to massage the facts and then present them to editors of newspapers and television producers who would give these slanted points of view to their readers and listeners."

"I don't get it." Sam was sitting way back in his chair, arms folded over his chest.

"Don't you see, DeBeque was pumping up his ego by playing big shot with the facts? He told me what a sense of power it gave him to 'make' the news, a sense of power over ordinary people."

Sam heaved a big sigh. "So this is true of anyone who lords it over others?"

"Pretty much so."

"By gawd, in that case, almost everyone I know is guilty."

"That's probably true," Ryan said. He did not smile.

"And institutions that put their own good first are feeding off the fear of those they control?"

"The IRS is a good example," Ryan said. "Fear is the basis of compliance. Fear's also used by the medical industry: 'We're suggesting you might have a certain disease. Dwell on it. Ask your doctor about it, he'll give you one of our pills to make everything okay.'"

"I'm beginning to get the picture." Sam's lips twisted into a frown. "And I don't like what I'm seeing."

"Sam, we've just scratched the surface." Ryan leaned over and put a hand on his boyhood friend's shoulder.

"A terrorist incident." Sam almost jumped up and yelled out loud; instead he leaned closer to Ryan. "They believe there's another terrorist incident coming. That's the connection. Don't you see? That's the reason they've kept at the story about the nuclear explosion and a terrorist base. That's the reason the President pulled me off the job. It all ties together."

Ryan smiled. "We've made a start. Do you have time for lunch?"

Glancing at his watch, Sam hurriedly put on his coat. "No, I promised Julie Tulagi I'd meet with her, and I want to check on something at the National Earthquake Center. I am free for dinner."

"How about the 14th Street Grill, a couple of blocks east of here, on the corner? You can walk from your hotel. About seven?" As soon as Ryan said it, he regretted his suggestion. The 14th Street grill was an upscale restaurant he had frequented in his prior role as a successful CEO. And he was going to have a difficult time finding something healthy to eat. Before he could correct it, Sam was out the door. The man with the iPod left not long afterwards.

That afternoon, Ryan drove west on Mapleton Avenue to a trailhead. With his backpack and water, he started out on the familiar path up Mt. Sanitas, a name he had used for his company. At first the trail was moderate, winding up a pleasant valley in which a small stream flowed when there was snow melt. This year it was dry. He said, "hello," to a few hikers coming down, and passed two women who were chatting away.

Then the trail began to climb. Ryan remembered his mantra, one foot in front of the other, no matter how steep, never step just to catch up, never pause. It felt good to be back on this trail again. At an overlook, he spotted the man in the blue sweat suit; he was a quarter mile behind. So those two guys had been interested in Sam and him.

Ryan topped the twelve hundred-foot elevation gain in a little under his old time. His heart was beating, but some of his agitation had receded.

Looking to the west he saw a few patches of snow on the high peaks, nothing in the lower mountains between. It looked like late August in the high country. The air smelled of pine, smelled fresh and clean. Turning east, he studied the town before him, no trace of the usual haze. The grass in most lawns and parks was brown, despite the balmy weather. The morning paper had reminded everyone that lawn watering was prohibited due to the dry winter, and the high cost of energy to process and pump water.

As he sat on one of the rocks at the summit, Ryan had glimpses of the shadow government he had seen through Sarah's pictioning and his own experience with Ernest Steiger. He thought about the media affiliates from Steiger's diary and from talking to John deBeque. His personal financial situation loomed large. Finally he glanced skyward and wondered when the humans from other star civilization, humans aboard the ships of the vast starship armada, would make their appearance. Sarah had told him that they were waiting until enough humans were awake and open to receiving their assistance, receiving such assistance without labeling it adversarial or evil, without worshipping them as gods.

He thought about Sarah's comments about how an entrepreneur would approach everything: without fear, without worrying about the competition, just focusing on getting the job done. But what was his job? Given everything he knew, what was it that he was to do?

He used his cell phone to call Ed McCain. The banker had nothing for him. Then he hiked down a different trail from that on which he had ascended, approaching his pickup from side streets that ran across the base of Mt. Sanitas.

He drove to the office of his former broker on Walnut Street, finding a parking place almost in front of the door. In the storefront next to it was a precious metals dealer. The electronic sign in the window read: GOLD $3,626 SILVER $59.26. Fascinated, Ryan watched as the price fluctuated by a few dollars in the case of gold, a few cents in the case of silver. The economy was in a new era.

After pleasantries with the man who had succeeded his broker, they carefully went over each of Ryan's accounts.

"I've never seen such simultaneous havoc," the man said. In the end, they concluded that Ryan might recover a few thousand dollars.

"If you have any spare cash, I can recommend some real bargains in today's market," the man said. "Nowhere to go but up." He pointed to the electronic ticker across the room. It showed the Dow Jones Industrial average hovering around six thousand, little changed from the prior day's close.

He looked at the man on the other side of the desk. In the face of near collapse of the financial system, how could he be recommending stocks? Ryan looked at the man's plush office and glanced at the rest of the establishment. People who did not see the larger reality were desperate to maintain their 3rd dimension lifestyles.

Ryan thanked the man and departed. He glanced at the quote on silver and saw that it had advanced by twenty-five cents; gold was up five dollars.

He stopped in his tracks and took out a slip of paper. John deBeque and he had researched to find out that there was about one trillion dollars worth of American dollars in circulation, and an additional nine trillion in treasury securities. The latter were mostly held as reserves in the treasuries of foreign governments. This made a total of ten trillion loaned by the government. As things stood today, they could only be redeemed if someone, or some country, was willing to take additional debt in the form of dollar bills.

John deBeque and he had also discovered, again according to published sources, that U.S. government gold reserves in Fort Knox and other places were about two hundred and sixty billion ounces. Ryan did a quick calculation: To cover America's outstanding debts, each ounce of gold would need to be valued at about $35,000.

As Ryan walked back to his pickup, it hit him, because he had been defending Sarah and speaking out, his accounts had been targeted. It did not matter that he had so carefully concealed them; he had been stripped of his financial resources in order to stop further activity.

'*Find a way to proceed,*' the voice communicated. '*Stay under their radar.*'

'*How do I do that?*'

'*We will assist you.*'

SEVENTEEN

At 7:00 PM, Ryan met Sam Wellborn in front of the 14th Street Grill. "I think we should eat somewhere else," Ryan said as soon as he saw his friend.

"Why, what's wrong?" Sam asked. "It smells great." He put an arm around Ryan's shoulder and pulled him into the restaurant.

As they were being seated, Ryan explained, "If we eat here, I'm going to have to ask you to pay."

"Sit, sit. I have my cash advance." They were seated at a small table in the middle of a crowded room.

Ryan looked around the restaurant. The tables were close by, but noisy conversation would cover theirs. In halting words, he explained his deteriorated financial situation.

"Wow, that's really tough, old buddy. I don't know how I'd react to something like that. So what are you going to do?"

Ryan shrugged his shoulders. "I'm working on it."

The waitress came. Sam ordered steak; Ryan ordered salmon. The prices were three times what Ryan remembered.

Sam leaned back in his chair eyeing his friend. Did Ryan's financial disaster make him any less trustworthy? And his new eating habits? After weighing his alternatives, Sam decided that he had no option other than to trust his childhood friend. After all, Ryan along with Sarah had shown him a glimpse of a much larger reality.

"I've been giving this a lot of thought since the President told me what was going on," Sam said, "and I've talked to a few people who have verified my information. I've suspected for a long time that some of the top people in the government have been compromised in one way or another. For some of them its sex, some do drugs, some take money

121

they shouldn't, some have family problems. Almost everyone has some sort of a skeleton that can be used to manipulate him or her -- if they allow it. There are those, of course, who have avoided it. However, it's almost impossible to tell who has and who hasn't."

Ryan said. "I've been doing a lot of research, and it looks like we've been taken for a ride for a long, long time. As far as I can tell it started way back in history with some off-planet guys convincing people here they were gods. They set up a hierarchical system, taught us to compete, and to reject anyone who was the least bit different -- it's been that way ever since."

"I don't know much about history," Sam said. "We have a system here in America that works pretty good. I'm not ready to jettison the whole thing because of a few bad apples. And I'm not buying your ideas about religion being at the heart of all our problems."

"Religion makes people believe there is something wrong with them," Ryan said. "I don't believe that's true."

"Religion lifts people out of the gutter, shows them how to overcome all kinds of problems," Sam stated.

"What about the spread between the wealthy and the not so wealthy?" Ryan asked before Sam could continue. "And what about us here in this country leading the good life while other countries starve?"

"It's always been like that."

"Sam, don't you see, this hierarchy was a set up? We've been led to believe it's always been that way; that it's something ingrained in human nature. In reality it's a scheme to keep those at the top in power."

"But the rest of us do live pretty good." Sam pointed to his steak as the waitress set it before him.

"We are what? Five percent of the world's population?" Ryan asked. "Five percent that consumes way out of proportion."

"When did you become so critical of your country?"

"When my country began to use military power to support its corporations. When we started to ignore the rights of indigenous people. When the American dream became all about earning and accumulating enough money so that people could buy whatever they wanted. I'm just waking up to a lot of this. I'm watching our country reap the rewards of overreaching at the expense of others.

"Our economy is failing because the dollar has been debased to insure comfort for ordinary people so they won't complain, and to cater to the power of the wealthy. The war on terrorism was created on a false premise, blown out of proportion for reasons not connected to national security, and funded by the printing press. Now we are reaping the results of all of this."

"Boy, we sure see things differently. You are a new person since you've been spending all that time in the desert."

"I think I'm finally seeing things as they really are, and I don't like what I see. By your own admission, you probably wouldn't be here without your government ID. Remember we talked about people lording it over others. Look in the mirror some time."

Ryan and Sam concentrated on eating, each lost in his thoughts, neither wanting to break off their conversation.

Finally Ryan said, "If we are going to get anywhere, there are things we're going to have to disagree on and let them pass."

"I just want to put our government in a place that's responsive to the people," Sam said. "That's why I got mixed up in politics in the first place."

"Knowing what you know, how are you going to pull that off?"

"I don't know. I honest to God don't know. I see a lot of people who want to keep things going the same old way. I know a few activists who I think will help. This is going to require organizing people, and money, lots of money."

"Don't you just wind up with another structure based on money and power?" Ryan asked.

"Not if we're careful and structure it right."

"I feel there is another way," Ryan said. "It's based on what I've learned from Sarah, and my own research. I feel if people understood that their soul voluntarily incarnated in a physical body, under the terms of a contract to which it agreed ahead of time, a contract that sets them up to play a particular part in the drama of this time and place, then they would understand that there is nothing wrong with them. When our contract is up, we die, simple as that. We do our thing, we move on. I feel this is really beautiful, and powerful, very powerful. However, at this moment it's all being played out on a really dark stage, a stage set up by those ancient gods."

Ryan paused to finish off his last bite of food. "As far as this world being overwhelmed by darkness, that was true about fifty years ago. But right now, there's a whole armada of star ships in this solar system. They are sending energy to our planet to counteract the damage done to Earth by fear, to shine the light of truth on the control mechanisms used by the darkened souls, and they are offering to coach us to a higher way to live.

"How would a nation, no, a world, full of people who understood what I just said be governed? Just how would you convince people who know that they are incredibly beautiful and powerful beings that you are going to control them?" Ryan asked.

Not waiting for Sam's reply he continued, "Not likely they would listen to anyone or anything outside what they know to be true, outside the leading of their own inner voice. That is what Sarah calls a new civilization. Now with a civilization like that you could really build a new structure."

Sam ordered a desert of crème brulée; Ryan had fruit. Agreeing to disagree, they discussed how they might help each other, until the restaurant closed.

Each man clung to his own perspective. Sam remained determined to restructure the government by assembling a cadre of activists to recreate a government without the pitfalls of the old, a government according to the original U.S. Constitution.

Ryan argued that the only way toward permanent change was to empower people by helping them understand who they really were. He insisted that revolution had been tried before. After untold revolutions, the people of this planet were still enslaved by the powerful, still in a hierarchical system of one sort or the other, still subjected to the beliefs that made religions so powerful. Structures were handed down from one generation to the next.

Sam felt the problem was more immediate: He was going to shatter the power of the cabal. He thought the political process was broken, but capable of being fixed. Both agreed that change would come from the common people, not the current leaders, nor the wealthy who wanted to hold on to what they had. Sam accused Ryan of being an idealist; Ryan accused Sam of being short sighted.

In the end, they agreed to find ways to cooperate, and to keep each other informed. Tiffany Wheeler was to become the focal point of Sam's extra-government efforts. He handed Ryan a hand written card with the address and phone number of her new office in Virginia. Then he added, "We need a secure way to communicate. I came up with this. We can post messages for each other here." Sam indicated the URL of a hidden page on a web site Tiffany had created. "No one else, except for Tiffany, has access to it. You understand how it works?"

"I like it." Ryan nodded. "Very creative."

As they were getting up from their table, Sam said, "By the way, earlier today I got people from NOAA to admit that they knew from their undersea sensors that a tsunami was likely to hit the West Coast. In both cases, they were stopped from informing anyone about it."

"There's your secret government." Ryan shook his head. "Let me know what you find out from Glenn and Tony, and also about Jake Ashton."

"Yes, sir, they're coming out now." The driver spoke into a headset connected to a cell phone. "They met once this morning and now a second time for dinner."

The muscular man in the leather jacket sat in a white van across the street from the 14th Street Grill. The van, with rebuilt engine and suspension to give it sports car speed and maneuverability, had been re-painted. JIMMY'S ROOFING had replaced the sign that had previously read HUBBLE PLUMBING. From the rear compartment of the van, a listening antenna was aimed at the restaurant. An elaborate collection of equipment both recorded conversations and maintained communications via satellite. Another piece of equipment could project low frequency energy for a hundred yards.

An hour earlier, a Boulder City Police Officer had approached the van and demanded that the driver move it from its illegally parked spot. The driver had casually flipped open his badge and picture identification: Federal Government Police, Department of Homeland Security. The police officer had walked away shaking his head.

The driver waited for a response before he continued. "No sir, I was unable to make much sense out of what Wellborn said, just enough to implicate him. The listening device we planted on his clothing was not sensitive enough." He paused again, "Yes, sir, I recorded everything and, yes, sir, I am sending it."

"Ryan Drake? I think he's a nut case."

"Oh, is that right? Maybe I'll change my mind."

He waited again for the person on the other end. "Yes, sir, I will continue on Wellborn."

He turned to a man in a blue sweat suit sitting in the passenger seat, "You're to stay with Drake." He pointed to the two men as they emerged from the front door of the restaurant.

"I was on him a few months ago -- piece of cake," he said as he climbed out of the white van. With a wry smile, he leaned back into the van and added, "He's not traveling far, took care of his checking account a few days ago. He's already on the no-fly list."

"You lost him earlier today."

"Yeah, he went up into those mountains. The guy's like a mountain goat. Boy am I out of shape."

"I told you to work out. Don't lose him again."

"I still say he's harmless, just another do-gooder."

"Just follow him, damn it."

"Okay, okay." The man in the blue sweat suit slammed the door of the van as he stepped out to follow Ryan.

Early the next morning, Sam Wellborn drove north out of Boulder on US 36. He passed though the small town of Lyons and in forty-five minutes found himself at the intersection with CO 7, just before the downtown area of Estes Park. He turned south.

A few miles from town, he headed west on a paved road. He soon found the entrance to Pleasant Valley Treatment Facility.

Sam's arrival was announced to the facility's director, Gertrude Steiner. He interviewed her for an hour. After swearing her to secrecy, Sam disclosed the name of the person he represented and Margaret, the name of his wife. They shook hands and Sam went away believing he had solved his most immediate problem.

On his way to Denver International Airport Sam called Tiffany to thank her for a job well done. In prearranged code words, she told him that she had something to discuss. He ran to catch the first available flight to Washington, DC, pausing only long enough to set up an appointment with Chuck Brown.

That same morning Ryan Drake ambled along the Pearl Street Mall. He was headed to the Boulderado Hotel for an early lunch with "Brauk" Braukington, the technological genius behind his former company, Sanitas Technologies. As he turned onto 13th Street, Ryan slowed. He thought back to his days as the CEO of Sanitas. It had been one of the more successful companies around Boulder.

Seated behind an impressive oak slab, he had surveyed his domain. His custom-made desk was at the north end of his office. From here he glanced west at the rugged features of the Flatirons, rock formations that dominated the landscape west of Boulder, Colorado.

Various awards and business mementos, the trophies of a distinguished career, covered the wall to his left. The sun glinted off a plaque on the wall, an international award, recognition of his company's position at the leading edge of pollution monitoring technology. Many in the industry regarded Ryan Drake as a visionary, a futurist, someone able to see commercial possibilities while repairing the environment. His speeches, or his presence on a panel, insured a large turnout. Farther along the wall was a framed certificate, signed by the Governor of Colorado, appointing him to the Colorado Conservation Commission.

A Nepalese tapestry hung on the far wall, a memorial of one of his hiking adventures. At the time Nepal had seemed exotic. That was before he had visited another planet.

"Ryan, Ryan Drake. Is that you?" The unfamiliar voice startled him from his recollection.

Ryan turned to see a dark haired woman with a flowered hat a few paces behind him. She was only a little over five feet tall, a bit over weight, with a heavy tweed coat. She was hurrying to catch up with him.

"Oh, I am so pleased that I ran into you." She was panting heavily. Her green eyes sparkled with friendliness. "You probably don't remember me, but I was at Peter's funeral. Sarah met with me to talk about the larger reality. How is she doing?"

"Sarah is well," Ryan replied. "May I tell her who I ran into?"

"Oh, excuse me. I was so excited to see you. My name Emily Malloy."

"Nice to meet you Emily."

"I read about how you and Sarah helped to save the President. That was so wonderful. Are you going to be in Boulder for a day or two? I would love to have you talk to my Wednesday group. You know, tell them all about how things really are. We have our monthly get-together this evening."

Ryan thought for what seemed like a long while. He had planned to head back to Harmony Center in the morning, but there was some other business he could attend to here, a couple of people he wanted to see.

"Okay, Emily, let's do it. How many people?"

"We usually get about fifteen to twenty. Mostly local people, sometimes Lucinda Ross comes from Fort Collins. If I tell everybody you are going to be there, I'm sure we'll fill the house."

"What time? And give me the address."

Emily pulled out a piece of paper and jotted down an address. "This is John and Marcia Van Patten's home. Seven o'clock. We'll have coffee, tea, and desert. Oh, and here's their phone number just in case." She patted his arm and turned away.

Ryan walked the remainder of the block to the Boulderado Hotel. He found Brauk waiting for him in the dining room. Meeting with his old business associate, in this room where he had spent so many hours, plunged Ryan back into his old business role. Judging from Brauk's expensive business suit, Ryan guessed that his former nerdy business partner had absorbed a little East Coast culture. He learned, almost immediately, that Brauk was engaged to a woman from TTT's corporate staff, Linda Chapman.

He inquired about Sanitas, now a subsidiary of TTT Instruments, and learned that there were problems integrating two very different cultures. TTT was an older firm based just outside Boston; Sanitas, only a few years old, reflected the easy-going style of Boulder.

Brauk, now TTT's Vice President of Technology, as well as being responsible for the operations of Sanitas here in Boulder, had a couple of issues to bounce off his former boss. Foremost of these was the recent price of TTT's stock.

Brauk told Ryan that his fiancé, Linda, TTT's financial guru, was worried about the health of the company, not just because the stock price had tumbled, but because the U.S. dollar was continuing to depreciate. According to published government reports, domestic inflation running at five percent. Linda's calculations showed it at two or three times that number. TTT was keeping some of its funds in European banks. Yes, a depressed dollar helped their export business, but the countries into which they sold were also experiencing problems. They talked about fiat currencies, a term that Brauk was just learning about, and how Linda had invested all her personal savings in gold and silver.

TTT had been forced to raise prices on all of its equipment by about thirty percent. This was due to higher prices for parts coming in from overseas, higher energy costs for heating and cooling its facilities, and higher costs for keeping installation and service people in the field. This had depressed sales by around twenty-five percent, causing the company to experience operating losses as it struggled to shed costs.

Truman Thompson, TTT's CEO, had informed all officers and directors that they would be well advised not to sell shares of the company at this time. He predicted that the economy was in a temporary slump and that things would get better. He reminded them of SEC regulations about insider trading.

Brauk and Ryan commiserated that at the present share price they would receive only a fourth of what they had expected. Brauk had exchanged eighty percent of his Sanitas stock for shares of TTT; Ryan had received eighty percent in cash. "If I could sell all my shares today, which I can't do because of the lock-up," Ryan said, "I'd get about fifty thousand. No telling what it will be by the time it's tradable."

Ryan reflected on how his own behavior had changed in the months since his departure from Sanitas. His experiences with people of star civilizations, the explosive situation with Carlton Boyle, and finding out whom he really was had altered his personality. Without the daily demands of running a business, he was no longer the aggressive CEO, expert in everything.

Brauk and Ryan chatted about Brauk's recent move to Boston. Two thirds of his time was now spent at TTT's corporate headquarters. Many of Sanitas' development people, formerly Boulder residents, had been moved east; some of them were not happy.

Ryan told his former employee how all the funds he had received from the sale of Sanitas had disappeared in one way or the other. Brauk immediately responded, "Hey I've got a company room in this hotel. Sits empty when I'm not here. I keep my clothes here so I don't have to lug my stuff back and forth. You're welcome to use it. I'll tell the people at the front desk to give you the key."

Brauk had already explained that he was leaving after lunch to head to Houston. One of TTT's corporate jets was waiting at Jefferson County Airport, not far from Boulder. "Given what's going on right now, it's the only way I could travel as much as I do," Brauk had said. For just a moment, Ryan had a tinge of jealousy at his former business associate flying about the U.S. aboard a flashy corporate jet. Then he reflected on other aspects of the world of business, and reminded himself of the larger reality.

Ryan asked if he might borrow one of Sanitas' instruments that measured air quality. Brauk made a quick call to the local facility and told them to have one ready for pick-up that afternoon. "It's one of our demos; works great."

"I don't know when I'll be able to return it."

"Not to worry, we've got more."

Finally Brauk asked, "How's Sarah?"

Ryan smiled. Here was his opening. "She's good, sends her best."

Ryan watched as Brauk also shifted gears. "Tell me what she's up to."

They talked for another hour before Brauk called a halt. He had to run to make his appointment in Houston.

"Oh, by the way, Bill London died, that real bad kind of tuberculosis," Brauk said as he put on his overcoat. "Doctors couldn't do a thing for him. His funeral is the day after tomorrow. You may want to attend. If I didn't have an emergency, I'd be going."

Bill London had been Sanitas' Vice President of Sales when Ryan ran the company. When the companies were integrated, he had been demoted to product manager for Sanitas' products. Ryan imagined that this had been rough on someone with Bill's ego. It had also resulted in numerous international trips.

Hearing about London's death from Brauk reminded Ryan how he had lost touch with his old business associates. Attending the funeral would be one way to catch up with them.

It also reminded him of the article he had read in the Daily Camera. Just how bad was this TB epidemic? There had been so many pandemic scares Ryan wondered if anyone believed the stories any more.

After Brauk left, Ryan sat for a few minutes reflecting on their conversation. He had watched first himself and then Brauk slip from the business world and economic worries into discussing a larger picture. In a way it was quite natural; in another way it was eerie. It was like they each had stepped through some sort of a portal between two dimensions. He decided to attend London's funeral.

On his way back to his current hotel, Ryan was feeling better. He was settling into the shock of his financial situation. He did not have any answers as to how he was going to make ends meet, but he had put aside the idea that he had nothing. Maybe his shares of TTT might eventually be worth something. In a better frame of mind, he called his friend, Sheriff Tom Ertl, to tell him he was in town.

"Been wondering when I'd hear from you; rescued any Presidents recently?"

They exchanged brief updates, then the Sheriff said, "I'd like to talk, but I'm headed off to a problem. How about coming out for dinner? Nancy will be happy to see you." They agreed on dinner for the following evening.

He called McCain again. The bank's wire transfer department had made the transfer without the proper documentation. They were processing paperwork to get the funds returned to Ryan's account.

EIGHTEEN

That evening Ryan found his way to John and Marcia Van Patten's home, one of the older houses on Mapleton Street, just west of Broadway. When he arrived, there were several cars parked in front of the house. Since Boulder did not allow overnight parking on this street, he guessed the cars belonged to people whom he would soon be meeting. He also noted a number of bicycles parked near the front porch.

An attractive woman of about forty greeted him at the door with a hug. "Welcome, Ryan, I'm Marcia. We are so pleased you were able to make it tonight."

Marcia walked him into a large living room filled with people of all ages. Emily was there. Marcia introduced him to older men still in their business suits, to a long-haired college student in a sweat shirt and his girlfriend in a long dress with beads, to several middle aged women in flowered dresses, and to her husband John. Everyone seemed to know each other. He found coffee and deserts in the kitchen.

After about fifteen minutes of casual chatter, during which Ryan consumed a large piece of pecan pie, Marcia called the group to order. With a very southern accent she said, "As I told you all, in place of our video this evening we have the honor of having Ryan Drake with us. Ryan has agreed to say a few words to the group, and take questions." She smiled at the group, then added, "Now, you all be nice to him. Remember, he is our guest."

Since running into Emily, Ryan had been thinking how he was going to handle things and had prepared a few thoughts. First he asked that the chairs be arranged into a circle. There was just enough room to squeeze everyone in, including a slender woman with dark hair who arrived late.

131

"I'd like to ask a couple of questions to get us started," Ryan said. "How many of you have seen a UFO? Let me see a show of hands."

Everyone raised a hand.

"How many of you have had a contact experience? By this I mean contact with non-humans, spirits, celestials, star people, people from inner Earth, or people who have ascended. Let me see a show of hands."

Again, every hand was raised.

"How many of you think you understand the current situation on this planet? No. Let me rephrase that, how many of you feel this is the best of all possible worlds?"

This time no hands were raised.

He smiled and continued, "Very good, looks like this is a pretty conscious group. So, let me give you some things to think about, and then I want your questions.

"I have been told that this planet is an abnormally dark place to live -- that's by comparison with other third density planets. By that I mean most of the people on this planet experience a lot of fear, and they broadcast fearful energies.

"There are two ways of looking at this: One, it provides an opportunity for souls to incarnate here and experience what it's like to live without much of The Creator's light, or love, if you prefer. It's a great chance for a soul to decide what it wants, or doesn't want, by experiencing it first hand.

"The second is to examine the current situation to see if we can change it. That's what I'm going to focus on tonight." Ryan paused to see if they were following him.

"Eons ago, four races of beautiful humans were brought here: red, black, yellow and white. This was part of a grand experiment to meld the best these four races had to offer into a new race, something that had not been accomplished before. Earth was chosen because it was a pristine planet and had the greatest diversity of plants and animals anywhere in this galaxy. The races, knowing full well who they were, where they had come from, and their intended goal of amalgamation were introduced into this veritable paradise."

Everyone was nodding as Ryan spoke these words. It was as if they knew exactly what it was that he was about to say, and they were urging him on.

"A race of entities from whom the light was nearly gone, not third dimensional, and not associated with those who had brought life here, saw this sphere as ready-made for their needs. They undertook genetic engineering and energy controls to enslave the four resident races. The result is what we have today: We have hierarchical societies. We have competition in place of cooperation. Most people feel fearful, at least part of the time. No one, and I mean no one, escapes some aspects of the enslavement that was imposed thousands of years ago. As an example we live in a world in which religions and philosophies have laid the foundations for our culture. Even if we do not believe in the philosophy that was the foundation of a particular country, that foundation is still in place, still influencing innumerable aspects of that country. Capitalism is another philosophical foundation. Most importantly, as a result of these foundations, people are blinded to who they truly are.

"We don't have much time tonight, so I want to focus on the situation in this country. I imagine it would surprise no one in this group to know that things are not what they appear to be on the surface. I know, first hand, that the media is being used to further the aims of a small group of elites, humans, who think they are better then the rest of us, and who are determined to hold onto their power, power that comes from wealth and position.

"The enslavement of people in America comes in many ways. Our government officials are more interested in their personal welfare than ours. Most people work extremely hard to maintain lifestyles they have been led to believe they must have. All of us receive confusing messages about what to eat and what to wear, where to shop, what car to drive, where to live, etc. We have the highest cost for medical care among the industrialized countries, but far from the best, primarily because the insurance and pharmaceutical companies who control medicine are so profitable. We, along with much of the rest of the world, have become addicted to burning hydrocarbons to power our materialistic society, thereby enriching those who control the oil and coal companies, thereby polluting our land, water, and air.

"We put up with all of this because the media tells us that this is the way things are, and, more importantly, this is the way things have always been. Our history has been so cleverly rewritten that we have come to believe this lie. Is everyone with me so far?"

All heads nodded.

"It is my belief that most people, and I'm speaking just of people in the U.S. right now, do not see themselves as enslaved. Life is pretty good. Most people are comfortable. There are exceptions, of course, but they are exceptions. How many of you feel enslaved?"

Twenty hands shot up.

"Let me go a bit further then I'll take questions." Ryan continued to talk for another ten minutes. He focused on helping people see who they really were, how powerful they were, and why they did not utilize that power. He talked about the consensual paradigm and how they were creating it with their every thought. Finally, he gave them a list of practical things they could do to help birth a new civilization.

"If I were to have given this talk a couple of years ago, I would have told you to turn your backs on the consensual paradigm. What I would have been talking about were practical things you could have done to tell our enslavers that you were no longer interested in playing their game. Little things like refusing to buy items shipped from other continents. Things like grapes from Chili, papaya from Brazil, and pine nuts from China. It's not that I didn't like these things, I still do. Rather, it's that they took a tremendous amount of energy to transport. Did it really make sense to ship bottles of water from California? Did it make sense to ship strawberries from California to Florida?

"The good news is that most of these things have taken care of themselves. You no longer see water from California in the supermarkets, or grapes from Chili, or nuts from China. The high price of fuel coupled with the erosion of the dollar has taken care of them.

"So what are the most important things you can do today? They are quite simple, yet contrary to conventional wisdom, contrary to the consensual paradigm. One, stand up for who you are. You are a soul having a physical experience. No one has a right to enslave you. Two, if you desire it, you can have a direct conversation with God; take God's invitation to do this. Three, invite our sisters and brothers from the star civilizations to assist us in our transformation.

"And number four," Ryan paused, "see the world from a place of light. Base every thought in love. Make every interaction based on love. Create your intentions, your beliefs, from love. If you will act in this way, we can re-create this planet to become utopia."

After a ten minute break, Marcia hustled everyone back into the their seats. "Before we ask Ryan to respond to your questions," Marcia interjected, "I have one. What do you mean by difficult times? I thought we were already experiencing them."

"Before I answer Marcia's question, let me ask one of my own." Ryan felt himself lift into a lighter density. He was very calm, very sure of what he was about to say. "How many of you understood what I just said about functioning from the basis of love."

About half of the people raised their hands.

Ryan remained very still, not sure how to pursue the subject further. In the silence, Martin, his spirit guide, communicated, 'All will come to see that which you say is true.'

After a moment Ryan looked around the group and said, "If there is but one idea that you leave here with tonight, it is this, the only path to lasting change is through love. I hope you can see that and begin to live from your hearts."

After a couple of deep breaths, he was ready to plunge back into the 3rd dimension. "Now to Marcia's question, I noticed that most of you arrived by car tonight. I did see some bicycles. Let's take a moment and project things forward. I believe that we will ultimately arrive at a place where there are no more gasoline-powered vehicles. However between then and now, is what our sisters and brothers from distant star civilizations call 'interim time.' What is that going to look like? Are we going to be able to attend a gathering such as this? Am I going to be able to travel from Arizona?

"And how about food? It's spring. Vegetables are just beginning to grow, nothing to harvest for a few weeks, or months. What are you going to eat during the interim time?

"Water is a necessity. Is the City of Boulder going to be able to process and deliver water during the interim time?

"I am not talking about becoming a survivalist. I am addressing how you good people will make it through interim time so that you can be part of the New Earth. And I am suggesting that since you are conscious, you probably need to be thinking about how you are going to help others to make it to the future -- and which others you are going to help, since you can't help everyone.

"I believe times will get rougher, and very soon. I also believe that we are approaching the point where our brothers and sisters from the stars will come to assist us.

"The most important question in all of this is, 'Why do you want to survive?' If the answer is to be of assistance to the transformation, I say, 'Hurray and welcome aboard.' If your answer is that you're afraid of death, then I suggest you look more deeply inside yourself."

Ryan felt himself slip into a higher density. "And as you are looking inside, see where you are operating from, what are your intentions? Are your actions based in fear, or are you coming from a place of love? Are you connected to God? Are you functioning in your own best interests, in the best interests of others? Think about this before you speak, before you act."

Ryan called on the young man in the sweatshirt who had raised his hand several times. He recalled that his name was Chuck.

"How do you know there are these elitists?" Chuck asked. "I haven't run into any of them."

"And you probably never will, Chuck." Ryan was rooted in the 3rd dimension as he said the words. "I know about this cabal because I have friends who have run into them. The only one I ever encountered was that guy, Ernest Steiger, who captured Sarah Smith. Everybody know that story?"

Most of the heads in the group shook no. Ryan gave an abbreviated story of Sarah's capture and rescue.

Chuck asked another question, "What about the evil aliens? I hear they are the ones who are really running things."

"I have no direct experience with anyone like that," Ryan said. "I have been told they exist. If my experience changes, I'll let you know. By the way, I'd like to have everyone's email address -- if you want updates."

After she found paper and a clipboard, Marcia passed the sign-up sheet around.

The next question was, "I don't see why we have to go through such hardships. It looks to me like things are getting gradually better, and really hopeful that, in time, we will transform things."

"Good question," Ryan replied. "Let me see a show of hands that believe we treat each other much differently today than we did two thousand years ago."

When no one raised their hand, the questioner said, "But a lot of things are so much better today, can't we just keep improving little by little?"

"From where I sit, I do see material improvements," Ryan said, "Sure, as an entrepreneur I believed the products of my Company, Sanitas, were making a big difference. But if I look at the situation worldwide, I see hunger and extreme poverty, I see people who don't have clean water to drink. I see that those in power in this country are bleeding the rest of us just enough that the majority won't openly rebel. To me it isn't much of an improvement over what I understand about the way the Romans occupied other countries.

"A wonderful saying that I picked up from a Shaman in Ecuador goes something like this, 'If any man is not free, then all men are not free.' In my book, this applies to hunger and poverty as well as freedom.

"So, if we are interested in making a radical transition to a better way of life, we need to get enough of us thinking and behaving differently so that we can initiate the hundredth monkey effect. I feel tougher times, particularly in this country, will help pull us together.

Look at what it has already done -- I see signs of going back to basics all over this town. Now if you can support each other during the interim time I envision, we can flip the surviving people around this entire planet into a new way of behaving. Then if we add the assistance of our off-planet friends, we create a whole new civilization."

Chuck was back again with another question about the off-planet race who had enslaved everybody. Ryan told him about the Annunaki. Everyone seemed familiar with the story.

Chuck's girlfriend raised her hand. "I don't see the terrible things you are talking about. Everything in my life is perfect. Everything is beautiful and joyful."

Ryan was taken back for a moment; he then replied to her in a gentle voice. "My sister, yours is a different way to see. I honor you. Apparently you have chosen to live in this harsh world without being touched by it. My path is different. I choose to see this world for what it is, but not get caught up in it. I choose to observe the machinations of those who create fear, but not give in to that which they create. I honor you and encourage you on your path."

The others in the circle focused their remarks and questions on what was going on at this time and when the transition to better times would occur. Ryan responded by saying, "I have been told that the interim time is underway. Just look around, the power structures are shaking, the financial house of cards is crumbling, and everyone's beliefs are being challenged. I believe we will see even greater changes in the very near future."

The questions lasted until 11:00 PM. Ryan was amazed by his ability to field their questions. They were listening to him, just him, without Sarah at his side for support. What amazed him more was the level of consciousness in the group. All of a sudden he saw a light at the end of the tunnel. If people in groups like these could seek out and convince others of their individual power, and if they could get enough groups radiating energy, they could make the difference.

Then it hit him. He had been able to function in both the dimensions. He had watched himself slip in and out, just as Sarah did, just as she had coached him to do.

Words interrupted his reflection. "Mr. Drake, my name is Lucinda

Ross." The slender woman with the dark hair extended her hand. She had waited until most of the others departed.

"I know of another group like this," she said with a broad smile. "Could you speak to them on Friday evening?" She explained that she was from Fort Collins, a town about an hour away, and that she was part of a group of people who were aware of the cosmic paradigm and Sarah Smith.

Ryan explained that he had not planned to be around the Front Range that long. However Lucinda was extremely persuasive, offering to pick him up from his hotel and drive him north. In the end, Ryan agreed to stick around another day to speak with the group. With the price of gasoline on the rise, there was no telling when he might be here again. He saw that this might be an additional group to radiate energy; if so, perhaps his visit there could make the difference. He also realized that it might be another chance for him to play with his newfound ability of moving between the two densities.

NINETEEN

On Thursday morning, Sam Wellborn was escorted into the outer office of the Assistant Director of the Federal Bureau of Investigation shortly after 9:20 AM. He waited until Chuck Brown cleared a last minute matter.

After a cool handshake and greeting, Brown asked, "So what can I do for the President today?"

"This is not an official visit, Chuck." Sam saw Brown relax a notch, but he still preserved the demeanor of an important government official. "You remember that incident a few weeks ago when I was assaulted in the driveway of my house?"

"Sure. My people are still working on it, nothing so far. Is everything okay?"

"Yeah, except the security firm I hired went out of business, and somebody broke into our house. Guess I need a new security company, but that's not the reason I'm here."

Sam settled into the chair and stared at Chuck Brown for what seemed a long time. They had known each other in college, been on the same swim team with Carlton Boyle, had been fraternity brothers. Finally Sam said, "If you knew that a friend of yours was in trouble, real trouble, and you weren't sure who you could trust to help, how would you go about finding out?"

"I'm guessing where you are headed, and I'm not sure I like it," Brown replied. "I've been around this town longer than you, and I'd say that there are very few people I'd trust completely. I've seen too many people compromised by problems that only occasionally surface in the newspaper. From where I sit, I see that the problems are very widespread. This goes to the heart of the trust issue.

139

"When I want to check someone out, I look at past performance, that and the issue of power. Anyone in a position of power fudges, once in a while."

"Does that include you?" Sam asked. He was gauging Chuck Brown with the keen eye of someone who had been in tight spots before. He also remembered that Chuck Brown had come clean with Carlton Boyle on the subject of UFOs and ETs.

"Yeah, that includes me. How's that for brutal honesty."

"I've discovered a secret government," Sam said.

Chuck Brown nodded.

"So you know?"

"Some of it," Brown said. "I know I'm being kept in the dark. I know my guys can't make headway in certain areas. I know the CIA can't be trusted. I know I can't trust military intelligence. I know that some of my men and women support the secret government, and I can't do a damn thing about it.

"As long as I play along, I get to keep my job. If I don't, some sort of a failure or wrongdoing will be laid at my doorstep, then I'll have to be careful the door doesn't hit me when I leave."

"What happened to Jake Ashton?" Sam watched the reaction of his old fraternity brother.

Brown shook his head. "I don't know. He disappeared."

"And you're not concerned? One of your agents disappears and you don't pull out all stops to find him?"

"Do you have any idea how crazy things have been around here with Tyler assuming the Presidency, with Boyle being found alive and coming back?" Brown rose out of his chair to perch himself on the edge of his desk towering over Sam "The FBI's focus is keeping a lid on terrorists who see this country as particularly vulnerable right now. That's where all our manpower is directed. I believe we are this close to a major incident." Brown held up his thumb and forefinger separated by a fraction of an inch.

"Yes, I'd like to know where Jake Ashton went. And I'd like to know what happened to that alleged fake alien he had in his custody. Sooner or later, I'll get to the bottom of it, but not right now. What's your interest in Jake Ashton?"

"Friend of a friend."

"I think there's more to it than that," Brown said through clinched teeth. "Just why does the President's bulldog come in here this morning, and ask me about a missing agent?"

Sam rose from his chair. Standing nose to nose he stared into the eyes of the Director of the FBI. After a tense moment, he said, "I got what I came for. Thanks for your time." He brushed past Brown and walked out of the room.

Sam left the Hoover Building by a different entrance than he had entered, leaving his car and driver on the other side of the building.

He walked to the nearest Metro station and boarded the Blue Line after an attendant scanned his American ID. In the Washington, DC area, along with New York, those in charge of national security had decreed that only an ID would be necessary to travel to the adjoining States. Alighting in Springfield, Virginia, Sam walked two blocks from the station to Tiffany Wheeler's new office.

"So what have you got for me?" he asked after he had brought her up to speed on his visit to Pleasant Valley.

Her computer binged; it had lost its connection to the internet. "That's the first thing I've got for you: Service here is lousy. I'm lucky to get on four hours a day."

"Is this any different than at the White House?"

"Oh yeah, I got spoiled; we never had these kinds of problems. The White House has some kind of a special connection. I've talked to other people in this building; they're all having problems. Here's one for you, the problems started only after I moved in."

"Okay, I'll keep this kind of stuff in mind," Sam said, "not dismissing them, but let's move on."

"Günter Von Hedemann is among the missing," Tiffany replied. "In fact, he's been missing for a number of years. I was able to trace his father back to Germany in the nineteen thirties. He came here as part of Operation Paperclip. Günter was born in the U.S. Smart guy, has degrees from M.I.T. and Princeton. He worked for a number of government labs and defense contractors. The last record of him is five years ago. He worked for Raymond Technology, a big defense contractor in Connecticut. Nothing since then."

"How about LNR Corporation?"

"You are going to love this one," Tiffany said. "LNR is a joint venture among three big aerospace companies. One of the companies is Raymond. Very little public on LNR, and none of the three partners mention anything in their 10-K filings or annual reports. I'm afraid this is another dead end."

Sam told her about his meeting with Gordon Moore, and Moore's "accident." He asked her to watch for articles in the Washington Post and New York Times that might hint at anything Moore had divulged. They discussed who should go talk to Moore's widow. The woman had been too distraught to discuss safety deposit boxes when he had been in Boulder meeting with Ryan Drake.

He also asked her to track down Glenn Koslowski and Tony Santori, the two Secret Service agents who had been with the President in the cave in Oregon.

"We need to think about making an end run around the President." He went on to tell her what he had learned from Ryan Drake. Then he launched into an assessment of how the situation in America was reaching the boiling point.

"Are things really that bad?" Tiffany asked. She too had spent months as a dedicated supporter of Carlton Boyle, and like everybody else involved with the campaign, had believed that the new President would solve everything.

"We're getting there." Sam held up the front page of the Washington Post; the headline read: BANKS FROZEN. In an unprecedented move, President Carlton Boyle had decreed that all banks falling under the control of the Federal Reserve were to freeze deposits. Individuals would not be allowed to withdraw more than they had deposited within the prior thirty days, or up to a maximum of twenty percent of their average long-term balances as of the end of the prior month. This latter was to cover any ninety-day period. Corporations, of course, were exempt from this restriction.

He added, "This has a lot of people upset; however, it looks like the only way to control runs on the banks. Eleven banks have been forced to shut their doors thus far."

"Is that going to cause us problems?" Tiffany asked.

Sam could see where she was headed. He was paying her salary and paying for this office out of his personal account. "I'm doing this through a corporation I set up a few years ago." Sam motioned to their surroundings. "If the paper is accurate, we should be okay." What he did not tell Tiffany was that one of the banks that had closed was where some of his funds resided; he had found out to his dismay that several thousand dollars had been frozen.

Sam pointed to a second article in the lower corner of the front page: SAUDI OIL AT RISK. "Here's where I think our entire economy's vulnerable," he said. "Even after adding in the newly discovered oil reserves in Alaska, we will still depend on imported oil. In the last three years we've been importing more oil from the Middle East than ever, and they keep raising the price. By my calculation, buying Saudi oil raises the cost of a gallon by a dollar. As I recall, when the problems in Nigeria cut that source to a trickle, prices jumped up a dollar a gallon. Mexico and Venezuela have been declining for years, that's good for another buck. Canada is our only reliable source, and it's maxed out. The exchange rate with the Canadian dollar is good for another buck.

"Add them up and you get to our current price for gasoline. Oh, and by the way, I don't think rationing will work. Poor people will sell their ration to rich people and go ride the bus. And as far as tar sands and oil shale go, they may be economically feasible, but they all require lots of water and make a huge mess out of the environment.

"Then we come to farmers and the food chain. Diesel is already in short supply. Most crops depend heavily on petrochemicals, and most food is transported over a thousand miles. Maggie is complaining that prices have almost doubled in the last year."

"I didn't know you were such an expert."

"Just one of the little things that came out of my Task Force -- looking at where we were the most vulnerable to future tsunamis. We were fortunate this last one hit the Pacific Northwest; not much oil coming in that way."

"My home heating oil supplier, Lawson, just announced an additional price increase of twenty-five percent," said Tiffany, "over the twenty-five percent they're already charging. The morning paper was talking about rationing heating oil. I'm sure glad I live out in the country where I can burn wood. Just got a cord."

After Tiffany and he finished, Sam retraced his steps, awakening a slumbering chauffeur who dropped him off at the White House. There he found a strange woman in Tiffany's old office next to his. "Hi, I'm Jessica Thurmond. They sent me to fill-in until you hire a new admin. Anything I can do for you?"

"Get me an appointment with the President, as soon as possible," Sam said.

She knocked on the door to his office in a few moments. Her eyes were very large. "He'll see you right away."

Sam slipped on his suit coat and headed upstairs.

Carlton Boyle was standing in the hallway talking with Henry Bustamonte. When he saw Sam, he motioned for him to come over.

"That will take care of it for now," the President said to his Chief of Staff and turned to Sam. "Let's take a walk."

Outside the building, the air was crisp. When they had walked a few paces into the brown grass, Boyle said, "Do you have news for me?"

"I visited a place where Margaret can go, Pleasant Valley Treatment Facility. It's near Estes Park, Colorado, about two hours from the Denver Airport, real nice place, competent people."

The President closed his eyes in thought. He opened them, clinched his jaw, and said, "I'm going to tell them that this is the way it's going to be."

Sam nodded. "What else can I do to help?"

"This is a lot, Sam. Thank you so much." He paused for a moment then asked. "How do you think I'm doing? You know, how am I running things?"

"Mr. President, may I speak frankly?"

"Of course, Sam, that's always been our agreement."

"Well, Mr. President, I think you have changed. You seem to have lost your vision for a better America." Sam watched as the President's anger rose to the boiling point. "I think you are acting more like the prior administration, or like Tyler than yourself. I understand you're under pressure, sir, but where is the old Carlton Boyle?"

With a clinched jaw, the President stared at his old friend. For a second, Sam saw Carlton Boyle's eyes turn yellow; a black slit replaced the round iris. Then he smiled and everything was back to normal. "I have people waiting." He turned and left Sam standing on the frozen lawn.

"Who are you?" Sam called after him. Sam shivered; it was not the chill in the air. The word disingenuous formed in his mind, and repeated itself; it was not a word Sam had ever used before, but he knew what it meant. What had he just seen? He definitely needed to talk to Ryan Drake again, and more likely Sarah Smith.

TWENTY

Bill London's funeral was held in the same church in downtown Boulder where they had celebrated Peter Jones' transition, including a journey to the afterworld, courtesy of Dr. Adamson. He recalled that Tom Ertl and Jake Ashton, as well as John deBeque, had been there. It was the extraordinary occurrences at that service that had moved deBeque to abandon his job at the media affiliates.

Most of Ryan's former employees were here at London's funeral. He greeted them with warm handshakes and hugs. He had a special greeting for Karen Borden-Banes, his former administrative assistant, now manning Brauk's office in Boulder.

As they settled into the dark wooden pews, organ music began the service. Then London's sister read a passage from scripture. This was followed by a traditional funeral service with the church's new minister. Brauk and Ryan had laughed yesterday that the former minister had been fired after Peter's memorial for conducting a "pagan worship service."

As the service droned on, Ryan realized how far he had come in the months since he had met Sarah. Before her, he would have considered this service normal. Now, since he understood the continuation of life, knew that death was a return of the etheric body and the soul to its origins, death took on a whole new meaning.

A fragment of one's cumulative soul was sent to this 3rd dimension to gain experience. It could be a lifetime of living in the light, or it could be to experience life in the darkness, diminished light. A life in the dark established for many what they did not want, a most valuable perspective, and sometimes a necessary price to achieve balance for their cumulative soul.

While friends and relatives could morn the loss, they could learn so much by seeing death in this light. It would undoubtedly help them to know that they could communicate with their departed loved one, and that the veil between lives in the two dimensions was not that dense. Ryan now had new respect for those wonderful psychic people who functioned as mediums, connecting people with those who had passed over.

Ryan also saw how conventional religions imposed their dogma on "sinners." Just the idea that all were somehow tainted led to the structure wherein someone more devout could dominate them. And he saw by merely placing people in this frame of mind that they were easily dominated by anyone who lusted for power. The structures created by the ancient gods were still working. He took what for him was the next logical step: religion was just another form of mind control.

'When are you returning?' Sarah's communication startled him.

'I was headed back first thing tomorrow; but then I agreed to speak to a group in Fort Collins, so it will be the next day.'

'Something has come up, we need you back here.'

'Should I go to Fort Collins?'

'Yes, I suppose so.'

'I miss you.'

'I miss you too. Travel safely.'

Ryan slipped into analyzing. Was it all religions, or was it just Christianity that was a form of mind control? Ryan had not studied other religions; in fact he had not studied any religion since graduating from high school. The structure of his boarding school had been enough to turn him away from anything that smelled of dogma. During his four years at Arizona State University, religion was the last thing to which he had paid any attention. When he returned to Harmony tomorrow, he would speak with Sarah and Ethete about how they viewed religion.

'Some of what is taught about Jesus is not true, some is. Do not condemn what you hear with too broad a brush.'

The communication startled Ryan. Was it something more from Sarah? However, it did not feel quite like her, so he asked, *'Who is communicating with me?'*

'I am he whom they worship in this edifice. However, the real story of who I am, is both much more glorious and magnificent, and at the same time it is much less. What is true in one dimension may not be true in all. Be open to new insights, you will learn.'

Overcome, Ryan could only respond, *'I will.'*

That evening, Ryan Drake drove from the Boulderado up Sunshine Canyon into the foothills west of Boulder. Tom and Nancy Ertl's home was on one hundred fifteen acres that they had inherited from Nancy's family. The single story home, which had replaced the old ranch house, was about ten years old. A dirt road of about a quarter mile led from the highway to it.

Nancy greeted him at the door with a huge hug and a peck on the cheek. "Welcome stranger."

The sheriff's wife had been a schoolteacher, had raised three boys, all grown now, had been a member of the local school board, and a political activist, as well as a loving wife to Tom. She had been Ryan's godsend when he was going through the divorce from Vicki, all that. and she was an excellent cook.

Nancy pointed him to the living room and went off toward the kitchen humming a tune Ryan could not quite place. She said over her shoulder, "Tom will be along in a couple of minutes."

When Ryan entered, a man was seated with his back to the entrance.

"Hello, Ryan." The man said before he stood and turned to face him. "Been staying out of trouble?"

Ryan's mouth fell open.

Jake Ashton thrust out his right hand.

Ryan grasped it warmly with both of his. "I'll be damned, Jake. Where have you been hiding?"

"Right here. Been getting fed and watered real good, since I 'disappeared.'"

"I figured you might like a little surprise," Tom Ertl chuckled from behind Ryan's left shoulder.

"I don't get it," Ryan said.

"I made enemies over that fake alien you handed off to me," Jake Ashton said. "My superior in Denver wanted him real bad. Then some real funny things happened when Tyler took over. Some of my friends got thrown in jail. In the end it was hang onto your fake alien or disappear; I decided to disappear. I still haven't figured out who I can trust, present company excluded."

"Trust is a big issue these days," Ryan said. After his talk with Sam Wellborn, he needed to determine with whom he could share a huge secret. Both Tom and Jake had been at Peter's memorial service and had glimpsed the after life. Sarah had pictioned her home planet for both.

147

Sarah had also shared her off-planet origins with Nancy.

After they were seated around the dining room table, there was a loud knock on the door.

Tom Ertl said to Ryan, "Had an idea someone might be following you, so I posted one of my guys along the road. I'm guessing he caught one." Tom Ertl went to answer the door.

From the living room they could hear the conversation at the front door. "Sheriff, I've got a man in the car out there. Found him snooping around."

"Take him in. Book him for trespassing."

"Yes, sir."

"Wait," Ryan said. He had walked up behind the sheriff. "Let me take a look at this guy."

"Sure," Tom Ertl said.

They walked to the deputy's car. Ryan recognized the man in the blue sweat suit as soon as Clyde illuminated the face with his flashlight. He was the one from the coffee shop; the same one who had tried to follow him up Mount Sanitas.

"Good going, Clyde."

As Ertl returned to the dining room table, he muttered, "He'll be out in an hour."

He pointed to Ryan and said, "Looks like you're up to your old tricks. Just can't stay away from trouble."

"All of which means I'm on the right track," Ryan said.

"I could tell you a few things about trust," Tom Ertl said. "Things looked like they were going to be okay, right after Boyle resurfaced, but then they went back the other way and then some."

"What do you mean, things went back the other way?"

"Let's see if I can help," Ertl said. "Going way back to when I was starting in law enforcement, the local guys could pretty well run their own show, even the guys from the State of Colorado left us alone. Then over the last twenty years, the feds, like this one," he pointed to Jake Ashton, "started to throw their weight around more and more. It wasn't like the old days when we would all cooperate; now it was like 'take orders or take a hike.' Jake here was an exception. He actually used to ask me for advice from time to time. I think it all has to do with States rights versus the federal government. The States have lost a lot the last thirty years.

"The part that's been added for me is this whole business of domestic surveillance. We all suspected that some government agency was peeking into people's private affairs; now it turns out they've been listening to phone conversations for years, pursuing bank accounts, and, most recently, checking on everybody's emails. This started well before Boyle came into office, or the guy before him. But it's all out in the open now, and they are demanding that local law enforcement cooperate in these efforts. They're going crazy over this latest terrorist threat."

They talked over dinner, a wonderful meal of pot roast and vegetables. Ryan told them about the cabal's control of the President. Given recent events, no one found it shocking. Nancy found the conversation so interesting that she stuck with the three men into the evening. The dishes were stacked next to the sink.

At last Ryan said, "There are going to be some worldwide changes coming along, changes like we've never experienced before, changes that will affect everyone and everything. The cabal is fighting to hold onto its power. The economic situation has already changed dramatically."

"That's why we're raising a few cattle up here," Tom Ertl said.

"The planet herself, Earth, is going to change," Ryan said. "We should plan on a ten-degree increase in average temperatures. For this part of the North American Continent that means little snow pack. And we can expect other changes too.

"So what do you want us to do," Nancy asked.

"I don't know quite yet, but I do know that it's women, like you, who are going to help us through this. Last evening I met some very interesting people; I want to introduce you to them. Do you have time for coffee tomorrow?"

TWENTY-ONE

"Boy, is it a mess out there," Sam said as soon as he walked though the door of Tiffany's office.

She held out her hand to accept the latte Sam had picked up on his walk from his car. On the salary Sam was paying her, she could not indulge in twenty-dollar lattes, the same lattes that used to cost five.

Tiffany nodded and sipped as Sam told his story about finding gasoline for his car -- like many top-ranking officials, he had a government limousine and had not paid much attention to the availability or price of fuel. He went on for another five minutes, fuming about pot holes in Virginia's roads and things about which his wife Maggie had been complaining: That there were no more seedless grapes in the stores, "Was it that hard to ship them from Chili?" Really good lettuce from California was twelve dollars a head. And despite everything costing more, their bank had not raised the amount of cash she could withdraw from the ATM; in fact their account had been frozen just like everyone else's.

Earlier today, after a meeting and checking his mail at the White House, Sam had his chauffeur drive him home. He had then used his own car to drive to Tiffany's office in Springfield. Sam had taken an hour to make the drive, detouring through the rolling countryside, stopping once or twice, all to make sure he was not being followed.

"Welcome to the real world," Tiffany responded from behind her desk.

"You knew about all this?"

"Oh, yeah."

Sam frowned, heaved a sigh, and then asked, "Anything from Ryan Drake?"

"Soon as my internet connection comes back."

"Again huh?" Sam plopped himself down in the lone chair across from her. Since the last time he had visited, Tiffany had added a filing cabinet, a desktop computer, and a copier. "Post another query on the site." He added, "This private page on the web site method may be cumbersome, but at least it's private. I'm sure he'll respond when he gets to a computer."

"Okay." Tiffany typed a few characters into her computer. "Sam, please don't get the wrong idea, I'm not discouraged, far from it. This arrangement suits me. I just get aggravated when my phone doesn't work, and when the price of office supplies is shooting through the roof."

She went on to report that she had located both Glenn Koslowski and Tony Santori. Santori was on leave, recovering from the bullet wound he had received defending the President. Koslowski was still with the Secret Service. He was assigned to a financial institutions investigations unit in New York.

"I want to talk to both of them," Sam said. "With all the recent news about bank failures, Koslowski is likely to be the more interesting of the two."

Tiffany dialed the number she had been given by his office, then handed the phone to Sam. "Glenn, this is Sam Wellborn. You may remember me from the day I discovered Carlton Boyle in the cave in Oregon."

Once they had established who each was, Sam said, "I need to talk to you, face to face." They set a meeting for the next time Glenn was due to be in DC, a few days from now.

Tiffany found Tony at his apartment in Annapolis, Maryland. He told Sam that he remembered him and would be willing to meet that evening.

After arrangements were made, Sam pulled a chair up next to Tiffany's desk. "I need to talk. Something is going on that I can't share with just anybody."

"Okay," Tiffany said as she put down the papers she had been shuffling.

"It's about this secret government stuff," Sam said. "I feel real conflicted. On the one hand I know this is a great country -- I've been to quite a few others, and most of them are nothing by comparison to what we have here. On the other hand, I now know that we're being run by a group of men, no, a gang, who are not looking out for anyone other than themselves.

"I've always loved my country," Sam moaned, "considered myself a patriot -- whatever that means. I am a highly placed government official; I report directly to the President. But I know things are not right.

"The stuff that Ryan Drake threw at me when we were in Boulder has been eating on me. I know we trample on other countries. I know money is what counts in this country, what buys influence. I know there are people starving, both here and in other countries. And I know these same people sew my clothing for one one-hundredth the price it would cost me in this country. So I see all this, but I can't make sense out of it."

"And you're just now seeing this?" Tiffany asked.

"Yeah."

They sat for a while not speaking. Finally Tiffany said, "Look, this is the way it's been for a long time -- little people and powerful people. Although I've worked at the White House, I'm still one of the little people. I see what the little people go through to make ends meet. What I don't understand is why we put up with it."

"Because they feel powerless?" Sam was not quite ready to put Tiffany in the same category as "the little people."

"So what are you going to do with your new insights?"

"I'm going to find a way through this mess," Sam said. "In the last couple of days, I've talked to people who know about the secret government, and who aren't afraid to go up against it. A couple of them have web sites and are out giving speeches."

"Anybody I know?"

Tiffany nodded her head as Sam rattled off names from a list of activists they had encountered on the campaign trail. Many of them had supported Carlton Boyle's run for the presidency, and had applauded his early actions as President. Since he had returned from the tsunami, they had become disillusioned by his inability to stop the economy from collapsing, and his attacks on personal liberties. "And a couple of billionaires," Sam added. "I don't think you know them."

"Why would they go against everything that got them their billions?" Tiffany asked.

"They see this crumbling economy destroying everything they've worked for. Their plan is to put things back the way the Constitution intended."

"What about the government that's in place already?"

"Everybody says it's not working. They're all pointing fingers at

Congress, at the Supreme Court, at the bureaucracy. Some of them want to recall Boyle, and I'm beginning to agree." Sam could hardly believe he had uttered the words. Here he was, going along with people who wanted to recall the same President he had just helped to get elected, a President for whom he worked.

Sam thought back to the campaign trail, how he had worked day and night to insure Boyle's election, how they had refused to be bought by major corporations who dangled money before them. He had kept Carlton Boyle clean of the taint that had dogged his predecessors.

President Boyle had come into office on the heels of a disastrous administration that had been unable to cure the problems left by its predecessor. In Boyle the country had seen a savior, had believed that they had elected a politician with no ties to the old ways.

Sam rambled on, "You know, during his first weeks in office, Carlton Boyle was remarkably proactive; Congress went along with many of his ideas. Then he had visited his ranch and was lost in the tsunami.

"After reassuming the Presidency, he really did the right things." Sam set down his espresso and ticked them off on the fingers of his left hand. "Rescinding Tyler's domestic terrorist decree. Releasing political prisoners. Declaring the West Coast a disaster area. Going after the members of the World League. And, last but not least, issuing amnesty decree for anybody who was part of covering-up contact with extraterrestrials, or who had engaged in reverse engineering of extraterrestrial technology, or who had been part of mind control operations. That was really acting like the President I helped get elected. Never mind that he had inherited an economy that was not doing so good, he had his priorities right.

"Now," Sam shook his head and threw up his hands. "Congress is just now considering legislation he proposed in his first days back. Then, a week later, he tosses them proposals to tighten security, support the financial system, and increase funding for oil exploration, and they go back to their committees to reconsider. In my opinion, the government of the United States of America has ground to a halt. It's mired in conflicting agendas, caught up in bureaucracies guarding their own turf. In the meantime, people are standing in lines to withdraw funds from banks, to find work, and to receive a bowl of warm soup.

"For the first couple of days after he returned, he acted like the old Carlton Boyle, then he began to resemble Richard Tyler. Too bad I wasn't around to kick him in the butt. I got to watch it by reading the Salt Lake City Tribune and the Deseret Morning News, plus emails you sent me."

Tiffany drained the final drops from her latte and tossed the cup into the recycle wastebasket. "Okay, let's say we find a way to maneuver Carlton Boyle out of the picture. Then what?" she asked. "If those people who control the President are so powerful, what's to prevent them doing it again?"

He thought for a minute. "That's where you and I come in. We've got to figure out how they have such a hold on him, then we make sure they can't do it to the next guy."

"Or woman?"

"Or woman," he conceded. He flashed back to the change in Carlton Boyle's eyes. Ryan and Sarah, where were you?

"So what's next?"

Sam pulled out a square envelope and handed it to Tiffany. She opened and read the personal note to Sam from Carlton Boyle. The note instructed Sam to accompany Margaret Boyle to Pleasant Valley. It stated that the President had cleared the way for Margaret's removal from the White House. The press was not to be informed. Jessica had handed it to him as he packed up to leave.

"So when's this going to happen?" Tiffany asked.

"Tomorrow, I'm hoping that I can gain some insights from traveling with Margaret. I'm going to see if I can stop off in Boulder and talk Moore's widow into opening that safety deposit box."

"Wait," Tiffany said, "here's a reply from Ryan Drake." She was staring at the screen of her desktop. "He wants to know when to call you. He's still stuck with going to a pay phone."

"Damn." Sam shook his head. The only secure phone was right here in Tiffany's office; no way was he going to talk to Ryan using his cell phone. "Tell him I'll be away for a couple of days. When I get back to DC, I'll post a time."

Then Sam added another thought. "Tell Ryan that I'm escorting Margaret to Pleasant Valley."

"Before you leave," Tiffany said, "let me give you a thought to take along on your trip. If you do figure out how to put the country back on track, what about the little people in this country, in other countries? This government was designed to preserve the hierarchy of the wealthy. So what changes for the little people? What changes for mankind?"

That evening, Sam met Tony at a third floor walk-up apartment in Annapolis. The Secret Service agent had said that he lived alone, however pictures of a pretty girl, several of them with Tony, were prominently displayed on the table next to the sofa. Hand weights littering the living room supported Tony's contention that he had recovered from the bullet wound.

Tony was wearing a grey sweat suit that did little to hide his muscular body. His dark hair was cut very short, and he was clean-shaven. A full-sized German shepherd greeted Sam with a plea to be petted, and followed him as he took the seat Tony offered. He learned her name was "Dolly."

"You said on the telephone you had some questions about the Secret Service," Tony said. "I'm curious why someone who's been around the President as much as you wouldn't already know everything."

"All right, let me cut right to it. Things have changed around the President. I see a lot of new faces among the agents. I'm wondering why Glenn is no longer assigned to the President. I'm wondering why you're still on sick leave."

Tony sat back in his chair and stared at Sam. His silence lasted a long time. Finally he said, "I don't understand why they haven't put me to work either. I'm healthy, probably healthier than before I was shot. My old boss, James Batcher, is no longer around. Nobody seems to know where he went to. Yeah, things have changed."

They sparred for a few more minutes, testing to see who knew what. Tony wanted to preserve the secrecy surrounding the Secret Service, and it was clear he wanted his old job back. Sam did not want to disclose what he knew until he felt sure of Tony, although his recent conversation with Ryan had cleared both Tony and Glenn from any part in the secret government.

At last, Tony said, "So what can I tell you?"

"I want to know about the new agents. I understand some of them have not gone through training. I want to know who they report to. And I want to know anything you have heard about changes in the President's behavior."

Tony lowered his head. When he raised it, he had a tear in his eye. "You know, I took a bullet for that guy. Do you think he has even once said thank you?

"And yes, I talk to guys who are still on duty. Most of the old White House detail has been reassigned or laid off. Some are like Glenn, spending time chasing financial bad guys. Some of the others are overseas trying to ferret out counterfeit money. My friends in the Service tell me that everything got out of whack when Tyler was in. He's the one who brought in all the new guys. A few days after President Boyle came back things got even worse. Now there are thirty-two guys, two shifts of sixteen, no women, who are in charge of Boyle's security. They call the shots; everybody else is second-class. I'd like to tell you more, but I haven't been to work in a month."

"Let me tell you a few things I've discovered," Sam said. "Regardless of whether you decide to get involved or not, I need your word that you'll keep this strictly to yourself." Sam was desperate to find people in the DC area whom he could count on.

Tony said that he could do that.

He went on to tell Tony about his conversation with the President, and about the two men who had searched Tiffany's office.

"I need to think about all this," Tony said. "If what you say is true, then this so-called secret government is really well entrenched. And if that's the case, it's going to be real difficult to do anything without them finding out. So, what can you possibly do?"

Sam explained his thoughts about taking the government back to basics, back to the constitution. He even went so far as to suggest a movement to oust President Boyle.

"We'd need to get the military on our side," Tony said.

"I don't want to use force, but a show of force might be necessary."

"Hey, I thought you were a tough guy. You were always right beside Boyle when the going got tough. Do you know what your designation was on the campaign trail?"

"No."

"Bulldog," Tony said. "We all thought you were the candidate's muscle. What happened?"

"I'm a lot smarter nowadays."

"Keep in mind, those people can make you disappear, just like that." Tony snapped his fingers.

They parted with Tony promising to nose around. Sam felt he had made contact with an ally.

TWENTY-TWO

The next morning Sam walked Margaret Boyle from the White House to the waiting helicopter. She felt lighter on his arm than he remembered her, and she walked slowly. A few members of the press corps waited a respectful distance as she waved good-by. The official release was that she was traveling to visit her sister in Washington State and did not want any press accompanying her. The gossip columnists speculated that she had some sort of terminal illness.

The Marine guard stood by as Margaret's two Secret Service agents boarded. They identified themselves as Jesse Hardinski and Marvin Bushnell. The helicopter flew them to Andrews Air Force Base where they boarded a small military jet; it took off almost immediately.

Sam took the seat next to Margaret. When Bushnell offered her a sleeping pill, Sam brushed him off. Nonetheless, she fell into a drowsy state as soon as they lifted off.

They had just passed over the Mississippi River on their way to Buckley Air Force base near Denver when Margaret whispered, "Sam, you've got to help me." Her words barely floated from her mouth. "They keep giving me those damn pills."

"Everything will be fine as soon as we get you to Pleasant Valley," Sam said. "It's a very nice place. I checked it out myself."

"Sam what's going on? I never see Carlton any more. Is he okay?"

"Carlton's having some problems right now," Sam replied. "He wants you to be in a safe place. That's why I'm taking you to Pleasant Valley. It's a safe place, Margaret."

"Good." Then she slipped back into a drowsy state.

As they were landing, she awoke with a start. "Is this it?"

"We're going to take a car from here to Pleasant Valley," Sam said.

He helped her down the stairs and into the waiting black limo. Hardinski sat in front with the driver; Bushnell slipped into the back with them. He said to Margaret Boyle, "You'll be more comfortable, if you take one of these." He held out a blue pill and a small glass of water.

Before Sam could intervene, she reached for it. Sam looked up at Bushnell; he wore a crooked smile.

After three hours they pulled into the grounds of Pleasant Valley. Gertrude Steiner walked to the limousine to greet her important guest. Sam helped the attendant put Margaret into a wheelchair, while the two Secret Service agents unloaded luggage.

During check-in, Bushnell explained that he and his partner would remain at the facility, and that two more agents would arrive later today. Steiner said that, yes, she had received instructions from the President's Chief of Staff that Margaret was to be in the company of one agent at all times.

After Sam wheeled Margaret to her room and settled her in, he walked to the waiting limo for the trip back to the airport. Bushnell said, "Thanks for your help."

Although he was agitated by the constant presence of Steiner and Bushnell, Sam tried to relax in the spacious rear seat of the limousine as it retraced its route. Somehow he had to get Margaret away from them.

As the limo pulled into the north end of Boulder, Sam rapped on the glass and said, "I'm going to get out in a few blocks. I'll let you know."

"But, ah, Mr. Wellborn, my orders are to take you to Buckley."

"Hey, go home early."

"Sir, I have my instructions."

"Tell your boss, whoever that is, that I jumped ship."

"I don't think I can do that."

They were still discussing it when the limo stopped for the light at Pearl Street. Sam calmly grabbed his briefcase and opened the door. "Have a great day," he said as he caught a glimpse of the perturbed driver in the rearview mirror. He dodged a car and was on the sidewalk in a couple of strides. He began walking north, back the way they had come.

When the limo disappeared in heavy traffic, Sam reversed his direction and darted into the Golden Buff Motel. He secured a room for the night, paying two hundred and fifty for a room that should have been seventy-five.

Once in his room he called the number for Dr. Gordon Moore's widow. The phone rang several times before she answered.

Sam explained who he was and why he was calling. She agreed to meet him the next day at the bank.

Sam then called Tiffany. He was fairly sure that the phone in her office was secure; he had paid a lot of money to buy the very latest equipment.

"So how did it go?" she asked.

"A bust, she slept most of time. What little conversation we did have indicated that she knew she was addicted to the drugs that her guardians were foisting on her."

"I feel sorry for her."

"Yeah, me too. I hope that Pleasant Valley will be a better situation -- for the time being. Now, we need to figure out a way to get her out of there."

The next morning Sam met Moore's widow at the Wells Fargo branch on Pearl Street. Sam told her how sorry he was for her husband's death, said that he had done a great service for his country, and thanked her for meeting him.

For some reason the bank did not know of her husband's death, so they admitted her to the safety deposit box area without question. In a few minutes she returned with a large brown envelope.

"It was buried under our family's financial papers," she said handing it to Sam. "Gordon told me that you would be coming to get this. It was the last conversation we had. He was so proud of this project, said it was the best thing he had ever done. Is it possible he sensed he was going to die?"

To relieve the widow's mind, Sam replied, "Mrs. Moore, I believe Gordon had an automobile accident, just like the papers say."

Sam thanked her again for accommodating his schedule and hurried to catch the shuttle to Denver International Airport. The bus was empty, so he peaked at the papers in the envelope. They were Moore's hand-written notes of his conversations with the people who had come forward. Each note was referenced to a name and phone contact; some of them contained addresses. Not wanting to expose things further, he folded the envelope and stuffed it into his briefcase.

At Denver International, Sam waited in a long line to get to the ticket counter. He was told the next available seat was in three hours, and that it would cost him fifteen hundred dollars. It was one of those times he wished that he could avail himself of the privileges of other people on the President's staff and search out a military jet. On the other hand, given what he was learning about the secret government, the price for those privileges might just be too high. He used his government issued credit card to pay for the ticket.

During the four-hour flight Sam reflected on his conversation with Tiffany the prior day. She was smart, she challenged him, and she looked at the world differently. What about ordinary people, would they have it any better if he and his billionaire friends put the republic back together again? What could be done about the people in other countries? Maybe Ryan Drake was right; maybe it called for a whole new way of seeing things.

Sarah dialed the private number for President Boyle. She had waited until she was sure he was not in the White House to make this call. Remembering her previous conversation with him, she was more than a little apprehensive as she touched the last digit on the satellite phone.

When she explained who she was, the woman on the other end asked her to hold on while they put the call through to the President. Sarah heard several clicks before the line became clear.

"Good morning, Sarah." His familiar voice had a nice ring to it. "I've been wondering when I'd hear from you."

"Hello Mr. President. Thank you for taking my call. I am interested to learn if you have reconsidered my offer to help you reconstruct the civilization of this planet?"

"Sarah, you know I'm open to your suggestions. Are you available to come to Washington?"

"Before I commit to doing that, I would like to know a couple of things. The last time we talked about creating a new civilization, you were hesitant. Where are you now? Are you open to recognizing that people in other countries have the same rights as those in America?"

"As we discussed when we were holed up in that cave, after you were kind enough to let me visit your home planet, I see the desirability and necessity of what you are asking. Now if that answer satisfies you, call my secretary Sally O'Hara and set up a time. You can stay at the White House."

Barely able to contain herself, Sarah said, "Thank you, Mr. President. I'll get back to you." She pushed the button to disconnect and heaved a sigh of relief.

Across the room, Ethete roused herself from her semi-conscious state. "They routed you to the real President Boyle," she said when her eyes opened. "I watched as he talked to you; he seemed so enthusiastic to hear from you."

"The enthusiasm I agree with, but he seemed disoriented. First, it's not morning. Second, he made no reference to our prior telephone conversation, only to talking with me in the cave."

"Guess they aren't keeping the real him up to date."

"Which tells us what?"

"I don't know yet."

When the two Phantians reported on their conversation with Carlton Boyle, Ajax said, "The guy underground seems like the real McCoy, but after what you've told me about that facility, I'm not sure I want to try rescuing him."

"That will not be necessary," Sarah said. "We have others who are ready to help out. What I do need help with is figuring out what we can do."

TWENTY-THREE

The four drove north from Harmony Center on the paved road that ran up the valley between Fortress Mesa and Black Mesa. Ajax, still dizzy from his ordeal, chose not to come along. Unlike a similar trip Sarah and Ryan had made a few weeks earlier, when they were fearful because they were so sure they were being watched, the drive tonight was filled with pleasant chatter among Sarah, Ethete, and John deBeque. Sarah's attitude of fearlessness buoyed them.

Ryan was lost in thoughts of his trip to Colorado. He had arrived back at Harmony this evening, shortly after dinner. On his trip he had seen numerous vacant storefronts, had noted the increased number of homeless, and had experienced outrageous prices for everything. All of these were signs of a depressed economy and of high inflation. Added to that were the numbers of people sick with tuberculosis and other respiratory diseases. At London's funeral he had learned that another one of his former employees, Glen Castillo, had been diagnosed with TB.

Reacting to this chaos, and his own desperate financial situation, Ryan had returned to his mountain home to dig up a bucket of old silver coins he had buried beneath the deck outside his home office. At current prices, he reckoned this single bucket, weighing about seventy pounds, would be worth about seventy thousand dollars. He had paid fifteen thousand for it. When he stopped in Monte Vista, the price of gasoline had been a dollar higher than when he had stopped a week earlier. Prices on the menu had been scratched out; prices higher by a dollar had replaced them.

When he had inquired of Sarah how it was that she financed Harmony and her activities, she had shown him a gleaming five-ounce gold bar. Their discussion had been truncated by preparations for this trip, but he intended to inquire more about Harmony's treasure.

More important than his own financial situation, or the economy, or widespread sickness, was the pictioning that Sarah had given him of Carlton Boyle and his double. Ethete and she had found that he was being held in a colony of N'Roids and that the N'Roids who were in charge of the World League had a headquarters just to the west of Denver, Colorado. If this was true, and he had no reason to doubt it, except it was so far-fetched, then it was even more incredible than a U.S. President under the thumb of others.

"We must face the reality that there are forces greater than can be overcome by human intervention alone," Sarah had said after she told him about the N'Roids. "We must look for another solution." Seeking that other solution was where they were going tonight.

He concentrated on the roadway. Gusty wind buffeted the light-weight electric vehicle. With a cloud cover, no other traffic, and no lights alongside the road, the car's headlights were all that penetrated the darkness. The clock on the dash read 1:13.

"I'm all for new adventures," John deBeque said, "but can one of you shed a little more light on where we're going?"

"Patience, John, patience," Ryan said with a smile deBeque could not see from the back seat of their vehicle. The younger man was still having trouble coping with sudden appearances by Dr. Adamson, and now this mysterious trip.

As they rounded the side of a bluff, a few lights from Kayenta came into view. Gone were the red, yellow and orange from the neon signs at the intersection with US 160.

To the north, a dimly lighted sign announced TEEDIUDEEH SHOP-PING CENTER, but the stores were all darkened. Ryan paused at the stoplight, the brightest glow to be seen. A man and woman, bundled against the fierce wind, hurried to cross before it changed.

Farther north along the lighted four-lane highway through the town, a man in dirty overalls sat beside the road sipping from a brown paper bag. The town lay in darkness. Only two lights glowed from windows in the federal government housing project to the east. Ryan slowed to allow a chicken to wander out of the road.

North of town there was only darkness. Suddenly snow flurries began to dance in their headlights. As they progressed farther north the snow began to stick on the road. Since cacti were blooming at harmony, thirty miles to the south, snow was the last thing Ryan expected.

They approached the Utah border wondering if it would be guarded or open. On his way back from Colorado, the radio news had reported that, based on renewed terrorist threats, President Boyle planned to institute martial law. This was confusing everyone because the first day he had returned to office President Boyle had relieved the restrictions on movement placed during President Tyler's reign.

Signs on both sides of the highway reflected in the car's headlights: SPEED LIMIT 25 MPH. Ryan slowed from fifty. At the border, there was a checkpoint in the middle of the road, however the gates for both northbound and south were raised. There were no lights in the temporary housing for the guards, but two vehicles labeled HOMELAND SECURITY were parked nearby. In one, a man, apparently fast asleep, slumped in the driver's seat.

A mile later, they turned east onto the road leading to the Navajo Tribal Park. The snow stopped as the clouds dissipated to reveal a star-studded night sky with a half moon. But, more than that, Ryan had a sense of peace, a sense of security, a sense that it was important that the four of them be here. The chatter of the others diminished; it was replaced by awe of the dark buttes rising up on either side of the highway.

As before, the metal gate at the entrance to the Park swung open before them. Ryan drove through the parking lot, and then headed down the winding dirt road into Monument Valley. As soon as he rounded the first hairpin curve, he caught a glimpse of Merrick Butte glistening in the moonlight. It was only after they had descended to the valley floor that the vertical sides of the butte, towering over a thousand feet above their vehicle, displayed their majesty.

"Awesome," John deBeque said. "Hey, this was worth waiting for. I'd like to come here in the daytime."

Ryan grinned.

They turned onto the same rutted road as Sarah and he had taken before, and parked in the same spot. Sarah had told them to wear only windbreakers, so, despite a steady breeze, the four walked from their vehicle with only light clothing.

Ryan followed Sarah, her uncovered blonde hair glistening in the moonlight. The others trailed behind winding their way through dense clumps of sagebrush.

After a hundred yards, they emerged into a flat area. Unlike last time, the bushes were not flattened against the ground. Looking at John deBeque, Ryan saw him taking in the unfamiliar surroundings. They formed a circle. Hand in hand, they took in the splendor of the night sky, millions of winking lights, the great glow of the Milky Way.

As Ryan watched, all of this became distorted. In the place of singular points of light, squiggly lines now appeared, as if he were looking up through a layer of water or ice. The moon was no longer shaped like half of a pie; it too had an irregular shape.

As John held his bare hand, Ryan noted that the younger man was trembling with excitement. He could see John's bearded face. White teeth, in a mouth open in wonder, glistened in the moonlight. John was a city boy; he had told Ryan that his experience with stargazing had been limited to planetariums.

A bright light from directly overhead dazzled his vision. Ryan felt like it was embracing him. In an instant, he was transported upward.

In another instant, they found themselves in the domed space of a starcraft. It was much larger than last time Ryan had been on board the craft of someone from another star system. The sides of the very large space were not apparent beyond the rows of seats that surrounded them. Gentle lighting was supplied from overhead, but there were no lines or points of origin. The floor was pliable yet glistened as if it were metallic.

'This starcraft is call the Star of Bethlehem,' Sarah communicated to Ryan. *'I have not been here before, only heard of it. You will learn more about it later.'*

A much larger crowd was present than the last time Ryan had been on board a starship; most of them resembled Earth-humans. A jumble of phrases and thoughts flooded his mind. He had learned from his experience with Sarah that he could not readily discern between a native of Earth and those who had been transplanted, let alone those who had been trained elsewhere and incarnated to assist at this time.

Mixed with those who looked human were a few beings of mixed sizes and with different features. A few among them were quite unique, beyond what he could have imagined. As before, he stared at the people of the star civilizations; they were all exceedingly handsome.

Ryan spotted a pair of beings who resembled a being he had encountered on his last visit. This pair, a male and a female, were dressed in clothing that one might find on any American street. They had no visible hair, no ears; their glossy skin had a scaled look about it. With inquiring yellow eyes, the male turned and looked at Ryan.

'They are A'Roids,' Sarah communicated. *'As I explained last time, they are present on Earth, although you would not recognize an A'Roid when they are cloaked in their human visage. On board a craft such as this, those*

who have natural physical bodies must appear in them. A'Roids are being quite helpful at this time.'

'Different from the N'Roids you viewed in Colorado?'

'Very, the A'Roids are cooperating with us; the N'Roids are not. There are many millions of non-humans on your planet,' Sarah communicated to Ryan. *'Only about a million of them are the N'Roids of which I spoke. Many visitors from distant star systems, such as myself and Ethete, are represented here.'* She pointed to other very human looking beings scattered within the three tiered circle. *'No N'Roids are present.'*

Ryan glanced at John deBeque. The bearded younger man was stunned by what he had been thrust into. Ryan picked up a snatch of transmission from Ethete to John. *'You are on-board a starcraft... ...benevolent interest in this planet...'*

"Am I dreaming?" John exclaimed.

His utterance caused the room to fall silent. A life form wearing a long white cape over a robe of light blue moved to stand in front of them. Her beautiful face set Ryan's heart to pounding; she looked like Sarah's twin, an elegant, but older J'Li D'Rona, before Earth's caustic environment and Peter's death had taken their toll on her.

'Ryan Drake?' The non-verbal communication came through as clear as if the words had been spoken against an absolutely quiet background.

Without hesitation Ryan returned the communication, *'Yes.'*

'It is good to meet an Earth-being who is so aware. J'Li has told me of her love for you and how you have guarded and assisted her. I am very pleased to meet you.'

'This is my D'Ct-Elds mother,' Sarah communicated to Ryan. She stepped to embrace her elder twin. Ethete loosened her grip on John deBeque's hand and joined in the embrace.

Ryan overheard Sarah's D'Ct-Elds mother communicate to Ethete and Sarah, *'I am so excited to be here. The entire academy has been transported to observe this wondrous transition. You two are so lucky to be on the surface, in the middle of it all. Is John deBeque as aware?'* She nodded to the younger man.

'He is learning,' Ethete replied as she returned to John's side.

'Aren't we all,' Sarah's D'Ct-Elds mother communicated.

Sarah and Ethete pointed out a number of other Earth-humans to John deBeque and Ryan. Ryan thought he recognized a couple of Hollywood stars. Ethete did not know them, but had knowledge of their activities. What was more interesting to Ryan were the numbers of those who appeared to be Earth-humans but, like Sarah and Ethete, were visitors from other star systems.

'*We will meet some of them later,*' Sarah smiled. '*You are becoming adept at recognizing their true identity, congratulations.*'

'*I think these rarified surroundings help a lot,*' Ryan communicated.

'*True.*'

TWENTY-FOUR

On the far side of the area Ryan noticed the short, elf-like creature he had dubbed, "Jasper," at the last on-board gathering. He was conversing with Dr. Victor Adamson and a woman, both of whom towered over the shorter creature. Jasper, and his globes, had been responsible for the cave in which they had sheltered Carlton Boyle and for getting them out of a number of tight spots. His globes were the ones who had guided Ajax back to Harmony.

The white-haired architect of Harmony Center walked to where the four of them stood. He greeted Ryan with his usual bear hug; he then turned toward John deBeque, who seemed less startled by the antics of Dr. Adamson now that he was onboard a starcraft, and did the same.

After Dr. Adamson had greeted the two women, he motioned to the tall female with similar gray hair and pleasant features that accompanied him and communicated, *'This is my sister Crita. She came from Earth's Center for this gathering.'*

In the middle of the space, a brilliant being slowly materialized. It radiated a brilliant white light, almost too intense for human eyes. Ryan had the impression of a human form; it wore nothing on feet that did not touch the floor. Once again, Ryan felt a surge of overwhelming love. The being was accompanied by two other brilliant life forms who stood beside it. While fully visible, the being's brilliance appeared to undulate. Ryan guessed that he was dampening it so as not to overwhelm those nearby.

The celestial moved to greet each individual. Ryan watched as it treated each with great respect and tenderness.

'We welcome you, Ryan Drake,' the being said as it grasped both of his hands. Ryan was surprised to be recognized, as this was a different

being than had been present before. More impressive was the exhilarating energy that flowed from the celestial to Ryan.

'*And John deBeque. You have done well.*' Ryan overheard the being communicate. John looked like a deer caught in the headlights of an oncoming truck.

'*This is Jesus,*' Sarah's D'Ct-Elds mother communicated as the being enveloped her in a mighty hug. When they stepped apart, she continued, '*But he is not the Jesus of your Earth religions. Much of that Jesus was created by the imaginations of men of lower density.*'

Jesus smiled at her last remark and moved to greet others.

As this process was concluding, Dr. Adamson indicated seats on the first row of the three-tiered circle. Ryan was preparing to sit to his right, but he indicated that Sarah should sit next to him with Ryan on her other side. As if some sort of orchestration was in charge, Ethete went to sit on the other side of John. Crita occupied the seat to Dr. Adamson's left. The seat between Ryan and John deBeque was left unoccupied, as were one or two others in the front row; most of those in the other tiers were occupied.

Standing in the middle of the circle, he opened the meeting with the following communication. '*I am most pleased to be present at this important gathering. What a privilege it is for all of us to assist in Earth's transformation.*

'*The God of this universe thanks each of you for your efforts on behalf of the enslaved humans of Earth.*' He paused for emphasis. '*Although I do not need to do so, I remind each human with us -- those from Earth and elsewhere -- how wonderfully beautiful, powerful, and loving you each already are, and how incredibly beautiful, powerful, and loving you will yet become. As we go through these difficult times, it is good to remember this truth, along with the unconditional love of God for all his children.*'

Recalling how he had felt the last time he had heard a communication from a celestial, Ryan glanced over at John deBeque. Ethete was gripping his hand. Ryan hoped this was sufficient for the young man to receive every word of this wonderful telepathic communication.

Pointing to John deBeque, Jesus communicated, '*It may seem to you, the newest among us, that you do not comprehend what I have just stated, however in the higher dimensions, your cumulative soul is well known. You have been a part of the evolution of this planet for millennia. I congratulate you on choosing to live with those of the light. We are pleased that you are fulfilling the contract of your incarnation.*'

John deBeque's face turned white, then flushed. Ethete's grip on his hand tightened so that her knuckles turned white. A smile of understanding crossed his face.

Jesus then glided to an empty seat on the far side of the space and sat down. His companions floated to station themselves behind his chair. He continued, *'As we all are aware, Earth is transitioning herself. When it is complete, she will glow as a beacon so all may see her true beauty.*

'Some Earth scientists are sensing energies coming from outside the planet. These energies, supplied by the starcrafts of many who are here, along with Earth's own internal source, are shifting Earth's climate to become more moderate. Some will interpret these energies as fearful; some will sense the joy in them.

'I would now paint for all the vision I have of Earth after she comes into her fullness, after her human children have chosen to live from love, after they have chosen to see the consciousness of all, conscious water, conscious rocks, conscious plants, conscious animals, conscious humans, conscious food, conscious manufactured products, and, most importantly, consciousness at the quantum level.

'Earth in her transcended state of light has become a shining orb; her waters are clear and pure, as is her air and land. Her climate is moderate and welcoming in all regions of the globe. She radiates love to all who dwell on her surface and beneath, and to all who visit. Her oceans abound with fish; her land is fertile. There is no competition among the animals that dwell on her, no survival of the fittest.

'Peace reigns among her human inhabitants, because there is no fear, there is no violence. Communities of humans live and work together for the benefit of all. Communities link with each other for trade and education. People govern themselves with small locally oriented structures. Humanity enjoys unlimited free energy, unlimited wealth, and unbounded freedom for individuals to be. Technology is beneficial to all.

'This vision for Earth-humans will be accomplished as a quantum energy shift. When enough choose it, it will take place. However, Earth is not waiting, thanks to the energy of the armada, she transforms even as we gather here.

'As Earth shifts into lighter densities, those who embrace these energies will ascend with her. Those who resist will depart to take up lives that will offer them new opportunities for growth in lower dimensions. All of this will take place gradually during what is called interim time. Although the shift will become quite apparent soon, its completion will take many years.

'Some of our cosmic brothers and sisters, those in whom the Creator's light has diminished, have been resisting this transformation. Eons ago their dark ancestors laid claim to this planet, asserting that they had the right to control

life here, and that the peoples of Earth were rightfully under their auspices. Their darkness was on Earth during my incarnation. For millennia their darkness has enveloped Earth and her people, to the extent that seventy years ago Earth's light had faded, and she was choking. The light energies from the ships of the armada have now caused that darkness to retreat; now Earth once again breathes freely. Although remnants of the darkness lingers, it is rapidly retreating from this sector of the galaxy.'

Heads nodded in understanding. Jesus continued, *'Now, it is only rogue brothers and sisters who reside on Earth's surface, who still wish to retard her transformation. There will be no thermonuclear war, nor planetary shifts of great magnitude. The efforts of those represented here, along with the rising consciousness of the humans of Earth, have mitigated such potential cataclysms. Those remaining, who embrace the darkness as their master, will be removed so that Earth-humans may determine their future.*

'Turmoil, from the crumbling of the many institutions created by souls in which the light has dimmed, will accompany Earth's ascension. We are gathered here to find ways to mitigate any attendant hardships and dissipate the power of those who still wish to exercise control over the people of Earth. We are here to find ways to help the humans of Earth create institutions based on the highest needs of all.'

Indicating a dark complexioned being with a bright orange tunic, Jesus addressed it with a name that Ryan could not understand. *'You asked to address this gathering.'*

When the being stood, Ryan could see that she had the shape of a female. She communicated, *'We believed that we had accounted for all the nuclear weapons on planet Earth. Until the recent detonation we did not realize that this was not so.*

'When the craft, constructed by the Earth-humans, came into our area of vigilance, we believed that it was being powered by a new type of nuclear reactor. Since we have all agreed that these will not be allowed outside the atmosphere, my crew proceeded to return it to the facility from whence it came. They escaped just before the explosion, but were severely damaged by radiation. Fortunately, it was a small device. Little radiation escaped to Earth's atmosphere. However, the effects of the detonation were felt by many.

'If my crew had known it was a thermonuclear device, they would have disabled it. After that unfortunate incident, we now know where three more of these small nuclear devices reside. We have disabled all three. I apologize for my crew's actions, and for our earlier oversight.

'When we are so authorized,' she motioned first to Jesus, and then to the others in the circle, *'we will deactivate all thermonuclear devices on*

the planet.'

Standing and opening his arms wide, Jesus asked, 'Who would comment?' Several indicated they wished to address the group.

As they were speaking, Jesus moved about the circle to focus attention on each speaker. Ryan felt love and joy; he glimpsed for only an instant the incredible power he too possessed. It seemed to Ryan that Jesus was purposely allowing others to feel their own power in his presence. He was amazed at the fluidity with which this gathering was being carried on; it seemed to have a rhythm of its own.

Sarah's D'Ct-Elds mother stood. Her golden hair draped her shoulders. She communicated, *'We are indeed honored to be present at this great moment of planetary transition.'* She paused to take a graceful step forward, then continued, *'My ancestors from the Pleiades were among the first to seed this planet with their progeny. They nurtured the embryonic earthlings until the ancestors of those who continue to menace this planet prevented them from doing so. The peoples of this planet are truly my brothers and sisters.*

'To further this ascension process, we would address two issues. First, the cabal of Earth-beings and N'Roids are threatening our ships and others of the assembled armada with scalar weapons. These same weapons may be used against Earth-humans. There are such devices in place in this planet's orbit and on its surface. What can be done about this situation? I now yield the floor. I will come back to my second point.' She returned to her seat.

A being, this one quite short and with a decided yellow cast, asked to be recognized. *'Along with the civilization of our allies from the Pleiades,'* he motioned to the previous speaker, *'we too brought life here. By our inattention, we have allowed the current situation to develop. My fellow citizens, we must not stoop to the level of those addicted to the dark energies. We too know that the off-planet puppet-master has withdrawn, leaving that which it had constructed to crumble. In the desperation of their last moments, its former puppets seek to have their way or destroy all life. Although we must find ways to stop this insanity, we say no to conflict. We believe that we have an opportunity to reach out to these former puppets, to help them overcome their fears, to offer them a hand along the path to enlightenment.'*

A being less materialized than others requested recognition; he then arose. His radiance had a distinctive red aura. In an ethereal voice he communicated, *'We too believe that it would be most desirable to help the dark souls reconnect with the Creator's light. However, we are not wise enough to know if that is possible during the interim time. The souls of the billions of Earth-humans who are enveloped by the darkest of third density are what I wish to address.*

'For them life on this planet is all they know, so many are unknowingly content, despite their hardships and lack of joy. A few enterprising ones, and those who possess an extraordinary desire to dominate, have found ways to make the consensual paradigm work to their self-centered benefit. However, this is not the situation of the vast majority. Most have been so disabled that they are unable to see clearly, or make reasoned decisions. What can be done to assist them?'

Others around the room gave their opinions of how the current situation should be dealt with, and how they could proceed without dropping their energies to the dark levels. They also addressed how elitist humans and N'Roids were living so well at the expense of other Earth-human brothers and sisters, and what could be done about the diminished light in their souls.

Twelve of the twenty Earth-humans who were present on board addressed the situation from their perspective. A woman, who said she was from France, talked about gathering a million people to focus benevolent energy to counter the N'Roids. A man in the robes of the Middle East talked about domination by corporations and the continuing Christian crusade against his part of the world at the insistence of the U.S. A woman in the traditional garb of a Tutu pointed out that wealthy nations were standing by while genocide was committed in her country. An asian woman, dressed in a business suit, talked about the plight of women in Japan. All agreed that the elitists and *N'Roids* were at the center of their problems. Each speaker also recognized that the only way for humans to assert themselves was by using their collective energy.

TWENTY-FIVE

Jasper, the elf-like being asked to be recognized. *'I address my remarks principally to the Earth-humans among us,'* he communicated. *'Please understand that the warming of the planet is the result of energy supplied, at Earth's request, by the armada of those gathered here today. It is required for her movement into lighter density.*

'Nor has the intentional polluting of Earth's atmosphere been the cause of this warming. The gases and particles from aerosols are intended to diminish certain beneficial energies directed to Earth-humans from the armada, as well as provide a vehicle for transmitting fear-based energies. When the ships of our star nations brothers and sisters are able to materialize and remain in the atmosphere, it will be cleansed of all this.'

Sarah's D'Ct-Elds mother was recognized again. She stood and communicated, *'I would like to address my second point. In this, the final hour before the Earth transition, the cabal plans a last desperate effort. Let me explain my understanding of their plot.*

'As we are all well aware, using the media and movies, they have painted certain Earth-humans as evil, as people to be feared and killed. This perception of terrorism and terrorists has served them well. Media around the globe have concocted the story that the recent nuclear explosion was connected with terrorist activities.

'The N'Roids' have a plan to stage a worldwide coordinated attack that will be attributed to terrorists. The public will be bombarded with exaggerated reports of casualties and property damage from around the planet -- much as they did with exaggerations at the time of the recent tsunami. The instinctive responses of governments has been to restrict personal freedoms with even more repressive tactics.'

Several beings excitedly sought to be acknowledged. Jesus pointed

174

to the dark complexioned being.

'*If this is a coordinated effort, how do they plan to achieve it?*' She asked.

Sarah's D'Ct-Elds mother replied, '*They have hundreds of thousands of their own kind willing to undertake sabotage. In addition, they have enlisted many Earth-humans in their scheme by promising wealth and safe places in which they can hide.*'

'*What exactly do they hope to gain?*'

Sarah's D'Ct-Elds mother closed her eyes and stood for a moment. Everyone waited for her words. Then she communicated, '*I am sorry to have brought this news to you. We became aware of the particulars because of Sarah's monitoring of the situation. By implementing this scheme, they hope to regain control of the planet, and thereby discourage us enough that we will withdraw our starships.*' She returned to her seat.

Using telepathy, Ryan indicated that he wished to speak. When his turn came, he stood and asked, '*How do the rogues propose to accomplish this without everyone knowing what they are up to?*'

Sarah's D'Ct-Elds mother responded, '*They began the process in earnest with the attacks of September eleventh. They have recovered from a mistake on the part of one of their own by claiming the nuclear explosion in Utah was the act of terrorists. Keep in mind, they have been planning this for many years, have been softening people's beliefs with movies and books about terrorists, and have innumerable variations of the plan thought through and through. They are desperate, this is the last gasp of their dying effort; the final moves in this chess game will be the most intense. Many in whom the light is dim, believing they are better than their fellow man, are involved,*'

'*So what are we to do?*' Ryan asked.

'*We do not know enough as yet.*' She communicated from her seat across the space. '*We will advise you.*'

The discussion went on for some time without resolution on many of the issues. When it appeared that the group was preparing to adjourn, Ryan's training as a businessman emerged. He did not like leaving the meeting without some decisions.

'*How can we just adjourn?*' He communicated to Dr. Adamson.

The reply was not what he expected. '*Ryan, remember that others in this group have almost instant access to each other through telepathy and pictioning. You would do well to practice your skills. The only reason that this gathering was arranged was for the benefit of you and other Earth-humans.*'

When he recovered from this piece of information, Ryan communicated, '*How can the humans of Earth avoid seeing you as gods and turning* to worship you?"

'It is your job, Ryan, and the job of other aware Earth-humans to convince them we are their brothers and sisters, not gods,' Sarah's D'Ct-Elds mother said. 'Tell them of your experiences; remind them of the many like Sarah, Ethete, and Ajax who walk among them.

'The unique nature of Earth, after the transition, will be determined by her humans; only they are allowed to design their future. Those who assist from starships may not impose their ideas upon another world. We are not gods; we are merely your sisters and brothers from other star systems. At one time you knew us as such, but that memory has been purposely dimmed.'

Ryan slumped in his chair. This was getting to be too much.

Sarah squeezed his hand to get his attention, then communicated, 'You are a proxy for many American Earth-beings. Remember this gathering as we walk the next steps of our journey.'

Ryan looked around the space to see the smiling faces of many focus on him. They all understood what he was just now beginning to glimpse.

Jesus took the seat between Ryan and John deBeque. The visage of he whom Ryan had adored in his younger days was gentle and loving. 'Ryan, remember that the members of the cabal are God's children also. While He wishes that all could be balanced in the light, he loves dark souls just as much as he loves you and me. Some of them are souls who volunteered to come to this planet to play dark roles so that you and others could see their actions and choose the light.

'As Dr. Adamson has told you, you can gain access to the opinions and actions of those who are not of the third density through the skills that Sarah is teaching you. She will act as an intermediary between you and the others gathered here, until you are sufficiently adept, but you would do well to learn to communicate directly.'

Turning to the others in the circle, Jesus communicated, 'Please stand.' Without further words, those around the circle joined hands. 'My brothers and sisters, this is the glorious time of Earth's transition. Let us all continue to work together to assist this beautiful planet and her people. The end result is assured, now we can do much to smooth the way for all. I leave you now with my love.'

Turning to Ryan he communicated, 'I want you to remember something and share it with me. When you tell people that you were onboard an ET craft with people of other star civilizations and spirit beings from around the galaxy and that you were holding hands with Jesus, remember their reaction.' Then Jesus smiled broadly as if he already knew what the reactions were going to be.

Ryan wondered if this night were but a dream, maybe that would be an easier way to tell people about it than if he tried to convince them it was real. But he looked around at those assembled here and knew in the very depth of his being that it was not an illusion.

Then Jesus communicated, *'Ryan, when you come to see this life as but one that your cumulative oversoul is living in this physical density, it will free you to experience it to the fullest. As you go about your day, look around and feel empathy for those whose path is different than yours. You too have experienced lives that were immersed in the dark, and lives in which you were blinded to the larger reality. Fragments of your cumulative soul are incarnated on this planet today; such has been the case for millennia -- one was a contemporary of mine when I walked here. We who have tread on this planet are most grateful for all that you have done, both in this life and in your past lives. This is the last of your lives in this dense reality; be grateful for it and live it well.'*

He then released Ryan's hand, stood, and glided to the center of the space. There he dematerialized before the eyes of those gathered. Sarah wandered off to say farewell to her D'Ct-Elds mother.

Two A'Roids from Philadelphia, Banue Randall and Stefan Duncan, came over to Ryan and introduced themselves. They knew of Sarah and him through the publicity surrounding the rescue of President Boyle. They were also in more or less constant communication with others of their kind who occupied one of the large ships of the armada. They explained that they were in contact with an N'Roid in the U.S. Navy. They were quite upbeat about convincing her to move into the light. *'Please let us know if we can be of assistance to you,'* Stefan communicated.

Pia Mehan, who introduced herself as a visitor from Andromeda, approached Ryan. *'As one who can observe without being observed, I have been very close to you and your activities for many years. The event the N'Roids are planning is calculated to engender great fear; they hope it will throw the entire planet into darkness. Remember to remain open as you become more aware.'*

Sarah came up to Pia and placed her arm around the woman. *'This is one who is helping in many ways.'*

Sarah then moved to Ryan. When she embraced him, he felt himself descend as if in an elevator. She was still holding him tightly as he found himself standing in the desert of Monument Valley. John deBeque, Ethete, Dr Adamson, and Crita were with them.

Ryan glanced at John deBeque; the young man's eyes were filled with tears as he stared at the first light of dawn. Ryan walked over to embrace the younger man; it was all that kept him from crumbling to the ground.

Pink began filling the sky, from the horizon to the edge of wispy overhead clouds. But the clouds resisted, refusing to assume the new color, preferring their gray. Ryan could see the silhouette of distant mountains, far to the east. Pink intruded more intensely into the gray of the pre-dawn sky, which in turn pushed the darker gray to the west. A few of the brightest stars continued to shine. The light to the east intensified.

Trees were now visible in the expanse between Ryan and the giant monoliths. As he glanced to the north, pinkness touched Mitten Butte; its face was bathed in the dawn light, at its base a slope of shale and boulders had sloughed from its sides. The vastness of Monument Valley became apparent as he stared at the eastern horizon; the hugeness of its monolith hard for one's mind to capture, distances and sizes vast. As the light intensified, the sheer faces of the monoliths showed themselves complete with clefts and ridges. The stars had disappeared, but the overhead clouds were barely touched by the pending event.

The stage was set. Pink faded. It was as if a giant inhale were taking place.

Suddenly the sky became alive. The clouds took on incredible colors of pink plus gold. The brilliant orb thrust itself above the horizon, and dawn broke. Now pink and gold bathed the monoliths. The intensity increased until Ryan's vision was overwhelmed with this incredible display. It was as if this morning had been made for him alone.

After the sun was fully up, Dr. Adamson said to Ryan. "I have, quite recently, made contact with a young man who wishes to leave the service of the cabal. He sees that his military unit, which possesses scalar weapons, will be forced into service against mankind. For some reason, the mind control programs to which he was subjected failed to dull his sense of ethical behavior. He sees the potential damage to humanity and wants to avert it. I am visiting with him as frequently as possible.

"Crita," he motioned to his sister, "has established a similar relationship with a young female N'Roid in the military. She is talking to Stefan Duncan whom you met. If we can find more like these, we may be able to thwart the cabal's final grasp at power."

"Will you return to Harmony with us?' Ryan asked.

"Not at this time," Dr Adamson replied. "I still have a situation at Earth's Center with which I must deal."

As soon as they passed through the front gate of the Tribal Park, they found themselves in a whiteout. Drifting snow had almost obliterated the road. The clock on the dash read 7:44.

They drove at twenty miles per hour. John deBeque, in the front seat, helped Ryan spot the sides of the road. In forty-five minutes the lights of Kayenta became a beacon, and the snowstorm subsided. Only then did Ryan realize that they had passed through the checkpoint on the Utah-Arizona border without stopping.

"What did Jesus mean when he said that the rogues would be removed?" Ryan asked. "It seems like a huge undertaking."

"At this moment I do not know how that will happen," Sarah replied. "I feel that we are to concentrate on filling the void left by such an event."

TWENTY-SIX

Ryan slept into the middle of the afternoon. Ordinarily the almost total silence and the lack of light in Harmony's underground facility made for an almost perfect sleeping situation; however, this night Ryan was restless. His sleep was filled with questions. He had awakened more than once and jotted words on paper he kept by the bedside. Not wanting to disturb Sarah, who slept soundly, he had written in the dark.

So much had been presented during his time on board the starcraft that Ryan's mind was a jumble. Now, as he deciphered his nighttime scratching, he pensively wrote complete sentences on sheets from a yellow tablet. Ajax, who had been awake since early morning, sat reading in the corner of the great room.

Who were the dark entities who believed Earth belonged to them? Were they the Anunnaki that he had read about? Are N'Roids the same as dark entities? What did Jesus mean when he talked about the influence of the darkness lingering, while it was retreating?

He had read about scalar weapons, some sort of energy devices, but did not understand the technology. How could his fellow humans even consider using them against starcraft that were helping the planet? What did they not understand?

What would happen to those humans who had been so disabled by conditions on Earth that they were unable to see clearly, or make reasoned choices? How anyone could reverse the course of wealthy and powerful elitists was beyond him.

Then there were the questions that his trip to Boulder had raised: Just how bad was his own financial situation? Was the economy doing a repeat of the depression, or was this something else?

180

Sarah found him with yellow pages scattered about the long table in Harmony's great room. "I'm trying to organize my questions -- so we can talk about them," he said, as he rose to greet her with a hug and kiss.

"I'd like some food, then we can talk," she said. Since she had given Singing Bird and the rest of the staff the day off, Sarah headed for the kitchen.

Ryan trailed after her. "I could make some pasta," he volunteered. "I'm really quite a good cook."

By the time the pasta dish, a combination of shrimp and vegetables in a feta cheese sauce, was ready, Ethete and John had poked their heads into the kitchen.

Ryan brought it to the table in the dining room in a huge bowl. Ajax, looking better than at any time since his return to Harmony, found his way to the table.

"Were you this discombobulated the first time?" John asked Ryan.

"Oh, yeah. It'll take a while to get your feet back on the ground. And then, just when you believe it all might make sense, they take you for another ride. Welcome to life in the transition lane."

Sarah, Ethete, and Ajax were all smiling.

"So you think it's funny," Ryan said. "Switch places with us." He took a large bite of pasta sucking in a straggling noodle.

Sarah put her hand on his arm, "Ryan, you've come a long way, but there is more."

"I know," he said, "I know." He passed around his sheets of questions.

"The N'Roids are aggressive members of their race. They came to Earth eons ago," Sarah explained. She went on to make it clear that not all members of that race had allowed their souls to darken. The N'Roids, pursuing what they believed was a great opportunity for their race, had enslaved the primitive peoples they had found on this planet through a combination of genetic engineering, mind control, and energy management.

"Appearance-wise they're not too different from humans and have the ability to change so that they appear to be human, thus they're able to mingle with the general population." When Ethete and she together had viewed Carlton Boyle, they had seen an N'Roid practicing to impersonate him.

"There are many N'Roids on Earth at this time," Ethete said. "In the distant past, the N'Roids aligned themselves with a powerful celestial entity whose soul, except for one buried sliver, was completely dark. Together they set out to control this entire galaxy, using Earth as the focal point of their nefarious activities. N'Roids inhabit not only on Earth, but also other planets in this solar system. Seventy years ago, the light of Earth had almost been extinguished by the machinations of the N'Roids and fear broadcast by the humans they had enslaved. Only the appearance of the armada saved the situation."

Ryan felt the pasta in his stomach begin to churn as he heard these words. He could not prove it, but he was willing to bet that Ernest Steiger had been an N'Roid. He had done battle with one of them, and won. John deBeque, who sat across the table from him, had worked for an N'Roid. Ryan could tell by the expression on the younger man's face that this realization was beginning to dawn on him.

"How can you tell if someone's an N'Roid?" John deBeque asked.

"Not by looking at them," Sarah replied. "Look to their actions. They function from an amoral belief system."

"They think humans are theirs to use," Ajax added.

The conversation subsided as Ryan scratched notes on his tablet. The three Phantians watched as the two Earth-humans digested this new perspective.

"So, are we ready to talk about Jesus?" Ethete asked after Ryan stopped writing.

Ryan nodded and reached for his glass of water.

"Jesus incarnated on this planet, in much the same way that you did. He was born by the act of human parents, as were his brothers and sister.

"However, in the case of Jesus, his soul was of the highest realm, very close to that of the Creator. In your language, you would call it Christ Consciousness. He incarnated to teach the people of that time, and to imprint his energy here. Some of the stories contained in your Bible are true, others are distorted accounts of his life and teachings, and others are pure fabrications.

"What is true is that he set an example of and taught about the highest way to live -- that is what attracted people to him. He taught about a God of love, not an angry God. What is left out of the Bible is that he taught about star civilizations, that he married and had children, and that he traveled to Europe and to India.

"I am sure you recall our discussions about various levels of density. What is contained in the Bible is a third dimension, or third density, account of what the people of that time experienced. From a higher density perspective, Jesus was banished from the land of the Jews because of his teachings. Furthermore, the physical body of Jesus, in third density terms, did not experience the crucifixion; rather it was a holographic representation of him on the cross. So, if you witnessed events from a third density perspective, Jesus was crucified; from a fifth density perspective he was not.

"The story of the crucifixion later became the center piece of the New Testament, as it was assembled at a much later date. Those who wanted to twist the story of Jesus for purposes of controlling others dwelled on the horror and blood surrounding the crucifixion. The cross has become the symbol of Christianity, not the teachings of Jesus."

"How do you know all this?" Ryan asked.

'Because I told her.' The voice of Jesus in Ryan's head was unmistakable.

The others around the table looked at each other in amazement. They too had heard the unambiguous communication, even John de-Beque. Ryan closed his eyes to visualize the Jesus who had so recently held his hand.

After a few moments, Ryan asked, *'And what about me learning who I really am?'*

Jesus replied, *'Ryan, your cumulative soul has had many, many lifetimes; you were individuated from it for this one, individuated but not separated. In some lifetimes, an individuated fragment of your cumulative soul incarnated into a body that became powerful in some physical dimensions; in some it did not. In some, a fragment of your cumulative soul experienced the dark, in some only the light. Some incarnations have been on this planet, some on the planets of other star systems. In short, your cumulative soul is an incredibly experienced and powerful being. Since you are an individuation of that soul, not separate from it, your soul also is powerful and wise. In time, you will learn to tap into that power and wisdom.'*

Ryan got up from his seat and walked to a corner of Harmony's great room that was used as a meditation area. The others quietly busied themselves with refreshing their drinks and clearing the dishes.

When he returned in a half hour, he took a deep breath and said, "Before we move on, tell me about the holographic image."

Ethete smiled and said, "Thought we were trying to slip one past you, huh?"

"Too much." Ryan shook his head.

"Jesus knew that he was going to be crucified in this lower dimension. Rather than taking on the physical suffering he slipped back to the Star of Bethlehem and created a hologram of himself. It was the hologram that was crucified, not the real physical Jesus."

"And the soldiers and others didn't catch on?" Ryan asked. "Must have been a super hologram."

"It was."

"So how can I tell when something or someone is a hologram and when it's real?"

"A real person has a soul," Ethete said. "Look into their eyes."

"Is this how they do clones?"

"Sometimes. Remember everything is energy. A hologram is an energy projection."

"Is my body an energy projection?"

"Something like that combined with DNA, family history, and a mind plus what memories you have of this lifetime."

Ryan sat back in his chair. No one said anything for some time. At last he said, "Okay, onward."

Pointing to the next question on Ryan's sheets, Sarah said, "Some of the ships in the armada are many miles in diameter. Colonies of star civilizations live on them more or less permanently. They have more than enough power to impact the energies of a planet. A collection of them, such as those attending Earth, is able to benevolently transform an entire planet. Earth's gradual warming is a manifestation of that process. Keep in mind, as you wrestle with all of this, that Earth, and everything else connected to this physical reality, is a manifestation of energy.

"As to Earth's internal source, at the center of Earth, as with most other planets, lies a fiery hot energy source, similar to your sun, only much smaller. Beings, like Dr. Adamson, who live in 'the center' rely on it for light and heat."

John deBeque shook his head as if clearing out his old ways of seeing and believing.

Ryan looked at his written questions and asked, "So, if everything is energy, what does it mean that humans are to design Earth's future?"

Sarah answered again, "You have seen Phantia, as has John. Phantia has a unique ecology, a unique civilization, a unique way to govern, and a unique way in which its inhabitants relate to one another. At this time in its evolution, it is a sphere of light, but it was not always that way. It evolved from a place of less light to where it is today. Earth too has its unique features, albeit they have been clouded by the activities of the N'Roids. However, with time and proper attention, Earth's ecology will return to its original beauty, but at a lighter density. Earth's inhabitants can now decide how the civilization that will replace the one here, the one dominated by the N'Roids, will be reconstructed when Earth is at that lighter density.

"There will be human inhabitants, and there will be human institutions. What will they look like? This is a way to exercise the power you have. Think about it, what would a successor civilization look like?"

The conversation went on like this for another hour, until Ryan held up his hand. "Enough, I'm in overload."

Across the table, John deBeque mouthed, "Thank you."

"Can I ask about those little gold bars?" Ryan placed his hand on top of Sarah's.

"I was anticipating this," she smiled. She dug into her jeans and placed one of the glistening bars in the middle of the table.

John deBeque, who had not been part of their earlier conversation, reached for it. He examined it closely, weighing it in his hand, turning it over and over. "At today's prices, this could be worth a small fortune," he said, "I'm guessing fifteen to twenty thousand dollars."

"Pretty close," Sarah said, "we converted some of them at eighteen thousand about a month ago."

"So this is how you pay for this place?" John asked.

Sarah nodded once.

"Just exactly how does this work?" Ryan asked.

Sarah looked at Ethete and Ajax. They both nodded.

"Once a month, Johnny Black Raven takes a few of them to a dealer in Phoenix. Others, who are here from Phantia and other planets, take theirs to dealers in other cities. Because they are such pure gold, five nines is the way it is expressed, they command a premium and a market has grown up around them."

Ajax offered, "When Ethete and I were living in San Diego, we made a monthly exchange. The dealers have been very quiet about their sources for these little gold bars, despite repeated government inquiries. They make a nice profit trading them to collectors. There's a federal regulation that came in with Tyler; it requires that dealers report all sales and purchases of gold over twenty thousand dollars. Selling them one at a time will be a real pain."

"What are five nines?" John asked.

"Ninety nine point nine, nine, nine percent pure," Ajax responded.

"I need exercise," Ryan said standing. "Anyone want to go for a walk?"

TWENTY-SEVEN

A half hour later, Sarah and Ryan strolled up the gravel road toward Ben Tsotsie's dig. The two of them had stretched their legs in this way many times, yet it was still special. On either side, the cactus flowers and other desert blossoms presented a brilliant carpet of yellow, orange, and red.

"So where do the gold bars come from?" Ryan asked.

"I manifest them," Sarah replied shyly.

"You create gold?"

"Just energy manipulation."

"So I guess I could say you have the 'Midas touch,'" he joked.

"I can create only enough to support the activities of Harmony."

"This is too much," Ryan said, placing his arm around her. "Is there no end to this higher density stuff. Or your higher consciousness?"

"It keeps getting better the further you go."

They walked arm in arm for a quarter mile. Neither said anything.

"Despite your extraordinary abilities, and I assume you are not the only visitor that has them, I don't see the way through all of this for us mere humans," Ryan said. "If the N'Roids are in charge of everything, and they've been doing it for thousands of years, why isn't it going to be a repeat of the same old same old. Jesus said they had the planet under their control when he was here."

"Never before have the ships of the armada settled around a planet in such numbers," Sarah replied. "Never before, in Earth's history, have so many visitors like myself been here to help. Never before have so many Earth-humans seen the truth, and been ready to do something about it."

"And exactly what is that truth?"

"That this planet, like all material creation, is energy. It is energy that has been slowed into a material reality, a stage upon which a grand drama is being played. We are here to assist."

"I hear the words, but I don't understand," he said.

They heard the beating of the rotor before they saw it. The dark shape of the helicopter became more distinct as it flew north in the valley between them and Black Mesa. Suddenly, it made a right turn toward them.

"Run," Ryan grabbed her hand, but she shook him off. The helicopter was still a quarter mile away, but he knew what they wanted: Sarah.

She quietly stood in the middle of the road with her eyes closed.

Despite the deafening sound of the helicopter, Ryan shouted again, "Sarah, get down."

She did not respond.

Just as the helicopter prepared to land on the road, it vanished. In the next instant, the desert returned to its tranquility.

"What was that?"

Sarah turned to where he stood and smiled. "While you were in Boulder, I was busy making some new friends. The helicopter and its occupants are now in their custody. It will be returned to this dimension a few miles away with no memory, human or electronic, of what just happened."

"You are amazing."

"So are you, you just don't know it yet. You just witnessed different dimensions, or densities, interacting with each other. You have experienced moving between one and the other. The next step is to be in more than one simultaneously."

They walked together, hand in hand, for an hour, discussing all that Ryan had learned in the past few weeks. They returned to Harmony's facility as it became dark.

After a late evening meal, the five once again gathered around Harmony's long table. Ryan asked, "I understand that Earth is a conscious being, but how can something that huge be impacted by the actions of puny people on her surface?"

Sarah responded, "Mining activities, oil wells, and pollution of Earth's land, water, and air all affect her. In addition, she is sensitive to the energy of her inhabitants and how they treat each other. Fleas trouble an animal. Bacteria make a human sick. However those are all third dimensional perceptions. Viewed from a higher perspective, it is all about energy; all is interconnected.

"Look at what was happening during the early nineteen forties: There was war. There were death camps. The majority of the people of the planet were operating from intense fear.

"The beneficial energies from the armada are like an antibiotic for a sick patient. The energies of light are driving out the dark energies, supplying vital nutrients. This has two additional effects for humans, both beneficial: The light is showing the lies for what they are; the truth about everything is emerging. The light, or love, is illuminating the souls of all, both those in which it already shines brightly and those in which it is dim.

"Enlightened soul fragments see death as a transition; because they are unafraid, they are willing to sacrifice themselves to make change happen. Enlightened souls see that their energy alone impacts everything around them; they know that collectively their energies could transform the consensual paradigm."

"I have to tell you," John deBeque shook his head, "I'm not getting all of this."

"You will, John, you really will," Ethete said. She grabbed him around the shoulders and hugged tightly. "Even if I have to transfer it directly."

"I've got so many questions," Ryan said glancing at his hand written pages. "One more, then we'd better call it quits for now. Tell me what you can about the crumbling of human institutions."

"This could take a while," Ajax said.

"You're sure you want to go there this evening?" Ethete asked.

"Sure," Ryan said.

"As we understand it," Ajax said, "all the institutions created by humans and corrupted by N'Roids are going away. That is what happened on Phantia, although we didn't have any N'Roids involved. Our monetary system, also with fiat currencies, crumbled because it had replaced real money and served the wealthy and powerful. The monetary system here on Earth is in much worse shape. You have already seen the dollar lose most of its value. On Phantia, when we installed our new form of government, it took the monetary system away from the bankers. Interesting parallels aren't they. Wonder why they selected us to come to Earth?" Ajax grinned at both Ryan and John deBeque.

"So what comes next for Earth?" Ajax continued. "As I see it, and this is just me talking, I see a return to precious metals as the basis for the monetary system. That means that any paper money has to be exchangeable into gold or silver. I've done a little scratching and figured out that gold would be worth about thirty-six thousand U.S. dollars per ounce. Silver would sell for about six hundred dollars an ounce." Seeing the shocked look on deBeque's face Ajax added, "Makes each of those little yellow bars worth a lot of dollars, right? Or, is it that we're just figuring out how little an American dollar is really worth?"

"So how do we get from where we are right now to a new monetary system?" Ryan thought to himself. But he was too tired to voice the question out loud.

Sam Wellborn met Glenn Koslowski at Reagan National Airport. Glenn had come back from New York to spend the weekend with his family and was taking a mid-morning flight back to New York. The two men found coffee and headed toward seats in a vacant waiting area not far from Glenn's departure gate.

Sam had used his top-level government ID to talk his way through airport security. High security conditions favored government employees with the proper credentials; without them, individuals found it increasingly difficult to cross state lines or travel by commercial airlines. Most business executives employed private jets, which were exempt from restrictions at commercial airports. Many sales calls were conducted using the internet or by telephone. Repair and delivery people were given advanced clearances, as were truck drivers, but cargos were searched repeatedly. Vacation travel had come to a standstill except for the wealthy who could buy their way anywhere.

"I talked with Tony a few days ago," Sam said as he pulled the chair from the small table.

"He told me."

"Did he tell you what we discussed?"

"I find it hard to believe."

"Me too."

"I thought you were close to President Boyle," Glenn said. He took a sip of his coffee and sat back in his chair.

"I thought I was too, but he's changed a lot." Sam changed his tack. "What can you tell me about your investigation in New York?"

Glenn eyed Sam before responding. "I'm sure you understand that there are insufficient funds for banks to pay out. I'm also sure you have read about big banks doing some 'unusual things' to keep depositors from withdrawing their funds."

Sam nodded.

"I'm part of a task force to monitor all this. No, I'm not happy about being pulled off the Presidential detail, but what I'm doing is very important."

"How bad is it?"

"It's bad. With inflation running at twenty-five percent, those who can afford to have already paid off their loans, but that was a small proportion of the loans outstanding. Now banks and other credit issuers are stuck with loans in default, and it's getting worse every day."

"What about credit card debt?"

"Exploding," Glenn responded. "All those credit cards that banks pushed at people. People have used them to pay off their mortgages."

The lights in the airport flickered then dimmed. "Not again," Glenn said, "up in New York, I go through this at least once a day. They tell me that utilities are rationing electricity with rolling brownouts -- all due to the high cost of fuel."

"We haven't seen many of these around here."

The two men fell silent as people, knocking chairs over, running into each other, scurried about in the dim flickering lights. After a few minutes the airport's emergency lighting kicked in and things returned to normal.

"So what are you working on?" Sam asked.

"Counterfeit American Eagles."

"Counterfeit gold coins? You mean making them out of something other than gold?"

"No, they're gold all right. Actually they're better gold than in American Eagles, but the U.S. mint isn't making them."

"Why would anyone go to all that trouble? Why not sell the gold in big chunks, or whatever it was before they made it into coins?"

"Whoever is doing this is trying to hide the source of the gold," Glenn said. "We track the output of every mine in the U.S. Every shipment of gold, in whatever form, that comes in from outside the country is recorded. This gold, coming from an unknown source, is screwing up the system."

"Any idea about the source?"

"We've discovered five ounce bars of extremely pure gold that someone is supplying to coin dealers in a dozen cities. I'm headed to Phoenix next week."

They talked for a while longer then Glenn said, "Look Tony told me what you're trying to do, all right. I'm not sure whether I believe it or not, but that's not the point. I have a family, I have a career with the Secret Service, and I just got a promotion. I believe this country is in pretty bad shape, but I'm not going to jeopardize what I've worked for. It doesn't matter what you and Tony have found out. Thanks, but no thanks."

"If you change your mind, let me know." Sam handed Glenn a card with Tiffany's phone number on it.

On his way out of the airport, Sam used a pay phone to check in with Tiffany at her office.

"Ryan Drake finally responded to my hundredth post. He's at his computer and waiting for you to set a time to talk."

"I'll come to the office. Tell him to get to a pay phone as soon as possible."

Ryan's call came in an hour later as Sam paced around Tiffany's small office. "You're a hard man to track down," Sam said.

"We've got to talk," Ryan said from a pay phone in Kayenta, "and not just over this phone. Everything's been confirmed by our allies, and a whole lot more we've never discussed. With all the new regulations, I can't travel -- barely made it back from Colorado."

"I get your drift," Sam said. "I'll see what I can do to come your way. Where's the nearest major airport?"

"Phoenix."

"I'll get a government pass and fly out there. Then what?"

"I'll meet you there. Let me know when you'll be arriving."

TWENTY-EIGHT

At the urging of Henry Bustamonte, Carlton Boyle made arrangements to visit Douglas Windfree's home in the mountains west of Denver. The five thousand acre estate had been acquired from an old Colorado family when the youngest daughter decided she could no longer live on it. The 9,000 foot elevation of the main house, a southern colonial mansion transported from Georgia, was not compatible with her failing health.

At 10:07 AM, Air Force One landed at Buckley Air Force Base near Denver. As he walked to the waiting electric cart, the President paused to make brief comments about looking forward to a rest in the mountains of Colorado; he then fumbled to make a joke about the location being far enough away from the nearest ocean. Amid questions about the reason for this vacation, he was whisked to a waiting limousine. Reporters were barred from accompanying him.

Grant Clever and Henry Bustamonte climbed into the limousine behind the President's. Everyone waited until aids and Secret Service personnel were seated, then the parade of vehicles pulled out amid the sirens and flashing lights of its motorcycle escort. A black Chevrolet Silverado preceded each limo; each had Secret Service agents in addition to the driver.

Clever and Bustamonte glanced at each other, nodded, but said nothing. Clever closed his eyes, retreating into one of his legendary power naps. Bustamonte pulled out his laptop and connected to World League Headquarters, via a secure satellite link. He typed three words: PACKAGE ON WAY.

The motorcycles moved traffic to one side on Interstate 70. Lights flashed on the vehicles, but there were no sirens. The limited access highway from east of Denver into the mountains to the west was not crowded, but traffic was sidelined as the column of black vehicles sped by.

HIDDEN VALLEY CENTRAL CITY EXIT 243. A smaller sign read: IDAHO SPRINGS CITY LIMITS. The vehicles turned off the Interstate and headed north on the Central City Parkway. The divided highway climbed more steeply than was common for most Colorado roads. It had been built ostensibly to give gamblers easier access to the casinos in the mountain towns west of Denver. Local residents, noticing how swiftly the highway had been constructed, had attributed it to money provided by the gaming industry.

In a few miles, the limousines and security vehicles pulled through the entrance to Windfree's estate. Secret Service agents closed the wrought iron gate after the motorcade had passed through. A mile up the newly paved road, the caravan pulled into the circular driveway in front of the main house.

Douglas Windfree greeted Carlton Boyle. "Welcome, Mr. President. Let me show you around."

They meandered through the house while luggage was placed in the President's room. "You look tired Mr. President," Windfree said. "Would you care to take a nap?"

"Now that you mention it, I do feel sleepy." The President yawned. "A nap would do me good. After all, I am on vacation."

"It's probably the altitude," Windfree said. "Be sure to drink lots of water. You'll find a pitcher beside your bed."

On the floor above the President's suite, Henry Bustamonte was unpacking his things when he heard a knock on the door. The girl was dark haired and slim, just the way he liked them. He guessed she was from somewhere in Eastern Europe.

As soon as he shut the door, the girl knelt before him and attacked the belt on his trousers. He could feel himself getting hard as she unzipped his fly. With his ample belly, he could not see her.

After a few seconds of delicious pleasure, he grabbed her by her hair and pulled her to her toes. She was young, and quite beautiful for a human, but drugs and electroshock clouded her eyes.

Her overly large breasts on such a diminutive frame looked almost painful. Good, the growth hormones for dairy cattle were continuing to work their way into the human sheep. Bustamonte felt a supple breast with one hand. Maybe this one really was a virgin. Inches from her face, he slipped off his façade to reveal his true identity. She gasped and struggled to get away. Keeping one hand entangled in her hair, he pushed her back to her knees. Without his façade, his stature as a muscular young adult shown forth. He studied the top of her rocking head with delight.

After he was sufficiently aroused, he used one finger to slice through the front of her clothes. To satisfy himself that she was indeed a virgin he mounted her. After he had impregnated her, he pushed her away and pointed to the door. "Tell no one."

The terrified girl ran for it, leaving her tattered clothes on the floor. He could tell from the look in her eyes that his secret was safe. It did not really matter, where she was going there were others like her who also kept secrets.

After a quick shower, he changed into a blue sports coat, khaki slacks, and loafers. Glancing at his reflection, he smoothed his right bushy eyebrow. Then he grabbed his laptop and walked down the hall to a set of double doors marked PRIVATE. Closing the doors behind him, he crossed the room to an elevator and pushed one of the buttons.

As the elevator dropped, Bustamonte relaxed. As he did so, the laboriously constructed façade he wore in all public places once again dropped from his body. It felt good to be himself again, at least for a few days.

When the elevator stopped, two hundred feet below, he offered his ID to the red-uniformed guard. He then made his way to his World League office.

They had waited until the sensors in the room indicated that Carlton Boyle was asleep. The sedative in the water was the same fast acting compound that the CIA used.

A team of men dressed in light blue scrubs rolled him onto a stretcher and wheeled him down the hall to double doors marked PRI-VATE. Beyond a second set of locked doors was an elevator designed to accept the stretcher.

When that door opened, there was a similar stretcher, upon which another male lay. After the teams exchanged stretchers, the blue scrubs wheeled the second sleeping body back down the hall. They placed the sleeping form in the bed.

Forty-five minutes later, Carlton Boyle awakened from his nap feeling rested and relaxed. He showered and put on fresh clothes that had been laid out for him. The room seemed oddly familiar, as if he had slept and showered there before, but he knew that was not the case; he had arrived by limousine only two hours earlier.

He found Douglas Windfree in a garden room filled with tropical plants. Over a whiskey on ice, he told Windfree how he and two Secret Service agents had stumbled into a cave near his ranch in Oregon, and how a rockslide from the tsunami had fortuitously closed the entrance. There, cold and thirsty, they had waited out the tsunami. Rescue workers had found them on the third day. Carlton Boyle likened it to the resurrection of Jesus.

The following morning, the Executive Committee of the Board of Directors of the World League gathered in a conference room on the same floor as Henry Bustamonte's office. The room was quite similar to another room in which prior meetings of the League had taken place, only much larger. That other room had been on the lower level of the Pentagon. Actions from the first Gulf War to the invasions of Afghanistan and Iraq had been coordinated from that room. From this room, deep within the new headquarters of the World League, they were planning much more.

Lapping up a small dose of white powder from his goblet, Warren Ophir watched as Bustamonte strutted to his seat at the diamond-shaped conference table. The eighty-four-foot table, made from four massive slabs of granite, was set with its two extremities pointing to either end of the rectangular room. White-haired Grant Clever, looking much like a king, sat in an elevated chair where the two center slabs of the table came together. On the opposite side of the table, the other five members of the Executive Committee sat facing the Chairman.

Jonathan Olson and Justin Ridgway were in quiet conversation to Ophir's right. Jeremiah Goldman sat beyond them, eyes closed. Since the Executive Committee also functioned as the administrative arm of the World League, Clever was, in effect, the autocrat who controlled the United States. He made no secret of his desire to be the first to control the entire planet.

Seeing that the World League's Executive Committee was finally seated, Clever said, "Before we invite the others to join us, I would like to hear what recent word any of you might have received from off-planet."

"His Eminence's ability to influence events on this planet continues to diminish," Goldman said. His eyes returned Clever's aristocratic gaze. "Light from the armada is too powerful. Our brothers on other planets have been neutralized. We are isolated."

"More from the star civilizations have incarnated here than anyone thought possible," Bustamonte said. "Visitors like Sarah Smith, along with the light from the armada, are awakening the sheep."

"I know about this nonsense," Clever said. "Anyone want to add something?" The chairman lapped a small amount of white powder from the large goblet that he held in his left fist.

"This also is probably not new," Warren Ophir said, "but I continue to receive messages from the armada demanding that I depart from this planet."

"You are correct; it is not new," Clever said dismissively. "As usual, we have no intention of responding."

Silence enveloped the six. Each man closed his eyes.

At last Justin Ridgway spoke, "I just received a message that we have lost our nuclear ability."

"What?" Clever exclaimed.

"I was told that all of our nuclear weapons have been rendered inactive. I'm going to check." Ridgway picked up his specially designed cell phone and dialed. He spoke for a few moments then hung up. "They'll get back to me."

"Anything else?" Clever asked.

"One of our overseas associates has failed to keep her human charge focused," Goldman said "I will deal with her when they join us."

"Anything else?" Clever asked.

No one responded.

Clever examined the face of those seated across the table from him. Ophir sensed that Clever knew they were holding back, but it had always been that way. No one completely trusted the others.

By mutual agreement the members of the World League addressed each other with the names they had adopted for the particular roles they had assumed. If desired, each could "disappear" and reemerge in a different role; for each of those seated here, this had already occurred during several human life spans. However, the members of the Executive Committee had become quite comfortable in their current assignments. It was unlikely that any of them would easily relinquish their hard-won portrayals.

At last Clever said, "Let's get the other Board members." He pushed a button under the edge of the table.

A door to the right of Ophir swung open. Eleven males in dark business suits filed in and found seats on the same side of the table as the Executive Committee. A pyramid, with a name on each of its three sides, marked each place. At each place was a pitcher of ice water, a glass, and an electronic writing tablet. At most of the places there was a goblet filled with white powder; one did not have a goblet. At each place was a microphone that led to recording equipment.

When they were seated, Grant Clever said, "Before our associates from the Planetary Council join us, I want each of you to give us the latest on your area; highlight anything that is new. Byron, you go first."

Byron Greylock, the overseer of the news affiliates leaned toward his microphone. A middle-aged human, he wore his blonde hair long and wavy; a former producer with a major television network, he had been working with the media affiliates for ten years before being selected for his current job. Testing had revealed that he would take orders from non-humans and that he would keep his mouth shut about all that transpired with the news affiliates. This had been assured with mind control techniques and with threats against his children.

Because of the voids left by the departure of Ernest Steiger and the defection of John deBeque, the media affiliates had been split into news and entertainment. Along with mind control, they fell under Jeremiah Goldman's oversight. The head of the entertainment affiliates was not present. Being merely human, neither he nor Greylock were qualified to be members of the Board of Directors.

This reorganization had been a sore point with Ophir, since it was he who had stepped in to oversee John deBeque when Ernest Steiger had met his untimely death. In a classic move, Clever had reorganized the leadership of the World League by stripping Ophir of involvement with the media affiliates, placing him in charge of facilities and support functions, while simultaneously promoting him to become a member of the Executive Committee. Over everyone else's objections, Clever had not stripped Ophir of the intelligence affiliates which Ophir had originally organized, and which he now, with Clever's concurrence, was in the process of reinvigorating.

Greylock said, "First of all, thank you for opening this new facility to me. It will simplify my work greatly to have an office here, where I can interact with the rest of you. And those underground trains, wow!

"Now for my report, as you are aware, after John deBeque's release of information on our operations, several of our previously loyal editors and news directors stated that they would no longer cooperate. We have since persuaded several of them to rejoin us; others have been moved to one side, and replaced with humans who are in concert with our agenda. However, we are losing ground due to alternative news sites on the internet. I am hopeful that modifications to search engines will effectively restrict access to these sites; I think this will be particularly important in the days ahead.

"At first our initiative on terrorists was quite hard to sell. We have, after all, played that scenario for many years. However, after the explosion in Utah, and comments about battles with terrorists, we have hit a home run. We will continue to emphasize that all dark strangers are evil; tomorrow we begin the campaign intimating that an attack is expected soon.

"All in all, I would say that we are as well positioned as could be expected, and will be a major contributor in the coming days of crisis."

Ophir noted the man's nervousness and thought back to how he had handled John deBeque. After this meeting was over, he would make it a point to talk with Goldman about management of humans. He reflexively felt for the gun he used to wear in his shoulder holster. There were times he regretted that no firearms were allowed in this facility, except those worn by men in red uniforms, a dictate he himself had instituted.

Greylock was preparing to say more when Clever preempted him. "You will not make equivocal comments to our associates from outside the United States. You are a guest at this meeting because some of the European and Asian associates want to know how we are going to manage news in the days ahead. Answer questions only when asked. Emphasize how effective your program will be, not its problems. Is that understood?" Clever raised the goblet to his mouth; his tongue lapped up a trace of the white powder.

"Yes, sir," Greylock said, cringing before Clever's unblinking gaze. Ophir wondered how he would react when he learned that this facility was his new home, his only home.

TWENTY-NINE

"Dr. Goldman, where does the index stand today?" Clever asked from his kingly perch. After berating Greylock, he had directed those assembled back to the agenda of the World League Board meeting.

Jeremiah Goldman, still smarting from Clever's reprimand of Greylock's presentation, replied, "The index stands at seventy three worldwide. It ranges from fifty-seven in this country, to forty-nine in Europe, to ninety-three in sub-Saharan Africa."

"If asked, you will say that our programs are all having their desired effect. Try not to be more specific about the numbers."

"But this is lowest for the last seventeen hundred years."

"You will say that our programs are having their desired effect. Do you understand?"

"I am not so sure this is the right approach. Our associates from the Planetary Council need to understand that some of our programs like HAARP are no longer working as predicted and that..."

Interrupting him, Clever said, "Did you not understand what I just said?"

Goldman narrowed his eyes to meet Clever's stare. "All right, I will go along with you -- for now. In any case the Admiral's proposed plan should push the index higher -- if it is successful."

Like other members of the Executive Committee, Goldman had not cowered before the alpha male's display of authority. It was not that long ago that Clever had been on their side of the table, and Delta Kingman was the leader. Ophir saw Clever's desperate battle to remain on top, and decided to support it for the moment. In time the truce that Clever and he had reached regarding the intelligence affiliates had the potential to thrust him into the top dog role.

Relaxing into an altered state, Ophir sensed the concern of others around the table. The energy supplied by darkened souls provided a livable environment for him and his race. If the numbers dropped too low, they would be forced to retreat to a less lightened area of the planet. Before his time, they had contained the enlightened civilization of Atlantis on its continent; eventually they had corrupted the Atlantians and set them against Numeria, all of which had allowed his race to regain its dominance worldwide. Now the energies coming from the armada were re-lighting the planet's human race. He calculated that their days were numbered unless they could dramatically increase fear in their human subjects, particularly in the developed countries.

Justin Ridgway's cell phone rang. "Yes." The admiral listened, his face darkening as he received the news. He slowly closed the connection. "The information I received earlier has been confirmed: We are without a nuclear capability. They are checking the situation in other countries."

The newly arrived members of the Board asked for clarification. Ridgway gave them the full picture.

"So, the armada has struck another blow," Clever said. "We will show no mercy to those who seek to protect the sheep with this illegal action."

Clever turned to the impeccably groomed and well-dressed male seated next to Olson. "Vincent, you are next."

Vincent House oversaw the corporate affiliates, a group of five thousand carefully positioned males in major American corporations. Homes leaned toward his microphone and said, "Our network of interlocking directorships has proven itself time and time again. Through it we are assured that only those in tune with the new world order are allowed to rise to the top. In the past year, we have purged six undesirables by fabricating illicit or illegal activities. Although the public is demanding changes in the make-up of Boards, so far we have blunted their attacks by introducing new faces from our race.

"Turning to the next item, we have continuing resistance in Europe to our programs of genetic engineering of crops and growth hormones for livestock, however in this country they have been more successful than we had originally envisioned. Now with the price of food inflating nicely, genetically altered products enjoy a significant price advantage, thanks to government subsidies. Despite the almost daily emergence of new organic food companies, our corporations are acquiring any that reach significant sales revenues. All of this will be exaggerated as we move into the days of crisis.

"Thanks to your fine work," House nodded to Clever, "I am most pleased with our ability to garner government backing for our programs, including military intervention. Our campaign to secure reserves of petroleum has stretched the military a bit, but I am pleased to report that we now have one hundred percent of our imports under control of one of our corporations, with our military on the scene ready to enforce these arrangements."

"What happened in Nigeria?" Warren Ophir asked.

House hesitated for only a second, then responded, "As you are all aware, the Nigerians constructed their own refinery rather than sell crude oil to our companies under prior agreements. For some reason, the locals became upset that ninety percent of their country's refined petroleum products were being shipped overseas, leaving them little." He chuckled, then continued, "They actually had to import oil from Angola. Despite Nigerian government security, terrorists infiltrated the installation. The rest you can read about in the newspapers. Any other questions?"

"What about set-backs in South America?" Jonathan Olson asked.

"Seems that not everyone wants water privatized. We plan to have another go after we rid ourselves of certain indigenous leaders. Anything else?" House paused to check the face of each Board member.

"In summary I'd like to say that the civilization we have created is very much intact. Our plan to addict the sheep to cheap petroleum worked as planned. Now, they do whatever is necessary to pay for high-priced gasoline and corporations rule every aspect of their lives."

"Thank you, Vincent," Clever said icily. "Please keep in mind that some of those who are joining us today are new to the tactics of American corporations."

Ignoring what the Chairman of the Board had just stated, Vincent House said, "If I may wax philosophical for a moment, Grant, I continue to be amazed at how well corporations work, how many humans we have who will dedicate their lives to their jobs, how many entrepreneurs are willing to sell out their companies for money, and how people will shop at major retailers just to get a better price. It's a marvelous system we've created. I cannot conceive of what might replace it."

It had become obvious to the others that Clever felt threatened by the power that Vincent Homes wielded as head of the corporate affiliates. He was the only member of the Board of the World League who attended public gatherings like the World Economic Forum. The other members of the World League wielded their power from the shadows.

Clever said, "Michael, you're next."

Michael Reedy was the overseer of the religious affiliates. In addition to being the oldest member of the Board of the World League and a long-time member of the Planetary Council, he was a high-ranking American within the inner circle of the Vatican. His human visage of an overweight man with a bald head and ring of dark hair reminded Ophir of a monk; his real visage, which he displayed at this meeting, was that of a sleek young male of Ophir's race. Reedy was seven hundred years old. Ophir, who knew religion to be as two-faced and secretive as the covert arena, planned to integrate more religious fanatics into his revitalized intelligence affiliates. He and Reedy had discussed this yesterday, but had not reached an agreement.

"Vincent, you may think you rule the sheep through their stomach's and pocketbooks, but we have ruled them through their beliefs for thousands of years," the cleric said in a sardonic voice. "Now for my report, little has changed since my report of one year ago. While our victim blueprint continues to work in most segments of the population, as it has over the centuries, the advance of the light is causing problems. The old stories are simply not holding peoples' attention. Without them, there is no guilt and inferiority, and without guilt and inferiority there are no victims. As I have stated before, a sizeable percentage of the sheep appear to be outgrowing their dependence on us.

"At the same time, Christianity is so well ingrained in Western economies that I doubt they could exist without its trappings. Military expeditions to 'free the citizens' of obstreperous countries so that they might become 'democratic' reminds me of similar words and practices by those who conquered in the name of Christendom." He paused to turn his large head toward Olson and Homes.

"The evangelical movement has substituted for traditional churches, but, with the failing economy, contributions are falling even faster than attendance. I find myself repeatedly imploring my good friend Henry Bustamonte to increase contributions from the U.S. treasury.

"I might add that we have stepped up our funding to religions spawned by the New Age, but they are so diverse and too many that we have yet to find a viable lever over them. The sheep who have rediscovered their connection to God are the most worrisome. Once they have achieved this, their light enlarges until they are no longer a source of sustenance for us.

"At this juncture, I would like to thank my colleagues," he motioned to others who had entered the room with him, "whose work in their specific areas has been so supportive of my efforts: The history affiliates who reinforce traditional perspectives of the Jewish, Christian, and Muslim religions. The scientific affiliates who are so valuable in keeping humans ignorant of truths about energy and the connectedness of all. The truth, you know, would so interfere with our dogma. The medical affiliates whose focus on the physical causes of disease assists our teachings about man's damaged soul. The psychological affiliates who label anything to do with the paranormal as a sickness. And last but not least, those of you who assist our efforts by supplying drugs, movies, video games, chemicals, and other mind control aids."

"As usual, Michael, you underestimate your importance," Clever said. "We have relied on your organization for eons."

"I would like to know why you have not influenced the political process more successfully," Warren Ophir asked.

Michael Reedy looked with distain at Ophir before he responded, "Warren, you seem to think that we have our hand on the lever of the political process. We do not. Despite harangues from the pulpit, people vote however they wish. In Carlton Boyle they got what they voted for. Personally I hope he reincarnates as my slave."

Ophir did not respond. Obviously, Reedy did not know that the Carlton Boyle he loathed so much was two floors below the very conference room in which he sat. Knowledge of the specifics surrounding Boyle would remain with the Executive Committee, particularly Henry Bustamonte, whose task it was to manage the President of the United States.

"Everett, do you have anything to add?" Clever asked a male in a black suit, black silk shirt, and white tie.

Everett Cox was highly placed in one the churches that had sprung up in the United States. In deference to Michael Reedy's long standing as a Board member and representative of major religions, he attended meetings of the World League as an alternate, not as a member of the Board.

"Our esteemed colleague from Rome has stated our case quite eloquently. I would add only that my team working behind the scenes in Hollywood and television studios has functioned superbly these last few years." Everyone around the table nodded in agreement. "In the days ahead, many will call on religion to make sense of terrorist invaders. You can be sure through dogma and obtuse references to ancient writings that we will provide the required doses of confusion."

THIRTY

After a brief break in the proceedings of the World League's Board meeting, the overseers of the history and education, science and technology, medical, and psychological affiliates spoke briefly. Each had been a member of the Board for several years; each recounted only the most important aspects of their particular area. None of them handled matters directly; each spoke for the thousands of their race that they supervised in institutions across the United States.

Humans in key position to distort knowledge of history were being supported with grants from foundations controlled by the overseer. If efforts to open the secret archives of the Smithsonian or other museums were successful, it would dash much of the commonly held view of history. Educators who stressed curriculums for the lowest common denominator were supported, but there was a growing movement against such discrimination. Government contracts continued to be directed toward scientists who supported traditional physics, chemistry, and biology, despite pressures for more funding for quantum physics, new energy, and research into the paranormal. Radically new technologies were starved; those promising advancements in line with World League objectives were provided funding from one of the several funds controlled by agents of the overseer. The medical model created by the World League continued to dominate the practice of physicians in America. Despite an aggressive campaign to discredit everything outside the model, and to control all natural supplements, alternative medical and nutritional approaches were making inroads. Psychological labeling continued to be a successful way to marginalize people and engender distrust. Without funding for proper care, many of the most disturbed humans were mingling with the general population, until they were imprisoned. No effective measures were allowed to surface that might halt drug or alcohol addiction.

"Mr. Bustamonte," Clever said. It was abundantly clear to all members of the Board that Clever and Bustamonte had a close relationship. "Tell us about your charge."

Bustamonte relayed that the stand-ins for the President were working well. He had observed a brief moment when the latest stand-in had confronted Sam Wellborn, one of Boyle's long-time friends, and was worried that the façade might have broken momentarily. Investigations of Wellborn were continuing to determine how he might be reacting to the event.

Ophir knew that shape shifters had not been employed before to replace a sitting President. The process had been tried on members of the Cabinet and on members of Congress with great results. Older processes of cloning had produced superior physical specimens, but their psyches were not well matched to the goals of the World League. Now the volunteers' psyches were tested for malleability and compatibility before the shape shifting process was begun.

"Zeno," Clever said, "give us your report."

Zeno Carletta was the overseer of a network of patriots outside the United States; he was not a member of the Board. In some circles his contacts were known as terrorists or mafia. Unlike the others who worked through well-placed people in existing organizations, Carletta worked hands-on. Recognized for his brutal ways, he had been one of Ophir's most trusted operatives until he assumed his current function.

He and his agents dispersed money to patriotic organizations that assisted goals of the World League. He also made sure that organizations that did not fit were starved for money. With the recent shakeup, Carletta reported directly to Clever.

"I am very happy to be here in these plush surroundings," he began. "My most recent adventure was in Central America where I funneled funds to an opposition guerilla group. Typical of the way in which I squander Jonathan's money, I lived in a hut for ten days," he chuckled.

"Indigenous peoples throughout the world are finding their voice. They see examples in Bolivia, Ecuador, and Venezuela and want to follow in their footsteps. I am supplying funds to the opposition in every case. In the end I believe that money will win the day, as it always has.

"In the Middle East we continue to fund everyone. The latest threats against the United States are in line with our plans to continue the climate of fear, and we are actively funding jihad groups.

Carletta continued down the list of projects that were calculated to continue to destabilize governments and populations in Africa, Asia, and even Europe. He finished by saying, "In light of what is about to transpire, I am most happy to take advantage of your hospitality for the next few weeks."

"And finally we come to Martin," Clever said in his haughty tone.

Martin VanOosterhoot was the League's overseer of planetary resources, and a member of its Board. Speaking with a Dutch accent, he said, "Despite reports to the contrary, the population of this planet has begun to decline; deaths now outnumber births. Our programs in energy, water, food, and disease are taking their toll." He went on to talk about successes in creating artificial shortages and escalating prices by withholding land from production, diverting food crops to biofuels, polluting water supplies, and by increases in the costs of transportation. Drug-resistant diseases had made significant advances and were now at epidemic levels in many countries. While acreage for genetically engineered crops had dropped, shortages of all foods and much higher prices for organic items had happily resulted in renewed demand for GM crops. He said that he found it quite amusing to watch humans try to figure out which foods were safe to consume.

"Our atmospheric aerosol program is exacerbating respiratory diseases everywhere coincident with the spread of drug-resistant tuberculosis. We've had some success controlling humans with electromagnetics, which the aerosols enhance, but we've been totally unsuccessful in stopping, or in modifying, the light energy coming from the armada. While we have induced a general condition of lethargy among the sheep, particularly here in the United States, we have had less success spreading this condition elsewhere. The light in humans of this planet continues to resist our best efforts at control. We are being further thwarted because the star nations have inserted overwhelming numbers of their kind into the population.

"I will conclude by saying that without a new agenda, we will soon slip from planetary domination. I am looking forward to taking an active role in coming events. I am sure they will put us back on the right track."

"Some of what you just said is not good news," Ophir said, fighting to keep a straight face. "I am going to check it against my sources." He repressed a laugh, knowing full well that VanOosterhoot knew they enjoyed poking holes in each other's presentation. They had discussed this banter earlier in the day.

"You're just looking for an excuse to grab a larger role for your intelligence affiliates," Bustamonte chimed in.

"As you well know, that is already underway," Clever said to Bustamonte. Turning to VanOosterhoot he said. "If asked, you will reply that our efforts are meeting expectations, nothing more."

Clever said, "Thank you gentlemen. I will expect detailed reports tomorrow. Now let us greet our associates from other parts of the world." For the first time since he had initially entered the room, Grant Clever stood and smiled. The others followed suit.

The great doors at the end of the room opened. Wearing mostly traditional dark western suits, sixty males and females, along with a smattering of humans streamed in. Each began looking for their assigned places around the unfamiliar table. Five wore military uniforms, three wore thoubs, shumaggs, and ogals, and two sported head wraps from India. Two females wore long dresses under jackets. The top males from Europe and Asia took seats next to Clever.

Zeno received hugs from two particularly rough-looking humans as they passed by. One human headed up the wrong side of the table, then went back around the far end rather than intrude into Clever's space. Two humans of the yellow race sat down at the far end of the table. Four red-uniformed guards followed the group in and posted themselves in the corners of the room.

The members of the Planetary Council, other than those who sat on the Board of the World League, had arrived at this facility from around the world over the past five days. They had come by the underground tram system from terminuses like Buckley Air Force Base near Denver, Peterson Air Force Base near Colorado Springs, or Kirtland Air Force Base south of Albuquerque, New Mexico. Their incognito arrival in the U.S. had been arranged via one or more clandestine agencies. Since their arrival, a series of less formal meetings had been conducted. This combined assembly was a showcase and rubber stamp of carefully negotiated positions.

Each member of the Planetary Council had an organization under him or her of ten thousand males and females, plus an equally large number of committed humans. The few humans attending today were guests of honor, selected for their service to the Council's agenda or their integral part in the next phase of its plan.

As the newcomers took their seats, Ophir's mind wandered to the starships clustered about the planet. They were at a higher frequency, so the eyes and instruments of humans did not detect them. However, the more sophisticated instruments of the rulers of mankind observed their presence with increasing concern. Ophir could only hope, in addition to the secrecy surrounding the meeting, that the electromagnetic shielding and underground location would be sufficient to thwart their prying eyes and ears.

It was Ophir's opinion, one that he had expressed to the other members of the Executive Committee, that this unprecedented build-up of craft signaled their final days of control over this planet. Grant Clever and Henry Bustamonte had rebuffed his recommendation that they send word to ready their craft and that all six of them travel to Antarctica for an immediate escape.

When the newcomers were seated, Clever said, "Welcome to the annual meeting of the Planetary Council, and welcome to the new headquarters of the World League. We are pleased to be your hosts.

"We hope your accommodations are comfortable. If you need anything, please do not hesitate to speak to one of the humans at the front desk. Now to business, we are most anxious to hear of your progress."

Ophir was always amused when he heard the wording of the names of the two organizations. He was sure it angered many of those present. Males from the United States, under the pyramid of the World League, had dominated the Planetary Council for the last fifty years of its six thousand year history.

"Let me interrupt," Jeremiah Goldman said. "There is one among us in whom the light shines too brightly." He pointed to a female who Ophir recognized as an overseer from France. Among her other duties was that of handling the newly elected French President. "Remove her."

"No," she screamed, "I belong here. I have something of great import..." She then lapsed into French which few of those present understood.

Two of the guards moved to her. They lifted her from her seat and dragged her from the room.

When calm was restored, Grant Clever said, "Let us continue."

A large black human leaned toward his microphone and said, "If I may, I would like to report on my country." He went on to say that the dictator whom he supported had successfully thwarted a plan to overthrow his government and that the opposition was imprisoned or dead. The prior year, in his country the death rate from malaria had reached an all time high. In conformity with the Planetary Council's desire to reduce planetary population, the government was continuing to refuse entry by the United Nations and by all NGOs.

The second male to speak up was from Israel. Although they had met, Ophir knew Isaac Eppler mainly by reputation and rebuff. Eppler had categorically refused to cooperate with Ophir's intelligence affiliates. This left a sizeable hole in his network of operatives. Before going underground, Ophir had set out to remedy the situation, but it was proving to be difficult to recruit in the middle of continued fighting. He had enlisted Zeno's help, but it had produced only one defection.

"As we have come to appreciate, the situation in my arena continues," Eppler said. "In cooperation with Zeno, we supply funds to all sides, but more importantly we stir the religious fervor of the masses. Those who report to me are well placed within the Wahhabi, the Shia, the Sunni, the Kurds, the Turks, and the children of Zion. Some of our major supporters are the Christians for Israel. It is hard to tell whether we have already started Armageddon, or it is just around the corner. I am most pleased to be working in the eye of the storm."

The meeting went on like this for two hours as overseers to governments, central banks, relief organizations, charitable foundations, and multi-national corporations reported on the status of their efforts. Ophir was amazed at the narrow points of view that some of them held, particularly the humans. How could they not understand that they were witnessing the final hours of planetary domination? The cracks of a few years ago had widened to canyons; humans around the planet were waking up. When enough awakened, their long reign would cease.

At the end of the reports from the guests, a break was called. Women in scanty blue uniforms brought all manner of delicacy to a side table: lobster from the nearly depleted fishing grounds of the Atlantic, real caviar from Russia, salmon from the cold waters off Alaska, prime beef from America's heartland. The feast was cooked to perfection, arranged in opulence. The favorite dish of each guest was present.

Continuing their display of hospitality, the guests of the World League ate last. Ophir and the other members of the executive committee stood back as food was heaped on plate after plate, food in which only the wealthiest of this planet could indulge, food that had cost a small fortune in today's dollars.

As he waited in line, a male approached Ophir, "Our new chairman seems to be enjoying his role."

Heinrich Durfenberger resided in Germany; he ran the back-up communications center that mirrored the one at this facility. In an earlier role he had been one of Hitler's close advisors. "As you and I both know, life on this planet takes on many faces. Today Clever is the Chairman; tomorrow it might be you. I believe you are in an envious position, Warren. May I offer you a proposal?"

"But, of course."

"In addition to my center, I have certain males at my disposal. They are, shall we say, better placed in countries where yours are not. I believe it would be to our mutual benefit to coordinate some of our activities, particularly in light of what is about to happen."

"And what do you understand is about to happen?"

"We all know of Admiral Ridgway's plan. I also know of the armada and know that they will not sit by as he plays out this latest move. They have already disabled all nuclear weapons. It may or may not work out as Admiral Ridgway, Bustamonte, and Clever expect. Either way, there will be a need for intelligence and communications."

"Yes," Ophir said, "there will always be a need for intelligence."

THIRTY-ONE

After lunch, Clever asked Henry Bustamonte to give an overview of the situation within the U.S. government.

"I am happy to report that the government of the United States of America is functioning in line with our modifications: We have control of the money supply. The President has control of all operations and decisions -- by presenting first a newly elected, Carlton Boyle, then a tyrannical Richard Tyler, then a revived but weakened Carlton Boyle, and now a totally confident President Carlton Boyle, we have the sheep completely confused. Congress is mired in procedural red tape and conflicting agendas. The Judiciary, most of whom were appointed several years ago, are waiting for our signal to rule on any number of cases. In short we are able to carry out our agenda without interference, and we can marshal military forces and private manpower as required."

"What about the ability of your populace to vote in new people?" a male from South Africa asked. "Aren't you vulnerable to a grass roots movement?"

"I believe we have that base covered," Bustamonte chuckled. "The voting mechanism has been ours for many years. There are always one or two exceptions; just to give the people hope, we allow them to elect a Carlton Boyle. Rest assured, no one is elected to top federal or state positions without our financial or organizational assistance, whether they realize it or not. Then after they are elected..." He did not finish his sentence.

"What Henry is trying to say is that we have sufficiently compromised the system so that democracy now works totally to our advantage, while appearing to work for the sheep," Clever smiled. "It is messier than some of you involved with totalitarian regimes, but humans in the U.S. are consistently much more productive than yours. The action they were proposing will eliminate the remaining trappings of the republic. With Mister Bustamonte managing the President and my influence in other branches of government, we form a powerful team. It was this team that had allowed us to assume the leadership of the World League."

What Clever did not say was, "and offer up Delta Kingman to a special prosecutor." Ophir had insisted that it was suicidal to believe they could rule from this hidden outpost. But his dissent had been overridden. Now if the majority of those present approved, they would go forward with what he saw as a most desperate scheme to extinguish the light -- under the very nose of the armada.

The next speaker was Jonathan Olson who had slipped out during a break to check on currency fluctuations, economic data, and stock markets. "If I am reiterating information already submitted to you, please bear with me," he said. "Our fiat currency program continues to maintain the façade of planetary stability in the face of bankrupt nations and falling economies. Debt, government and personal, acknowledged and hidden, is at an all time high. Here in the U.S. we are creating more debt to retire that which is already outstanding. Our planned disruption will spell new opportunities to reclaim control of assets from desperate debt holders; I urge you to take advantage of the situation. Please stay connected to the network for an updated list of opportunities.

"What might be new is that over the past six months we have brought speculation under our control; we are now able to move vast sums of debt instruments and derivatives undetected. Thanks to the assistance of those of you in this room, all governments and central banks, I repeat, all governments and central banks now rely on the World League to fix the value of their currency. At the push of a computer button, we can create inflation or depression and can manipulate any stock or currency market, all of this behind the façade of a free market. As with many of you, the World League's powers are being used to manipulate more and more assets. Our proposed action will make control even easier."

Ophir watched as a male, the overseer of a group of economic affiliates based in London, squirmed at this news. He was seated next to an advisor to the government of Qatar, which government had created its own currency, "barrolas," backed by its oil and natural gas reserves. A human advisor to the Saudi Royal family, which was considering a similar move, sat next to him. If allowed to happen, petrocurrencies would replace the dollar and the euro as world standards.

Olson's plan, which he had discussed with Ophir two days ago, and which he was not ready to reveal to the members of the Planetary Council, was to roll over all debts of the United States, public and private, into a new class of very long-term debt instruments. This would create a massive devaluation and such chaos that other governments would attempt the same, making the debts of those who did not play worthless. From such chaos, he planned to create a new economic order, a World League economic order.

Olson continued, "Although the public believes that we have passed the peak of oil production, the truth is that our reserves have never been higher. By creating the perception of a shortage we have finally been able to return oil's price to acceptable levels. A side benefit to this is that we have raised the price of food so that an additional twenty percent of the world's population now falls under the poverty level. Keep in mind here that we are treading a fine line between damage to growth of the desirable aspects of the world economy and obtaining the maximum price for black gold.

"Speaking of gold, congratulations. I am happy to report that collectively we have amassed the largest stockpile in history. My estimate is that those of us around this table control eighty percent of the gold on this planet. We have maneuvered governments into borrowing against their precious metal reserves, then defaulting on their loans. They are now safeguarding our gold while they assure their people it belongs to them. After we have purchased all desirable assets with worthless currencies, we will convert to a precious metals backed currency." Smiling, he leaned back in his chair and, with his long tongue, took several laps from his goblet.

For the next forty-five minutes, Olson answered questions. With the Planetary Council's clandestine communications network, any overseer could get a question answered within minutes, but some saved theirs for meetings like this. Ophir's people monitored all such communications between overseers; also they were in charge of posting the recordings of these meetings.

"How do you see economies faring with the proposed assault that Admiral Ridgway is going to talk about?" The question came from a male who was a director of the European Central Bank.

"I do not wish to upstage Admiral Ridgway," Olson said, "but if his plan is carried out as envisioned, all debt-based economies will crash. The last time I checked, this was everybody." He smiled and continued,

"This will mean much hardship, many lives lost to starvation, and fear beyond people's wildest imaginations." Olson smiled. "This is what all of us are counting on, isn't it? As your financial advisor, I am telling you to secure your assets before that time."

The males from Britain, Qatar, and Saudi Arabia hurried to the door. Only after Grant Clever nodded to the guards were they allowed to exit. Others asked for a brief break. "Ten minutes," the Chairman grinned. "Justin Ridgway is next. The most important part of the day is ahead of us."

When they returned, Clever said, "Members of the Planetary Council, we must focus on the most important issue of this meeting. As you are all aware, we had detected traffic from the armada. We tracked it to a location in South Dakota where they are installing something which they cloaked before we were able to determine its precise nature. So we must conclude that they are preparing something of a surprise for us. Does anyone have anything they would like to add?" This latest news surprised a few around the table, as it had not been broadcast on the network.

When no one offered anything, Clever said, "Okay Admiral Ridgway, give us your plan."

"Before I launch into the plan before us, I must comment on the superb job everyone is doing in the Middle East. While we control the flow of oil and gas to those who favor our agenda, the indigenous peoples of the region fight over century-old grievances. Our token military forces would be unable to act without this constant chaos. Job well done.

"Now let me turn to the most urgent item on today's agenda. The loss of craft in the recent Utah explosion crippled our first plan beyond recovery," the admiral said. "So we are now moving forward with the revised plan as outlined to each of you over the past month. Because we will be depending on ground forces, our own and human, it is most important that you disable your military.

"In actuality, the worldwide publicity accorded to the nuclear explosion, and the purported terrorist battles, makes for a near perfect situation: the public is now more convinced than ever that the threat from terrorists is real. I believe we should strike within the next month."

"Exactly how will a worldwide event do this?" a male from Canada asked. "It is one thing to have reports about battles with terrorists that few have seen, or about a nuclear explosion out in some wasteland; how do you propose to bring it home."

"We are looking to involve several cities. I am still working out the details and will consult with those of you whose cities are to be involved. Believe me this event will be most convincing, and will further our aim of population reduction. We will inform each of you in plenty of time to seek refuge. Our next step is to work with humans like Byron Greylock to step up fear of terrorist invasion."

The questioning of Ridgway went on for almost an hour. They set up a series of messages that would serve to coordinate the attacks in various locations while disabling local forces. These same messages would alert the members to seek their shelters.

"I would like to have a show of support for Admiral Ridgway," Grant Clever said, as he stood before the most powerful assembly in the world. "All in favor signify by pushing the green button on your pyramid. All opposed, push the red button. The vote will be displayed on the panel behind me."

It took a few moments for the tally to be published, during which there were several yelps of approval. Sixty-two were in favor, four opposed. The ten humans were not allowed to vote.

"I consider this to be a resounding vote of confidence. Admiral, proceed as planned.

"Now my friends," Clever's words were like honey. "We have an evening of festivities planned with young humans available for your pleasure. Please join us in one hour. I declare this meeting adjourned."

What none of those seated around the World League's conference table had detected were the non-physical entities who observed these proceedings. Among them was Sarah Smith, relaxing in a chair in the quiet of her room at Harmony Center, her etheric body transmitting the event to her consciousness. She spoke into a recorder in order to recall the lengthy proceedings.

She had chosen a vantage point behind and slightly to the left of the chair of Henry Bustamonte, opposite Grant Clever. Ever since her first encounter with Bustamonte in the Oval Office, she had, from time to time, monitored his activities. Today's proceedings, several hundred miles to the northeast and two hundred feet under a mountain, had been by far the most interesting.

At first she had been unsure, thinking that she had traveled to the wrong place. If she had not previously witnessed Henry Bustamonte when he had shifted into his non-human form, she would have been totally mystified. The way she knew it was him was by his voice, it did not shift with his facade. As it was, she had double-checked her intention to view him and had indeed arrived at this most interesting meeting with not only Bustamonte, but with the same men who had been with President Boyle that morning they had spoken by satellite phone.

The presentations and conversations fascinated her, but she found the sleek scaled faces and hands of those present even more interesting. Since all displayed the faces and uniforms of their race, Sarah could only distinguish between the men and women native to this planet and the males and females who were not.

Just days ago, again from the quiet of her room at Harmony, she had decided to check up on President Carlton Boyle, deep within this same underground complex. She had watched as they fitted him with a helmet from which wires were connected to a bank of electronics. In that same room other humans were connected to similar electronics. She recognized one as the Speaker of the House of Representatives.

This had led her to locate the men who had been in the Oval Office that day. Today she had found the five of them here, their facades dropped, meeting with other N'Roids. At least she assumed that they were the N'Roids she had learned about before coming to Earth.

When the proceedings ended, Sarah opened her eyes. Ethete sat across the room from her. In about five minutes Ethete's eyes opened; she grimaced and said, "How long has this been going on?"

"This particular play, or this whole façade?"

"This whole scheme."

"I found it very difficult to tell exactly who was speaking, except for the humans who maintained their form and clothing. However, I believe these are the descendants of the N'Roids that enslaved the humans of this planet hundreds of thousands of years ago," Sarah replied. "Their involvement has become more entwined since the demise of Atlantis. The Earth-humans of today are a mixture of those who fled that enlightened civilization blended with indigenous peoples who were devolved from the four races that were originally brought to this planet."

"I know of that history," Ethete said. "What I do not understand is how N'Roids have infiltrated the top echelons of human society so successfully."

"I believe they recreate their own kind in the top echelons as needed. As humans evolve, the N'Roids just keep reappearing in new guises, but always at the top of the ladder. Did you notice their motto, 'Riding The Wave?' They see themselves on the backs of humanity having a grand old time."

"Despite their current problems, the N'Roids seem well organized," Ethete said. "How can it be that they are losing their grip?"

"Their supporter, the dark one that Phantia never experienced, has withdrawn from this part of the galaxy. Our brothers and sisters from other civilizations brought such brilliant energy to this star system that Earth was able to heal herself, and the combined energies became so brilliant that the dark one was forced to withdraw.

"If we had come here sixty years ago, the energies would have been so dense that we could not have functioned. As it is, I am just now getting my faculties accustomed to the dense energy of this planet.

"Although they hide it from each other, the N'Roids are desperate. I believe they know they are playing out the last days of their control over this world."

"I believe you are correct," Ethete said excitedly. Then she added, "I will track the two religious ones to see how to best proceed. We need to communicate what we have learned to our star brothers and sisters."

"When the Planetary Council broke for lunch, I talked with them. Two of our brothers from Sirius were already there."

"What is the white powder they are all licking?"

"Monatomic gold. It is treasured throughout the universe for its mind enhancing properties. Gold was the N'Roids original purpose in coming to Earth. Egyptian pharaohs, some of them were the N'Roids ancestors, were depicted with cups of monatomic gold. I am going to go back to that facility to find its source."

"Be careful, they are not without abilities to sense our intrusions."

THIRTY-TWO

"Sir, I have something I think you should be aware of," the young male had knocked on the doorframe to Warren Ophir's office at 8:00 AM. He stood ramrod straight, in the red uniform that denoted he was a member of the facility's security service that reported to Ophir.

"Go ahead, ensign."

"Sir, last night, we had an intruder on level nine."

"Level nine?"

"Yes sir."

"Go ahead."

"Well sir, I would not have detected anyone, except it was about one AM and everything was very quiet. I was at my station near the elevator. So I decided to slip into alpha, like you showed us. And bang, I sensed her immediately."

"At what time?"

"At eleven thirty six, sir."

"I take it this visitor was not materialized," Ophir said.

"That is correct, sir, but with a signature that she was human. Whoever she was, she was looking for the generator. Once she found that room and looked around, she disappeared."

"Human, huh?" Ophir's attention was now riveted on the ensign.

"Yes, sir."

"Why am I just now learning of this?" Ophir rose from his desk and walked toward the ensign.

The young male stiffened. "Sir, I fell asleep after my shift, sir."

"Next time something like this happens, stay awake and tell me immediately, do not wait until morning."

"Yes, sir."

"Thank you, ensign. Shut the door behind you."

As soon as the young male left, Warren Ophir slipped into that relaxed state where his spirit self would do his bidding. He traveled back in time to the prior night. In space he positioned himself in the generator room at 11:30 PM.

In a few minutes, the energy trace of the human appeared. She was of the light, a beautiful visage. He observed her as she watched the operation of the monatomic gold machine; he then followed her as she further explored the lowest levels of the facility. When she departed, he tracked her back to a site in the desert of Arizona.

After he returned to full consciousness, Warren Ophir checked with the surveillance teams that were covering Ryan Drake and Sam Wellborn.

The Washington, DC team reported that Wellborn seemed to be following his normal routine. His chauffeur reported every movement, and most conversations had been recorded.

"Chauffeur be damned, his behavior is too pat," Ophir said. "I know he's meeting with that woman who used to work for him. I want a full team on him, everywhere he goes, and I mean a close tail."

"Yes, sir, right away."

When he called the team watching Ryan Drake, he was similarly frustrated. "You lost him when?"

"Three days ago. He left the site, in a vehicle with three others, in the middle of the night. They drove north. I followed the vehicle past Kayenta, toward Utah. Then I got into a freak snowstorm. My SUV went into the ditch, and I got busted up."

"Where are you now?"

"At the hospital in Flagstaff."

"Still?"

"Sir, they tell me I have a concussion and three broken ribs. I just woke up a few hours ago."

Ophir slammed down the phone. Damn, he hated being bottled up in this underground maze; it was time for some sunshine.

That same morning, Ryan, John deBeque, Ajax, Sarah, and Ethete were gathered around the table in Harmony Center's great room. The three men were aghast as they listened to Sarah and Ethete relay the details of the meeting of the N'Roids they had viewed the prior day. Both women, exhausted by their intense efforts, had gone to bed immediately after the meeting had adjourned.

Sarah had awakened in the middle of the night, and without disturbing Ryan, had revisited the underground facility to discover more about the white powder that the N'Roids were ingesting. After wandering about for some time, she discovered a small room in the facility's deepest level, where the source of electricity and air handling machinery were located. During previous explorations, she had ignored the room because it was darkened and the machinery therein was not operating. She now saw that at this late hour, when the needs of the facility were at a minimum, excess electrical power was diverted to a machine in this room. This room was isolated from the rest of the underground facility by an airtight entry and extensive air filtering equipment. Two N'Roids, dressed in white gowns, fed chunks of pure gold into the machine. From its other side poured a steady stream of white powder. They treated the white powder with extraordinary care, sealing it into glass jars.

"So, maybe we should get some of that gold powder," Ryan joked. "I'm sure I'd make good use of it."

"There's more," Sarah said, "as I was wandering about that underground facility, I saw something else." She paused to close her eyes and take a deep breath. "I found the entire group, N'Roids and humans, in a room lighted only with candles. They were dressed in black robes with hoods that covered their heads, but I'm sure it was them; I recognized their energy signatures. They were chanting words that I did not understand. I watched as they concluded with a ceremony that involved sacrificing a young girl." Sarah shuddered and again closed her eyes.

No one said anything for a long while.

At last John deBeque broke the silence. "I listen to what you two have told us, but I've got to tell you I don't see what we can do in the face of it." John deBeque shook his head. "They have their hands on every lever, plus they're totally amoral."

"On the contrary, I see signs that things are falling apart, that they are clutching at straws," Ajax said. "This goes along with the information you and Ryan are picking up from the internet."

"I'm with you, John, it does look pretty intimidating." Ryan said as he glanced down at the notes he had made. He addressed the three from Phantia. "Did you know about all this when you came here?"

"Most of it," Ajax said, "but until you have lived here, you really can't get a feel for it. Nobody back home would believe."

"I communicated with my D'Ct-Elds mother and others who are involved with the transition," Sarah said. "They also monitored some of the meeting. At this moment there is a discussion among the members of the armada on the next steps. Their only conclusion so far is that they are prepared to confront the N'Roids." Seeing the question on Ryan's face, she added, "Because the N'Roids are classed as intruders on this planet."

"Well that's something," Ryan said, "but what does it mean."

"Ryan, as we have discussed, this reality is a unique energy manifestation," Sarah said. "The physical bodies that you and I wear are but patterns of information and light condensed into a very slow form of energy called the physical realm. All of this energy is constantly interacting, both with all else in this third dimension as well as with all in the lighter densities.

"When our allies focused their attention on this star system about seventy years ago, at the pleading of Earth, their light energy was very powerful. Initially they were repulsed, but with additions to their fleet, the darkness began to retreat. Now they are saying to us that they have more than enough light to overwhelm the N'Roids. All that is missing is for the humans of this planet to wake up and ask for their help." She gestured to Ethete and Ajax and smiled. "What it means for us is that our mission can be successfully completed."

/*"Let me try," Ethete said. "At this unique moment in history, mankind has the opportunity to make a fundamental change in the way in which life is lived on this planet. This is different than what has gone on before in two respects. First, Earth herself is transitioning to a lighter density. This will happen regardless of all else, because the light from the armada has given her sufficient energy to accomplish this long ordained transition.

"Second, for thousands of years, mankind has been shining the light of love at its enslavement -- during brief moments in history, such as the Renaissance, or the founding of the United States, it has seen gains, but in the longer term little has changed. This is because the darkness overwhelmed that which began as good and twisted it to its own aims. So you see, it does no good to skirt discussing the reality of the slavery that has gripped this planet for eons, and simply focus on the light. Only by understanding the depth of the darkness can you come to understand how much courage and pressure must be applied to overcome it.

"Mankind's historic opportunity comes about because the light from the armada has forced the non-physical overlord of darkness to withdraw from this galaxy. I don't know that I understand the implications of what I just said, but I do understand it is huge and makes everything else possible. Now all that is required is for sufficient numbers of humans to awaken and to request that the power of the armada be focused on the N'Roids. When this is done, your brothers and sisters from the stars will show you the way to transform the people of this planet."

During a break just before lunch, Ryan and John deBeque went to the corner of the room to check on news coming from the internet. A major exposé, just published by the New York Times, was carried on several sites. TERRORIST DEMANDS, the headline read. They motioned the others to gather round as they scrolled down the article.

The story reported that, "Secret conversations have been held between the U.S. government and the terrorists whose base in Utah was destroyed by the U.S. military. The terrorists are demanding that the military immediately withdraw from the site and that they be allowed to collect their dead. They are threatening widespread destruction if these demands are not met.

"During a lull in the battles between the terrorists and the military, the terrorists had secretly constructed the base. When the U.S. government discovered it, they had tried a ground and air assault. Failing that, they had used a small nuclear device to eradicate it."

"Nuked a terrorist facility on American soil? Well, we all know where that line of bull came from," John deBeque declared when he showed the article to those gathered around the computer. "The sad part is that, if I was still in my old job, I would've been the one that wrote it. I am so glad I got out. More than that, I think the one the N'Roids call Warren Ophir is the same one who was my boss; no wonder I always thought he was ready to blow my head off."

Ethete reached over to hug him. "We're all glad you walked away from that awful situation."

"I have to get together with Sam about all this," Ryan said. They took a quick break while Ryan moved over to his computer to type an urgent message on the hidden web page.

When they reconvened, Sarah said, "Let's start with the media. John, is there anything we can do to get the truth about this out there?"

"In my opinion, it is not possible to get anyone's attention by reporting that we've been on board a craft or that you remotely viewed a secret meeting.

"However, with this latest news about terrorists' demands, the alternative sites will be hungry for anything they can get their hands on. I'll get to work on an approach. And it may be time to get in touch with some of my old employees at the media affiliates. I just wish we had pictures or something like that."

"Are you up for this?" Ryan asked. "Sarah just told you that Warren Ophir, the man who was your boss at the media affiliates was in reality an N'Roid."

"Yeah, I heard it," John replied, "and I'm really having a problem admitting it. Ophir never showed me his true identity, nor did Ernest Steiger, who I now suspect was also one of them. Quite frankly it scares the shit out of me to think how close I was to becoming like that man Greylock."

No one said anything. John deBeque spread his arms on the table and put his head on them. Ethete placed her hand on his shoulder.

With her hand still on John deBeque's shoulder, Ethete said, "I'd like to tackle the whole issue of religion and how to overcome its influence. It seems to me that religious beliefs are at the heart of people's unwillingness to face up to their enslavement. And those awful N'Roids masquerading as clergy, what could be worse than misleading people about what to believe?"

"That's the toughest one of all," Sarah said. "It's been going on for thousands of years. It was the way in which the original N'Roids got primitive people to do what they wanted."

"I heard the one say that people were outgrowing religion," Ethete said. "I'm going to work from that angle. If we can find a way to cut religion's influence, we can help Earth-humans accept the larger picture. Besides, I've been coasting for too long; time I did something. I feel my first task will be a search of the Vatican library."

"How are you going to do that," John deBeque raised his head and asked. "That's an all male society over there."

"From right here," Ethete said, "I just need to figure out how to record the information I retrieve. I can't very well make a photocopy."

"What do you feel you're going to find?" Ryan asked.

"There is a curious arrogance with people like that man they called Michael. I wouldn't be surprised to find a document or a diary that shows how they use dogma to control people."

Ryan smiled, "Men like Ernest Steiger, a couple of thousand years ago?"

"Exactly."

"Our allies have been telling us about this," Sarah said. "Maybe they can help."

John deBeque straightened in his chair. "I want to help. Let me work on the best way to tackle the media."

"Don't be doing it to get back at your former bosses," Sarah said. "The only way to a lighter density is with love and light."

"I understand."

'But does he?' the voice in Ryan's head asked. *'Does he really understand that fighting the N'Roids' control of the media will not transcend the consensual paradigm?'* Ryan glanced at Sarah. She nodded to indicate that she too had heard the message from their spirit guides.

"I'll take on the whole N'Roid thing," Ajax said, "after all I was an off-planet guy impersonating an Earth-human, and I did pretty well at it."

"That you did," commented Ryan, "that you did, until you blew it by admitting the whole thing."

"You just put your finger on it," Ajax said. "We get an N'Roid or two to show themselves. Out of a million, I bet there are several who are fed up. Maybe we start with that woman they threw out of the meeting."

"If she's still alive," Ethete said.

"Perhaps the two people Crita and I are working with can help." As he said the words, Dr Adamson became visible to the others. The white-haired giant stood near Sarah at the end of the table. He walked to a chair next to Ryan, pulled it from the table, and sat down.

Ryan shook his head. How Victor Adamson was able to control his physicality was beyond him. At one moment he appeared to be a human, the architect of Harmony Center, the next he mysteriously passed his hand through a solid surface like this table. As if reading Ryan's mind, Dr. Adamson allowed his hand to drift through the table. Then like a magician with a Cheshire cat grin, he pulled it out from beneath.

Across the table, John deBeque just shook his head.

Dr. Adamson's smile vanished. "They have told us that there are many within the military who do not like what is going on. If we can identify one or two, we can get our star brothers and sisters involved."

"I'll go with that approach," Ajax said. "Let me know how I can contact them."

"Now, I know that you five could continue this discussion for hours, and you probably will," Dr. Adamson said. "However, may I borrow Sarah and Ryan for a while?"

THIRTY-THREE

With Dr. Adamson crammed into the space behind the front seats and Sarah in the passenger seat, Ryan drove Harmony's pickup to Kayenta then turned east on US 160. Ryan could not tell, but he suspected that Dr. Adamson had partially dematerialized in order to squeeze into the tight space.

The familiar landscape buzzed by: Slender rocks at the base of a bluff. A hogan surrounded by a junky yard with a rusted pickup. An expanse of smooth red rock that went on for a mile. Scrawny horses eating sparse grasses amidst the sagebrush.

Sarah told Dr. Adamson what she had observed in the N'Roid's meeting.

He listened, commenting only that, "I am not surprised." After a period of silence the white haired giant asked Ryan, "When you were on board the starcraft did you ever wonder what powered it?"

"I have to confess," Ryan chuckled, "everything else was so overwhelming that the source of its power didn't cross my mind."

"I invited you out here this morning to witness something. It will play a large role in the coming weeks."

As they drove farther east, Ryan remembered that this was about where he had seen the huge spacecraft descend as he traveled to Colorado. He was about to ask about it when Dr. Adamson said, "Slow down and take the next left." He pointed to a barely visible opening through the sagebrush. The faint path did not appear to have been used recently, as there were no tire tracks in the dust.

They drove about a half-mile, twisting through openings in the ground cover. Then they dipped down the dusty side of a steep hill; Ryan had all he could do to keep the swaying pickup on track. They had reached the bottom of a wide valley, when he looked up. He gasped.

Just ahead was a large starcraft with a black top and a silver underside. It hovered just above the floor of the valley. To Ryan's eye it measured almost a quarter mile across.

Dr. Adamson motioned for Ryan to keep driving. In two hundred yards he said, "Pull over here."

"About time," Sarah said, as she squeezed out of the pickup. They walked the last quarter-mile toward the ship.

Beneath the craft was a circular structure erected in a deep hole; its top was open as if someone had peeled off the top of a can. Ryan could make out what appeared to be a steel superstructure with an outer skin that blended with the surrounding earth. Heavy wires could be seen leading away from its center; they disappeared through the skin.

In its central core was a mass of what appeared to be giant chunks of quartz. They watched as a crystal was lowered from the craft as if by an invisible hand. It glowed briefly, as it exited the underbelly of the ship, then turned quiescent. It awakened momentarily again as it was maneuvered into place among the others.

"They look like they are alive," Ryan said.

"Everything is conscious," Sarah reminded him.

Ryan noted the wires of the electrical grid a few hundred feet away. "Are they stealing electricity?"

"On the contrary, they are getting ready to supply it," Dr Adamson replied with a smile.

"Supply it?

"Yes, those crystals are the same as those that power the starships. They are a gift from the star civilizations to the people of this planet. In time, technologies like these will replace all hydrocarbon-burning electrical generation plants."

"But why out here in the middle of nowhere?" Ryan asked.

"For the moment, this must remain a secret. The ship is masking its activity from the spy satellites of the N'Roids. These crystals, along with others, will soon power the electrical grid."

"This is so amazing," Ryan said. They watched as another crystal was lowered into place. He saw no beings. "So this is all done by remote control?"

"This is the loading operation," Dr Adamson said. "The crystals are too energetic to handle directly. The construction of this facility was done in a similar fashion, but then there were people on the ground directing the activity."

"Will the ship remain here?"

"No, the site will be sealed. It will appear as a natural landscape. Neither the crystals, nor their connection to the electrical grid, will be detectable from either the ground or from space. Human engineers will only know that an immense new source of power has entered their system, like a new generating plant coming on line."

"Why the secrecy?"

"If this were to become known," Dr. Adamson replied, "the N'Roids might turn it to their advantage. Now, where the electricity comes from will remain a mystery, at least in the short term. Keep in mind that our sisters and brothers from the stars have repeatedly suggested advanced energy generating technologies to inventors going all the way back to Nikola Tesla. In each case their discoveries and inventions have been sucked into the shadows, and either depressed or developed into weapons."

"If they exist, can't we get at them, use them beneficially?"

"In time that will be the case. Some of them will be used for transportation; others will be used where there are no electrical transmission lines. Crystals are being utilized in countries where there is an existing electrical grid."

"Countries?"

"Yes, they are being installed in many locations."

"Does this have anything to do with the terrorist attacks that are getting so much publicity?"

Dr. Adamson nodded. "Possibly. But before we go there, think about the implications of a vast, clean source of energy."

"It will overshadow the power of the oil companies, and completely upend the entire world economy," Sarah suggested.

Stunned by the thought, Ryan's jaw dropped. "You are right, so right. A whole new civilization."

Sarah and Dr. Adamson smiled.

"How long have you known?"

"Since I came here," Sarah smiled.

"We use crystals like these to power our civilization at Earth's Center," Dr. Adamson said. "That is the major reason the World League wishes to enter our domain.

"Now back to the terrorist attacks, somehow the N'Roids learned that crystals were being installed in South Dakota. They suspect that a new source of electricity is to be made available. Like you, they realize its implications.

"They have modified their plan for terrorist attacks. Now they will also destroy enough electrical generating and distribution capacity to cause widespread blackouts. These blackouts, along with widespread terrorist attacks, will create fear and distrust which the media will direct toward anyone or anything coming from off-planet."

"When will that be?"

"They wish to act before the crystals they discovered at the Lakota's Pine Ridge Reservation in South Dakota can supply energy, before they can be seen to be beneficial. It could be very soon," Sarah said.

"Why here?" Ryan motioned to the bleak landscape around them.

"This is the final implantation of phase one. Like other phase one sites, this one was chosen because it is remote and the activity of a large ship can take place without observation. Within the last two years, the Navajos have regained possession of this land and formed a legally independent Nation within the United States. They, and other indigenous peoples like them around the world, are receiving crystals. They will offer free electricity to their former conquerors.

"Crystals are already in place in Canada and Mexico, as well as on every other continent. Their activation will coincide with the awakening of the crystals at this site."

"Free energy will totally disrupt the existing economic scheme of things," Ryan repeated it as if it were a mantra. "Totally disrupt. Totally disrupt. The world economy is built on oil, and it's so fragile this will totally disrupt everything: corporations, governments, money, debt, prices, salaries, everything."

"It will also correct the ecological imbalances due to burning hydrocarbons," Sarah said.

"That too," Ryan acknowledged. "This is so perfect."

Dr. Adamson motioned Ryan and Sarah toward the ship. "Step closer, there is someone who would like to meet you."

As they approached, the sleek hull of the starship towered over them. When they were a few yards away, a door opened in the bottom of the ship, and a ramp extended downward. A very tall human-looking being with black hair walked down the ramp and stepped toward them. As it approached, Ryan could see that she was over seven feet tall. A tight fitting suit that sparkled with a bluish hue covered her slender figure.

'This is Commander Huenda of the starship Afilia,' Dr. Adamson communicated to Ryan and Sarah. *'She wishes to say something to you.'*

'Good day, my friends, I am most pleased to meet you who are doing such

valuable work on the surface.

'As you can see, we are building an energy source to power your grid. These crystals are the same as power starcraft across the galaxy. They also power my home planet. They are a gift from my people to the people of Earth.

'We wish to insure that our gift is well received and used in the proper way. Please tell your people not to be afraid; our gift is benign. It will supply electricity for many years, until you are able to construct your own energy converters. Use this electricity with our wishes for peace and love.'

Seeing that Ryan was too stunned to respond, Sarah stepped in. *'Thank you, Commander,'* she said. *"On behalf of the people of this planet we accept your gift. We will begin a campaign to help all Earth-humans know that yours is a gift, and nothing more than that. You have done a courageous thing to bring this energy to us. Again, we thank you.'*

Commander Huenda turned and walked back to her ship.

"May I ask something," Ryan blurted out.

His words startled the Commander. She turned and looked at him. *'Yes?'*

Ryan quickly switched to communicate, *'Exactly when can we begin to tell others about this new energy source?'*

'We will be finished here by the end of this day. It will require a day to coordinate with others around the planet. I will inform Sarah of the exact time of initiation.'

'Would it be possible to get pictures of your craft?' Ryan asked. *'It would help us publicize that starships and craft of people from other star systems are not hostile.'* Ryan went on to explain what he had in mind in the way of publicizing the beneficial aspects of the new energy and the benevolent attitude of those who had brought it to Earth.

'I will inquire,' Commander Huenda communicated. As she stepped through the opening, the ramp retracted and the portal closed.

"Why me?" Ryan asked.

"I believe you already know," Sarah smiled. "You are in a perfect position to explain the benevolent nature of this gift. Translate the desire of the star people to help their human brothers and sisters. Help people understand that it is a friendly gesture."

Dr. Adamson said. "You have credibility as Sarah's companion, and as a former entrepreneur and CEO. John deBeque will assist you.

"We are entering into the days of the interim. People will become even more afraid during the deprivations they will experience. Many will decide to leave the planet.

"Your job is to help as many as possible see the larger reality. Then help them see that their brothers and sisters from the star civilizations are ready to lift them from their slavery; they need only request assistance. Most importantly, help them see that their individual energy affects all, that for thousands of years people have been misled into using their personal energy against their own best interests, and that it is their collective energy that is upholding the consensual paradigm. In addition to seeing the darkness, help them see that they can change it by turning their backs on it, by redirecting their energies."

"Okay, the signs are everywhere that the consensual paradigm is falling apart," Ryan said. "However, it is one thing for me to see it, it is something else for those who are just awakening to embrace a whole new life style."

"The days ahead will see many opportunities for everyone to rethink their beliefs and attitudes," Dr. Adamson said as they walked from the starship to the pickup. "Now, I must return to Earth's Center. I assume you two can find your way home." With those words the white-haired giant disappeared.

"This is so damn exciting," Ryan said. They had returned to US 160 and were driving toward Kayenta. "I can see it remaking our entire civilization. Just think no more oil or coal. Free energy. Wow, this is fantastic. It's going to change the entire economy."

"It's true, the energy produced by the crystals will give people relief from domination by the N'Roids," Sarah said, "and it will reshape the economy, however it is not a permanent fix. To truly fix things will require that the majority of people change their beliefs and behaviors. How far they are willing to go in that direction is dependent upon how they treat each other during the interim time, how well they use that time to throw off their shackles."

Ryan said, "Knowledge of the crystals will lead to knowing that they were supplied by people of other star civilizations, then people will have concrete evidence of other beings in the universe, and that they are benevolent. That alone will shake things up. And when they figure out that they no longer have to work to pay for energy, or pay for the energy component in products, services, and transportation, they will see that they no longer need to be enslaved."

"As I said, I am hopeful," Sarah said, "cautiously hopeful. However, the attitude of slavery is embedded in peoples' psyches. It remains to be seen how far they will go toward a new way of behaving. Those of us, the visitors, feel that the difficulties which everyone will experience during the interim time will help them shed some of their distrust of each other and will provide impetus for permanent change.

"Those who isolate themselves will find life most difficult. It is only by connecting to others that the human race on this planet can be restored to what it was before the influence of the darkness."

"This sounds socialistic," Ryan said.

"What I am saying goes well beyond socialism. When everyone is connected, there will arrive a mind-to-mind awareness of each other. This is what I have with others of the armada. You see we truly all are one. The most severe obstruction imposed on earth-humans was to make you believe you were not."

"I think I see the extent of what you just said. I feel it; I'm not sure I'm comfortable with it. Isn't it like the communication within a bee hive?"

"Exactly." Sarah leaned over to kiss Ryan's cheek.

For the next few miles, Ryan mulled over what he had just seen and the conclusions he had reached. As they approached Kayenta he asked, "How do you square experiencing the difficult times of the interim with the armada providing the crystals?"

"The people of star civilizations are not heartless," Sarah replied. "They recognize that the enslavement was done against the will of Earth-humans, by beings not of this world. Fear and victimization is ingrained at the level of DNA, in fact some strands of your DNA were disconnected by the ancestors of the N'Roids to facilitate your enslavement. The energy coming to this planet from the armada will correct the faulty DNA, but still it is up to the people to learn how to relate to each other out of love rather than fear. The interim times will force people to help each other, or die. This will be a most beneficial experience. Keep in mind that many will choose to exit rather than experience the interim time."

"Changing the subject," Ryan said, "there are a lot of entrepreneurial people out there. They're just itching to find a better way. I feel that if we give them a chance, they'll make the switch."

"Aren't most entrepreneurs driven by money?"

"In my experience, really good entrepreneurs want to change the world. That's what I was doing at Sanitas. Men and women who start businesses primarily for money rarely succeed. I feel we can get a whole bunch of motivated people to help remake this country, this world. However, my more immediate need is for some pictures to go with a really great story."

"You already know several visitors, and I believe Ethete can convince one or two Hollywood people to pose beside a ship."

THIRTY-FOUR

"So what was that about?" John deBeque turned from his computer to greet Sarah and Ryan when they returned to Harmony's great room.

"Just another meeting with another Commander of another Starship," Ryan grinned. "She has a little job for you and me."

"Another Commander?"

"Yeah, about this tall." Ryan stretched his hand above his head. "Really quite attractive."

"Okay, so what's the deal?

Ryan walked to where John deBeque sat in front of his computer. "Remember the splash you made with Ernest Steiger's material?"

"Sure."

"We are going to do it again, only this time we are going to have pictures of starcraft and pictures of people from other star civilizations. This time we are going to convince the people of this world that our sisters and brothers from other star systems are benevolent, that they can help us remake our society, and that a whole armada of starships and people are ready to pitch in."

"We are enlisting a number of easily recognizable people to help us," Sarah said. Seeing the puzzled look on John deBeque's face she held up three fingers, "My brother, Ryan, and me. And others that Ethete will connect us with."

"What am I going to do?" Ethete asked as she joined the group.

"From your Hollywood days we are hoping you know a few people who would be willing to have their picture taken alongside a starship or saucer," Sarah said.

Ethete paused for only a moment, "I can think of a few. Where are you going to get a starship?"

"We just saw one," Ryan said, "in broad daylight."

Sarah said, "Commander Huenda has just informed me that she will divert her ship to our location when it is finished with the crystals. Also, saucers will be available when we have people lined up."

"Can someone please tell me what's going on?" John deBeque asked.

Sarah and Ryan spent the next hour telling John deBeque what they had seen and their ideas for helping to publicize the benevolent nature of it.

After that, Ryan went off to fire up the Sanitas particle monitor that he had brought from Colorado. It did not measure any aluminum and barium particles in the outside air intake for Harmony. Thinking this strange, he took the machine below. When he used it to sample particles inside the electrostatic filter, it registered a very high concentration of the base metals, plus an unknown biological substance. Coupled with the clear skies that he and the others had been observing, he could only conclude that although the aerosol spraying had stopped there were still residual particles left in the filter machinery. Feeling pressure to work on other things, Ryan made a note to dismantle and clean the filter mechanism another day.

At the urging of his spirit guide, Ryan worked to create a bulletin board for the site. Then he sent messages to the groups in Boulder and Fort Collins, inviting them to post messages that they wished to share with others. In this way he hoped to create an interconnected network of similar groups.

One page of the site was not activated: On it was an explanation of a new source of electrical energy to be supplied to the grids of countries around the globe. It was complete with pictures of Sarah and Ajax standing next to Commander Huenda and her starship, against the background of Fortress Mesa.

Ethete had contacted five readily recognizable actors and three actresses who had agreed to pose next to saucers. The backdrop was to be their homes in Malibu or Beverly Hills, California. One of the men was in Bangkok, Thailand, another in Nice, France. The critical and timely nature of their participation was explained to them, without giving them details of the crystals. All had been informed that they might be criticized for participating in this; all agreed nonetheless.

John deBeque contacted a direct mail house with which he had worked before. He made arrangements for them to distribute a flyer to every postal address in the United States. Then he set about making an attractive single sheet to explain that a new source of electricity was being furnished to the country's electrical grid from several locations. Each flyer featured a picture of Sarah with Commander Huenda and her starship. The flyer went on to make it plain that this gift, from humanity's sisters and brothers of another star civilization, was to tide humanity over until humans figured out how to produce their own sources of free non-polluting energy. John deBeque stuck in a link to the Civilization of Light web site for people who wished to stay up to date. Later that afternoon, he transmitted it from his computer to the direct mail company. They would distribute the flyers within two days.

The following day, when high definition pictures had been received from France, Thailand, and California, John deBeque drove to a pay-phone in Kayenta. There, he contacted four of his former employees each independent of the others, each of whom he was fairly sure was not an N'Roid. He had selected each of them for their relationships with powerful people in television. It was the first time they had heard from him; each was surprised to learn that he was still alive.

He told each of them that he wished to distribute a sensational news item, promising each a carefully worded press release with pictures. Based on deBeque's record of supplying insider information, three of the four agreed to receive the material, although they were skeptical of its content. The fourth said she would not participate in something that was going to be so obviously against the wishes of Mr. Greylock, regardless of how sensational it was. DeBeque then called several newspaper editors with whom he had established special relationships. This done, he drove Harmony's pickup to Flagstaff to deposit nine envelopes with FedEx.

The evening of that same day, the Executive Committee of the World League met. The six had remained at their underground facility since the meeting of the Planetary Council. Overhead, President Boyle had extended his vacation. The press was admitted for an announcement, which included the Secretary of Homeland Security whose office was temporarily at Windfree's estate, about new measures to combat terrorism.

After the meeting with the Planetary Council, a cadre of government officials and bureaucrats had been transferred to this and other underground retreats. Warren Ophir had been assured that between the numbers here and those in other protected sites they had sufficient numbers to continue the government in the face of the upcoming terrorist attacks.

"Everything is ready," Justin Ridgway said. He stood and walked to a world map that was projected onto the wall opposite Grant Clever's seat. Alongside it was a large map of the United States.

"I want to emphasize that our plan is surgical; not mass destruction, even though many humans will die." He paused as Clever shifted in his seat.

Seeing that the Chairman was ready to continue, he said, "The sheep are addicted to electricity and oil, now we will take away their narcotics, but not so much as to destroy productive capability in the long term. Coupled with the stress caused by economic failure and disease, the weak will call it quits; we will be left with a strong, but totally dependant population worldwide. This will ensure our continued leadership of the Planetary Council."

The others nodded their understanding of the plan's objective. Bustamonte gave Ridgway a yelp signifying his concurrence.

"The cities in red are our primary targets. Rather than merely bringing down tall buildings, as we did with the World Trade Center, we will disable entire metropolitan areas with EMP pulses from large scalar weapons. This will permanently disable anything electrical, and should raise the fear factor to its very highest. Without their accustomed comforts, many will not be able to cope." Toronto, Chicago, Washington, DC, and Los Angeles were highlighted. Paris, Moscow, Tokyo, and Hong Kong were also in red.

"Not Hong Kong," Olson said.

"Changing it will delay things," Ridgway said.

"Do it," Clever said. Ophir suspected that Clever was catering to Olson in order to secure his vote.

"Since you're wiping out the competition, why not Hong Kong?" Ophir asked.

Ridgway glanced at Olson for a response. "Our associates there have fallen into line," Olson replied over his shoulder as he had turned back to study Ridgway's maps.

"All our 'terrorists' in place?" Ophir asked.

"In position for the last week," Ridgway replied. "Now if I can focus everyone back on the maps, our forces will sever the main arteries of the U.S. grid as indicated, here, here, and here." At the touch of a button on his hand-held controller, yellow hash marks appeared. "You will notice that we positioned these to surround the crystal emplacement in South Dakota. Just to make absolutely sure, we will sever it in several other places and repeat that pattern in other countries.

"We will use small scalar impulses from mobile emplacements to bring down important buildings in cities around the globe." Small flashing white lights illuminated the major cities on every continent.

"And we will hit these refineries." Orange lights appeared on the map near Caracas, Baton Rouge, and Singapore.

Ridgway pushed more buttons and blue dots sprinkled the maps.

"What are these?" Jeremiah Goldman asked.

"Electrical generating plants. Our males, along with humans, are in place to disable them."

"Isn't that going too far?" Goldman asked.

"Not at all. Disabling these should create massive fear, plus it will overwhelm the armada's crystal generator. We suspect there may be more generators than the one we chanced to find on the Lakota reservation. This should take care of them also."

"We have enough personnel for all this?" Warren Ophir asked motioning to the two maps. It was obvious to him that additional preparations had been made without his knowledge. The scale of this attack was much greater than he had anticipated.

"Yes," Grant Clever replied.

"Why shut down DC?" Ophir asked. "I thought we needed people to run things."

"We will govern from here," Clever said arrogantly. "We must not allow others of our kind to take over what we have achieved. We will alert only our allies to seek shelter; those who oppose us will perish, along with the sheep."

"What about ships from the armada?" Jonathan Olson asked. "I have received additional warnings."

"We have not detected the movement of craft other than transporters," the Admiral replied. "Despite our precautions, I believe the armada has plans to install other sites, but is waiting to see how its first installation is received. If we act now, we can thwart their plan."

"The armada has touched nothing on this planet since they assembled seventy years ago," Ophir said. "There is more going on than supplying electricity."

"What about the nuclear warheads?" Goldman asked. "That's certainly touching something. And they already disabled HAARP and stopped our aerosol program."

"Any source of free electricity has huge implications," Olson said. "It spells the death of our refinancing plans. We must counteract it."

"Regardless of how this turns out, we still hold the strings to oil, the government, the military, and corporations," Clever said. "If the fear level increases, as we anticipate, we will not only tighten our grip, but may very well flip to planetary darkness."

"You are living in the past," Ophir said. "Never since our initial occupation of this planet have we seen the index at this level. There is more going on here than terrorist attacks will correct. That is why our overlord withdrew. As I have said before, I think we should depart and seek an easier target."

"I will not tolerate this kind of talk," Clever said.

"Depart to where?" Jeremiah Goldman asked. "As far as I know, this is our last stand. Let's face it, we have been abandoned to fight a rear guard action."

"Are we sure this plan preserves our communications network?" Jonathan Olson asked. "Without it our financial structure is back in the dark ages."

"Think about it." Ophir's right hand sketched lazy circles. "We get to hole up here, all nice and comfortable, without a clue as to what's going on outside. Not a pretty picture."

"We will not disturb the internet's arteries," Ridgway assured Olson. "We have calculated our disruptions to circumvent such problems. And we have satellite communications as a backup."

"I hope you're right," Ophir said. "I'd like to see the details."

"Of course," Ridgway replied.

"How about media management?" Clever asked.

"Our news affiliates have placed several versions of events in the hands of cooperative newspapers and television networks," Goldman said. "However, I am only cautiously optimistic that they will be used during the turmoil of blackouts and starvation."

"Stop, stop," Clever wailed. "I've had enough. This type of defeatist talk does no good. I say back Admiral Ridgway's plan -- only modifications as we discussed today. Who agrees with me?"

Henry Bustamonte, who had said nothing during the discussion, said, "I vote for moving forward."

"Yes," Olson agreed.

With four out of six members of the Executive Committee backing the resolution, Clever declared, "Admiral, proceed." He brought his heavy goblet of white powder down on the table for emphasis.

THIRTY-FIVE

The following day, Johnny Black Raven, along with Ryan and Ajax drove to Phoenix, Arizona, a three hundred mile trip. Ryan had driven there one time since he had returned to Harmony from rescuing Carlton Boyle. That time, it had been to visit his daughter Danielle and her family. Danielle's husband, Roberto, was focused on a new job that might mean relocation. Danielle was not at all sure she wanted to leave a community that she had grown to like. It was causing strain between them, so Ryan focused on his two grandchildren, Galen, three, and Catherine, six months.

He remembered sitting with Danielle and the two kids. The mood in the room was very quiet, as Galen played first with one toy, then another. He seemed quite content to amuse himself. Catherine lay on the floor softly cooing to herself, seemingly aware of all in the room. Ryan had been up since 5:30 making use of Danielle's computer to keep abreast of the news; the girls had arisen about 7:00; Roberto had gone out to an early morning appointment.

Ryan recalled other quiet moments such as this when he and his wife, Vicki, had enjoyed times with Danielle and her older brother, Darren. That was many years ago, before the kids grew up, before Vicki and he had divorced. Ryan had not seen Darren since returning to Harmony. His son had promised to visit as soon as his job allowed. To Ryan's great disappointment, neither Danielle nor Darren seemed to be interested in learning more about the larger reality.

After Johnny pulled his Ford Taurus into the parking lot for AMERICAN COIN, a storefront in a small strip mall near downtown Phoenix, Ryan got out and stretched from the five-hour drive. The idea for this trip had started when the price of the gold bars jumped another

238

thousand dollars apiece. Ryan had decided Johnny, who stood only five nine could use the company of two larger men. Ryan was over six feet tall; Ajax, who still retained some hulk from his football days, was six five. After convalescing, Ajax was feeling back to normal, but not quite as physically fit as when he had played professional ball. As things evolved, Ryan and Ajax planned to make other uses of this trip.

Not wishing to show a change of pattern, Johnny went into the shop alone. As was his custom, he pulled a rolling briefcase behind him. Through the front window, Ryan could see the manager greet Johnny and show him into the back room.

As they waited, Ajax and Ryan continued their discussion. "Our allies in the armada believe the N'Roids are desperate," Ajax said. "They have two ARVs, and can't produce any more because their production facility was wiped out. They have scalar weapons, but they don't want to start a fight with the armada, a fight they know they can't win, so they are planning other uses for the weapons.

"So what's left to them? We foresee that they will start a ruckus here on the planet's surface. Make people believe there are terrorist attacks going on everywhere. Engender lots of fear."

Ryan asked, "Won't the conventional military fight back?"

"That depends on whether the military brass are in on this. Some of them are N'Roids; others will lose their jobs if a positive transition happens."

"Good point."

"Think for a moment. What's your current civilization's greatest vulnerability?"

Ryan pointed to the signs along the strip mall.

"Right," Ajax nodded. "Take out electricity, you bring the whole country to its knees. If it continues long enough, the economy will tank, and lots of people will die. That's their plan; after all what do the N'Roids want from Earth, now that their puppet master is gone."

"What if the puppet master was still here?"

"All he cared about was sucking people's energies."

"Sucking energies?"

"Yeah, that's what he lived on: The dark energy of fear."

"And some of his influence is still here?"

"That's why it's taking so long to work our way through this. Some of the most enlightened people are being targeted with all kinds of mysterious problems. From what you've told me, I'd speculate that your financial losses -- everything crashing at one time -- had something to do with the dark one."

"And this dark entity still has that kind of power?"

"Everything is energy."

Johnny returned; he had been with the coin dealer a half hour. "He wouldn't take all we wanted to cash in," he said as he hefted the now much heavier briefcase into the back seat next to Ajax. "People are still buying gold, but they want coins like American Eagles and Maple Leaves. The process to turn the bars into gold coins was shut down two days ago by the Secret Service. I had to fill out some paperwork, some sort of a new regulation. I did get the bag of silver coins."

After leaving the coin dealer, Johnny then drove to Banc One, Wells Fargo, and Bank of America, where he deposited the checks he had received from the dealer into accounts in the name of Harmony. At each bank he received $9,500 in cash, the maximum cash allowed without reporting the transaction. He explained that the staff and gardeners at Harmony Center liked to be paid in cash, plus Sarah had never used credit cards. She had mentioned to Ryan that she withdrew money from "cash machines" when she needed it.

"So how do we sort out this whole economic situation?" Ryan asked as they pulled out of the parking lot at the last bank.

"I don't feel anybody knows for sure, even our brothers and sisters up there," Ajax said. "The N'Roids have constructed a very elaborate system based on debt, layered on debt, rolled over with more debt, and converted into debt-backed derivatives. I have some theories if you want to hear them."

"Sure." Ryan directed Johnny to the Marriott Courtyard, a hotel in Scottsdale he knew from his business travels.

After checking in, the three of them, with Johnny pulling the briefcase, went to Sam Wellborn's room.

Sam had arrived earlier that day. He had told Jessica Thurgood, his still temporary secretary at the White House, to set up an afternoon appointment with Guido Sproule to discuss tsunami-warning technology.

"This trip had better be worth it." Sam pointed a finger at Ryan as he ushered them into his room. He was dressed in a dark suit. The collar of his white shirt was open. He had been perspiring.

For the next ten minutes, the President's Special Assistant complained about having to fly out of Dulles International, because Ronald Reagan was closed, about his connection in Dallas Fort Worth, and about interminable security checks and delays. Due to increased ticket prices, which were being blamed on rising fuel costs and fewer passengers, the number of flights from DC to Phoenix was down to two a day, no non-stops. The increased security was due to an attack yesterday on a refinery in Venezuela, the number five petroleum supplier to the U.S. Venezuela had constructed its own refinery to supply gasoline and other processed products, rather than shipping crude oil to U.S. refineries.

After introductions and making sure the briefcase would be locked in the room, Johnny called a friend on the Pima Indian Reservation. It was not far from the eastern border of the Phoenix metropolitan area, a short drive away. He pulled a white envelope from the briefcase and put it in his back pocket. "This is from Sarah. I'm delivering it to my friend."

Sam, Ryan, and Ajax drove a short distance to a Mexican restaurant, La Cantina. As they drove, Ryan explained that Ajax was Sarah's brother. "I remember you now," Sam said, "the football player, great hands, very fast. I still think you should've won the Super Bowl."

After they were seated, everyone checked around to make sure they could not be overheard. They concluded that the Mariachi music and the other noisy diners would keep their conversation private.

Sam told Ryan and Ajax about his mysterious encounter with Carlton Boyle. "I'll never forget those eyes, very spooky."

"You came to the right people," Ajax said with a smile. "I feel we can help you."

They were served chips and salsa with their iced teas. Sam ordered carne asada from the attractive Mexican-American waitress. Ryan ordered shrimp fajitas; Ajax did the same.

"I'm having the damnedest time with all of this," Sam said. "On the one hand I love this country, love my job, and love my lifestyle, also my wife and kids. One the other hand I'm beginning to see what you've been telling me." He pointed his finger at Ryan for the second time that evening.

"I have now talked to enough people to believe a group of elitists is running this country -- for their own benefit. I've been so busy doing assignments for the President, and before that getting him elected, that I missed this entirely. Oh sure, there were wealthy contributors, and they wanted favors, but this is different. I saw something in the eyes of the guy I helped get elected that I can't explain."

"What you just said is going to make what we're about to tell you a whole lot easier." Ajax paused as their food arrived.

Ryan told Sam about his latest onboard visit. Remembering the words of Jesus, he paid close attention to Sam's expression of awe as he casually mentioned holding Jesus' hand -- Sam had attended the same Catholic grade school as Ryan.

While Ajax and Sam delved into their food, Ryan explained what he had learned about the explosion in Utah, about how it had been a nuclear device aimed at members of the armada, and how it had been returned to its maker just before it exploded.

"I'll be damned," Sam said, "something told me that site wasn't an alien base, or a terrorist hideout. So it's true, they were making ARVs there?"

"Looks that way," Ryan said, "planning to use them in a fake alien attack."

"For what purpose?"

"What do you remember about September eleventh two thousand one?" Ajax asked. "Where were you?"

"I was in Washington State, Boyle was the Governor. I was work-ing for him on policy matters and interfacing with the legislature. I remember very clearly being glued to the television the whole day. I also remember following things for the next few days."

"And how did you feel?"

"I was uh, horrified. The whole thing, the lives lost, the clouds of dust, all the people in New York who were affected. The way it changed everyone's perspective, just like that." Sam snapped his fingers.

"Right, the same as most people," Ajax said. "What you may not realize is that people who did not see it on television were also affected. There was a worldwide horror engendered by the event, an energy that all Earth-humans felt at some level. Their energy was registered by others throughout the galaxy."

"We're that connected?" Sam asked.

Ajax nodded as he forked a large bite of fajitas into his mouth.

"I thought nine eleven was staged," Ryan said. "If that's so, then why did it register as so horrific?"

"Most people now realize that it was not carried out by terrorists from another country," Ajax said, "but was a deliberate act by those in this country. Because we are all intimately connected, that realization, at a gut level, has been present for most people since the time of that event, even though many refuse to admit it. Humans were deliberately sacrificed to further an agenda. It is this realization, conscious or not, that made the event so horrible that we on other planets also felt it.

"That event worked so well, that the cabal is now planning an even more horrific one. By staging widespread terrorist actions, actions in which many people will die, the cabal hopes to flip the energy of this planet permanently into the dark. It's their last desperate act. If they are not successful in flipping it, they hope to generate enough fear to continue their grasp on power."

Sam sat his fork down very slowly. He said nothing, just stared with a blank look into the distance. Without disturbing him, Ryan gave the waitress a debit card that Sarah had loaned to him.

"You'll really like this next part," Ryan said as they walked from the restaurant. "There are millions of humans on this planet who are not Earth-humans."

"I don't understand."

"What I'm saying is that there are millions of men and women like Ajax here; they look human, but they were born on another planet, then migrated here. They are known as 'visitors.' More than that, there are millions of Earth-humans who have had other lives as humans and non-humans on other planets, and who have been trained there, who are waking up to the realization of that training. All are here to help the transformation of our planet. I met some of them on the starcraft."

"So we're back to my original question. What about Carlton Boyle's eyes? Are you telling me he's not human?" They climbed into Sam's rental and headed to another spot to talk.

"What happens if the wrong people overhear this conversation?" Ryan asked.

"We might be dead by morning," Sam said. He had told them about the death of Dr. Gordon Moore. "The real question is why are we still alive?"

"Because we still have some value to them," Ajax commented.

"Look, Sam, what I'm saying to you is that the Carlton Boyle you've been interacting with is not the real Carlton Boyle."

They pulled into the parking lot for the Cactus Rose. Ryan had asked the concierge at their hotel for his recommendation of a noisy bar. When they were seated at a table and their drinks were served, Ryan placed his arm around Sam's shoulder, his mouth close to Sam's ear. He told Sam about N'Roids, how they were the puppet masters of the elite cabal, and how they had the ability to shift into human shape.

Sam digested this while finishing his drink. He ordered a second Margarita on the rocks.

Ryan then told him how Sarah and Ethete had remotely viewed both the real Carlton Boyle and his stand-in. He did not say anything until he had drained the glass. "Thank God, I wasn't going crazy after all."

"Hard to believe, isn't it," Ryan said. "It has taken me over six months and two on board visits to get my head around this. I can only imagine what's going on for you."

"If it was anyone but you..." Sam did not finish; he just shook his head as if clearing it.

The President's Special Assistant looked across the table at Ajax. "So you're really Sarah's brother, huh?"

"Yeah."

"What the hell am I going to do?" Sam threw up his hands.

"Nothing at this moment," Ryan said. "Sarah told me I don't get to rescue Carlton Boyle a second time. That there's a bigger job she wants us to take on."

"Oh?"

"Yeah, our country, our world is about to get torn apart. We get to help put it back together."

"How?"

"Let's start small. Remember our conversation in Boulder?" Ryan asked. "Who have you determined you can trust?"

"With what you are telling me, probably damn few. Tiffany for sure, beyond her?" Sam shook his head "I had a feeling about Sally O'Hara; now I'm definitely steering clear. Chuck Brown is probably not one of them, probably honest, but he's too tied up in his career. Tony will find it hard to believe, but in the end he might come around. Glenn is too committed to the Secret Service." Sam ticked off the names of those he thought he could trust. He wrote them down on a slip of paper and handed it to Ryan. "Trouble is, I don't know if any of these are N'Roids. Check these out for me, will you?"

"Sure, but there's more," Ryan said. He went on to tell Sam about the N'Roids' underground facility in Colorado, and how Clever and Ridgway, both men that Sam knew, were N'Roids.

"I say we grab one of them," Sam said, "and parade him on television. Now all I have to do is figure out which one and who in the media will cooperate with me."

"John deBeque can help with the media," Ryan said.

They talked for another three hours. At midnight Sam said, "Guys, I'm in total overload. Can we grab some breakfast before my flight in the morning?"

THIRTY-SIX

When they returned to the hotel, they had expected to find Johnny, but his six-year-old red Ford Taurus was not among the few cars in the lot. They checked his room; he was not there.

'Johnny is dying.' The voice in Ryan's head startled him.

He fumbled for the slip of paper Johnny had given him and called Johnny's Pima friend, Michael Hightree.

"Johnny never came," the Pima said. "I've been waiting all this time."

"Where do you live?"

Ryan dialed the police who said they could not institute a search until twenty-four hours had elapsed. Ryan called Johnny's friend again and told him to start searching. The man gave Ryan directions to his house.

Twenty minutes later, as Ajax and he turned onto the dirt road to Michael Hightree's house, they saw the lights of police cars and an ambulance. As they crept forward, they saw Johnny's Ford; its front wheels were in a ditch on the side of the road, its windows were smashed. A stretcher being hoisted into the back of the ambulance; Ryan knew, without question, that it was Johnny.

Was this related to what Ajax and he had been discussing with Sam Wellborn, and why Johnny? The older Navajo had not been privy to the discussions among Sarah, Ajax, Ethete, John deBeque, and him. He was just a gentle grandfather helping out around Harmony Center.

"That man is my friend. Where are they taking him?" Ryan stopped a tribal policeman.

"Banner."

"Where's that?

"Mesa, Dobson Road."

They followed the ambulance, but soon lost it in traffic. Ryan used his cell phone to get the address and directions.

By the time they arrived at the emergency room, Johnny was already in surgery. They waited.

A half hour later, an older man wearing overalls and sporting a long gray braid approached them. He asked if they were Johnny's friends from Harmony. A younger man, in the uniform of the tribal police, was with him.

The tribal policemen wanted to know everyone's connection to Johnny. After he took down their statements and contact information, he left. The four sat down to wait.

With his head in his hands, Johnny's friend blurted out, "I'm responsible. I told people about Johnny bringing me money for the tribe." He went on to explain that the members of the tribe were in a bad way because the government had not increased their checks despite the inflation. Sarah, whom he had never met, had learned of it through Johnny. Whenever Johnny came to town, he brought $5,000 to help the most needy.

At midnight, a doctor approached the group. "We lost him. His internal injuries were just too severe. I'm very sorry."

"Internal injuries?"

"Yeah, his stomach was sliced open and his intestines pulled out, and he had claw marks all over his body. Almost looked as if a puma had attacked him. We'll have to wait for the autopsy to be sure. Oh, by the way, until we put him on anesthesia, he kept mumbling something like 'warn Drake,' over and over."

With a heavy heart, Ryan went back to the hotel. As soon as they entered the room, they saw that the briefcase was gone.

Knowing he could not call Sarah by phone until the next morning, he tried going into a meditative state, but his mind was too cluttered.

When he finally talked with Sarah the next morning, he discovered that Ajax had kept her informed on an almost minute-by-minute basis. Ajax and she had concluded that an N'Roid had attacked Johnny. In addition to the loss of a good friend, she would have the unpleasant task of telling Singing Bird about her husband.

He told her about his conversation with Sam and asked her to have John deBeque supply the name of someone in the Washington, DC area who would be willing to put an N'Roid on television and expose their scheme. Before they hung up John deBeque supplied a name. Now all Sam had to do was capture an N'Roid.

"You kept me awake all night," a bleary-eyed Sam said when they met for breakfast. He was downing his second double espresso. "Now this." Sam scooted a copy of The Arizona Republic across to Ryan and Ajax.

Half of the front page was filled with a color picture of James DeLuzia, a well-known actor. He was posing alongside a twenty-foot saucer shaped craft in front of his Malibu home. The headline read, THEY'RE HERE. Under it was a sub-heading: AND THEY BROUGHT A GIFT.

Ryan flipped the paper open to the third page: Three more photos, these in black and white. One of the photos was of Sarah with Commander Huenda and her starship. Sarah was reading a statement from the High Council of Star Civilizations, the coordinating body for the armada.

The statement, that Sarah, John deBeque, and he had composed, in cooperation with the Council, spoke of the gift to mankind. It offered additional assistance, but only if requested.

"Do you have any idea how huge this is?" Sam asked. "We're talking about a concrete gift from people of other star systems."

"This ought to convince people that their sisters and brothers are friendly."

"It ought to make people look at Sarah and me a whole lot differently," Ajax said.

"Wonder how this will affect the economy?" Sam asked.

"Why do you mention the economy?" Ajax asked.

"Because in this country everything is tied to oil."

Ryan smiled. "The interim time is definitely here. Wonder how the N'Roids will respond?"

"If I do capture one, how do I get him to drop his guise?" Sam asked.

"We need to find one who's willing," Ajax said.

"And how are you going to do that?"

"Give me a few minutes." The tall Phantian said as he got up to find a quiet place.

"Before this electricity thing came along, I would have said that things were beyond help," Sam said. "Now I'm a lot more optimistic. Tell me what to do."

"We need help figuring out how to restructure government," Ryan said. "Every time someone with high ideals is elected, they get submerged in the system. It's the system that's broken, and the N'Roids did it deliberately. If you closely examine history, you can see how they infected every new institution.

"People still have free will. Now it's up to us to choose a new way of getting along with each other. What I've come to understand is that fundamental change is called for, not just manifesting the next good thing for us individually -- I'm ready for a radically new way in which people relate to each other."

"How do you get people to overcome years of conditioning, a whole lifetime of living in fear?"

"With difficulty," Ryan replied.

"Everything is energy," Ajax said as he took his seat again. "That's the secret to changing the darkness. Light, or love, is the purest form of energy. My people and others like us are working to make this happen. Light is being beamed to the people of this planet. The very DNA of Earth-humans is changing. This is a truly historical moment; I hope Earth-humans will rise to the occasion.

"Do you remember meeting Stefan on the starcraft?" Ajax addressed the question to Ryan.

"Sure."

"I communicated with him." Turning to Sam he said, "Get in touch with Stefan Duncan; he knows an N'Roid that's willing to come over." He handed Sam a folded piece of notepaper from the hotel.

"And if that works out, here's a recommendation from John de-Beque." Ryan had printed the name and phone number of the television contact in his notebook. He tore out the page for Sam.

They talked until it was time to head for the airport for Sam's return flight. Since the police were holding Johnny's car as evidence, Sam told Ryan to drive his rental back to Harmony. They could return it to the agency when they came back to Phoenix to pick up Johnny's body.

"Things look good so far," Ryan commented. "Maybe we caught the N'Roids unprepared."

THIRTY-SEVEN

After Ryan Drake and Ajax Johnson wound their way out of Phoenix's Sky Harbor Airport and were on I-17 headed north toward Flagstaff, Ryan turned on the rental car's radio. Every news broadcast was filled with reports about the pictures of the craft and the announcement about free energy.

"You know if James DeLuzia is willing to have his picture taken with this thing, it's got to be real," a caller to a talk show said. "He's the president of the NRA."

From Florida came a report of a public utility leveling charges of unfair competition. The State Assembly in Vermont had met early this morning and voted to give all users, households and business, a one-month holiday from paying utility bills, and to direct the Vermont Public Utilities Commission to recalculate utility rates.

"How do we know they're friendly?" one caller moaned. "Maybe this is just a ruse to lull us into stepping aside so they can invade and take over."

"I say we wait and see," another caller retorted, "sure, I'll take their free energy, but I want to know their real intentions. I want to know where this free energy is coming from."

During an interview, a congressman from Texas was quoted as saying, "I believe the sovereign rights of this great country have been trampled upon. What gives them the right to offer free energy in competition with legitimate oil producers? This is against God's law. We must refuse this unholy gift."

Scanning until he found a public radio station, Ryan and Ajax listened to reports from the BBC. A junior member of the Saudi Royal Family said that he welcomed the gift of free energy. "Now my country can produce oil for use as a chemical feedstock for higher value products. We will build petrochemical plants on our soil, rather than selling our black gold to others. This will free my country from depending on the military might of the West."

The President of India said he welcomed the gift of free energy so that all his people could now improve their lives. Companies in India would benefit in major ways from energy independence. Recognizing that the crystals might be a temporary measure only, he nonetheless proposed a plan to immediately extend the electrical grid to under-served areas.

With the stocks of public utilities, the financial sector, and all oil company stocks under extreme selling pressure, the New York Stock Exchange stopped trading. Foreign stock exchanges had taken similar measures. The Federal Reserve offered to make up to a trillion dollars of new debt, at virtually zero interest, available to companies affected by free energy. A congressional panel promised to begin an investigation into the legality of free energy.

In a message from the estate of Douglas Windfree, where he continued to vacation, President Boyle stated that he did not believe free energy was legal. He promised the American people that he would personally do everything in his power to make sure the current situation, which was so disruptive of the very basis of capitalism, worked out to their best interests.

He also said that the current rash of bank failures should not discourage people from getting out and going shopping. Despite the high cost of gasoline and food, there was never a better time to stock up on those little extras for family and friends.

Radio reception came and went as Ryan drove north. They turned east on U.S. 160. During the off periods, Ryan and Ajax discussed the history of financial disasters on Earth, the way money was used on other planets, and ramifications of the death blow the imploding U.S. economy had received from free energy. They both agreed that neither the U.S. economy, nor the government that backed it, would last. This was going to happen, whether or not the N'Roids carried out their fake terrorist attack.

"This is Earth-humans' big chance to start anew," Ajax said. "Your sisters and brothers from other star systems are easing the way with the crystals; the institutions that have been supporting the N'Roids are collapsing. What more can you ask for?"

When Ryan stopped at Tuba City to find fuel, he encountered a long line at both service stations. The price for unleaded gasoline had dropped by two dollars.

After buying a tank full, they returned to US 160 and continued their drive east. As the miles passed, each man was absorbed in his own thoughts. Ajax closed his eyes.

Suddenly he jolted awake. "I just got a communication from Sarah. Did you receive anything?" he asked Ryan.

"Nothing."

"She said something about N'Roids and Harmony. Then it faded. Let me see if I can view it."

The Phantian closed his eyes. After a few moments, with his eyes still shut, he said, "There is a contingent of N'Roids at Harmony. It appears that when she sensed them approaching, Sarah secured the steel doors over the entrance from the large hogan. They are now trying to break in through the dome."

"I watched Sarah fend off a helicopter attack," Ryan said. "Why is this any different?"

"I'm guessing the N'Roids threw some sort of an energy barrier over the whole facility."

"So what can we do?"

"I've already let our allies know what's going on."

Ajax went silent again for a few moments. Ryan pulled over to the side of the road and dug out the map of Arizona the car rental company had supplied. It showed a minor road across Black Mesa to Pinon. Ryan reasoned that from there they could approach Harmony from the south, maybe even hike the last mile.

Ryan pulled open the map and showed the alternate road to Ajax. "Too far," Ajax said, "besides what did you think we were going to do against armored vehicles. Let's keep going. I want to get close enough to see the action. I'm also interested to see what that N'Roid in the car behind us is going to do."

Ryan glanced in the rearview mirror; a black car, a speck in the distance, was stopped at the side of the road.

An hour later, Ryan and Ajax pulled onto the road leading to Harmony Center. The front gate, a twisted pile of metal, had been pushed to one side. As they drove closer, there were no signs of vehicles or N'Roids. They parked Sam's rental before the large hogan.

"What's that smell?" Ryan asked.

"The vehicles of the N'Roids were dematerialized," Ajax said. "I would have loved to have watched that."

'Be cautious. There is one among us.' Sarah's communication resonated in Ryan's head.

"Did you get that?" he asked Ajax.

"I sure did."

Ryan and Ajax rushed into the large hogan. The thick metal door blocking the stairway was still in place. "We're not getting in this way," Ryan said. "You said you saw them enter through the dome."

"Right. Is there another way?" Ajax asked. "I'd like to enter quietly."

Ryan thought for a moment, then pointed toward the small hogan that stood a few yards away. He had not been in it since the first tour of the facility Sarah had given him months ago.

"The incinerator, of course," Ajax said. "Come on."

The door to the small hogan hung by a single hinge. Upon entering, Ryan saw that there was a large pile of trash next to the six-foot high metal incinerator in the middle of the hogan. It was waiting for Johnny's return.

The door to the stairway leading down was closed. Ryan tried the handle; it was locked. "They didn't get in this way," he said. In frustration he banged on the door, "damn it."

"Who is there?" a quiet voice from the other side of the door asked.

"Singing Bird? Is that you?"

"Mister Ryan?"

"Yes."

The latch on the door scraped. When it opened, Ryan saw the face of the white haired grandmother. She had her finger to her lips. "He has Sarah, Ethete, and John."

"Where?"

"The great room."

"It's safe. Come out here." He motioned her through the door.

Ajax and Ryan stepped onto the landing and listened. All was quiet.

After descending the metal stairs to Harmony's major hallway, Ryan motioned right. He and Ajax crept toward the back door to the kitchen.

Without a sound, they moved through the kitchen to the swinging doors leading to the sound of voices. Ryan took a peek through the glass portal in one of the doors. He motioned for Ajax to do the same.

A sleek headed being in a black military uniform stood with his back to them, one claw resting on a cane. The gun in his other claw was trained on John deBeque, who along with Sarah and Ethete was standing against the far wall of the great room. Ryan estimated it was about twenty feet to the creature.

"You were to infiltrate these." He motioned to Sarah and Ethete. "You did not follow your orders. You are a traitor to our way."

"I found them to be more than you could ever imagine," John deBeque said. "They are truth and love. You defile the planet that has given you so much."

"Do you have any idea how much damage you have done? You have ended it all."

Before Ryan or Ajax could react, the gun barked three times.

John clutched his chest.

Ethete screamed. "No, John, no." She rushed to him. Then there was silence broken by the sound of Ethete sobbing as she rocked back and forth, holding John deBeque's limp body.

Ryan nodded once to Ajax.

They burst through the doors, covering the intervening distance in a matter of seconds.

The creature whirled, one claw clutching his cane. He brought the pistol up to fire.

Remembering his former NFL training, Ajax was already plunging toward Warren Ophir. He tackled the N'Roid around the ankles.

"No," Ophir yelled as his bad leg buckled beneath him.

Right behind Ajax, Ryan grabbed for the gun, but not before Ophir got another shot off. The bullet whizzed by Ryan's head, embedding itself in the ceiling. Ryan landed on top of Ophir, knocking the wind out of both of them. Ryan recovered first and grabbed Ophir's cane. He was about to bash him in the head when Sarah shouted, "No."

In one swift motion, Ajax rolled Ophir onto his stomach, pulling his arms behind him.

Ryan loosened the belt from around his own waist. He lashed the N'Roid's wrists, tightening the belt as firmly as possible.

But Ajax did not climb off. "Get me some of those plastic ties from the kitchen," he said. "This guy is really strong."

A half hour later, Ajax and Ryan waited next to the large hogan. Warren Ophir lay on the ground at their feet. Sarah had remained in the great room with Ethete.

Ajax had communicated with the A'Roids to tell them they had missed picking up the leader of the invaders; he also told them to capture the N'Roid waiting in the car where the road to Harmony intersected the main highway.

"So how did Warren Ophir manage to hide?" Ryan asked.

"He impersonated one of the A'Roids who was hunting him down," Ajax said. "This is a good rehearsal. Now they know the abilities of those who they're dealing with."

"I feel very bad about John," Ryan said, "particularly for Ethete."

"John did what he came here to do," Ajax said, "move from the dark to the light. His story demonstrates it for everyone."

A white Ford pickup roared into the parking lot. Ben Tsotsie and two other Navajos jumped out. "What's going on? Me and my crew watched the saucers come swooping down. All of our gear went dead. My truck wouldn't start until just now."

"Another raid on Harmony," Ryan said.

"This is getting to be a habit." With a startled look, Ben pointed to Warren Ophir on the ground. "Man, that is one ugly dude."

Ryan smiled, "Things are about to get real interesting. You may want to find a TV and watch." He went to the rental car and handed Ben a copy of this morning's Arizona Republic. "Wish we had one."

"If you'll supply me a little gas, I know where there's an extra TV," Ben said.

"Deal." The lack of TV at Harmony had been a source of pride for Ryan. The satellite company had even supplied a TV tuner along with its communications link, but Ryan had not bothered to purchase a television set.

At that moment, a saucer materialized a few yards away. Two A'Roids in dark green garb descended from its underside.

Ben's two Navajo workers ran for cover behind the pickup. With his mouth open, Ben stood rooted to the gravel of the parking area.

'Sorry we missed him,' one of them communicated. *'You say he was their leader?'*

'Not only the leader of these invaders, but most likely a member of the Board of the World League,' Sarah communicated.

'We will know soon enough.'

'And the other?' Ajax motioned toward the main highway.

'We have him already.'

The larger of the two A'Roids picked up Warren Ophir and slung him over his shoulder. Their ship dematerialized shortly after they entered it.

"Am I gonna have stories for my grandchildren or what," Ben said.

"Yes, you are going to have stories," Ryan said. "And it's not over yet. I'd like to get that TV."

"I'm headed to my folk's home in Kayenta," Ben said. "My days of digging are over. There's no more money to pay for anything. We were just cleaning things up and getting ready to head out when all the excitement happened."

"Come on," Ryan said, "Let's get your gasoline."

"Pick up our stolen briefcase when you drive by that N'Roid's car," Ajax shouted after Ryan as Harmony's pickup followed Ben's out of the parking area. "I told the A'Roids to leave the car; we can use another vehicle around here."

THIRTY-EIGHT

Sam's flight back to Washington had been uneventful, despite a delay of three hours leaving Phoenix. The first-class meal reminded him of the old days when most airline food had been tasty. The whole time he had eaten, he had thought about the amazing information Ryan Drake had given him about N'Roids, about free energy from crystals, and how Sarah and Ryan had orchestrated the appearance of benign UFOs. Amazingly, the part about free energy had made it into the newspapers and onto the TV. How would the economy react? Would people now behave differently? He dozed off with thoughts of what an altruistic government would be like.

Sam was jolted from his nap. "This is the first officer speaking. We have been diverted to Richmond, Virginia. Traffic coming into Dulles International from overseas has taken priority over domestic traffic. Immediately place all your things under the seat in front of you, and return all seats and tray tables to their original position. We will be descending rapidly."

In less than twenty minutes they had landed. Through the gathering dusk, Sam could see that they were taxiing toward the terminal. Without further explanation, the plane came to a standstill; the engines were shut down.

The captain came on the speaker and said, "Folks, sorry about that abrupt landing. We were told that we must divert. My instructions are to keep you onboard until I get further details. I will keep you informed."

Sam tried to use his cell phone to call Maggie. It rang and rang; Maggie did not pick up.

Sam motioned to the cabin attendant and asked her to lean toward him. "Tell the captain I want to talk with him," he whispered. He handed her his White House identification. "I'm the President's Special Assistant. I believe I know what's going on."

In a few minutes, the cabin attendant returned, "The captain says he'll speak with you. Act as if you are headed to the restroom; knock and he'll let you slip into the cockpit."

A few moments later Sam was introducing himself to Captain Lawrence Osage, a middle aged veteran of twenty years with the airline. "So, Mr. Wellborn, what can you tell me? I hope this is not another nine eleven."

"It's a little like that, only bigger," Sam said. "It's going on all over the world."

"No wonder they forced us down," Osage said.

"Okay, so let me tell you what I know, then I want you to let me off this plane. I've got to get back to DC."

Since it did not look like his airplane was going anywhere anytime soon, the captain excused his first officer and told Sam to take the copilot's seat.

As Sam began to talk, he became more confident that fate had placed him in the hands of the one airline captain who might actually believe his incredible story. It turned out that Captain Osage, who was based in Denver, knew about Sarah Smith, remembered that she and Ryan Drake had rescued the President, and was a student of conspiracies surrounding the attack on the World Trade Center. Once Sam heard this last part, he was pretty sure he could unload enough information to get himself off the airplane. They started with the attack on the World Trade Center.

"I've seen sufficient evidence to know that an airplane could not have brought down those buildings," Osage said. "No way that jet fuel can burn hot enough to melt steel. It was a controlled demolition. I know it was, just like you see with other buildings. How they did it, I don't know, but there are too many unanswered questions. So count me as a total skeptic of the government and media's line. This bull today reminds me of what happened when they grounded all of us then. What a mess. It took days to get back in operation."

"Don't lose that thought," Sam said. "This is another false flag operation."

At that moment, the cockpit radio crackled. "To all aircraft at Richmond International Airport. We have been advised that the United States of America is under attack. All military forces are on high alert. I am relaying the following message from The Federal Aviation Administration." The message said in simplest terms that all commercial and business aircraft were prohibited from flying. All craft that could not identify themselves as U. S. military would be shot down. A separate announcement from the Department of Homeland Security said that martial law was now in effect and would be strictly enforced. All passengers would be deplaned at their current locations.

Then a message was relayed from the President, speaking from a secure location in Colorado. The captain put it on the cabin speakers so that all passengers could hear. "My fellow Americans, at 6:01 East Coast Time terrorists attacked Washington, DC, similar attacks have been reported around the world. This unwarranted assault will be repulsed with all available force.

"I am requesting that all citizens take shelter. Do not venture out unless absolutely necessary. We will keep you informed."

Sam said, "The next thing they will report will be the destruction of the electrical grid, then blackouts of major cities."

"Why do you say that?"

"I've been given their plans."

A half hour later, Sam had convinced the tower to allow Captain Osage's plane to taxi to one of the unoccupied gates. In another half hour he had talked his way into the last rental, a nine passenger SUV, at a rental rate of two hundred fifty dollars a day, plus an additional two hundred for a full tank of gasoline. Skirting the city of Richmond on I-295 he headed north on an Interstate void of traffic.

He switched on the SUV's radio and found a familiar station out of Washington. "We are under attack, please seek shelter. This is an emergency broadcast." The message kept repeating itself. "We are under attack, please seek shelter. This is an emergency broadcast."

Sam switched to a station out of Richmond. "We have no reports out of Washington; the entire city, plus surrounding areas, is completely blacked-out."

He found an area with cell phone service. He called Maggie to tell her he was on his way. Again, the phone rang and rang with no answer. He then called Tiffany at her home; she did not answer, so he left a message.

He switched the radio back on. The newscast was saying that things in Richmond seemed to be operating normally. They were experiencing no power disruptions. Then the commentary was interrupted for a report from Baton Rouge, Louisiana. A gasoline and chemical refinery was ablaze.

At exit 104 from I-95, Sam pulled off at a truck stop. Everything seemed to be operating normally, but its back lot was filled with semis. Inside the crowded truck stop he found a pay phone and dialed the number Ajax had given him.

"This is Stefan."

"Ryan Drake told me to get in touch with you," Sam said.

"I have been expecting your call."

"You have?"

"Can you meet me in Maryland?" Stefan asked.

"You have what I am looking for?"

"Yes."

"Will tomorrow be soon enough?"

"I understand," Stefan said. "Call when you leave Virginia. Here is the address. Stay completely away from DC."

Sam continued north, turning off I-95, onto the darkened road leading to his home.

THIRTY-NINE

The following morning, April 1st, Sam drove to meet with Stefan Duncan. Skirting the Washington, DC area, he picked up US 15 at Opal, Virginia, and drove north. At the border with Maryland, traffic was at a standstill. Ahead Sam could see where two Abrams Main Battle Tanks were blocking the road, funneling traffic into a single lane.

As he waited in the lineup, he listened to a broadcast from Baltimore. Los Angeles and Washington, DC were without electricity. Portions of the nation's electrical grid had gone down. Crews were out everywhere trying to restore electrical power. The broadcasts were a jumble of conflicting reports. All of them attributed the situation to multiple attacks by terrorists.

The prior evening Sam had arrived at his home to find his neighborhood of expensive homes on large wooded lots totally in the dark. He had pulled the SUV into the driveway, leaving the lights on. Sam unlocked the side door and pushed the button to raise the garage door. Nothing happened.

After stumbling through a dark garage he managed to raise the door manually. Maggie's car was gone. He fumbled through shelves in the garage to find a flashlight.

He had entered his house from the garage. From the dim light of the flashlight, Sam saw that Maggie had left a note on the kitchen table. Not taking time to read it, he put it in the pocket of his coat. Feeling like an intruder in his own home, he fumbled around in shadows for a set of fresh clothes. Their second car, a three-year old Mercedes SL550 was in the garage. The engine turned over, but that was the extent of it.

Back in his rental, he had read Maggie's note of the prior day. It was a rambling letter that talked about being left alone, about her favorite shopping center closing, that there might not be enough food to eat, and that, after the latest burglary, she did not feel safe in their house. She had driven to her sister Adriel's home in Roanoke. Not knowing the extent of what he might be dealing with here, Sam was not about to undertake the three and a half hour drive to Roanoke.

After he locked his house, Sam had driven south toward Fredericksburg. In a few miles, lights were once again working, although few vehicles were on the roads.

Apparently the cell towers here had not been affected, as he was connected to Maggie's sister's number. No one answered, so he left a message saying he was okay.

It took Sam a while to find a motel with a vacancy. Along the way, he took the opportunity to top off the tank of the monster he was driving. After searching for an hour he found a motel not far from I-95.

As soon as he had entered the motel room, Sam switched on the television. He soon discovered that each of the channels out of DC had a similar notice: SERVICE UNAVAILABLE. The only local information was to be found on the channel out of Richmond where a weary anchor was repeating what he had learned from the national news. By comparison everything in Richmond was normal.

CNN was reporting that it had lost communications with its reporters and correspondents in Washington, DC. There were reports of no telephone service and no traffic moving. Reports of buildings collapsing were coming in from other cities along the East Coast.

During the hour he watched, Sam saw more pictures of famous personalities posing next to benign looking saucers. He saw one picture of Ajax Johnson playfully holding up a large starship.

Knowing that he had no chance of contacting Ryan Drake until he could post something on the hidden web page, Sam had gone to bed feeling like a frontier scout in an old Cowboy and Indian movie -- alone in enemy territory and very tired.

Now as he sat waiting to cross the border into Maryland, he reflected on his personal situation. Maggie had never wanted to face up to the possibility that their comfortable lifestyle might be interrupted. Since moving to the DC area, she had become accustomed to constant parties and shopping in expensive stores. He was sure that she would tell him that without electricity their house was not habitable. He was very glad she had gone to be with her sister. But what was he going to do? He felt that he had to stay in the DC area. He repeatedly dialed the number for her sister's house. It was constantly busy.

The line inched along as vehicles were inspected and either allowed to proceed or turned back. The whole process reminded Sam of an international border crossing. If similar restrictions were in force at every state border, it was bound to foster fear and would further inhibit the already disintegrating economy.

He recalled his conversations with Ryan and Ajax. Had he been in Arizona just yesterday? In his mind he went over everything they had discussed. Holding hands with Jesus? He should have gotten up and walked out of that Mexican restaurant, except something inside had told him that Ryan Drake was telling the truth. Holding hands with Jesus on board a starcraft. Wow, it was really a lot to swallow, until he thought about the other things.

About a vast armada of starcraft, hovering out of sight, beaming energies to Earth and its inhabitants. How people from civilizations in distant star systems were cooperating to ensure the transition of Earth and her people.

How the energy of individual humans affected everything, from plants to other people. He had learned that incredible energies would be expressed if humans learned to work together, focused their collective energies in the right direction.

An unwelcome nuclear device had been in the process of being returned to the Utah site when it had exploded. That facility had been used to manufacture ARVs. The explosion at that facility had stopped a fake alien attack.

There was a race known as the N'Roids, who had, long ago, enslaved the primitive population of Earth, and who had managed to retain control of the planet, in one way or the other ever since, despite mankind's growth and development. There were cousins of the N'Roids, known as A'Roids, who were opposing the enslavers. And how both the N'Roids and the A'Roids were able to shift into human form. And how an N'Roid had replaced his friend, President Carlton Boyle. Grant Clever and Admiral Justin Ridgway, men that Sam knew, were in reality N'Roids.

How this false flag terrorist attack was part of their scheme to create fear, fear that all humanity would feel in their guts, and how humanity's collective fear would be registered by all beings in the galaxy. And how in one last desperate attempt the N'Roids were hoping these events would flip the energy of Earth's remaining people permanently into the dark. The N'Roids did not really care that vast numbers of people would die, as long as they stayed in control.

There were millions of beings from other planets on Earth at this time, working for the benefit of mankind, most of them humans. Humanity's sisters and brothers from other star civilizations had been assured that their contributions would lead to success, that the planned darkness would not take over. And how it was now just a matter of playing out the drama, a matter of seeing how long and how dark the tunnel was before they emerged into the light.

As he inched past the treads of the two massive tanks, Sam noticed how they seemed to be binding. He studied it more closely and saw that some of the rollers were fused to the treads, as if they had been hit with a welding torch. "These sure aren't going anywhere," he muttered to himself. Sam had spent two years in a tank battalion; he knew a piece of crippled hardware when he saw one.

Sam thought about the gift of free energy, thought about the pictures of Sarah, Ajax, and other famous people, pictures of them next to craft from other planets. And he thought about how the beings who had brought free energy were offering additional assistance. And he compared it to the attitude toward aliens being portrayed on the television and radio.

He called Ester Randall, the mid-day program director at WZQY in Baltimore. This was the person that John deBeque had recommended. He briefly explained whom he was, and that he wanted someone to interview a non-human. With national coverage hogging her time slots, Ester was eager for a local story, even if it was something really weird. Sam told her he wasn't sure exactly when they might arrive.

"Mr. Wellborn, are you sure this is not an April 1st joke?"

"Absolutely. I will show you my White House credentials. I report directly to the President."

Eventually it was Sam's turn to cross into Maryland. He was asked to open all door locks and step out of the vehicle. He showed his government credentials.

"First one of these today," the sergeant said. He was dressed in battle fatigues. "How'd you get out of DC?"

"I wasn't in."

"Lucky you," said a second man who was inspecting the underside of Sam's vehicle with a mirror.

"Purpose of your visit to Maryland?"

"Classified."

"Okay, have a good one." He waved Sam ahead.

"A question Sergeant. What happened to your tanks? I notice they are not functioning. I know because I used to man one of those things, Third Battalion."

"Sir, we were hoping no one would notice."

"Don't worry, they won't son. So?"

"As soon as we parked them here last night, everything went dead, mechanical, electrical, everything. It was like it just froze."

Sam smiled. His instincts told him that a beam from space had done it, a small demonstration from their benevolent cousins with superior technology. No one got hurt, just a gentle nudge in the right direction. "Thank you Sergeant. And have a good day yourself."

In Frederick, Maryland, Sam turned down a side street. He made two additional turns, arriving at a two-story colonial mansion with a large front lawn and a circular driveway. He pulled in behind a brown Chevrolet Malibu.

As he was walking toward the front door of the house, it opened. A man in his forties greeted him, "I am Stefan."

Sam entered and the door was quickly shut behind before any further words were exchanged. When he looked back at Stefan, the man's eyes had changed to the vivid yellow of an A'Roid. Sam stumbled away.

"I will not harm you," Stefan said. "I met your friend Ryan Drake on board the starcraft, along with Sarah. We are on the same team." More of his A'Roid features emerged.

"But..." Sam was lost for words.

"Relax." Stefan smiled through jagged teeth. "I am not one of them. Martial law has interrupted the N'Roids' ability to follow you since you left the aircraft in Richmond. At the border crossing the equipment was unable to report you to their computers because of electrical failure. Rest assured, I am an A'Roid."

Sam relaxed a notch when he recalled his discussion with Ryan Drake.

Stefan's human façade returned. Smiling through humans lips, he said, "Come, I have a very special person I would like you to meet. She works at Navy intelligence."

They entered a room with a very high ceiling. On the sofa was a young woman in her twenties. She was dressed in a conservative blue skirt and a white blouse.

"Sam, I'd like to introduce you to Rosemary."

Sam extended his hand to greet Rosemary as she rose from the sofa. As she extended her hand, it turned into a scaled claw with pointed talons for fingernails. Her face assumed a radically different look.

Sam took a deep breath. His hand went limp. "I sure wasn't ready for more of this," he said turning back to Stefan.

Rosemary motioned him to a seat on the sofa next to her.

Stefan said, "Rosemary is an N'Roid. Her family members are all N'Roids. Her brother was a pilot who had manned one of the ARVs that was destroyed in the explosion. Her father is a highly placed man at the Justice Department. Her mother is politically active."

"Why are you doing this?" Sam asked.

"I see the problems my kind are causing," she replied. "For some reason, I am more sensitive than the rest of my family to the light. I have known this since I was a little girl being raised in the underground nursery. It has been a real challenge to hide it from the others. My mother suspects, but she has said nothing."

"And you are willing to show your ability to shift on television?"

"Yes, if it will help."

"What about your family?"

"They will disown me."

She said it so dispassionately that Sam was taken back. He stared at her.

"My kind have much less connection to family and things of the heart than humans."

"What will happen when you go public?"

"Do not be concerned for me. Stefan has made arrangements."

The way in which she said it bothered Sam, but it was too late to turn back now. "I have talked with someone at WZQY in Baltimore. How soon can we do this?"

"How about now?" Rosemary shifted back to her human façade.

"You're going to make a huge impression."

"I know."

"I have arranged for her protection," Stefan said. "She will be taken on board after she shows herself."

"And what about you?" Sam directed the question to Stefan.

"I too will leave this planet. I will lose my anonymity after I shift before the cameras; N'Roids will hunt me down."

"Wow." Sam stood and shook his head. What had he gotten himself into? Well, at least he wasn't going to be in front of the cameras. "Okay, let's do it."

FORTY

The television that Ben had traded Ryan Drake for gasoline was old. Last evening Ryan and Ajax had spent an hour wiring it to the control box of the satellite dish and getting reception authorized by the satellite signal provider. They had placed the set on a table in the sitting area of Harmony's great room, oriented so Ryan could also see it from the chair in front of his computer.

Ajax, Ethete, Sarah, and he had stayed up late, scanning the various channels, watching interviews with frantic reporters from around the country. Most were discussing the numerous explosions and fires, along with pictures of emergency vehicles. One network had developed a map marking where the terrorists had hit.

Ryan had arisen early and returned to the television, scanning the major news networks, stopping when he saw something of interest. As day had dawned on the East Coast, the reports had changed. This morning, there was footage of rubble and fires, and interviews with hysterical people who had been rescued, and pictures of people searching for loved ones.

Sketchy reports were coming from other countries where there had also been explosions and fires, where substantial damage had occurred and lives had been lost.

The networks focused on the blackout out of Washington, DC, and the surrounding area. As day broke, a few people had straggled out of the darkened area of Virginia across the Potomac; others had emerged in Maryland, several had ridden bicycles. Their stories were much the same: Computers, even laptops, and cell phones were not working. No vehicles were moving. No electricity.

U.S. military personnel in full battle attire had surrounded DC to prevent looters from entering the city. A similar situation was being reported around Toronto. Ryan noted an absence of heavy military hardware; also there were no pictures of military aircraft. News helicopters were banned from flying in the afflicted area around DC on the basis that terrorists might somehow utilize them to inflict more damage.

Scattered reports, via telephone and the internet, from cities in the Mid West told of damage to tall buildings. Large areas of the country were reportedly without electrical power.

Two buildings had collapsed in New York; otherwise it was largely unaffected by attacks or by electrical blackouts. Stock and commodity markets had not reopened, since they had been shut down by the announcement of free energy. Many retailers had shut down because people had already left the city due to a lack of food and its high price. There were reports that trucking companies were unwilling to deliver to New York and other cities due to restrictions imposed by martial law.

By 7:15 AM, Mountain Time, heavy trading in gold had pushed the price of one ounce to a new record of nineteen thousand six hundred forty three dollars.

At 7:30 AM, Mountain Time, President Boyle issued a statement from Colorado. He assured the people of America that terrorists who were behind the attacks were being pursued. He went on to say that since the Nation's Capital did not appear to be functioning, he and his top advisors would remain in Colorado and govern from there. "We have been unjustly attacked; we will respond with courage. Please stay calm and cooperate with law enforcement agencies.

"I am hereby directing military and law enforcement authorities to detain all people who are not citizens of the United States. Martial law will remain in effect until all terrorists are apprehended. All law enforcement agencies are hereby required to submit to control by federal authorities.

"All federal employees are to report to their local offices, which offices have been supplied with directives in the case of just such a national emergency. Key government functions like Homeland Security, the FBI, ATF, the CIA, NSA, and the IRS will continue to operate normally."

Ryan thought it was interesting what the President did not say. He did not address the failed monetary system, did not address food supplies or shipping issues, and did not talk about the free energy being supplied by the crystals. Nor did he mention the military.

Television networks were reporting that electricity was out in many areas across the Northeast and the upper Midwest. It was reminiscent of the blackout in 2003. That time it had been a cascading of the grid shutting itself down. Experts were claiming this power failure had originated in Toronto, which appeared to be in the same situation as Washington, DC. Repair crews from electric utilities were busy repairing the damage.

Television signals coming from satellites appeared to be unaffected by the electrical disruptions. In fact, new channels seemed to have begun operations since Ryan had last paid attention to TV -- that wretched night in Boulder, after learning of his abysmal financial situation. Signals coming from satellites appeared to have been undisturbed by the terrorist attacks.

Reports from the West Coast said that San Francisco and Seattle had suffered damage to tall buildings, however there were only minor disruptions in electrical service. In Portland, the Wells Fargo Tower had been decapitated at the thirty-fifth floor; fires were still burning within its steel shell. There were still no reports from Los Angeles, although Orange County, to the south, and Ventura County to the north, were functioning almost normally. National Guard units, along with local police, patrolled the streets of all cities, strictly enforcing martial law.

One report from downtown Detroit told how the central building, the Detroit Marriott Hotel, had collapsed on itself, falling to the ground in the matter of a minute. "Just like the World Trade Center," the man had said. Photos taken, with an old thirty-five millimeter camera, showed the walls collapsing.

By 9:00 AM new reports from across the United States told of explosions at coal-fired generating plants. One channel pinned these on environmental groups who somehow had coordinated their attacks with those of the terrorists. Military and police units were sent to guard power stations that were still active. Many utilities had begun the process of shutting down their older generators in the face of free electricity. One web site proposed that the sabotage was the work of the so-called benevolent beings who were trying to corner the supply of electricity.

A fire at the Baton Rouge refinery complex was given only a cursory report. It was linked to the wave of sabotage at utility power stations. A National Guard unit was dispatched to guard the facility.

Reports coming in from around the globe were similar: Buildings destroyed. Explosions at coal-fired plants. Large areas without electricity.

The leaders of other countries uniformly blamed the chaos on attacks by terrorists and called for the populace to stand up to the attackers, obey the law, and cooperate with established authorities. An expanded war on terrorists was declared; people were called upon to defend their homelands.

Ryan looked at the panic that was being fostered by the news channels. He understood how easy it would have been to fall into that trap, except he had been on-board a starship and knew the truth, except he had been told it was coming.

One small news item that others might have overlooked amidst the sensational was the increase in global temperature. The report said it had gone up by a full degree in the last year, causing further melting in Antarctica and Greenland. To be sure of this number, he had logged into the web site for Sanitas Technologies and queried its data. One of his last acts as CEO of his old company was to secure a contract to automate temperature monitoring around the globe. Sure enough, the system was up and running. It had showed historical data along with the most recently collected. The temperature, as calculated by Sanitas' equipment, was up three degrees worldwide over the last six months. When he showed this to Sarah she said, "Earth is entering the final stage of her transition."

FORTY-ONE

Turning to his computer, Ryan felt the absence of John deBeque. The younger man's machine lay untouched on a table not far from his. He went to the Civilization of Light web site, and posted a long article comparing the current round of terrorist attacks to the attacks on the World Trade Center, asking people to keep in mind who had been responsible for September 11th. He questioned how terrorists had been able to coordinate attacks worldwide. He also posted a message of reassurance, asking people to support each other.

Checking on visits to the Civilization of Light web site, Ryan saw an astonishing number. He checked his email; there were over a thousand new messages. Unable to deal with these at that moment, he hoped people would look at his commentary on the site and begin to question media reports.

Using a different email account, he sent emails to those with whom he had recently spoken. Almost immediately he received a response from Lucinda Ross and other members of the group in Fort Collins. They were meeting this afternoon to discuss what they could do. He told them to contact as many people as possible, both locally and around the world. "Tell them that the consensual paradigm has been destabilized. Recent events are creating chaos, shaking already dysfunctional institutions. Remember everything is energy, and as such can be manipulated by our intentions. Now is the time to reorder everything -- based on love." Liking what he had written, he sent the same message to other groups. Then he posted it on the web site.

Nancy Ertl responded next. She had joined the group that met at Van Patten's house. They too were meeting. High on their agenda was buoying the local economy and supporting local farmers. Ryan encouraged them to look at creating a local currency based on old U.S. silver coins. He gave them the same message he had given to the Fort Collins group. Nancy said she was active in the movement to take Colorado out of the United States.

Two new groups had posted messages on the Civilization of Light bulletin board. They talked about the steps they were taking to support the other members of their groups. They also said that they were working on raising their personal energy levels so that they might influence the transition. They each provided an email contact. Ryan posted a message encouraging them to get in touch with the groups in Boulder and Fort Collins.

After he finished reading the group messages, Ryan sat back and reflected on them. Some of the messages were about concerns and struggles with 3rd dimension realities. Other messages were about going beyond fear, about operating from a center of love. The latter he saw as a lighter dimension, as if those who written them had somehow ascended beyond the day-to-day.

He posted words to encourage everyone to leave behind the vestiges of the old. Attachments to money, old friends, land, power, collections, status, entertainment, or lifestyle would all be altered in the days ahead. Only by detaching could one hope to encompass what was coming. He encouraged those of similar mindsets to seek out and rely on each other.

Later in the day, Ryan got an email from Truman Thompson. He had not talked to the president of TTT Instrumentation since he had sold his company, Sanitas Technologies, to TTT. They arranged a time to speak by satellite phone.

"Well you called that one, congratulations," Truman said. "Now I see what you've been talking about, the ETs, the old paradigm, and all that. When we are able to travel again, I'd like to sit down with you and learn more."

"Thanks, Truman, it's been a lonely road at times. Thank goodness I had my connection with some fantastic humans from another star system."

"I'd like to meet them."

"You will."

Truman said, "May I suggest that, as you are encouraging all these local organizations, you do not forget that there are some things that it makes no sense to manufacture locally. I am meeting with other manufacturers to determine what we can most efficiently produce, and how we can get it shipped around the country."

"You're right. Let me know what you come up with, I'd like to let my network know what's available."

"I've stumbled on a very interesting over-unity device. Once you get it started, it produces electricity at one twenty hertz until you shut it down -- no fuel, no outside energy whatsoever. I've got Brauk engineering it for production."

"Wow, where'd you get your hands on that?"

"One of the local research outfits had developed a hundred thousand watt transportable unit, under a contract with the Army. They said the Army had given them quite a bit of help from one of its reverse engineering projects. Since it looks like Washington is out of business, they are going to license commercial applications to TTT."

"I see some great possibilities. Can you make it small enough to power a vehicle?"

"That's where we're headed. Probably will require batteries for acceleration, like the hybrid cars use, but it looks promising. At the very least we can make one to power a house, take care of those folks that those crystals can't reach via the grid."

"The crystals were always meant to be temporary, until something like this showed up," Ryan said. "The armada wanted to help out, and offer concrete proof that they were friendly."

"Well, they certainly convinced me."

"Going back to distribution, what are you guys thinking in terms of a currency that everybody's willing to accept?"

"You've hit on a major stumbling block," Thompson replied. "We don't have an answer yet. Any ideas?"

"Not right now. I'll let you know if I stumble across anything."

Traditional news channels were all about spin. Unfailingly they would have the perfect commentator talking about an event, helping people "understand" what was going on, invariably it centered on the darkest aspects of the situation. Ryan posted his analysis of what was transpiring, not to create fear, but to reassure people. More emails piled up.

"Are you watching this?" Ajax exclaimed from the corner of the room to Ryan's left. "Sam got it done."

Ryan hurried over. One network had interrupted its coverage of terrorist attacks and blackouts to carry a story out of WZQY, Baltimore. Right before Ryan's eyes, Stefan Duncan, shifted from his human façade to that of a handsome lizard and back again. Then a young woman, whom neither Ryan nor Ajax knew, performed the same feat. Both were interviewed as to who they were. The woman, who said her name was Rosemary, explained that she worked for the U.S. Navy as an analyst. The Federal Bureau of Investigations employed Stefan.

Stefan went on to say that he had come to Earth as a young man and had worked his way through college and into the FBI. He insisted that his mission, and of other non-humans like him, was to be helpful to the humans of this planet.

Rosemary explained that she had been raised by a family of beings who did not have the best interests of humans at heart, and whose primary mission was to instill fear. She said that her mother was a political activist and her father a DC bureaucrat. She had not heard from them since the blackout. When asked what their future plans were, Stefan and Rosemary responded that for reasons of safety -- theirs and the station's -- they would not be available for future interviews.

She went on to outline the way in which N'Roids had dominated humans for thousands of years, and how they planned to remain in positions of power in the future. When asked if she would name specific persons who were N'Roids she declined, "It will all become very apparent in the near future."

Ryan recorded a video clip of Rosemary and Stefan's shape shifting at WZQY and placed it on Civilization of Light, again with a brief explanation. He emphasized the message of the prior day about free energy, reminding people that it was more permanent than their temporary plight.

When Ryan accessed Sam's web site, he was glad to see the power outage around DC had not affected it. He posted a congratulatory message on the hidden message board and asked Sam if they could continue to keep in touch in this way. He also asked Sam to find out from Tony Santori who among the President's Secret Service detail could be trusted.

FORTY-TWO

"Where is Warren Ophir?" Grant Clever demanded.

The officer in his red uniform stood at rigid attention. "Sir, he left the facility yesterday with a small contingent. He told me he was going to capture some visitors and bring them back here. He said that he wanted to pump them for details on the armada's plans."

"Yesterday! Why wasn't I informed?"

"Sir, he told me that you were not to be disturbed, that you were busy with planning."

Without dismissing the male, Clever turned to the computer-generated map of North America. It filled one wall of the tiered war room on the third floor of the World League's headquarters. The current status of the terrorist attacks was displayed here and on a world map on the opposite wall. Information was updated every fifteen seconds.

"Why didn't we use more EMP?" he addressed the question to Justin Ridgway who stood watching as the display updated. Red blotches marked Toronto, Washington, DC, Los Angeles, and other cities that had been disabled by EMP energy pulses. Smaller white dots pinpointed cities where their operatives had inflicted damage with conventional explosives and/or scalar attacks.

"You asked me that a minute ago, the answer is still the same. We had only thirty large transmitters; we wished to cripple, not completely destroy. As it is, the pulse at Los Angeles disabled more than we had planned; all movie studios in the San Fernando Valley are dead. One of our transmitters aimed at Chicago was disabled by police before it could be used."

"And our smaller scalars?"

"The mobile scalar equipment has functioned exceptionally well.

Local officials believe the targets were destroyed by conventional explosives set by terrorists."

"How about our ground forces?"

"They have finished their assaults on the generating plants. They might not turn the tide, but they certainly are leaving their mark. Now the population will see what it is like to be without electricity. Now they will experience real fear."

"What about the power supplied by the armada?"

"It can't possibly compensate for the losses we are inflicting."

"Can you get some airplanes into the sky, bomb some more refineries, wipe out some more cities? Do something, damn it."

"No, I cannot. As I told you before, all military aircraft have been disabled."

Clever wrung his hands. "How about some missiles? Let's start something with Russia or China. Can Israel shoot something at Iran? We must do something!"

"Any improvement?" Jonathan Olson had joined the others.

"No," Ridgway replied sourly.

"The dollar is dead," Olson said. "Countries are declaring it worthless. Corporations are refusing to use it. I can only thank his Eminence that we have our gold."

"What about our allies at Camp David?" Clever interrupted. "It's time people heard from them. Let them know that the government of the United States is not dead." He turned to the male in red who was still standing at attention, "Get Robert Morris on the secure communications line. And I also want to speak with Beatrice Foster."

"Yes Sir."

"I told you we should have left when we had the chance," Goldman said. He had been standing in front of the world map. "The situation doesn't look any more promising over here."

"Sir?" The male in red addressed Grant Clever. "Beatrice Foster is no longer at Pine Gap. She left with a group for Antarctica about five hours ago."

"Smart woman," Goldman said.

"I have Robert Morris for you, line three."

FORTY-THREE

By 4:00 PM the collapsing house of cards was becoming evident; on the internet, messages about worthless money were posted everywhere. Most television news programs were still trying to make it look like terrorists were at the heart of all the world's ills. Despite the details they had provided on N'Roid activities, the shape shifting by Stefan and Rosemary was dismissed as clever theatrics.

However, Ryan Drake and the others at Harmony Center were able to watch developments with detachment. Their knowledge of the larger picture put things into a much different perspective. They watched as the price of gold continued to climb in response to a crumbling dollar. Without exchanges in New York and London, commodity exchanges like the Chicago Board of Trade had expanded their trading of gold, silver, and other precious metals. The currencies of other countries also tumbled in reaction to damage to their major cities. Blackouts were being mitigated as utilities switched to free energy from the crystals.

Sarah was told that two Sirians had remotely viewed Admiral Ridgway and Grant Clever as they finalized the details of the terrorist attack. They had alerted the armada who had dispatched craft to minimize the damage from scalar weapons and neutralize the military aircraft, ships, and armored vehicles of all nations. They also captured a group of N'Roids as they sought to escape from their spaceport in Antarctica.

She was also told that what had disabled all electronic circuits in Toronto, Los Angeles, and Washington, DC, were known as electromagnetic pulses or EMPs. Chicago had been spared when the humans in a crew that was supposed to fire one of the focused beams of the scalar weapon turned themselves into police saying that, "We could not fire such a monstrous weapon on our own people."

The U.S. grid had been severed in only six places, rather than the ten planned by Ridgway, but these were major interruptions. The explosion and fire at Baton Rouge, as executed by N'Roid ground forces, had knocked out a significant portion of the United States gasoline supply.

The United States had been the principal focus of the N'Roids' terrorist attacks, apparently due to the World League's desire to use it as a launching pad for tighter controls around the globe. EMP bursts had disabled Paris, Cairo, Tokyo, and Delhi, though not as completely as Washington, DC. A refinery near Singapore had suffered damage. In attempts to destabilize society and instill fear, N'Roid ground forces had disabled oil, gas, and coal-fired generating stations in every country. Lights remained on in many areas thanks to electricity supplied from crystals; all that remained in many places was to reconnect or re-route the grid. As it was, about 35% of the U.S. was dark; in Canada and Mexico it was about 50%.

People were emerging from the cities like Delhi with stories of how machines and computers no longer worked, and tales of people trapped in subways and elevators. Rescue workers entering the affected cities reported many people were unable to cope with the unfamiliar reality. Some had taken their own lives, some had killed for the bare essentials, and some had been heroes, helping those in dire straights, standing up to the fear oozing out around them.

The 6:00 PM newscast from Phoenix was interrupted by a breaking story from Camp David. The Secretary of Defense, Robert Morris, came on the television. "My fellow Americans, our country has suffered from multiple well-coordinated terrorist attacks. All of our military and law enforcement agencies are on full alert to prevent further attacks. We have captured several of the perpetrators and, using modern interrogation methods, will extract much from them in the coming hours and days about those behind these attacks. I have learned that similar conditions exist in other countries of this planet."

The Defense Secretary continued, "We have witnessed the destruction of Washington, DC, and the surrounding area, including the Pentagon. Nonetheless your government, now headquartered in Colorado, is fully functioning and stands ready to defend you.

"I call every American to arms. Arm yourselves. Prepare to do battle. We must not allow ourselves to be overcome by terrorists who wish to take our land, our families, and control the American way. At the same time, you must conform to the rule of martial law. I reiterate all law enforcement agencies are under federal control.

"Let us not be fooled by announcements of a mysterious supply of electricity. It is bogus. Our public utilities are taking it upon themselves to restore electrical service to everyone in this country. I have dispatched troops to guard their efforts. We will keep you informed as things develop."

"Talk about twisting things around," Ryan said.

"You have an interesting way of understating the obvious," Ajax said.

The networks began to show pictures of people clamoring for food from already bare supermarket shelves, long lines at gasoline stations, and crowded shelters for those walking out of Toronto, DC, and Los Angeles. Without the support of the Federal Reserve, banks across the country closed their doors. They informed depositors that they would have to "wait for their money."

Then it happened, a cable news network broke the mold. It started by picking up a local station in Kansas City that was broadcasting stories of people helping each other, of heroics, of sacrifices, and of leaders emerging from the ranks of the common man. Soon the maverick network had stories pouring in from cities across the country.

A second network followed the first with stories from around the globe. Together they pointed to a growing sense of empowerment -- mankind had survived another attack on its freedom. A third network began reporting that starcraft had landed with medical teams assisting injured humans. This news came from such diverse locations as Costa Rica and New Zealand. There were no such reports for the United States. Secretary of Defense Morris came back on the major networks; he threatened any craft that violated U.S. airspace.

Their most important insight for those at Harmony came late that evening in a communication between Sarah and her D'Ct-Elds mother. *The acts attributed to terrorists were deliberately undertaken by N'Roids. This last desperate act has failed, yet they cling to the idea that they will somehow regain their prior position.*

Rather than instilling overwhelming fear in the populace, the light in more and more people of this planet has actually increased as they reject stories of terrorist attacks and accept the truth that beings from another planet are helping avert worldwide calamity.'

"Not only has the playing field been leveled," Ryan said, "we are witnessing people rejecting the consensual paradigm." He posted all of this on the Civilization of Light web site, including the following analysis from Sarah, Ethete, and Ajax: "Yes it is true, Earth's nuclear weapon capability has been disabled, as well as military aircraft and ships. However, law enforcement agencies are still armed sufficiently to enforce domestic order.

"Now, it is up to you, the humans of Earth to create a new civilization. Your sisters and brothers from other star systems will coach and assist, but only after being asked. The only remaining questions are how long and how deep: How long will it take for enough of you to come together? How deep will you sink before you climb to a new way of being?"

Late that night, there was news that in several regions of the U.S., people were demanding action from the federal government. If they did not receive action from a government that now existed only by statute, they threatened to take matters into their own hands.

Sarah, Ajax, Ethete, and Ryan discussed how all of this was supposed to result in an enlightened civilization. The answer was not obvious. The three from off-planet insisted the solution rested in the proper use of energies to create morphic resonance. The problem was that currently there were too many conflicting beliefs, too many different approaches, and no apparent way to reconcile everything.

Phantia had never sunk as low, so they had no blueprint to suggest. Plus the three knew there were limits to their involvement; they could only advise and assist, they could not do.

Ryan went to bed that night wondering how it would all turn out. Could mankind create a new way to live, a way without fear? Would it be uniform across the planet? How long would it take?

FORTY-FOUR

After Sam said farewell to Stefan and Rosemary at WZQY, he re-traced his route back to Virginia. On the way he called Tiffany at her home. "I've been told that it's okay to talk on my cell phone," he said. "Seems the bad guys are busy."

"Are you okay?" Tiffany asked. "Where are you? I was worried."

"I'm fine, just driving back from Baltimore. Did you catch my gig at WZQY?"

"You were part of that? What a great piece of news -- in the middle of everything else. What was it like meeting those lizards?"

"Stefan was a gentleman. Rosemary was a little rough, but she'll be better after she spends a little time with Stefan and his kind."

"So what's next?" Tiffany asked.

"I'm headed back to my house. Maybe my electricity will be on by now."

"If it isn't, you and Maggie can come over here."

"Maggie's with her sister in Roanoke. I haven't been able to get through to her."

"The invite still applies."

"I'll let you know."

"Ryan Drake posted a message," Tiffany said. "Now I understand what the congratulations were for. He wants some names from Tony Santori. Should I take care of it?"

"That's all right, I'll call Tony."

Sam spent an hour in Frederick searching for gasoline. While he drove, he talked with Tony, filling him in on some of what he had learned from his visit in Arizona.

"I kinda figured the news channels had it screwed up," the Secret

Service agent said. "So what can I do?"

Sam waited in line an hour to gas-up the monster -- at twenty dollars a gallon he filled it half full. The attendant refused to take his government issued credit card, "Don't know if they're going to be back in business, cash only. And you're lucky our supplier is still taking it." Sam dug two one hundred dollar bills from the spare cash in his wallet.

With fewer vehicles on the road, Sam's return to Virginia was less of a chore than it had been driving the other way this morning. He stopped at the border briefly; his government ID worked its magic. The tanks on the Maryland side of the border were also disabled.

He finally managed to connect with Maggie and told her the electricity was off at their house. "Sam, I want you to come to Roanoke, at least Adriel has electricity. Everything in the refrigerator and freezer is probably spoiled."

Sam had seen Maggie like this before. Once she became emotional, there was no reasoning with her. "I have to stay here. Do what I can to help. I'm sure you heard about the trouble in DC."

"I'm not coming back there, Sam. You care more about that damn job than you do about me."

"Maggie, it's what I do. It's what I've done for thirty years."

"I've been miserable the whole time. And that robbery -- I can't take any more." She burst into tears and hung up.

In a few minutes, Maggie's sister called him, "She's in a bad way, Sam. You better come down here."

"I can't come right away."

"If you cared about your wife..."

Sam cut her off, "Our car won't start; I'm in a rental at ten miles per gallon. Give it a few days."

"She told me how you have so little savings. How you've been living high on the hog. Just what kind of a husband are you anyway?"

Sam bit his lip. The accusations had been the same since they married; he made the money, she spent it, and her sister bitched about him. "Like I told her, I'll see what I can do. It won't be today."

When Sam reached his home, it was late afternoon. He went in through the front door to find the living room in complete disarray. Jumping to the conclusion that they had been burglarized again, he tried to call the security company. Neither his house phone nor his cell would connect.

After Sam explored the rest of the house, it became evident that only certain things were missing, things important to Maggie. He checked her dresser. Some of her jewelry was gone, but not all; his was still there. He checked the closet; her favorite clothes were missing. This had nothing to do with a burglary.

He opened the door of the freezer; all the food was still frozen. Most of the food in the refrigerator was okay. In the pantry was enough gourmet food to feed him for a week. Concluding he did not want to stay here for the night, he packed a large suitcase.

As he drove farther south, his cell phone rang. "You've got to come here," Adriel whispered. "Maggie's really depressed. I'm worried about her."

"Is she drinking?"

"Yes."

"I keep telling you, keep her away from the damn booze." Sam pulled to the side of the road. From past experience, he knew that any discussion with his wife was out of the question. "Does she have her medication?"

"Yes."

"Try to get her to take it, and take the booze away from her."

It took Sam a while to find the house; when he arrived, it was dusk. The fruit trees in the back yard were full of pink and white blossoms. The nearest neighbor was fifty yards away.

She opened the front door as he hoisted his suitcase out of the trunk.

"Can I sleep on your sofa?"

"I have a spare room," Tiffany replied. She held the door for him. "Hungry? I was just fixing dinner."

She gave Sam a tour of her home, a three-bedroom ranch. He placed his things in a room reserved for guests. On the east side of the house was a sunroom loaded with plants. Trays of seedlings a few inches tall rested on an old table. "I see lots of work ahead for someone," Sam said.

"I keep myself busy." She smiled and pointed to a large garden plot outside.

In the basement Tiffany showed him how she had stored water in fifty-five gallon drums. She also had shelves of canned and dried food, all neatly arranged.

"You could feed an army," Sam exclaimed.

"Not an army," she said, "but maybe some hungry friends."

"Vienna sausages?" he reached for one of the small cans.

"I figured if things got tough, I'd trade them for something else."

"Same for the whiskey?" He pointed to the row of flasks.

"Yeah," she smiled.

"When did you find time to do this?" he asked.

"When you were out investigating the nuclear explosion in Utah, or off on some other project for the President. Something told me it would come in handy some day."

"I am really impressed."

"I learned from my neighbors. Most of them are doing this."

Over the next four hours, Sam told her about his trip to Arizona, and what he had learned from Ryan Drake and Ajax Johnson. They cried at the description of President Boyle in captivity, and his impersonator in the Oval office. They laughed at Sam's story about meeting Stefan and Rosemary, and how he had taken them to WZQY. Finally, at about 11:00 PM, they talked about Maggie.

Early the next morning, Sam's cell phone rang. Groggy from his all too brief sleep, he fished it out of the pocket of his sport coat. "Hello."

"Sam, this is Adriel. Maggie swallowed a bottle of her medication last night. I found her this morning. Sam, she's dead."

"I'll find a way to get there, soon as I can," Sam said. He was now wide-awake.

Sam showered and dressed before he awakened Tiffany. "Take my car," she said with a yawn. "It gets seventy miles to the gallon. I filled it yesterday."

Taking a few moments, Sam accessed the private page on his web site. He saw the congratulatory message from Ryan Drake on his WZQY gig. Ryan also informed him about the death of John deBeque and the A'Roids capture of Warren Ophir.

Sam posted a message back to Ryan, informing him of Maggie's death. He took time to tell Ryan what he had seen around DC, his whereabouts for the next few days, and added a sentence about the disabled tanks at the border. He also mentioned that, with the exception of a couple of news helicopters, he had not seen any aircraft since leaving the Richmond airport.

As he was preparing to walk out the door to the garage, Tiffany reached up and gave him a hug. "I know this hurts," she whispered. "Just remember, it was not your fault." They both had tears in their eyes as she walked him to her car.

FORTY-FIVE

The previous morning they had buried John deBeque between the small hogan and the geodesic dome. It had been his wish, as he had no other family. In accordance with John's wishes, there was only a simple ceremony to commemorate his passing through the veil. A flat rock, onto which one of their Zuni workers had chiseled John's name, marked the grave. Saying that she wished to be alone, Sarah, Ajax, and Ryan had left Ethete seated by the mound.

Feeling depressed at the loss of John, Ryan had walked with Sarah to the geodesic dome. It was the first time he had been there since he had returned to Harmony after the tsunami. At the outside door to the dome, six Navajo women waited to exchange corn, eggs, or a piece of lamb for some of the green harvest from within.

Inside, despite the intense midday sun, the humidity was quite a bit higher than that of the surrounding desert. With the exception of small walkways, every square foot was filled with benches lush with greenery, some were mature plants, others were just emerging through the rich soil.

In place of the unusual plants he had previously seen, there were row upon row of benches with lettuce, green beans, peppers, tomatoes, eggplant and squash. As a result of the raid by the INS, the dome had lost many of its panes of glass. These had been replaced as a part of the settlement with the government. The door that the N'Roids had recently bashed in had been repaired. Two older men from the Southern Zuni Reservation in New Mexico worked among the plants. A few Navajo women and men watched and listened as the Zuni explained the gardening techniques used at Harmony.

"So this is where you've been spending your time," he had said putting his arm around Sarah.

"Some of it." She gazed into his face; her large gray eyes open wide. "I foresaw the day when neither our neighbors nor we would be able to drive to Kayenta for fresh food."

"So how do they get here?" Ryan motioned to the line.

"Some walk, some drive."

This morning, for the first time since the raid by the N'Roids, and since John deBeque's death, Ryan drove Harmony's pickup toward Kayenta. He drove slowly to conserve fuel. Harmony's reserve of gasoline was such a precious commodity that they had not dared use it until their produce was ready.

It had rained for two days greening the grass alongside the road, as well as the sides of the mesas. "I hope people are taking advantage of this," Sarah said pointing to the greener than usual landscape. "The weather is warm enough for us to plant a large garden outside the dome." As they rounded the last bluff, Sarah exclaimed, "Look people are out everywhere."

Ajax pounded on the top of the cab. "Civilization."

Seven eighteen-wheelers were lined up at the truck stop on US 160. None them appeared to be unloading in Kayenta.

They drove past Bashas' Super Market at the intersection of US 163 and US 160. Ryan noted that the bank was closed.

Farther north, they pulled into the general store and trading post. There was a small crowd of Navajos milling about its muddy parking lot. When they spotted the crates of fresh greens in the back of the pickup, a crowd congregated like a school of hungry fish.

"I have piñon," one woman shouted.

"I have blanket," another one said.

Several men tried to climb onto the truck, but Ajax stood his ground.

When Ryan walked around to lower the tailgate, a woman with two children tugged on his sleeve. "Please, for my little ones. I will pay." She held up wrinkled dollar bills.

"We will tend to you first," Sarah said. Accepting the dollar bills, the blonde-haired Phantian reached into the bed of the truck and extracted a head of romaine lettuce and a paper bag of green beans. The woman thanked her profusely. With the produce, Sarah also handed the woman an envelope containing seeds and instructed her to go home and plant a garden. "You need to take care of yourself, for your children. When we come again, show us your garden. Then we will have more food for you."

"You are so great," Ryan said.

Sarah smiled at his compliment.

They handed out their supply of lettuce and green beans in thirty minutes, receiving in return small sacks of flour, beans and corn, a few eggs, and a quart of goats' milk.

With each bag of beans they supplied an envelope of seeds for growing more beans, lettuce, and squash. "Plant a garden," Sarah said to each. "Learn how to care for your needs. If you do that, we will help you."

"Not much to show for all the greens we handed out." Ryan pointed to the small pile of things they had received for their crates of greens.

"I would be happy to take nothing," Sarah said. "However, this way they learn about taking care of themselves, and about bartering. It also buoys their dignity. Hand-outs are what they used to get from the government."

Ryan watched as the woman he loved functioned from a center of love. He was getting better at it, but she was there all the time. He placed his arm around her and squeezed.

Ethete, still in shock at the death of John deBeque, wandered among the crowd. From time to time she would stop to help a child by placing her hands on them, helping their energetic body to correct itself.

Ajax passed out copies of a flyer. It was similar to the one that John deBeque had designed, and that the direct mail service had delivered to every household in the U.S. This one explained that some of the sources of free energy were on the land of the Navajo Nation, and lands controlled by tribes in other Western States, and in Canada. The star people had set things up this way because these lands were independent from national governments, and thus the free part of the energy could not easily be compromised. Also, this was a magnanimous gesture as Native Americans were now giving something back to those who had conquered them.

When the crowd saw that there were no more vegetables, they began to disperse. Most of their homes were within walking distance.

"Many of them will be unable to survive without government money or food in the supermarket," Sarah said gesturing to the people trudging from the parking lot. "Those that do will help create a piece of Earth's new civilization."

"What can we do to help?" Ryan asked.

"The Navajo already know how to raise sheep, now we are encouraging them to farm. Next time we come here, in order to receive lettuce or beans from us, we will require that they show us that they have made use of our seeds."

"We can't save all of them," Ryan said. "How do we decide?"

"We don't. Each determines his or her future. We can only assist. Remember, each soul incarnates here under the terms of a contract. When the contract expires, they die. Many of the details of their lives were agreed upon long ago."

Ryan was troubled with this view of human life. On the one hand, incarnation contracts seemed so callous -- you're born, you live, you die -- on the other hand, they diminished any guilt he harbored about not being able to save more of them from dying during the interim time. If souls really did know what they were in for, why did they choose a particular life? Why did they incarnate into hopeless situations? And what did a soul hope to learn by incarnating, only to give up its life during the interim time?

They headed into the market to find cooking oil. SILVER COINS ONLY a hand-lettered sign on the front door read. Ryan wondered how many Navajos had silver coins.

The only Navajos in the largely deserted store were the two who were stocking a new shipment of flour, cornmeal, and rice. There was a third at the register near the front entrance. One other person, a white woman whom none of them recognized, had a small shopping cart filled with staples.

Many of the shelves had been cleared of food items, probably before the silver coin rule came into effect. There was no fresh produce or meat; the only dairy products were chunks of cheese sealed in plastic.

They settled on two large rounds of cheddar cheese at twenty eight dollars. They found containers of canola oil; $20.00, the price tag under them read. They also found a bottle of vinegar and a box of laundry detergent. Sarah paid for everything with six silver quarters that the cashier told her were worth twenty-five dollars apiece.

"It can't continue like this," Ryan said. "The reason silver coins command such a high price is that there are so few of them. It doesn't make sense to buy a quart of cooking oil for a quarter."

"You are looking at things through old eyes," Ajax said. "Remember the American dollar has been distorted for so long it is hard to tell the real value of anything."

"It still doesn't make sense," Ryan insisted.

"In time the value of that quarter will bear some relationship to that quart of oil. Until there are enough quarters in circulation, things will continue to be distorted."

Ryan went to the hardware store next door to find a screw for the air handling system. Again silver coins were the only money accepted. He saw ink cartridges and paper for his printer. He purchased everything for two silver quarters.

FORTY-SIX

A burned-out Sam Wellborn returned Tiffany's car two days later. The drive from Roanoke had taken five hours, not due to traffic, but Sam's melancholy.

For a long time, the two of them sat on her porch sipping iced tea, not saying much, just sipping iced tea. There was crispness in the air as a light rain turned everything even greener. It was peaceful and quiet here; it had not been peaceful in Roanoke, nor quiet.

"I guess I won't be making any more long trips until things change a whole lot," Sam said, thinking aloud.

"You're right."

"I filled your tank, seven gallons."

"I know."

"How do you know?

"Because you are the kind of a man who would do that."

Neither spoke as they continued to sit, sit and relax. He enjoyed Tiffany's calm companionship, enjoyed sipping her iced tea.

"Do you want something to eat?" she asked.

"I need to get going," Sam said as the sky turned to dusk.

"Where are you going?"

"To check on things at my house. I'm sure there's something I should be doing."

"You can stay here. We'd have less trouble finding each other."

"Thanks, but I'd better check on things."

"Do you want me to go with you?"

"No, I have to do this myself."

"I understand." She wore sadness on her face. Her dark eyes squinted and the edges of her mouth turned down, as she walked him to his monster SUV.

When Sam pulled into the driveway of his house, it was dark. Using the flashlight, he made his way to the messy bedroom and climbed into the unmade bed.

The hamburger he had stuffed down, after he had left Tiffany, was not sitting well so he got up for water and some antacid. As he was crossing to the bathroom, he stepped on something sharp. It gouged the bottom of his foot.

Limping back to the bed, he scrounged for the flashlight on the nightstand. Through dripping blood, he saw that a piece of glass had penetrated the ball of his foot. He carefully pulled it out and wrapped the foot in a pillowcase.

Now in slippers, he tiptoed to the bathroom to wash the cut. There was no water. Searching under the sink he found a bottle of hydrogen peroxide. He sloshed it over the cut.

Back in bed, antacid on the nightstand, he tried to sleep. His foot hurt, so he lay there ruminating about his broken marriage, and about a wife who had committed suicide. The funeral, a hurry-up thing without many in attendance, had been a grim affair. Maggie's sister, Adriel, and her husband stood on one side of the grave; he stood on the other, while a minister intoned words he did not hear.

After a while Sam began to focus on what he was going to do the following day, what he was going to do with his life. He saw a new picture emerge and wrestled to find a place within it. He eventually fell into a troubled sleep.

It was dawn when he struggled awake. It had rained during the night and was chilly in the room. His foot hurt, but it had stopped bleeding. He examined it again, pulling out a sliver of glass he had missed. It started to bleed again, he poured on more hydrogen peroxide. He found a gauze pad and a shoe big enough to accommodate both it and his foot.

Looking to where he had stepped on the glass, Sam saw that it had come from a picture frame. He picked it up. Glass shards fell to the floor. It was his wedding picture with the imprint of a high heel through the photo. Maggie had purposely stomped on it. Finding this made him feel less guilty about her death.

Sam smelled a wood fire. Every house in this exclusive neighborhood had gas fireplaces with automatic lighters. He looked out the window. Dark smoke was pouring from the chimney across the street. Frank Tidwell was burning something to stay warm, probably furniture.

There were no signs of life in the other executive homes.

From the back of his closet he pulled out the suitcase he used for overseas trips. He filled it with clothes and shoes, mostly practical, and one dress outfit. Searching the drawers for anything else, he spotted his jewelry box. He added it to the suitcase. Then he struggled the suitcase down the stair and into the monster.

Sam packed the food from the pantry into boxes. Then he opened the freezer; the food seemed remarkably solid, so he packed it, wrapping it in blankets to keep it cold.

When the vehicle was full, he headed south into the area with electricity. After finding breakfast, his first stop was to hunt up a coin and jewelry dealer.

After limping into the shop, he traded all his jewelry for some old silver dimes in a plastic grocery bag. Before leaving the shop he inspected the coins; some of them were the newer composite type. He shoved them into the owner's face. The man got a different bag from the back room.

Sam inspected it, counting the coins to make sure there was $250 of face value. All the coins were of the old silver variety. "I ought to take my business elsewhere."

"Hey, I'm probably the only guy in a thousand miles who would even consider trading that pile of jewelry for coins." The man pointed to Sam's rings, wristwatches and cuff links on the counter. "I just happen to have a bag of dimes. You're the second guy this morning. A couple of more like you and I ought to be able to close up and go home."

Sam's foot was throbbing as he returned to the SUV. He stopped at the twenty-four hour clinic in the same strip mall. There was no receptionist, only a lone doctor and a nurse who was trying her best at all the jobs.

After waiting two hours a doctor looked at his foot. "Not good. There may be more glass in there. I'd like to open the wound and clean it out. This is going to hurt, so I'll give you a local."

"Do it," Sam said.

As the doctor worked on Sam's foot, the lights blinked twice, then glowed steady. "They've been working on them all morning," the doctor mumbled through his surgical mask. "Probably those damn aliens."

"More likely it's the new electricity being pumped into the grid," Sam said. "The utility is probably taking its generators off line. Pretty soon you'll have one hundred percent free energy."

The doctor paused, "You really believe that stuff about free energy?"

"I don't believe, I know its true. When you were growing up, did your parents ever give you anything?" Sam asked.

"I grew up in India," the doctor said, "we were very poor. But my parents made sure I got a good education. That's what they gave to me."

"The people from other star civilizations are our relatives. They are giving us this gift of free energy to help us through these difficult times."

"And you are sure of this?"

"Yes."

"All right, then I will accept it and be grateful."

A half-hour later Sam limped to his SUV. Now his whole foot was swollen. After the doctor had extracted one additional fragment from the wound, he had cleaned, sewed and bandaged the cut.

Sam drove slowly, not quite sure how this was going to work out. Moving his stuff into Tiffany's house was a big deal.

He recalled how he had met her on the campaign trail, at the moment he could not recall where. She had attached herself to him, becoming his assistant. When he got an office in the White House, he had put her in the one next to his. Then they had decided to move her out into an office of her own. When that happened, Sam footed the bill for both her salary and the office.

Over the last eighteen months she had done everything he had asked, sometimes with her own twist, most often accomplishing more than he had asked. He shared almost every bit of information with her, had introduced her to Ryan Drake, had seen Sarah's home planet along with her, had conspired against the politics in the White House, and most recently had told her about Carlton Boyle's double. Now he was going to be living in her house.

Sam limped up the front stairs and knocked on the door. She answered after a few long moments.

"Rent in advance." He handed her the quarter-bag of silver.

Surprised at its weight, she dropped it. The bag burst and the coins spilled onto the porch. "Pieces of silver? You think you need to buy your way in here?"

"All right, think of it as salary."

"Sam, we both know you probably have seen your last government paycheck."

He stumbled when he shifted his weight to his sore foot. She caught him under the arm and helped him to a chair on the porch.

After he explained everything, she said, "Well I'd probably better get that frozen stuff before it melts."

"I'll help get the frozen stuff, but first put those dimes away."

"The least you could have done was to bribe with quarters," Tiffany smiled as he scooped the dimes into a paperboard box.

With Sam maneuvering on his heel, it took them an hour to sort through the food and put the rest of his things away. "We're going to have to cook some of this tonight," Tiffany said, "I can't refreeze it."

"I have some great dishes," Sam said "I used to be a great cook. Haven't done much since we, since I, moved to DC. I'd like to help out."

"Okay master chef, get with it. How's the foot?"

"Pain killer's wearing off."

"Tell you what, you elevate your foot and tell me what to make."

"Deal."

After dinner they sat and talked until late. Tiffany was probably right; Sam would not see another paycheck from the Federal Government. That meant no income for either one of them.

"The coins in that little bag of silver are worth about thirty thousand," Sam said. "Let's see how far that'll take us."

FORTY-SEVEN

At 6:00 AM the following morning, a convoy of Jeeps and other SUVs breached the front gate of Douglas Windfree's estate. The two Secret Service agents who had been manning the gate stumbled away at their approach, and then collapsed into unconsciousness beside the road. They met no other resistance.

Five school busses, two first responder teams along with a convoy of ambulances, and three television crews from Channel 11 in Denver followed them. The crews set up their cameras at three positions on the front lawn. Shortly thereafter nine gleaming saucers positioned themselves a short distance in back of them; the saucers hovered noiselessly a few feet off the ground. One of the camera crews filmed male and female A'Roids as they descended from the ships. The handsome males and females were dressed in forest green military uniforms. Green berets covered much of their sleek heads, leaving only lizard-like eyes, nostrils, and mouths showing. The only sounds were conversations among members of the camera crews and reporters quietly speaking into their microphones.

The contingent of Secret Service men guarding the estate was quickly neutralized without a shot being fired. All were disarmed. Those who were N'Roids were sorted out and herded onboard saucers. Those who were not were allowed to watch from a safe distance, under the watchful eyes of two sheriff's deputies.

The front door of the main house was breached without noise. President Carlton Boyle's double was arrested by the leader of the A'Roids, allowed to dress, then escorted out to the waiting cameras. Henry Bustamonte, barely awake, was detached from his young sleeping companion and paraded out in pajama bottoms.

Minutes later, other members of the President's staff were hustled out the front door. Some continued to display human facades; others showed their lizard-like features. All were placid.

As the former conspirators watched, thirty of the male A'Roids returned to two of their craft. The saucers ascended a short distance, then headed straight down, dematerializing as they passed through the dirt in front of Windfree's house.

Douglas Windfree, in his bathrobe, wandered onto the front porch. "What is going on out here?"

"Sir, you are under arrest for treason." Jake Ashton stepped in front of him. "Turn and place your hands on the wall."

"Do you know who you are speaking to?" Windfree said, not moving. "The President of the United States of America is a guest in this house."

"Not any more he isn't." Jake motioned over his shoulder to Bustamonte and his puppet as they stood in front of a camera. Both were shifting in and out of human form. Bustamonte's naked upper body shifted in and out of his lizard-like skin.

The interviews with Bustamonte and Boyle's double, with and without their human facades, were broadcast live. The cameras continued to roll as they were escorted to a saucer.

An A'Roid escorted Windfree into the house where he dressed in a suit and tie before being loaded onto a school bus guarded by sheriff's deputies.

As instructed, Jake and law enforcement personnel from Clear Creek, Park, Jefferson, and Boulder counties waited in front of Windfree's house. Within an hour, people in uniforms of blue and green began stumbling out the front door. They were herded onto the waiting busses.

When their numbers kept piling up, Jake turned to Tom Ertl and said, "Sheriff, you'd better radio for some more busses."

The leader of the A'Roids asked first responder teams and ambulance crews to bring stretchers into the mansion. In about a half hour a parade of gurneys with obviously sick men and women emerged through the front door. Two television reporters commented on the identity of the well-known political, business, and entertainment personalities as the stretchers made their way to the waiting ambulances.

Jake again turned to Tom Ertl. Before he could say anything, the sheriff reached for his radio. "I know, more ambulances." Ertl radioed all area hospitals that they had a major medical emergency on their hands.

A little later female A'Roids escorted groups of young women with blankets wrapped around their shoulders out the front door. Most were scantily clad, many were noticeably pregnant, and some held the hands of small children. A newly arrived medical team from Clear Creek County, along with several A'Roids, hastily examined each and escorted them to one of the waiting SUVs or to a saucer. Most of the children went onboard a saucer.

Carlton Boyle, dressed in a dark suit with white shirt, was helped out the door. One of the reporters approached, but Jake waved him off. "Not now. He's very sick. We are taking him to the University of Colorado Hospital."

Margaret Boyle climbed from one of the Jeeps and rushed to his side. "I didn't know you were here," Carlton Boyle mumbled. His face had the look of a drunk the morning after an affair with a quart of whiskey.

"He got me out of that horrible place," she pointed to Sheriff Tom Ertl. "Took me to his house. Got me off the drugs."

As Carlton Boyle and Margaret were helped to one of the Jeeps, Jake walked over to the group of Secret Service agents. "Which of you is Arnold Schneider?"

A barrel-chested agent replied, "That's me."

"Back on duty agent, you've been cleared."

"I don't understand."

Jake pointed to Tony Santori, in a dark suit and white shirt. He stood next to the President's Jeep.

Jake then waved to three FBI agents whom he had personally selected for this job. They hurried over to the SUV behind the Jeep. Another SUV, driven by a sheriff's deputy, escorted it off the property.

Grant Clever, struggling against his A'Roid captors, emerged from the front door. The television commentators from Channel 11 did not know who he was until an A'Roid explained it to one of them. Then the reporters began to question him about his role as the Chairman of the World League and the President of the Planetary Council.

"This is not the end of anything," he shouted at the cameras. "There are too many of us to simply dismiss."

He pointed at one of the cameras, "You will see, you all will see chaos. Then you will be grateful for the discipline we have supplied."

He was taken to the same hovering saucer into which Bustamonte and the presidential double had entered. It lifted off and was out of sight within moments.

A while later, more humans straggled out, each supported by a female A'Roid. Jake recognized a few of them as well known political leaders, others as famous personalities from movies, sports and business. They were helped to ambulances or the waiting busses. Earlier the leader of the A'Roids had told him they had discovered a number of humans that were being held captive.

Tom Ertl counted a total of six hundred humans and N'Roids emerging from the underground facility. The humans who were waiting for busses were being interviewed. Many told stories of abduction and forced servitude. For some this was the first sunshine they had seen in years. Everyone said they were pleased to be out of the underground labyrinth.

As the television cameras recorded every conversation, the leader of the A'Roids approached Jake Ashton. "Mr. Ashton, some of the N'Roids escaped on their underground transport system; it goes for hundreds of miles. Others from the armada will join my team to search them out. It will take some time to follow all the routes. I suggest you and the others take care of the humans you have. I will inform you when we have others to be picked up."

"What will happen to the N'Roids you took on board your ships?" Jake asked.

"They will be taken to our mother ship and provided with every opportunity for rehabilitation." The words of the A'Roid commander flowed in perfect American English.

"And if that does not work?"

"We will give them many of your years to come to the light."

"And if that does not work?

"They will be imprisoned." The commander's face displayed no emotion. "I do have several more items."

"Oh?"

"On one of the floors below is a large amount of gold. Most of it is in the form of gold bars, plus there are jars of monatomic gold, a most valuable substance. It is all the property of Earth-humans. Will you provide for it?"

"We will safe guard it. How do I find it?"

"Take the elevator to the ninth floor." The A'Roid commander handed him a brass key. "You will need this to operate the elevator."

"And the other items?"

"On the seventh floor is a vast computer installation. We will leave it for you to examine. On the lowest floor below is the electricity generating system for this facility. It is quite advanced. I believe you will want your scientists to examine it. We saw no danger to it, so we left things operating."

"Thank you, for everything," Jake said.

"It has been a great pleasure to right a wrong imposed on Earth and its peoples for so many years by our cousins. I wish you well on reconstructing your civilization."

"Reconstructing?"

"Yes, after we remove the rest of the N'Roids from around the world, your institutions will no longer function. This is a process that may take several weeks of your time, but it will happen. None can hide for long, as they have a signature that identifies them.

"This will decapitate your institutions, and in the process shatter that which is familiar. It will also begin a new way whereby you see each other as sisters and brothers of the light, as opposed to the old way of seeing each other as flawed, or as someone to be feared or conquered. Then it will be up to Earth-humans to construct institutions based on the light. We are quite confident that, in time, you will do this, that they will be to the benefit of all, and that they will be unique to Earth. You are, after all, children of star civilizations.

"So, I leave you now with my peace and light." The A'Roid commander bowed to Jake in the manner of the Japanese.

"Good-by commander. Thank you." Jake returned the bow.

This exchange, as well as the prior proceedings, had been recorded as well as broadcast live to the world.

FORTY-EIGHT

Sam Wellborn was resting at Tiffany's home in the Virginia countryside. His foot had healed to the point that he could walk normally, which he did when they took daily strolls around the neighborhood. Most of Tiffany's neighbors were busy gardening; many of them raised goats, chickens, or cows. The few country gentlemen were busy learning how to survive.

Tiffany and Sam had established a pleasant routine where he arose early and scanned the internet for the latest news; she remained in her room until she smelled coffee.

He would have walked out to retrieve a morning paper except none were being delivered anywhere in the U.S. The only way they could get mail was to pick it up at the post office. Delivery of all but first class mail had been suspended.

Sam and Tiffany had watched events in Colorado on her television as the channels played them repeatedly. In the past ten days, more N'Roids had been rounded up and transported off the planet. Where television crews were available, the events had been broadcast both on television channels and on the internet, however with so many N'Roids, their human façades were not always recognizable.

The largest such event was from an underground bunker beneath Naval Support Facility Thurmont, also known as Camp David, in the mountains of Maryland. Top government officials, like Secretary of Defense, Robert Morris, were apprehended and shown to be N'Roids. Other top officials in government, in the military, in business and finance, and in other institutions were also apprehended and shown to be N'Roids.

"Wondered where this is all going to stop," Sam said after the Camp

David event. "I've met quite a few of those people."

"Not people," Tiffany corrected. "Monsters."

"They had it pretty sweet for a long time. Sure had me fooled."

"How could they do this?"

"Ryan Drake says they saw us as their sheep, figured they could do whatever they wanted. He says that the light had drained from their souls."

"They have souls?"

"I've come to understand that everything is conscious," Sam said, "like the plants in our garden, even rocks."

The second largest event was from the Vatican where the partially transformed body of Steven Reedy was displayed before the cameras; half of his features were those of a human, the other half those of an N'Roid. He had apparently committed suicide as A'Roids sought him out. A number of other N'Roids, still in clerical garments, were hustled aboard waiting saucers.

Similar events were broadcast near underground facilities at Zavidovo, in Russia, Chequers in Britain, Harrington Lake in Canada, Kultaranta in Finland, Pine Gap in Australia, in other countries, and at an underground spaceport in Antarctica.

The A'Roids had rooted out N'Roids hidden within intelligence organizations, state governments, military bases, corporations, banks, universities, medical centers, and at secret research installations. All were brought into the light, shown to be shape shifters, and in full sight of television cameras were hustled onto saucers.

Jonathan Olson and Jeremiah Goldman had been captured in an underground facility in New Mexico, three days after the event in Colorado. Other members of the World League and Planetary Council were still at large. Speculation was that they were hiding in some corner of the underground labyrinth. Unable to use their spaceport in Antarctica, none had left the planet.

Human accomplices of the N'Roids, those found in hiding with them or protecting them were handed over to residents of the local community in which they were found, again in front of television cameras. True to the prediction of the A'Roid commander, without their N'Roid controllers all institutions that they controlled slowly ground to a halt.

Events at the World League's headquarters were now imprinted in the minds of most humans; the footage had been played repeatedly by one network until the others had caved in to broadcast it, and similar events. People were finally waking up to the benevolence of their sisters and brothers from other star systems, waking up to the fact that they too were children of the stars.

One of the major results from the capture of N'Roids was that military units throughout the world began to dissolve and disburse. Almost without exception, they were no longer being paid because the economies of their countries were crippled, or non-existent. Coupling that with major voids in their top down command structure, and faced with superior technology and what appeared to be the overwhelming manpower of the A'Roids and others from the armada, most simply went home. Intelligence and law enforcement agencies, particularly national ones, experienced the same phenomenon.

Sam had sent emails to the people Ryan Drake had told him he could trust. He had heard from about half of them. Two had asked how they might get together with him. Tiffany invited them to her home. That was three days ago, they had not yet made an appearance.

Tiffany had created a page on the web site so that Sam and others could post things. Recently Ryan Drake had posted a long commentary about the demise of N'Roid-based institutions and how to use energy to create a new civilization of the light to serve the needs of all humans of the planet.

Most days Sam and Tiffany worked in a garden that had expanded as they had found seeds or cuttings to plant. A neighbor with a tractor had tilled a huge area so all Sam had to do was work the black dirt to where it was ready to accept whatever they wished to plant.

They had talked about a vegetable stand out in front of the house, but dismissed it for lack of traffic. Sam bicycled into Bristow and talked to the manager of the local market, who said he would welcome fresh produce, but wanted a hefty percentage to stock it. Tiffany and Sam looked at setting up their vegetable stand in Bristow, Buckland, or Gainesville.

Then they discovered that the farmers market in Manassas, Virginia planned to be open every day, an increase from its historical Thursdays and Saturdays. With the warmer weather, it was opening two weeks early. They purchased a space. They also discovered a community of locally owned and operated businesses in Manassas who had joined together long before the economy had crumbled.

Joseph Stamp, the owner of a local restaurant explained it to them. "We barter, buy supplies in quantity, and do business with each other. Local farmers supply locally owned restaurants like mine; we shop at locally owned hardware stores. Everyone gets paid a living wage. A few months ago, we adopted silver coins as our currency, adjusting their value every day to current market conditions. However, with the scarcity of coins, everyone in the co-op has agreed to support each other with credits for products or services that are bartered."

"This could be the model for a new America," Tiffany exclaimed.

"It's a beginning," Sam said, "but I don't see how we take it national."

"Maybe there won't be a national," Stamp said, "just a lot of little groups all networked."

"I'm not so sure about that."

"Guess we'll see."

"Yeah, guess we'll see." Sam paid for their lunch with two silver dimes.

FORTY-NINE

With repairs to the grid underway, Ryan learned that about sixty percent of the North American Continent was now receiving some of its electricity from crystals. Since there was insufficient capacity to service everyone, ships from the armada brought more crystals. The new installations were on land that was not being used for either farming or houses; many of the new sites were close to major cities. Pictures were posted of people watching the giant ships at work from such diverse places as the U.S., Canada, Ecuador, Spain, Egypt, India, Mongolia, and Australia.

Thanks to the redundancy of the grid, electricity was now flowing to most corners of the land. Many of the areas formerly serviced by the coal and oil-fired plants destroyed by the terrorists were functioning as if nothing had happened. With electricity, there was water; ninety percent of U.S. households depended on municipal supplies. Local communities were exerting their newly found powers; water that had been owned by private interests was returned to the public. Electric and water utilities had reluctantly agreed to charge their customers only enough to recover the cost of their distribution systems.

The bad news was that transportation of food had been severely curtailed. Supplies of diesel for semis, trains, and ships were still scarce, as were supplies for farming. Electricity was plentiful, but transportation ran on the refined products of oil. The fire at Baton Rouge had severely hurt an already strained production and distribution system. Until supplies of diesel could be increased, the only source of food was locally grown. The fortunate people were those who had stored up like squirrels; those without such foresight were starving.

Crops in California were being left to rot because there was no equipment to harvest them, and customary markets were often more than a thousand miles away. In the Midwest, because there was no way to get them to market, cattle, pigs, and chickens were allowed to roam fields formerly reserved for corn and grains, fields that had not been planted due to a lack of diesel and petroleum based chemicals. Much the same picture was true in other countries.

People in cities like New York were starving because they depended on food imported from other areas of the country. That supply had dropped to a trickle. They were also trapped because there was little gasoline to transport them to a place where there was food. This burden fell across all socio-economic lines. The rich were used to eating at fancy restaurants, most of which had closed, or buying whatever food they wished from supermarkets. The rich were also ill equipped psychologically to handle the strain of doing with less. Many of them left for their second homes, which were in almost the same situation.

The poor, better equipped psychologically and used to doing with less, could not afford the high prices for what food there was. Families took the electrically powered trains out of the city and spread out across the countryside of New Jersey, New York, and Connecticut. Among those remaining in the New York area, the death toll had now surpassed five hundred thousand.

In Toronto, Washington, DC, and Los Angeles, the picture was worse. Electrical power had not been restored. In none of these cities were electrically powered trains functioning. No vehicles that had been in the city at the time of the EMP discharges were operational. No computer systems, even battery powered ones, were working. There were no television sets, no electrical appliances, and no lights.

Emergency services were slowly making their way into the heart of these cities. What they found there was stunning. Many who could, had walked out the first few days; those who could not, had died, mostly from lack of water. With no bosses, and because there was no electricity, and no paychecks, most government workers had departed. Sam had run into a van full of them at the grocery store in Buckland; they told him that they were headed south -- until their gasoline or money ran out.

Another piece of bad news was the epidemic of multidrug-resistant strains of tuberculosis. It was killing up to sixty percent of the population in countries other than the United States, particularly in areas with crowded conditions and areas without sanitary facilities. Tuberculosis had been diagnosed in people who had walked out of Washington, DC, as well as people in every other major U.S. city. Now health workers, in protective garb, accompanied rescue workers into DC, and the rescue workers wore masks. Clinics had been established in every city and town to contain the plague.

After many at the Center for Disease Control had been apprehended as N'Roids, it was disclosed that under N'Roid direction little research had been done to find a cure for the multidrug-resistant strains of tuberculosis, and in fact there were indications that the drug resistance had been fostered by research at CDC. One human researcher claimed that one of the new strains bore a signature of having been genetically engineered.

Once this was published, something that those in the armada had only recently become aware of, relief teams were sent to the scene of major outbreaks. Under galaxy rules they were able to intervene like this when it was shown that non-indigenous beings had inflicted damage on the populace. Once again people watched as strange craft and strange beings ministered to those who were sick. For millions this help arrived too late.

Bodies of humans who had been replaced when N'Roids had shifted into their facades began showing up. Since most of these were beyond recognition, and because there was no way to tell where they were from, mass cremations were held. Earth-humans, their sisters and brothers from other star systems and celestials were invited to witness these; no television or pictures were allowed.

Television networks and internet sites reported more bits of encouraging news. One was that States in the Rocky Mountains were taking steps to form a confederation. They were circulating a draft declaring their independence from what was left of the government in Washington, DC. Arizona, Colorado, New Mexico, Wyoming, and Utah had tentatively agreed to unite, despite lack of support from southern Arizona and southern New Mexico, and part of the other former States. Declining to participate in this confederation, and after a brief fight between its north and south, California had declared itself a separate nation and was preparing to issue "California Coins" made from gold and silver discovered by A'Roids in an underground facility at Naval Air Weapons Station China Lake. Both the proposed confederation and the Nation of California declared their intent to appropriate all lands and facilities within their borders formerly owned by the United States, including military bases.

Wanting to avoid domination by California, Oregon and Washington were holding discussions with British Columbia. Nevada was talking to California, as was Baja, Mexico. Idaho and Montana were talking with the proposed confederation, with California, and with Canadian Provinces. The Navajo Nation, speaking as the largest Native American entity and with land in both Arizona and New Mexico, was negotiating with the confederation as a full member.

A refreshing development was that in every State, since the A'Roids had apprehended so many top government officials, ordinary citizens had taken over the job of creating a new government based on a loose affiliation of local entities. These citizen groups had declared all debts payable in dollars to be null and void. Strangely, banks and other lenders complied with the announcements.

The Declaration of Independence of the proposed confederation stated that theirs was an allying of equals: equal entities, equal citizens, equal rights, and equal obligations, and of freedom: free expression, free assembly, and free energy. They dismissed the concept of a top down structure. In the spirit of brotherhood, they agreed to do without an army -- like the country of Costa Rica had done since 1948 and to minimize the number of police. The proposed confederation was also preparing to issue its own precious metal coinage using the former U.S. Mint in Denver.

These developments were discussed on Sam's and on Ryan's web sites. One of Sam's contacts had become the leader of the proposed confederation. Ryan remembered meeting two of Colorado's new leaders at his presentation in Boulder. On the hidden page of Sam's site, Ryan and Sam discussed how they might get further involved, how they could insure that these new organizations were based on love, equality, and freedom, and how they could prevent the new institutions from becoming like the ones they were replacing.

The most encouraging signs of all were from the small groups that had been formed prior to the terrorist incidents. Each began to post their experiences on the Civilization of Light web site, asking to be connected with similar groups around the world. Their stories were of instances of morphic resonance between groups, and of teaching others not only to survive, but to be truly helpful to the new society. Most importantly, they talked about focusing their increased energies toward a new Earth, and of exchanging energies and experiences with others who were doing the same.

A delegation from the armada landed at United Nations Plaza. Four very human appearing beings, two female and two male, walked down a ramp that extended from the bottom of their circular craft. They were dressed in white flowing robes belted at the waist with gold chains. The complexion of one appeared to be distinctively red, another was yellow, the third was black, and the fourth was white.

They were met by a collection of quite ordinary people who escorted them to the speaker's platform in the room in which the General Assembly traditionally had met. Due to the arrest of so many N'Roids, and the impossibility of traveling, only a few of the seats of the member countries were occupied.

Speaking to the mostly empty room, but with television cameras focused on them, the red male spoke. "Greetings my sisters and brothers of planet Earth. It is my great pleasure to be here as a representative of your many sisters and brothers from the galaxy. With me here today are representatives from the other three races who brought human life to your planet." He motioned to the others that stood beside him. "We are happy to announce that your long enslavement at the hands of the N'Roids is now terminated." He spoke a few more words, then stepped from the podium.

A tall woman with oriental features and a yellow tint to her skin stepped to the microphone. "I too bring you greetings. Like the others I have slowed my energy so that I might appear to you as familiar. This is my tenth visit to your planet; in past incarnations I experienced much of what you have been experiencing. My starship has been in place above your planet for seventy years, beaming energy to Earth and her many children. I am most pleased that, in doing so, we have been able to help Earth and her human inhabitants."

The other tall woman, this one with pale skin and blonde hair, spoke next. "The task before you, the remaining human inhabitants of Earth, is to build a civilization based on love. Rely on your fellow men and women; build something never before experienced on this planet. We stand ready to offer you examples where this has occurred elsewhere in this galaxy, however this is to be your creation; we will not do it for you."

The final speaker was the extraordinarily handsome black man. "There is much joy about this planet. Joy because the human inhabitants are now free. Joy because the planet is now returning to its wonderful natural state. Joy because the children of this planet are now ready to become citizens of the cosmos. We who brought life to this planet now welcome you as you bring unique life, a melding of our four races, to the rest of the galaxy."

FIFTY

Sam received an email from someone he had become acquainted with during Boyle's campaign. It asked him to call a Virginia number.

"Mr. Wellborn, nice to hear from you," Edgar Cerroni said. "I guess since you are still with us, you're not one of those off-planet guys," he chuckled nervously.

"Yeah, I guess you could say that," Sam said. "Although I've met a few."

"How was it?"

"Scary, particularly in retrospect. Hard to believe I had dealings with them."

"Mr. Wellborn, the reason I wanted to get in touch with you was to see if you'd be interested in a job. We're putting the State government back together, hopefully the right way. We need someone with experience; all of us are real novices. Can you come to Richmond and talk?"

"It would have to be a completely new approach, nothing top down."

"We're open to almost anything -- just getting started with it. Don't have much real money as yet, but we'd be willing to pay for your gas."

"Can I get back to you in a day or two, I need to think about this and check my schedule. And, by the way, my name is Sam."

"Sure, uh, Sam, call me at this number."

After he hung up, Sam called Carlton Boyle at the medical center in Denver. He was told that the President was too sick to take calls. Sam left a message for Margaret to call him.

News channels were at a loss to explain how the country was going to operate since Vice President Malm, the Speaker of the House, and the

Secretary of State had all been found at Camp David and transported off planet. Despite this, the networks were reluctant to declare the government in Washington history. Internet sites were less diplomatic. Several of them declared that since most top government officials had been N'Roids and had been taken away, as had the fake President Boyle and his controller Henry Bustamonte, there was no government unless the people reconstituted it.

Many State governments were also without their leaders; many had been shown under arrest and boarding saucers. Citizen groups were forming, but with transportation difficulties, most organizations remained local, or were limited to communicating by telephone or via the internet.

The American military, without direction from the Pentagon, was restricting itself to its bases, fields and centers in the U.S. Elsewhere all action had been terminated and all personnel had returned to base. Many officers had been hauled away by A'Roids, their men having declined to fight on their behalf.

With food and supplies to last for some time, military bases posted guards at all entrances. Awaiting orders, they resisted all attempts by the States and local groups to appropriate their facilities. Because no one in the services had been paid since the alien attacks, and because there was little prospect of such in the future, many men and women went home.

The same had happened in every other part of the world. The A'Roids had disabled all killing machines of war; food and water was at a premium. There was no fighting because those who sponsored wars were without funds to carry on, and those who did the fighting had lost their incentive to fight. It was as if a consensus had been reached among mankind that there was to be no more war.

Always pointed out in the spotlight of television cameras, hoards of gold had been uncovered as the A'Roids searched underground facilities around the world. These were turned over to local authorities on the condition that they would be distributed to the people on an equitable basis. In the U.S., as soon as these were shown, people refused to take Federal Reserve dollars, instead demanding payment in precious metal. Banks and other lenders screamed, but promissory notes, payable in legal tender of the United States, were generally deemed worthless, such contracts rendered unenforceable. Wealthy people, who had relied on their collection of cash and securities, found themselves reduced to bartering their jewelry for food.

All countries that held U.S. currency and promissory notes in their treasuries declared them worthless. For most this meant bankruptcy, now it meant that each skeleton of a government had to appeal to its people. Most refused to accept any printed money unless it was tied to some precious commodity. In countries like Ecuador and Panama, that had adopted U.S. dollars as their own, there was a mad scramble to find a replacement. Most countries reverted to a barter system, supplemented by coinage with some intrinsic value or converted to a precious metal. Ownership of private property was temporarily frozen; mortgages and other debts were declared null and void.

Every government around the world found itself deprived of officials. Those countries whose cities had not experienced an EMP pulse functioned in rudimentary fashion, mostly due to confusion about monetary matters and loss of top government officials. Junior people, and some who had previously been excluded from the political process, tried to take on new responsibilities. The most successful form of government appeared to be a loose network of locally based entities.

Now, the major obstacles to creating a new civilization were hunger, disease, and people's intrinsic fear. After thousands of years of slavery, many of the newly freed slaves still were not sure how to behave as free men and women.

That evening Margaret Boyle returned Sam's call. "Carlton is recovering, but I'm not at all sure he will ever return to his old self. Sam, what is happening to this country? Is there still a place for a President?"

"It pains me to report that this country is disintegrating," Sam replied. "Maybe it's for the best, considering what's gone on behind the scenes. My very best to Carlton and you, let me know if I can help."

FIFTY-ONE

"Want to take a ride?" Sam asked over breakfast.

"Where?"

"I want to see DC for myself. It won't take much gas, and we might learn a lot."

"Okay," Tiffany replied. "Guess I won't need to get dressed up."

They pulled Tiffany's car around the big SUV that sat to one side of her driveway. Sam had tried to return the vehicle to the local office of the rental car company, but neither the phone for that office nor the 1-800 number had been answered. So it sat, running up charges on Sam's government credit card. They had driven it only once, when they hauled stakes for tomatoes, beans, and cucumbers that were too long to fit in Tiffany's car.

They caught I-66 at exit 43 and headed east, driving at fifty miles per hour to conserve gasoline. There was virtually no traffic in either direction. Lights in shops alongside the freeway were brightly lit until they neared Fairfax, then all went dark. They pulled off at the next exit to stop by Sam's bank; it was closed, no lights showing. "Mid morning on a weekday? Guess I don't really need those documents," he sighed and put his safety deposit box key back into his pocket.

They continued east until they saw the Washington Monument. Ahead emergency vehicles and temporary shelters blocked the Interstate. There were large signs posted: EMERGENCY PERSONNEL ONLY, CONTAMINATION GEAR REQUIRED. They were directed off the highway.

With no traffic behind them they paused. Sam smiled when he saw two Abrams Battle tanks as they sat awkwardly next to the highway.

"Why did you smile just then?" Tiffany asked.

311

"You see those tanks? They're no longer functional. They've been disabled, just piles of scrap metal."

"Why?"

He pointed upward.

It was Tiffany's turn to smile.

Sam pointed to a man in white protective clothing. "Guess the news about tuberculosis is true," Sam said. He checked to make sure the car's vent fan was turned off.

A car pulled up behind them and honked. They found a way onto VA 110, then proceded south. The car pulled around them.

The water in the Potomac River was the highest either of them had seen. As they pulled off at Arlington National Cemetery, an unusual looking car passed them; it made no sound. "One of those electric cars," Sam said, "bet we see a lot more of them. I wonder what we could trade for one?"

They walked to a point overlooking DC. "There're no lights anywhere," Tiffany said pointing to familiar buildings across the river. Looking up at Sam she said, "How's it going to end?"

Sam encircled her with his arms and pulled her tight. "I'm not sure when it's going to end, or what it's going to look like between now and then, but I do believe something better will come of it. You and I are going to be part of a new civilization, just like Ryan Drake and our relatives from Phantia have been talking about."

She rested her head on his chest. They remained like that for a long time.

They continued south on VA 110 past a darkened Pentagon, and kept going on US 1. The runway at Ronald Reagan Washington National was under an inch or two of water. It did not matter since no commercial airlines had flown since the terrorist attacks.

On the right, a large billboard had been papered over with a hand-lettered sign: CONVERT TO NATURAL GAS. It supplied a number for people interested in converting their gasoline-powered vehicles to run on "clean burning" natural gas.

"Maybe we should look into that," Tiffany said.

"Maybe."

Tiffany pointed to the west. "There're no lights in that hospital. What happens if someone gets sick? What about all the people from DC?"

"Big problems, I'm guessing. We probably ought to look at how we're taking care of ourselves. Not likely we can count on anybody for more than a stitch here and there." Sam pointed down at his foot. "Maybe family doctors will make a comeback."

"Some of those people in Manassas are holistic practioners," Tiffany said. "Maybe we can link up with them, practice preventive medicine, offer to trade them produce." She paused for a moment, a questioning look on her face. "Are they going to keep manufacturing antibiotics?"

"I'm sure somebody will. No telling what's going to happen to the big pharmaceutical companies without their FDA champions."

Sam turned west on VA 120 then took I-395 south. No lights on either side of the freeway. Southwest of Alexandria, after I-395 had joined I-95, they exited at Springfield. They parked in the deserted commuter lot for the Metro.

Walking the two blocks to Tiffany's old office, they passed Starbuck's where Sam had often purchased coffee; it was closed. Farther along the same block, the smells from a bakery caught their attention. They bought a cinnamon roll and two small coffees for two silver dimes.

"What a change," Tiffany said as she placed the last morsel of her half of the roll into her mouth. She pointed to her blue jeans and sweatshirt. "Somehow it tastes better, than the old way."

"Lots of changes," Sam agreed. "Most of them good." He motioned to her. This morning she had pulled her hair back into a ponytail fastened with a red ribbon.

She smiled and finished her coffee.

"I need to ask you about something," Sam said.

"Oh."

"Yeah, I got a call yesterday from a guy in Richmond. There's a group putting a new State government in place. They want to talk to me about a job."

"Do you know what the job is?"

"Not until we talk more. I wanted to see if it would be okay with you."

Tiffany smiled, hesitating for only a moment. "You needed to check this out with me?"

"Yeah."

"Whatever you want to do is fine, you're your own boss."

"Not anymore."

They went to her old office to see if there were papers they needed at her house. Both the lights and phone were working. Sam turned on the copier; it responded as normal. Apparently the EMP had not reached this far. "Let's leave it here, until we see if we really need it."

After driving four miles on winding roads they pulled up in front of Sam's house. Everything looked untouched since his last visit. The grass needed mowing; weeds had grown up everywhere. He opened the front door, and they went in.

"Look around," he said, "see what we can use."

"You're not coming back here?" Tiffany asked.

"Not unless you throw me out."

She smiled and headed for the kitchen.

An hour later, in addition to boxes of teas, spices and seasonings, and vitamins, they had packed all the silverware and fine crystal into Tiffany's car. Sam collected clothes that he could use around the yard, plus a set of tools. After determining that his desktop computer would not boot up, he settled for paper and print cartridges. Then they stuffed the car full of sheets, blankets, and pillows.

"All set?" Tiffany asked.

"There's one more thing, come into the house a moment." He led Tiffany to the upstairs master bedroom. Clothes lay on the bed where Sam had sorted through them. "Check that out," Sam pointed to a picture frame that lay upside down on the floor. "Watch out for the broken glass."

Tiffany stooped to pick the picture and turned it over. It was Sam's wedding picture. The imprint of Maggie's heel on it was clearly visible. "Sam, I'm so sorry it had to end this way."

"Me too, she was a very unhappy woman those last few years. You probably noticed all the empty booze bottles in the trash."

"Yeah."

A few blocks from Sam's former home, they passed a church. It had plywood over its windows. Motioning to it, Tiffany said, "I saw something on the internet just yesterday. It seems not many people are attending church any more. Somehow they have figured out that they could get along without it, that it didn't help during their desperate times. The article said it was really counter-intuitive, and that people should be flocking to church in times of crisis and hardship."

"On the other hand, maybe people have grown up due to hardships," Sam remarked. "Maybe they've learned to take care of themselves. Maybe, like Ryan Drake keeps telling me, they have found a direct connection to God, one they don't have to pay money for."

On the way back to Tiffany's house they stopped by a jewelry store with a sign out front: COINS FOR JEWELRY. They traded the set of twelve crystal goblets for a quarter bag of junk silver coins. "More rent money Sam said, handing it to her."

"You know, since I'm not paying a mortgage and my electricity is free, this will probably last quite a few years."

"I'm hoping," Sam said.

FIFTY-TWO

It was a familiar dream to Ryan Drake, one that had recurred several times since it showed up that night on Fortress Mesa, eight months ago. With each recurrence it had changed, as his understanding of the larger reality enlarged. It still felt like a prison because he was not totally free to come and go. He still felt alone in his cell. The walls of this bizarre jail were still transparent. He could still watch people next to him, above, and below. However this time there were no guards; no one sat in a central tower watching him and the others. This was a prison of his own making.

He went about his daily activities. He got up, ate, drank, interacted with the others at Harmony, worked on the Civilization of Light web site, and responded to emails. Yet he never left the prison. The cells were without sound barriers. As he went about his activities, he could hear others make observations, some were appreciative, others were in awe, and a few were critical. Censure did not change his behavior. From somewhere deep inside, he felt an overwhelming sense of confidence that what he was doing was right, noble, and very much needed. He commented on the activities of others in the jail, not from the perspective of superiority, but rather as someone who wished to share. He took delight when his sharing influenced them.

He recognized people from the groups in Boulder and Fort Collins. They were helping each other with the necessities of life, showing each other how to grow, how to transport, and how to organize. The two groups had adapted to use only electricity for lighting, heat, and transportation. Members of these groups were reaching out to other groups to tell them of their successes, posting stories on the Civilization of Light web site. The network his spirit guides had envisioned was becoming a reality.

Under the constant gaze of the other prisoners, he and friends in adjacent cells demonstrated how to live from a place of love. The jail walls faded, he was engaged with the others at Harmony; they were handing out produce to supplement that which Navajos had grown for themselves. There was a feeling that others were watching. He turned to see Peter Jones, Aza O'Sullivan, John deBeque, and Johnny Black Raven smiling at him.

He also saw Nancy Ertl as she worked at her desk at the head-quarters of the newly organized Territory of Colorado, Confederation of the West.

The walls of the prison suddenly disintegrated. He felt a tremendous sense of freedom. For the first time in his life, Ryan felt love for everyone who had been in the dream. He realized that he had only to come from a heart center to keep the jail walls from returning.

As he blinked awake, he recalled the dream and how it had changed from earlier versions. He smiled knowing that he had evolved. He felt a sense of freedom, love, and joy.

After he turned to snuggle with Sarah, drifting back into the alpha state, it happened. He felt his etheric body separate from his physical one. Drifting above the bed, he turned to look back at his physical form lying there.

As Sarah had coached him, he willed himself into a deeper state of consciousness; Ryan found himself in a place without boundaries. There were no shapes, no sense of anything except an awareness of self.

He willed himself to find Sam Wellborn. In an instant he was standing next to a sleeping Sam. In another room of the small house he saw Tiffany curled up under light covers. Not wishing to invade their privacy more, he willed his return to his place next to Sarah.

Ryan did not return to either sleep or the alpha state. In the clear light of dawn he realized that humanity had taken major steps toward creating a civilization of light. People were functioning from their heart center, making decision based on love, not fear. At that moment he was very hopeful.

FIFTY-THREE

Two and a half weeks after their earlier visit, the four from Harmony once again ventured to Kayenta with a load of squash, lettuce, and green beans. The grass alongside the road was still a brilliant green, the sagebrush a hearty grey. Everything smelled fresh and clean. It had rained for two days, unheard of in the desert. Today the sky was azure blue with a few puffy white clouds. Sarah commented that it looked more like a Phantian sky. The rain had helped them as they planted a huge garden outside the dome. They would get their first spinach in another three weeks, beans and lettuce from it a week or two later.

When Ryan diagnosed the air quality in their underground facility, as well as outside, he detected neither heavy metal particles nor biologicals in the samples. They had seen no planes spewing white aerosols since the terrorist attack; in fact they had seen only two planes, both single engine and both flying up the valley to the west of Harmony. According to the internet, all commercial flights had been cancelled for lack of fuel and because of confusion caused by lack of a viable currency. The military had finally admitted that all of its planes had been disabled.

Ajax, driving the vehicle left behind by the N'Roid, with Ethete in its passenger seat, had preceded them. In the rear seat of that vehicle were two of the Zuni gardeners. Ajax dropped them off at the community house in Kayenta, along with lunch and water.

Ajax then drove back to US 160, and pulled the black sedan into the service station. A large banner overhead proclaimed: CONVERT TO NATURAL GAS. The four of them had decided that since electric vehicles were still limited in their driving range, and Harmony's pickup did not get good mileage, that this was a good choice. The chances of getting Harmony's gasoline storage tank refilled were slim; propane was available. Ajax was told he could pick up the converted car in a week.

When Ryan stopped to pick up Ajax and Ethete, he filled Harmony's truck with gasoline. It cost $250; he paid with a few silver coins.

They drove the pickup through the residential neighborhood. Whenever they saw a house with a garden they stopped to talk to its owner, to offer squash, lettuce, and green beans until the garden could be harvested, and to ask for directions to the next garden. Emaciated people whose thin bodies and distended stomachs brought tears to Ryan's eyes approached them. Invariably Sarah or Ethete asked him to stop so they could offer them a burrito made that morning by Singing Bird, and invite them to a gardening class at the community house that afternoon. They discovered two community gardens that were being watered from houses adjacent to the formerly vacant land. Beans and lettuce were up, but a ways from being harvested.

One of the men tending the community garden was Ben Tsotsie. "Hey, amigo," he called to Ryan as the pickup pulled to a stop. "Do you like my new profession?"

"I am doing the same," Ryan motioned to the load of lettuce and beans in the back of the truck. "Come, take a look."

Ben took lettuce and green beans for his mother and father, both of whom were unable to work in the field. "Things are different now," Ben said, "people are learning to work instead of living off the government. There is not enough food to go around, so those who are not enterprising are starving."

"How can you just stand by...?"

Ben cut him off, "This land will not support everyone. It is an individual decision whether to survive or not. Those that sat around and drank alcohol were the first to go. Others are unwilling to stoop to the ground until they become desperate; by then they are usually too weak to work. It is very hard to see all of this.

"At the same time, my cousin who lives up near Monument Valley has become a farmer. Yes, there is a river north of there and fertile land. He is growing corn and Anasazi beans. When they are ready, I will take my truck and go there. Who would have believed that my cousin would ever become a farmer?

"And another cousin, over by Mexican Water is also farming. He was a sheep herder, but has decided farming is also good."

"How did they learn about farming?" Ryan asked.

"It is like magic; a week after we began farming our backyards and creating community gardens, I hear from a truck driver about my cousins. The old ones say that all Navajo are connected."

Ryan smiled. Sarah, who had stood by listening to Ben, walked over to him, hugged him, and gave him a kiss on the cheek.

"Wow, if I had known that was my reward for becoming a farmer, I'd have started months ago."

"Don't push it," Ryan said.

"I am very proud of you," Sarah said.

On the way back to the truck she whispered to Ryan, "I didn't have the heart to tell him that his cousin might be the hundredth monkey."

At 2:00 PM, Sarah stepped on the stage in front of a gathering of over a hundred people. "Thank you for coming. We would like to share what we have learned about gardening." She introduced the two gardeners. Ryan stood by to flip the large paper charts they had made for the presentation. The two Zuni, a man and a woman, explained Harmony's system for organic gardening, the system developed by George Tomichi their predecessor who had died protecting the dome from the rogue INS attack. They focused on farming techniques for the poor topsoil and normally dry conditions of the reservation.

Many in the audience were the same ones who had planted gardens from the seeds delivered two weeks previously. Others had purchased seeds from Bashas' or from the hardware store. Some had tended small backyard gardens for years; others were participants in the community garden. All were clearly hungry.

"As a special reward for those attending this presentation we have some canned food out in our pickup. You may claim it as you head home. In the meantime, join us for some refreshments."

In addition to burritos, Singing Bird had baked a huge batch of her special oatmeal cookies this morning. Their aroma had permeated the community center. Every one of the Navajos rushed to the side table. Sarah, Ethete, Ryan, and the two Zuni mingled with them. Ajax had stayed with the pickup to make sure that only those who had attended got the canned beans, tomatoes, peaches, and tuna.

"Many people have died," one Navajo woman said to Sarah. "We now understand that we must work together to survive. This is like the times that the old people talk of, when we were not confined to this reservation. Then we were a strong tribe, then we worked and lived together as one."

"I believe you are learning how to be one again," Sarah said.

"Including Ben's cousin?" Ryan asked.

"What's this about my cousin?" Ben had sat through the entire presentation making notes.

"Just commenting how neat it is that he has become a farmer," Ryan said.

FIFTY-FOUR

Ryan had seen advertisements on the internet for a new class of all-electric vehicles; they would be available within a year from six automobile manufacturers. They reportedly would have a range of two hundred miles and could be recharged within an hour from a standard 220-volt electrical socket. After consulting with Sarah, he placed an order for one.

In the meantime, according to the internet, natural gas supplies were being directed to power private vehicles. What little petroleum was available was going to diesel for delivery trucks, ships, and freight trains. With a lack of demand, coal mining had stopped; the trains that transported it were no more. The fuel they had consumed was diverted to other transportation needs. With fuel at astronomical prices, abandoned gasoline-powered vehicles were pictured alongside almost every road. Ajax had driven their new propane powered car back to Harmony yesterday.

Suppliers of fertilizer, seeds, pesticides, and herbicides rationed available supplies. With limited amounts available and high prices, farmers returned to the old ways of farming. However they found that their soil had been so depleted by modern farming methods that they had to nurse it back to health before it would produce. With predictions of stunted crops, yields were predicted to drop dramatically. Non-GM seeds commanded a premium. Commentators forecast a worldwide famine.

Shanghai had been most resilient city in the world in the wake of the EMP attack that had wiped out its electronic equipment and machinery controlled by electronics. Many Chinese people still cooked over their charcoal grills and heated with coal; they felt little that affected their brethren who had moved to more modern housing. Tall office buildings and modern apartment complexes remained dark; bodies were just now being recovered from elevators.

Most Chinese people had kept their old one-speed bicycles, so the streets were once again crowded with the black two-wheelers. Demand for bicycles, both domestic and for export, was so high that factories in China, Korea and elsewhere were put on twenty-four hour production schedules. Since the Chinese did not depend so heavily on supermarkets, their traditional central markets were booming. China was receiving electricity from crystals in Mongolia via power lines installed within the past year, but it was insufficient to meet the needs of the entire population. Despite these favorable factors, many millions of Chinese had died as the result of terrorist attacks against the coal-fired electrical generating plants and a lack of food production and distribution.

The transport ships of the armada were now seen on a regular basis. Additional installations of crystals were made close to what was left of major cities.

Truman Thompson contacted Ryan. When they spoke, Brauk Braukington was on the speakerphone at TTT headquarters near Boston. "We have a beta model of the over-unity device," his former partner said. "Tests show it will charge up a car battery pretty much like the gasoline engine in a hybrid."

"The brass ring," Ryan exclaimed.

"We like to think of it as gold," Truman said. "Sorry, my old mind set bled through. Mind you, we are not looking to make a lot of money producing these things; we just want to get them in the hands of as many people as possible."

"And as quickly as possible," Brauk added.

"How can I help?"

"Any ideas as to how we can pay for the production set-up? Truman asked. "Any ideas about a currency?"

"I'm tempted to speak for the people who control the load of gold discovered in that facility in Colorado," Ryan said. "I think they'd be interested in both your problems, and I just happen to know one of the people who is heading up that effort. Can I get one of your new vehicles as a beta test?"

"Possible. First, we need to convince the hybrid manufacturers to switch to our concept. In order to do that we need to show manufacturing capability."

"Put me down for one. I'll get back to you on the funding and currency issues."

FIFTY-FIVE

A month later, Sarah, Ryan, Ethete, and Ryan were sitting around the long table in Harmony's great room. Ryan had rigged up a speakerphone so that the four could hear the conversation on the other end. Sam and Tiffany had just dialed in, via satellite phone, from Tiffany's home in Virginia.

After catching up with everyone's good health, Ryan said, "There are so many changes that have occurred, I really don't know where to start. Let me try this on as a proposal.

"We allow the reader of this story to write the last chapter in this book. Yes, I know Mark Kimmel has his own ideas as to how things will be after the interim time, however, we all know he's not one hundred percent. So, why not let each reader complete the story?"

Before responding Sarah thought for a moment. "There are many loose ends that need resolution. The most important one for me is just how evolved Earth's new civilization is going to be, just how far will the imaginations of Earth-humans carry them?"

"I'm interested in what government's going to look like," Sam chimed in. "Just how differently will we organize ourselves?

"I'd like to know Earth-humans are going to perceive the larger reality," Ethete said. "Are they going to welcome their sisters and brothers from the other star systems as equals? What about new belief systems?"

"At what point do Earth-humans learn that all is energy," Sarah asked.

"I think that local groups are going to be the bedrock of a new civilization," Tiffany said, "but just exactly where are they going to flourish and how do they keep in touch with each other? Are people going to get along any better? How successful will they be at supplying the necessities of life?"

"I'm curious to know if there's going to be a larger economy," Ryan said. "I see that local groups are the bedrock, but they won't be able to manufacture all the things people need to prosper and stay connected." He pointed to the speakerphone in the middle of the table.

"For me, I'm curious to know whether that machine that Brauk was working on got into production," Ajax said. "It seemed to have a terrific potential."

"What happens to all the debt that governments issued?" Sam asked, "and all that gold the A'Roids discovered in the underground facilities?"

"What will the new Earth look, smell, and sound like?" Sarah asked.

After an hour of discussion, the six main characters of One decided to allow you, the reader, to finish this story, knowing that you might find even more things that needed to be resolved in your minds and hearts.

If you wish, you may submit your ending to Mark Kimmel at PO Box 270156, Fort Collins, CO 90527. For each submission along with proof of purchase* of **"ONE, Toward a Light Civilization,"** plus your address and email, you will receive FREE, a copy of Mark Kimmel's final chapter(s) of this book.

*Proof of Purchase = a photocopy of the back cover of *ONE*.

Do not read this until you have finished reading
"One, Toward a Civilization of Light"

This book is fiction, a story from the author's imagination. The characters, their thoughts, and their words are from the author's imagination. Events and their locations are from the author's imagination. However, truths about the larger reality, views expressed by the characters, and predictions of future events are based on the author's research, as well as direct contact with star people and celestials.

The following questions are provided as a study aid to navigating interim time. They are based on information contained in *One, Transition to a Civilization of Light.* These questions are suitable for study groups examining the implications of the larger reality and how we can successfully traverse the transition to a new civilization.

Additional information is available in
"Birthing A New Civilization"
by Mark Kimmel
and at www.cosmicparadigm.com.

• *Sarah, Ethete, and Ajax are humans from Phantia, a planet of a distant star system. They came to Earth to assist with the transition of Earth's humans.*

Do you think there are physical beings who are not of this planet walking among us? How would it change your life if you knew that humans from another planet were walking among us? Do you think they would look like us?

Are the stories about a star seed project true? Were the first humans brought to this planet rather than being evolved from monkeys, rather than being created here by God? How does that impact your belief system? Would this knowledge help you to see them as brothers and sisters and not objects of worship?

Would they look like us? How would they behave? What would they say about us, to us? Is it possible that there are millions of them?

Is it conceivable that non-humans have been on this planet for hundreds of thousands of years? Is it conceivable that they showed themselves to be non-human and were considered gods in ancient times?

How would the media react if a famous person declared that they were not born on this planet, but were from a distant star system?

Is it possible that beings from other star systems and celestials could be cooperating to assist Earth's transformation?

- *President Carlton Boyle is unwilling to openly acknowledge Sarah because she is not from this planet.*

Why does the government of the United States take the official position that there are no such things as UFOs and extraterrestrials? How do you explain the numerous sighting of UFOs? Have you seen one?

Have you had a contact experience? What was it like? What did you learn from it?

Do you think the government or private corporations could reverse engineer ET craft to produce alien reproduction vehicles? Do you think that there might be such a thing as scalar weapons? Could they produce an electromagnetic pulse that would destroy electronic equipment over a wide area?

- *The World League and the Planetary Council are at the core of a secret world government. They are comprised of beings who are not indigenous to this planet.*

Is there a secret government behind the ostensible government of the United States of America? Is it likely that the secret government is controlled by non-human beings who have only their selfish interests in mind and believe they have the right to "use" humans for their benefit?

Do secret underground facilities exist? Is there a network of tunnels connecting them?

Is it conceivable that there might be as many as one million non-humans on this planet who do not have our best interests in mind, and that they mingle unnoticed with the human population? Can the non-humans who are not favorable to humans be called "dark?"

Is it conceivable that these dark non-humans are in positions of authority, wealth, and power, and that they either direct, finance, and/or influence such diverse organizations as finance, banking, government, military, intelligence, media, medicine, research, psychology, education, religion, major corporations, as well as patriotic and/or terrorist organizations? Are the stories about an off-planet race taking over the entire planet true? How could they possibly accomplish this? Are the power structures cracking? What are the symptoms of this?

Is it possible that States might close their borders over issues of sovereignty, economy, immigration, or disease? Might they withdraw from the United States? What would lead to this?
- *Sarah makes a long speech about oil. Ryan and Sam pay high prices for gasoline, many times what we currently pay.*

Is it correct to say that our civilization is based on oil, that we are addicted to oil? What are the effects of rising oil prices? Will this change the U.S. economy, the world economy? Are governments willing to invade other countries to support domestic oil companies?

- *Sarah and Ryan notice changes in Earth's environment. Sarah says that global warming is part of Earth's transition.*

What Earth changes can we expect during interim time? If global warming is part of Earth's transition, then what role does pollution have? How about mining, drilling for oil? What impact does war have? Can we dismiss mining activities, oil wells and pollution of land, water and air as necessary evils?

Earth is transitioning to a lighter density. What does that mean to you? What does it have to do with the energy from the armada? Could a collection of starcraft provide enough energy to modify the energy of a planet? Is this the cause of Earth's warming?

Do you believe the U.S. government is involved in secret weather modification projects? Are other nations? Do you believe there is such a thing as chemtrails? What is their purpose? Who is responsible for them? Other than weather modification, what are their other intended purposes? What are the side effects?

- *Ryan finds articles about many deaths due to drug-resistant strains of tuberculosis in both newspapers and on the internet.*

What are the chances of a major epidemic killing billions of people around the world? Is it possible that tuberculosis or AIDS could mushroom into such an epidemic?

Is it possible that these diseases could be caused by an engineered pathogen? What would be the cure for such a plague?

- *Ryan Drake and Sam Wellborn are affected by the declining dollar and loss of personal assets. They both talk about problems with the U.S. government.*

Is the U.S. economy faltering? Is this a long term or a short term problem? Why is the U.S. dollar depreciating? What would cause the U.S. Treasury to take over a major bank? Has it happened in the past?

Is it possible for the U.S. to experience inflation such as seen in Germany and Argentina? What could lead to that? Is the price of gold a good measure of the value of a currency? Why not? Would it be possible to reconnect the currency of the U.S. to gold?

What is the best way to correct the problems in this country? Is returning to the original U.S. constitution the way to solve the current governmental and economic problems within the United States? Or is something else required, if so, what? What would create lasting changes, so that we do not return to the current ways?

Are corporations really beyond the control of governments? Have they privatized many formerly government run services such as water, prisons, and the military?

Competition and profits are taken for granted in the world of business. Is there another way in which essential services and products could be delivered to people? How could this take place if the transportation system breaks down?

- *Ryan, Sam, Sarah, Ethete, and John deBeque all express their views of religion and the media.*

Do you believe that religions originated when off-planet beings descended and people saw them as gods? How aware of off-planet civilizations were Earth's original inhabitants? Do you believe religions are a form of mind control?

Most would agree that Jesus set an example of the highest way to live, and that he taught about a God of love. Did he also teach about civilization on distant planets? How much of Jesus' life was fabricated?

Do our sisters and brothers from other star systems believe in God?

What has shaped your beliefs? What would it take to change them? Who do you believe you are? Why are you here at this time and place?

Do you believe what you see and read in the media, or do you believe the media is managed? How is this done? Do you think the media is a form of mind control?

- *When Sarah, Ethete, Ryan and John deBeque are hiking, deBeque falls, injuring himself. The two women heal him energetically.*

Is it possible to heal the human body using energy techniques such as accessing it at the quantum level? If this is so, could this be applied to erase fear? How does belief enter into this process?

Is Earth, and everything connected to this physical reality, a manifestation of energy?

Do you believe that your energy affects other people, other things?

How do you control your energy? What about the energy of fear?

- *When Sarah trades the vegetables that were grown at Harmony for things the Navajos can supply, she talks about bartering rather than giving.*

During interim time you will have few of the things we now take for granted. How will you treat those who have less, those who have more? Will you give others fish, or will you teach them to fish? Will you expect those that have more to help you?

What preparations have you made for yourself in light of what you know about interim time?

- *In ONE there are numerous references to the consensual paradigm.*

How do you understand this terminology? Do you believe that your thoughts, beliefs, and actions influence your circumstances, influence how you perceive life? Do you think it is possible that the humans of this planet are engaged in a consensual experience, that they are upholding the current paradigm? How do you change such a situation? Do you see yourself as enslaved?

Do you see yourself as a soul having a bodily experience? Have you incarnated here before? Have you incarnated on other planets? Have you incarnated to experience lifetimes in the dark as well as in the light? What does death mean to you?

What is the role of those in whom the light has diminished? Is it possible to ignore them and simply walk a higher path?

How would someone from another planet react to the consensual paradigm as expressed on our planet?

What would be the benefit of incarnating on earth to lead a life on the dark side? Do you think people do this, or do they slip into dark roles? Is it possible for someone in a dark role to turn to the light?

- *Starcraft of the armada play key roles in assisting Earth's transition. Sarah, Ethete, Ryan, and John deBeque interact with beings from them.*

Is there is a collection of starcraft surrounding Earth? What is their function? Is the armada beaming energy to Earth, to Earth's humans?

If people from other planets were among us, would they be able to communicate with the armada? Are all members of the armada operating in the best interests of mankind?

Will some from the armada intervene to remove non-humans who have the continued enslavement of Earth's humans as their agenda?

- *Energy producing crystals are bought to Earth by starships from the armada.*

Do you believe such a thing could happen? Do you believe it might already have happened, and that the crystals are already in place, awaiting the interim time?

What would be the results of a source of free energy? How would it impact your life? How would public utilities, oil companies and governments react? How would it impact our economy?

Would knowledge that the crystals were supplied by beings from other star systems help convince people of the benevolent nature of their non-earthly brothers and sisters? How could energy crystals be presented so as to become widely accepted?

- *Sarah, Ethete, and Ajax communicate with each other without speaking. They do this on a more or less continuous basis. Ryan discovers that he also can do this.*

This is an illustration of the entanglement of (ongoing connection with) all that is conscious. Do you believe that you are connected with other people, with other things? How has that manifested itself in your life?

Do you believe that one of the ways in which mankind was led into slavery was by severing our connection to each other, so that we saw others as separate? Do you think that we are all one, but that we just don't see it? What will happen when we reestablish our connection to each other? What would it be like to be a member of a hive? Are you prepared to function in this way?

If we are in constant communication with each other (entangled), then the concept of morphic resonance (hundredth monkey principle) makes more sense. Do you believe it is possible to entangle with all of humanity, with the universe? What would such a hive-based civilization look like?

By using meditation, or similar methods, can you communicate with non-humans? Is it possible to remote view a conversation many miles distant?

- *A'Roids capture N'Roids. The armada disables airplanes and other war-making machines.*

Is it possible that we will see intervention by beings from other star systems to assist our transformation? How do you picture that? Do you see it as interfering with our free will? What do you think should happen to those who have enslaved humanity?

- *Ben Tsotsie refers to the Navajo people seeing themselves as one. Sarah talks about the people of Earth coming together.*

What is the meaning of one? How does that relate to functioning with a hive mentality? What does it mean relative to our brothers and sisters from distant star civilizations? How does judgment and discernment enter into one? What about God?

- *What do you think Earth will be like after her transformation? How long do you think it will take?*

- *What will interim time be like? Do you believe that we will jump into a higher dimension, or will we slowly transform as depicted in ONE?*

- *Why is it important for the people of Earth to design their own future? How much assistance can our brothers and sisters from distant star systems provide us?*

- *How many people are required to instigate a hundredth monkey transformation and/or create morphic resonance for mankind? What are its characteristics?*

• Is it utopian to believe that a civilization based on cooperation and caring for others can exist?

• What makes this moment in history unique? 1: The assembly of the armada? 2: The number of people awakening? 3: The number of off-planet humans and non-humans present on Earth? 4: The presence of energy crystals? 5: The truth emerging about the secret government? 6: Earth changes? 7: God?

ACKNOWLEDGMENTS

First and foremost, I wish to express my gratitude to my sisters and brothers from other star civilizations, to my spirit guides, and to my friends and allies among the celestials. They have contributed greatly to my life experiences and to material for this book.

Second, I wish to acknowledge the many wonderful people who have shared of themselves, their contact experiences, and their understanding of the larger reality. Their very human experience of this planet has tempered and enriched that which I have received from non-humans.

Third, are my friends with whom I have had discussions on the topics within this book, they provided valuable grounding for what have been difficult rearrangements of my prior beliefs.

Fourth, are the books (some of which are listed on a following page), web sites, and newsletters from which I gleaned valuable insights into the larger reality.

Fifth, I am most grateful to Don Daniels (see his poem on the next page) and others who edited this manuscript, without their keen eyes it would not be nearly as readable.

Sixth, but by no means last, my beautiful and wonderful wife Heidi who supports me in so many ways.

Mark Kimmel

RECOMMENDED READING

Anastasia by Vladimir Megre
ISBN: 0-9763333-0-9

Atlantis Rising by Patricia Cori
ISBN: 0-595-20303-9

Birthing a New Civilization by Mark Kimmel
ISBN: 0-9720151-7-5

The Creature from Jekyll Island by G. Edward Griffin
ISBN: 0-912986-39-5

The Celestine Prophecy by James Redfield
ISBN: 0-446-67100-2

Confessions of an Economic Hit Man by John Perkins
ISBN: 0-492-28708-1

The Cosmic Code by Zecharia Sitchin
ISBN: 0-380-80157-4

Decimal by Mark Kimmel
ISBN: 0-9720151-1-6

The Great Turning by David C. Korten
ISBN: 1-887208-07-0

Hegemony or Survival, by Noam Chomsky
ISBN: 0-8050-7688-3

Illumination for a New Era, A Matthew Book with Suzanne Ward
ISBN: 0-9717875-3-0

The Intention Experiment by Lynne McTaggart
ISBN: 0-7432-7695-7

Lost Secrets of the Sacred Ark by Laurence Gardner
ISBN: 0-00714296-X

Matrix Energetics by Richard Bartlett
ISBN: 1-58270-163-6

Matthew, Tell Me About Heaven, A Matthew Book with Suzanne Ward
ISBN: 0-9717875-1-4

The Missing Times by Terry Hansen
ISBN: 0-7388-3612-5

No more Secrets No More Lies by Patricia Cori
ISBN: 88-901040-0-7

Path of Empowerment by Barbara Marciniak
ISBN: 1-930722-25-7

Power Versus Force by David R. Hawkins
ISBN: 0-9643261-1-6

Revelations for a New Era, A Matthew Book with Suzanne Ward
ISBN: 0-9717875-2-2

Rule by Secrecy by Jim Marrs
ISBN: 0-06-019368-9

Sanctuary by Stephen Lewis & Evan Slawson
ISBN: 1-56170-845-3

Trance Formation of America by Cathy O'Brien
ISBN: 0-9660165-4-8

Trillion by Mark Kimmel
ISBN: 0-9720151-2-4

The Ultimate Experience, Realities of the Crucifixion
By Verling CHAKO Priest
ISBN: 1-4251-0716-8

Voices of the Universe, A Matthew Book with Suzanne Ward
ISBN: 0-9717875-4-9

Before One, Toward a Civilization of Light, came...

FRIENDS IN HIGH PLACES

By Don Daniels

© 2000 Don Daniels

A bold New World awaits us
a spinning on this Earth,
an end to want and poverty
a time of happiness and mirth.

Abundant, free, non-polluting energy,
an end to hunger and disease,
the possibilities are endless
floating cars, if you please.

I have met with friends in high places
all this is possible you see,
It has already been given to us
and should be cause for much glee.

But there are those among us
who do not want these things to pass,
they would much rather
stick it to us in the Gas!

Our friends and neighbors we betray
their technology was given, stolen, taken,
all so these greedy people
huge profits could be makin.
(the relationship was adversely shaken)

Fossil fuels we keep on burning
our environment it is a cryin,
big money these people are making
while Mother Earth she is a dyin.

Minions of darkness
have caused us this plight,
the only weapon we have
is to expose them to the light.

Legions of covert workers
will then march out from their cave,
humanity will have to grow up
and learn how to behave.

There is a new Golden Age a coming
of that we can be sure,
we are working very hard
so you can stand the cure.

The Angels are on our side
that I truly suspect,
future generations untold
our actions will effect!

The world will get a lot bigger
when we all realize,
we are not alone in this universe
and see it with new eyes.

If we fix our problems
and do this as we should,
we then will be invited
to join the cosmic neighborhood!

We have friends in high places
they want us to succeed,
it is most important for us humans
to persevere in this momentous Deed.

You can certainly help us
in our epic quest,
join and work with us
if you can stand the tests!

A New Universe awaits us
a chance to visit many places,
an opportunity to meet new "people"
with many different faces.

New cultures, peoples, places
a much bigger view of creation,
a future to look forward to
with hope and great elation.

ABOUT THE AUTHOR

Since 1987, Mark Kimmel, author of *Trillion, Decimal, Creating the Cosmic Paradigm,* and *Birthing a New Civilization,* has studied the messages provided by our sisters and brothers from other star civilizations. By focusing on these messages in both his writing and speaking, Mark presents an uplifting vision for the future of humanity. Unwilling to ignore the reality of our current paradigm, Mark encourages those who would move forward to first acknowledge it, then turn their backs on it.

In a business career spanning 33 years, Mark founded and ran three of the most respected Colorado venture capital funds. In addition to providing capital, Mark served on portfolio companies' boards and helped them with strategy and tactics. He retired from business in 1996. Mark has been listed in Who's Who since 1985. He has degrees in engineering, marketing, finance, and psychology.

Mark is married with two grown sons. He spends his days writing and speaking about this, the pivotal juncture in human history, and how each person can help make the transformation positive for all on this planet. He is the founder of the **Cosmic Paradigm Network**, a group dedicated to manifesting such a transmutation.

TO THE OWNER OF THIS BOOK

The humans of Earth are engaged in a transition of historic proportions, one that affects this entire galaxy. Remember that although you may feel dwarfed by these events, your unique participation is vital to the positive transformation of our planet.

May you awaken to the realization that your sisters and brothers from distant star systems are among us, that they are already assisting us, and that transforming events are already underway.

Mark Kimmel

For comments about this book or for questions,
contact Mark Kimmel at: cp@zqyx.org

Interested in joining a global network of individuals dedicated
to awakening this planet? Find out more about the
Cosmic Paradigm Network at www.cosmicparadigm.com